Don Bull went to San Francisco State University. He studied art, science, and creative writing.

This book is dedicated to Sandy Vandenburg and Heather Bull.

Don Bull

Shiny Silver-Green Soul

Austin Macauley Publishers

LONDON * CAMBRIDGE * NEW YORK * SHARJAH

Copyright © Don Bull 2023

All rights reserved. No part of this publication may be reproduced, distributed, or transmitted in any form or by any means, including photocopying, recording, or other electronic or mechanical methods, without the prior written permission of the publisher, except in the case of brief quotations embodied in critical reviews and certain other non-commercial uses permitted by copyright law. For permission requests, write to the publisher.

Any person who commits any unauthorized act in relation to this publication may be liable to criminal prosecution and civil claims for damages.

This is a work of fiction. Names, characters, businesses, places, events, locales, and incidents are either the products of the author's imagination or used in a fictitious manner. Any resemblance to actual persons, living or dead, or actual events is purely coincidental.

Ordering Information
Quantity sales: Special discounts are available on quantity purchases by corporations, associations, and others. For details, contact the publisher at the address below.

Publisher's Cataloging-in-Publication data
Bull, Don
Shiny Silver-Green Soul

ISBN 9781638295396 (Paperback)
ISBN 9781638295402 (Hardback)
ISBN 9781638295419 (ePub e-book)

Library of Congress Control Number: 2023910882

www.austinmacauley.com/us

First Published 2023
Austin Macauley Publishers LLC
40 Wall Street, 33rd Floor, Suite 3302
New York, NY 10005
USA

mailto:mail-usa@austinmacauley.com
+1 (646) 5125767

I would like to thank and acknowledge Shirley Jackson, author of *The Lottery*.

Chapter 1

Found this unanticipated happening that should never have happened, but it did, or could this be a fantasy? I don't know for sure. Of all things, an old dusty, tattered manuscript found by his granddaughter, after Victor's death, in a shed behind the house. Did this man and his family keep a secret since the year 1977? The family moved away and left the house to their grandchild. Sarah, their direct descendant, turned over the manuscript to me. Sarah's seductive influence of her narrative for the beginning of it shocked me. My own skeptical incredulity of such a strange tale; when the girl discovered that I doubted this wild tale and thought it a falsehood, she showed me the reconstruction of the house in various spots, due to this incident.

I do not know if this story is true. I went to the school where her grandfather was last employed. The girl said he had many occupations and positions in his life, but being crucified by teachers for being left-handed, he became a teacher. I walked into the school where her grandfather had retired from teaching and asked the secretary for records of her grandfather's years of employment.

She replied, "No, he must've taught here when the school opened in 1975. If you go to the district office, I am sure they will have his records." Sure enough, they did have records of his employment. There is apparently no person still alive when this happened or maybe anyone didn't know that this incident happened because of the secrecy. The fact of telling it to you, I have taken fictitious names for the principal characters. There is quite sufficient evidence that it may be true.

The yellow and mildewed pages of the manuscript of a man long dead and the DVD record, plus the record of his adopted son's athletic achievements, has convinced me to read the manuscript.

Chapter 2
Chance

"Ma, do I have to take him, I take him all the time."

"He is your brother and you don't take him, you always dump him in the trash." Mother, Joy Martin, 35, 110 pounds, short hair, graying at the temples, ragged jeans, flipper footwear, no socks, left twitchy eye and a little red in the face from the kitchen heat, perhaps blood pressure.

"Georgie is not Elvis, he can't sing; he can't even speak. My friends think he is an animated dummy. They do a Shirley Jackson on him and he has bruises, they throw stones at him and try to win the 'Lottery'; if you win the Lottery in this 1950 story, you are stoned to death."

"He comes home crying to me," she said as she took a swipe with a belt but missed her teen kid Joey Martin, elegant dresser, custom Levi's, pin-striped shirt, three gold chains around his neck, hair smooth and spikes in the front, and a fledgling mustache.

He laughed while chewing gum and smoking a cigarette and said, "Ma, you're getting to old, you can't hit me anymore, I duck better then you swing."

"Are you selling again, you god damn punk?"

"No Ma," as Joey grabbed his little brother, Georgie's, hair to keep him from nodding yes. Georgie was slightly smaller than his brother Joey, just a year younger, dressed in Levi's, hand-me-down, a dirty shirt with holes, his hair cut by his mother six months ago; he spat at his brother and tried to stamp on Joey's foot. Joey pulled his hair harder and slapped Georgie across the face, and he screamed.

"Six months in juvie cured me. Ma, he keeps trying to talk to everyone and mumbles. No one knows what he is talking about, I wish the dumb shit would keep his mouth shut." Joey twisted his hair with added pressure, a scream from Georgie.

Their mother again took a swing with the belt and missed the older brother, Joey Martin. The belt wrapped around a hot boiling pot on the kitchen range and pulled it to the floor. Mother Martin screamed, "Get out of here, if only your father could you see now, Joey, a true drug pusher." The hot water splashed onto her legs, turning them red and blistering! She ran for the butter.

Joey grabbed his brother's hair again and pulled him out the kitchen door laughing and saying, "So long, Ma, I'll be back with some money."

She screamed through the kitchen screen door, "Don't dump him in the dumpster, Georgie always comes home when I go to work, he opens all the windows and starts howling like he is in some sort of pain. Then starts barking and gets all the dogs and the other dumb kids in the neighborhood making all kinds of noise. Then everyone starts throwing rocks at the windows. God damn it Joey, take care of your god damn brother!"

"OK…OK ma, I'll take the stupid idiot!" As they walked down the alley, Joey kicked and punched his little brother and by the time they reach the end of the alley, Joey was pulling Georgie by his collar. Choking, moaning and crying, Georgie was doing his usual for this time of night, since Joey got back from juvie. Georgie learned to bark and howl. Georgie's father died before he was born, when the brakes failed on a bus and crushed his father's car.

Georgie could handle harsh treatment; this was something he understood; it made him hate people and love dogs because they were beaten the same way he is treated. He was one year younger than Joey. After seeing the movie *Lassie* on T.V., Georgie was convinced that dogs were better than people, especially his brother Joey. Georgie was kept in a closet during the day, he thought it was Devil's Island. After staying eight and a half hours in the closet, he was soaked through in sweat.

His mother, after work, hosed Georgie and the closet down. Mother Martin and Georgie mopped the basement cement floor. She took his clothes off and wrung them out. The clothes line black with soot had been nailed to the ceiling of the kitchen by his father years before. It was a love-hate relationship for Georgie, he knew she was the only person that kept him alive. His hair was a rough cut that his mother did every other morning before she went to work at the wood mill.

Georgie stayed behind his brother who would throw him in the dumpster. Joey acknowledged he was leaving his brother in the dumpster by a grunt and a fart.

A restaurant was on the opposite side of the alley from the grungy apartment building where the Martins lived. Georgie always pulled the bones and meat from the garbage for his friends, the dogs. He used to eat some of the meat himself but got deathly sick and almost died; dogs have sturdier stomachs it seems. Georgie threw out the bones and meat on to the alley and calls the dogs from under the steps of the apartment building. Georgie always picked up the scraps left by the dogs after a run in with a bus boy over the mess in the alley. The bus boy had knocked one of Georgie's front teeth out.

He and the dogs have been friends for two years. Some jerk had thrown the dogs out of his car after mutilating them. But the mutilation was superficial. Georgie's dogs had no names; Georgie just grunted three times and they emerged from under the steps. He loved the two dogs although hideous in appearance; the dogs loved him, his dogs had no training, Pavlovian they were not. When Georgie was locked in the closet, he howled and barked so the dogs could hear him, they growled and barked back.

Georgie always waited until his mother left for work. He accepted the closet because he knew that was the only way his mother knew to take care of him, he thought. One day it was so stinking hot, the sweat from his head and forehead stung his eyes constantly; in the closet, he ripped open a box in the closet and found a plastic card.

He studied the lock that kept him from the rest of the apartment. The space between the door and the door jamb was enough so that he released the latch with the plastic card, he put the card back in the box where he found it. Georgie opened all the windows and barked while dashing from window to window; *everyone thinks me crazy, I'll act crazy*. His bark was deep and resonating and was heard for many blocks. His dogs began to bark. The neighborhood dogs went crazy.

Georgie knows when to quit so the cops won't make the scene. After several days, the tenants of the surrounding buildings began to pin point where the racket originated. The summer temperature was getting hotter and the tenants were beginning to boil with anger over the noise. Every day got hotter and every day the barking got louder until Georgie overdid it. He spent too much time at his game of barking. The screams and stones came flying through the windows of the apartment.

Georgie raced back to the closet and locked the door. The obscenities and rocks subsided as quickly as they began but not before two window panes were broken. Fortunately, the rest of the windows were pushed all the way open. Georgie knew he was in for a beating when his mother's friend got to their house and saw the broken glass. The sweaty monster of a man who had to fix them gave Georgie pain, pain. The next day, he took the plastic card from the box and slowly and painfully went to the alley so the dogs could lick his wounds.

Chapter 3
Brooding

Two weeks later, one night, after walking two blocks, Joey finally let go of Georgie's collar. Georgie, still with pain from his beating from the monster man, pulled his holey shirt back on straight. Georgie had given up the barking and howling for running in place in the closet, while he jumped over a cardboard box containing a sleeping drunk. He kicked it as he propelled himself over the box. The drunk murmured, "Fuck you." He then thought after making the successful leap about running away from his brother but he knew his brother was too fast for him, maybe not now.

For the fun of it his brother caught Georgie several times trying to run away and kicked the shit out of him, then he threw him in the dumpster. Joey, a grisly bloodthirsty individual, got his kicks by throwing big rocks at the dumpster that contained his younger brother.

The hose down came later that night, after being in the dumpster four hours, their ma couldn't stand the smell. She never sent him to school, thinking they didn't allow mutes. The next night, Georgie felt really hostile so he climbed out of the dumpster quietly, settled on splashing his brother from behind with his hand-me-down ragged shoes. A messy mud puddle lay just to the rear of his brother, while selling drugs to a couple of kids.

Georgie crept slowly and silently in the dark of the alley and splashed Joey, obscenities rang through the alley, then ran for his life down the alleyway; he thought that this was the way to get even with his brother for the dumpster and the bruises. Fear, happiness, and adrenalin was pumping through Georgie's brain. Georgie thought, attack now! Joey looked back and saw Georgie's eyes focused on the puddle. It had been raining earlier.

"Oh no you don't, you ain't going to splatter me with dirty crappie water on my new elegant shirt and pants, then run," screamed Joey as he uttered dumb shit for the millionth time. Georgie sidestepped the puddle; he whirled around and gave his brother a blank stare and tried to kick Joey in the balls but missed and hit him on the left shin and then dashed for the lights and for the crowd that always hung out in front of the Soft Stone Café. He hid behind three guys enjoying their evening wine and smoke, switching bottle back and forth. They were too busy staggering and smelling bad to really notice Georgie.

Joey was pushing drunks and yelling, "Get the fuck out of my way." Joey erupted, "I'm goin' to beat the shit out of you and stone you! You snotty nose brat. When I get through with you this time, no one is goin' to recognize your ugly fuckin' damn face, including ma! You're not goin' to look as good as those two grotesque dogs in the alley! I'm going to kill you and the dogs!"

That was it; Georgie grabbed a bottle in a brown bag from a drunk and hurled it at Joey. Immediately, there were two screams—one from the drunk that he took the bottle from and Joey. Joey still didn't see where Georgie was hidden. But Georgie knew where Joey was and this time Georgie grabbed two bottles and threw them in rapid fire; kind of like a Bazooka from WW2. He blitzed another drunk with the first bottle, he sank to the ground.

The second bottle got Joey on the side of the head, he had one side normal, the other side bloody with skin torn away. "Ahhh shittt," screamed Joey as he held his bleeding wound. The left side of his head began to swell. Joey ducked, the drunks covered his position.

He kept talking, "I'm not goin' to beat you up like Ma's friend did with red welts all over your body! I'm goin' to beat you until you turn blue that will tell people you're dead."

Georgie began to run and Joey was screaming when the drunks tried to jump Joey. Joey simply smashed through the drunks like a bowling ball through the pins. Joey could see Georgie halfway down the street running for home. Georgie knew he had no chance against his brother in a fight. He wasn't worried because he had a secret weapon that he can use against anyone. He could hear his brother's footsteps coming hard and his voice screaming obscenities. Georgie started to stretch it out, by lengthening his stride. He gained time by running out in front of a semi pulling two trailers, the brakes could be heard for miles.

Joey rolled under the second trailer and somersaulted to his feet. Georgie didn't anticipate the move. He must have enough time to make it to his secret hiding place.

He thought, *I have to do something unexpected. Hurry, hurry; what, what?* Joey's swearing was getting closer. Georgie heard his heart pounding and the pounding of Joey's feet hitting the cement. Five more steps by Joey and Georgie knew he was dead meat. Time…timing now; just as Joey grabbed his shirt, Georgie flipped over backward and his crotch hit Joey right in the face and knocked him to the ground. Georgie's scrotum twisted and torn, he landed on his head and back, screaming. Joey ripped Georgie's t-shirt off and in a fraction of a second, Georgie could feel the skin being shredded off his back by the cement, while Joey pulled him along; Joey flung Georgie on a continued assault, torrents of blood from Georgie's back created mumbled screams as loud as Joey's swearing.

Georgie locked his right knee and hit Joey in the gut as Joey ran at him. He passed over Georgie and landed on his hands, falling on his face after the force of Georgie's blow pushed Joey's legs in the air. This pulled Joey's head toward his chest onto the cement, obliterating the front portion of his scalp on the cement. Joey was so busy swinging at Georgie he didn't notice his injury until blood blinded him. Georgie jumped up running, leaving a trail of blood and agonizing pain.

Georgie couldn't scream; his brother would know where he was. He knew he would make it to his secret hiding place. Blood streaming down his back, Georgie ran twisted, his head high, his teeth set determined and clenched, ran into the alley where he lived. He jumped as high as he could and grabbed the aluminum square tubing from atop the cinder block wall that surrounded a new apartment building at the beginning of the alley.

Joey's mind was blown with pain and rage. He sat where he fell, after the blood blinded him, screaming and swearing. He then tried to rip off the part of his scalp that had fallen over his eyes, not knowing what it was. A crescendo of ear-piercing howls unmatched by any known living slum creature. Realizing his scalp, rubbing his eyes with his shirt, was loose.

Joey was up and running, keeping his right hand on his forehead preventing the blood from dripping into his eyes. Georgie then saw his brother staggering down the alley with blood still somewhat blinding his vision. His screams were now out of frustration and wildly swinging and swearing, "You'll never get away from me! I swear I'll kill your fucken ass!"

Georgie simply grunted for his dogs, they came before Joey could get to terminate his brother. Georgie petted his dogs, Dash and Bunker, he fed them, knowing they gave him protection.

The dogs were unfamiliar with the streets Georgie was taking them on. They sensed nervousness in their master and showed nervousness of their own. Georgie now had mixed emotions about his brother. And his own well-being, the adrenalin rush was over and the blood on his back was beginning to dry. Pain was developing with every passing second. Georgie stole cream from an open front store and ran painfully away.

"What about Joey? I've got to get to the medical clinic! I've got to get Joey to the medical clinic!"

Georgie stopped and turned around, still thinking of his brother; suddenly, he had a spasm in the back of his head. It felt as though his brain was trying to escape from his skull. His head felt lighter, Georgie felt dizzy, he put his hand on the back of his head, he had gouged out a part of his scalp. He could feel his skull!

The dogs hesitated; people were coming at them and they growled and attacked the closet person. Their master wasn't paying attention, Georgie's eyes rolled up and his body turned to mush. From the overbearing street noises and the screams, came an unnoticed roar approaching from the alley. A mini truck! Blood streaming down the driver's head, the truck bolted out of the alley, tires screeching on a collision course with the crowd scattering. The vicious dogs turned toward the truck and recognized the driver, they rushed toward the vehicle.

Joey cleverly outwitted the K9s and ran them both over. Georgie lay on the sidewalk in a blood loss daze, moaning. The mini-truck occupant was wearing a bloody green headband holding his hair and scalp together and screaming obscenities at the crowd: "Get the hell out of the way." Joey gave them the finger. Bodies fly off the mini-truck as it careened through the crowd; the truck ran over Georgie, lying on the sidewalk.

"Georgie," a voice said calmly, through the chaos as the mini-truck sped away.

"Georgie," the voice said again. "Georgie," for the third time. Georgie opened his eyes, then stood up and couldn't figure who was lying on the ground. His eyes opened wide and mumbled, "fa-da," in his almost inaudible pronunciation, then jumped into the man's arms and said, "fa-da," again.

Georgie planted kisses all over the man's face. He was crying and kissing so hard that he didn't realize his fa-da said, "I have been allowed to help you." He patted Georgie on the head. Georgie's mumbles turned into words in Georgie's mind but silently stared into his father eyes.

Georgie only knew him from his mother's pictures. "I'm here to give you a second chance in life!"

Georgie just stared. "What do you mean a second chance?" saying his first sentence ever.

"Life is so precious and you have had misery, not a life," his father answered.

"But father, you're dead!"

"Yes, and you are too! Turn your head and see what happened to you and your dogs," as he squeezed Georgie to his chest.

Georgie saw several bodies including both of his dogs and his own. "Father, father, why am I lying there when I'm in your arms?"

"I have my arms around your soul, son, you have been given a gift of a new life. Your soul will be placed in an inadvertent body that has no soul."

"Father, what is a soul?"

"Son, that is your essence of your thought process that makes you human and a child of the supreme order, your memory will stay intact so that you understand abuse. I must say goodbye and I hope he lets me see you again."

Georgie and his father slowly rose upward, ascend, everything went from clear to a blur then blackness. Georgie said, "Father, don't leave me! I am afraid, I only know you from mother's pictures of you. I have much to tell you now that I can speak!"

But as soon as Georgie uttered his last word, Georgie was engulfed in a mist and was swept away—oblivion!

Chapter 4
Solution for the Solution

In 1978, all toxic substances are banned from the classroom and that meant I have to shut down my gold and silver plating in class. I, Mr. Victor Vance, had to reluctantly put the solutions away that I have used for several years in my classroom. Now the kids won't be able to silver plate pennies and try to pass them off as dimes in the cafeteria. Of course, several hassles arose from such incidents but were amicably resolved and a briefing from Victor to all his classes on the futility of trying to dupe the cashier in the cafeteria into believing that a silver-plated penny is a dime will never happen again and those of you trying to sell silver sets of coins is a fraud, unless you tell the buyer that the coins are plated.

There is a penalty involved; you will have to serve detention after school and pay the money back. Some of the other entrepreneurs try to sell coins of any vintage as gold sets. The first thing that happened after class, the plating can no longer continue. Victor Vance's high school class gold ring that is serving as the replenishing gold anode disappeared from its perch on the positive wire in the solution of the plating emulsion; a search of outside lockers and the ring is found.

To his amazement, Victor Vance finds the gold ring in Johnny Two buck's locker, his student assistant. He confronts his assistant Johnny and he says, "I don't know how it got there."

The boy has a perfect record and is completely honest. "Wait a moment, I was standing at my locker, Peter tapped me on my shoulder so I would look away from my locker, two girls were giggling and I looked back at my locker, Paul was standing beside me on my right side and Peter was on my left then, the girls giggled even louder. That's how the ring got in my locker. Peter gave me a roofie that's why I have a Quasimodo-like gait and the girls broke loose with ear piercing laughter. That's why I've been walking funny."

"So, Johnny, you had an episode with the school sharks; they have big teeth and have a big bite; stay away."

The plating is made up of distilled water and sodium cyanide, which is, of course, poisonous, but with cleaning the milky layer off silver and gold with plain baking soda, it neutralizes the poison and shines the object plated to a bright luster. The school administration said it did neutralize the poison but a law is a law and the school had to abide by It.

My thoughts turned to how to make a solution that's nontoxic. Most of the students really appreciated finishing metal objects with plating. So, Johnny Two Buck, my lab assistant, still walking funny, and I began experimenting with various substances to replace the old forbidden tried and true majestically wonderful finish. After two months of trying just about everything non-toxic, we hit upon lemon and potato juice mix that worked but not as good as the old formula.

I crushed some ascorbic acid table commonly known as Vitamin C. The combination applied a very adhesive plate of silver coating. And in no time, I began getting complaints from the cafeteria about silver pennies being used as dimes again. I told the students if they did it again, I'd shave their heads, paint them black, put three holes in their heads, and use their heads for bowling balls. I had laughter but I never had another complaint.

Victor Vance graduated from San Francisco State University and had been teaching for fifteen years at the George Washington Junior-Senior High School in R-Coti district, California.

Chapter 5
Second Life

Two days before the President holidays, Johnny was stripping a wire with a razor blade. He had misplaced, or I had, the wire cutters and strippers. Two students were scuffling in the back of the room and one of the students hit Johnny Two Buck's elbow and he cut the skin of his left thumb with a razor blade. The skin fell into the plating solution. The Indian boy cringed in pain as he knocked off the orchid being cloned into the plating solution.

There was a sudden flash of light and Johnny looked down at the five-gallon container that held the makeshift solution. A greenish-silver tinge engulfed the solution and to his amazement, a cocoon shape formed. Johnny turned and grabbed the two fighting students and hurriedly took them to their assigned seats and said, "Look what you did to my thumb and the plating solution!"

Both said they were sorry and pleaded that they were just fooling around. First thing, a band aid for the thumb as Johnny walked to the teacher's desk. "Trouble?" asked Mr. Vance.

"Yes, I need a band aid," Johnny replied, holding his thumb with blood dripping on the cement floor. Mr. Vance opened his right desk drawer and brought out a disinfectant, Bactine, and a band aid box. In a second, Johnny was walking back to the counter where he cut his thumb and picked up the soiled batch of plating solution tub that he and Mr. Vance had sweated over on the patio behind Mr. Vance's room.

The potato peel and lemon peels were scattered on the cement that had to be picked up at the end of the day. Johnny was so happy when the final bell of the day rang. This flushed the room of bodies. Johnny yelled up at Mr. Vance, "What'll I do with the ruined solution?"

"Just put it in the cabinet with the other tub."

"What about the transformer?"

Two girls come screaming by the open door. Mr. Vance plugged his ears for a moment. "What?"

Johnny yelled, "What should I do with the transformer?"

By that time Mr. Vance had the door closed and again holding his ears, nodded his head side to side and took his hands away from his ears. Quietly, Johnny repeated, "The transformer?"

"Leave it there." (It takes nine volts of electricity and wire acting as a fishhook to deposit gold or silver on an object in solution.)

Johnny stopped at the door. "Don't leave, we have to clean up the patio, Johnny. You get the broom and I will get the big dustpan with the handle." Ten minutes later, Johnny and Mr. Vance were walking to the classroom door.

"See you after the holidays, Mr. Vance."

"Bye Johnny." Mr. Vance opened the door and Johnny stepped into the flow of bodies in their happiness of four days off.

Victor Vance looked around the room C5 checking to see if everything was in order. A few papers on the floor, all the stools placed on the tables so that the custodian can sweep up, and he said to himself, "I'm gone." The quiet serenity of the room was broken as he opened the door that led directly outside; there were no interior hallways in the school. As he looked back at the decorations in the exhibit case window, admiring the objects that his students produced, Mr. Vance noticed a streak of silver-green light passing across the exhibit window; he hesitated; two students plowed into him and almost knocked him to the cement.

Mr. Vance said to the students, "Look at the strange light streaming across the window!"

As the students and Mr. Vance started toward the door, the light disappeared as though it knew they were coming to investigate. The two students and Mr. Vance heard a rumble then lightning. *Better get to the car before it rains*, he said to himself. The two students disappeared around the corner laughing and giggling. Mr. Victor Vance unlocked the door and walked around the room, saying to himself, *I must be imaging things. I better get my glasses checked.* He walked out of the classroom scratching his head.

Chapter 6
Astonished

Victor Vance was married and had just bought a house. Fortunately, the U.S. government built houses for low-income families, after all, his salary for teaching was just six hundred a month. Victor Vance, 32, dark red hair, pushing five foot nine, sort of a disfigured nose from a childhood accident.

The next day, he had little to do but science test papers and putter around the house, playing with his two children and dog. He was on the floor of the living room, rolling around, tickling his kids, and fending off licks and play bites from his dog. The phone rang; from the floor of the living room, Victor Vance yelled, "Jan!" Victor's wife had a job with a dentist, twenty-nine years old and married for ten years. "Will you get the phone?"

"Yes." When his wife picked up the phone, it was the fire department. "Honey, your room is on fire!"

Up and running, Mr. Vance headed for his car while his wife, kids and dog stood on the stoop with an anguished look on their faces. The dog ran after him as he started down the block and stopped at the stop sign; the dog jumped up and through the open window of the driver side and landed on the passenger side with a smile on Tanny's face. The dog was a Vizsla, a Hungarian pointer retriever, capable of running at legendary speeds.

The dog was a happen chance; an elderly couple couldn't handle the dog so Jan's boss asked if Victor and she would like the dog.

"Thank you for coming. I'll need the support if I find what I think I'll find—that some student left an animal hidden in the classroom."

The school was five miles away and just one stoplight between home and school. As Mr. Vance turned the corner, he saw two fire engines in the school's parking lot. There was Mr. Acevedo, the principal, a man in his fifties, a nice sort, talking to a fireman. Victor Vance jumped out of his car and asked, "Why aren't the hoses out?"

The fireman reported, "There's no fire."

"Why are we all here?"

"A parent called me and said your room is ablaze inside with a silver-green light flashing," answered Mr. Acevedo.

Mr. Vance quickly unlocked the door and as he did so, the light disappeared. He slowly opened the door and Tanny rushed into the room and began nosing everything as dogs have a habit of doing. She started out calmly and the only thing heard was her sniffing and her toenails scraping on the polished cement floor. She continued the process, smelling every nook and cranny until she came to a hole in the plating cabinet.

"I don't recall a hole in the cabinet door," Vance said in a complaining voice. The slim wiry dog began a slow but distinctive growl coming from her throat and she began pawing at the door. Mr. Vance asked Tanny to sit while he unlocked the door.

Mr. Acevedo was looking over his shoulder, "That's a funny color, Vic, what kind of solution is that?"

Mr. Vance replied, "Plating solution."

"You know it's toxic and it's illegal in the state of California."

"This is my own brew and non-toxic. It took me six months to figure out the combination of chemicals to use."

Suddenly, Tanny picked up her ears and turned her head toward the container with the silver-green glob and raised her paw as though to shake and then rolled over and lay there as though her tummy was being rubbed. "What is your dog doing?" asked Mr. Acevedo.

"I don't know." Mr. Vance saw an almost imperceptible stream of silver-green light going over the top of the five-gallon container and hitting Tanny directly in the head. Victor Vance reached down and stuck his left index finger in the almost imperceptible stream of light and screamed, "Ouch, that hurts," as he pulled his finger away from the source of pain. There was a funny jiggling of the five-gallon container and an odious smell.

Mr. Vance and Mr. Acevedo stepped back but Tanny seemed happy as a dog could be. "I don't like it; get rid of that stuff in the bucket," Mr. Acevedo announced.

"I should have had Johnny throw it away when it was contaminated."

"What you do mean contaminated?"

"Yesterday Johnny was stripping insulation off a wire from the bucket to the transformer and he inadvertently sliced off a piece of skin from his thumb."

"Did he or did you report the injury to the office?" Mr. Acevedo the, principal of the school, asked as a person in the position of authority.

"Yes, we did," as Mr. Vance crossed his fingers behind his back. Then Mr. Vance went to re-lock the cabinet door, thinking, *I hope he doesn't check with the school nurse.* The door didn't want to close; finally, it did with a creak. They walked out together but Tanny lagged behind as though being caressed by something invisible.

Mr. Vance said, "Tanny, come!" Mr. Vance closed and locked the classroom door; a muffled sound emanated as though someone or something was murmuring in a hissing whisper. "What is that sound?" Mr. Acevedo said, startled.

"Oh, that's just the wind going through the cracks in the patio wooden fence." Driving home, Victor Vance noticed that his finger felt swollen and bleeding slightly, he put his finger in his mouth; it gave him a slight shock. *I wonder why the light didn't hurt Tanny?* He stared at his finger long enough to cross the yellow line and was headed for a collision but the oncoming driver honked his horn in time and Victor swerved back and almost steered into a ditch.

Victor Vance was over the white line on the right side of the road. He stopped to collect his thoughts for a few minutes and then drove home. The rest of the President's Holidays were uneventful.

Monday morning when he picked up Johnny Two-Buck, his student assistant and his friend walking to school, he asked Johnny, "How's your thumb, Johnny?"

"What thumb?" replied Johnny.

Mr. Vance turned and smiled keeping one eye on the road, remembering his close call. Nothing seemed abnormal as they pulled into the school parking lot, except a little pain in Mr. Vance's finger. Johnny's friend waved and was off to class. Mr. Vance unlocked the C5 classroom door and Johnny and Mr. Vance closed the door behind them so that no student can come in the classroom.

"Johnny, you better take the contaminated plating bucket and dump it in the large garbage dumpster." The cabinet door began to shake. The cracks around the door began to glow silver-green.

"I don't want to open it," Johnny cried out. "It looks too dangerous."

Mr. Vance approached the door hesitantly because it looked like the door was coming off its hinges. He tried to put the key in the lock but couldn't. "This is abnormal," as Mr. Vance and Johnny Two-Buck stepped back from the door.

The door rattled and shook, glowed bright silver-green and burst through the door and something flew over to the drinking fountain in a crescendo of silver-green blinding light and thunder. The fountain snapped on and a voice said, "I needed that! What is that stuff I was stuck in?" asked the voice from the tiny silver-green figure hanging on the drinking fountain.

Mr. Vance was sprawled on the floor with the cabinet door on top of him, what was left of it. Mr. Vance mumbled, "Plating solution," inaudibly.

"Answer the question pleaseeee? Close your mouth and stop staring at me as though I'm some kind of freak."

Johnny Two Buck closed his eyes and Mr. Vance kept his mouth open but couldn't speak. "Look at my skin, it's silver-green with leaves sticking out of me," the tiny body stuck its arm out and looked at it. "I'm a freak! Look how short I am and I don't stutter, wow! What kind of mess did my father get me into? Where are all the dead people in front of the Soft Stone Cafe? Speak up, you, so I know what's going on."

The greenish-silver naked body was sitting on the sink edge overlooking the drinking fountain. Mr. Vance and Johnny Two Buck stared wide-eyed at this tiny freakish person as Victor Vance pushed away the door and got up off the cement floor. "Speak up, where's your dog and what is this place?"

"My dog is at home and this is my classroom," Mr. Vance acknowledged.

The little silver-green body known as Georgie said, "My name is Georgie and what is your last name, sir?"

"Vance," answered Mr. Vance.

"I am Georgie, Vance. Who is the kid standing beside you?" asked the silver-green little person.

"He is my student assistant, helper and you're something he created inadvertently."

Johnny finally got his mouth working and said, "Who are you?"

"My name is Georgie Vance and I come from a terrible place where my brother ran me over with his truck. So, I'm dead but I will grow into a somewhat of a normal human being if I'm allowed to, I hope," said the little silver-green body.

"Georgie, first thing," said the startled and surprised Mr. Vance, "let Johnny and I recover from this truly amazing perchance happening."

The little voice from the silver-green creature spat out, "Johnny, what is he talking about?"

Johnny walked up to the front of the room and opened Mr. Vance's middle desk drawer and picked up a small mirror and took it back to Georgie. He handed it to Georgie; Johnny was immediately shocked with static electricity. Johnny's eyes widened with pain and he blew on his right hand and said, "Ouch, this guy is hot, Mr. Vance!"

Victor Vance hurried to a cabinet that had aluminum foil and towels. "Georgie, I'll have to wrap you up so I can move you, it is for your protection and ours."

Georgie takes another drink from the fountain then he looks in the mirror. "That's not my dad," said the tiny body. "I was to be given another life but not a silver-green midget life!"

"Johnny, tell him," uttered Mr. Vance. "As far as I can tell you are a duplicate of Johnny!"

"What does that mean?"

"You're a makeover of someone else, Georgie."

"Who am I and why do I have this awful looking skin and where are my dogs? Dead?"

"I can't answer about your dogs but I can answer about your skin. You were conceived in a vat of plating solution and an orchid that fell in at the same time Johnny sliced his thumb," acknowledged Mr. Vance. "And that is what made you, I think. lease let me wrap you up so I can take you home, so no one can see you're silver and green, and don't spark and don't shoot out bright lights, a thousand kids will encircle us if you do. I will never get you home and get me out of trouble with the school administration."

"This isn't an alley filled with trash. Where am I?" asked Georgie.

"You're at a school and I have to get you out of here before all the kids arrive for class, we would have complete chaos," replied Mr. Vance.

"What do you mean chaos?" cried the silver-green body.

"I mean all the kids will go nuts seeing a silver-green nude body."

"You mean I'm a freak?"

"No! You are a Johnny Two-Buck, sort of."

"Why can't I walk?"

"Because you are a baby." Mr. Vance wrapped up the tiny body. He put him on the wide edge of the sink with Georgie's legs out.

"I can fly but can't walk."

"Because you're a baby!" answered Mr. Vance. Mr. Vance tried to wrap him up in a towel; again Georgie came off the surface of the sink edge and hung in midair; he flapped his arms and legs for a second then stood still or lay flat in midair, so he could be wrapped up easier. "I seem to be able to fly without moving my arms and legs; why?"

"I don't know." Victor Vance leaped toward the door with Georgie in his arms and yelled to Johnny, "Keep the joint percolating, I'll be BACK!"

Mr. Vance's feet barely touched the ground as he exited the room. Students were gathering at the door for the first period; two students asked, "Mr. Vance, where are you going?"

"I have to get rid of this bundle!" Suddenly the bundle pulled Mr. Vance off his feet, his arms were stretched upward, allowing the bundle to slip away from his grasp and float. Victor Vance tumbled to the sidewalk with a thud, scraped his right elbow, and glanced at his shoe tips that were gone; his left big toe was without a sock, then he put out a pronounced ouch; his right elbow was bleeding.

The students ran to help Mr. Vance but the bundle making funny noises fell back into his grasp and picked him up. First period class students stood amazed as the bundle pulled Mr. Vance along with his shoe tips, what was left, grinding on the sidewalk then lifting Mr. Vance in the air while he shouted to the bundle, "My car is the fourth one on the left!"

The bundle pulled Mr. Vance over the three cars, banging his feet with Mr. Vance yelling, "Ouch," several times! Then the bundle dropped Mr. Vance on his butt on top of his car, causing a dent. Victor Vance ended up at the driver's door, he grabbed the bundle off the roof of the car and got in the car and pushed the dent up as the students ran toward the car.

"Now look what you've done to my roof, Georgie!"

"What do you mean; you just adjusted it."

"I hope so," said Mr. Vance.

"I can't seem to walk Mr. Vance but I can levitate!"

"How do you know how to float?"

"I was thinking floating," said Georgie, the voice in the bundle.

Chapter 7
Home

The entrance into Victor Vance's house was uneventful; everyone was still asleep. Both of Mr. Vance's children were sick, the flu was going around. Mr. Vance put Georgie on the floor by a chair near the wall and unwrapped Georgie from the towel. He noticed that the lower part of Georgie's body looked normal in coloring but his head and shoulders were still silvery-green and his body seemed to be bigger. Mr. Vance thought to measure the baby and take his temperature.

Victor with the baby in his arms moved to the kitchen and found the measuring tape in the bottom drawer. Then, moving down the hall to the bathroom as quietly as possible, he acquired a thermometer, from the dark ages, from the cabinet in the bathroom, a rectal one. He quietly and quickly put Georgie in the bathroom sink and the only sound emanating was the electric clock on the wall that made a tick-tick sound. Mr. Vance looked up. "Wow, Mr. Acevedo is going to be on my case for leaving school. Georgie, I want to measure you and take your temperature."

"Why?"

"Because you're growing fast and heat is radiating from your body more than normal."

Georgie spoke up, "I have never been measured and I have never had my temperature taken."

"Hold still. I can't measure you if you're twirling around in the air." Mr. Vance grabbed Georgie and said, "How do you twirl in place like that?"

"I don't know; this body has more energy than I can handle," said an exasperated Georgie.

Mr. Vance again grabbed Georgie by the shoulders and laid him on the rug in the bathroom. He took a measuring tape out of the cabinet and unrolled it.

"Hum, you're twenty-nine and ¾ inches long. Temperature…" As soon as Mr. Vance inserted the thermometer, the mercury shot out the end. "Wow, you are hot," as Mr. Victor Vance cleaned up the mercury from the rug with toilet tissue; he extracted what was left of the thermometer from Georgie's bottom and threw the residue in the trash. Immediately, he thought of the outside thermometer, he walked to the kitchen with Georgie in his arms and put him on the counter and held him down lightly with one hand; he opened the window and pulled the thermometer out of its holder, washed it with soap and returned to the bathroom with Georgie.

"Georgie, this may give you discomfort so don't cry out if you can help it." The thermometer only went up to a hundred and twenty, it was already at one hundred and ten and moving up. "Double wow, Georgie, I don't know why you're still alive, anyone in your condition is in deep trouble with anything over one hundred and four."

"You mean, I'm dead twice!"

"No Georgie, you're alive but your metabolism is abnormal. No wonder you're growing so fast."

"What's metabolism?" a convulsive Georgie was gagging and discharged silver-green light, which hit the protective cap in the wall plug and blew the circuit breaker.

"Georgie, I'll tell you what metabolism is later." Three screams in unison, their electric blankets shocked them, because Georgie was so full of electricity it went through the house wiring and shocked Mr. Vance's family. Mrs. Vance and the two children, Heather and Jason, got a high-pulsed electrical sting.

"What the hell happened?" Jan Vance came screaming into the living room.

Mr. Vance began to laugh and a funny squeak came out of Georgie! "What the hell are you laughing at? What's that you have in the bundle, why is your hair standing on end?" demanded Mrs. Vance.

"This is your new son!"

"What, was I in a coma for nine months?"

"No, this thing happened at school. I can't explain it right now, he is a unique character. Take care of him, I have to go back to work."

"Wait a minute; is this a baby or a creature, I leave outside in the kennel with the dog or do I feed it with a baby bottle?" asked Mrs. Vance.

Finally, Mr. Vance unwrapped the bundle. "What, a silvery-green twirling kid?" Mrs. Vance jumped back.

Mr. Vance stuck his finger in Georgie's mouth. "Feed him with a baby bottle; I gotta go!"

"Don't go yet; you haven't introduced me," squeaked Georgie.

"It can talk and it doesn't have teeth!" cried a vacillating Mrs. Vance.

"How do you do, Mrs. Vance, my name is Georgie! I can't walk but I can float and eat."

A voice came from the back of the house, "Mom, I can't sleep; there's too much noise."

Just as Mr. Vance was leaving the house, "What's Dad doing home at this hour?" another voice asked. Jason was home from school sick and as he rubbed his eyes, everyone laughed, even Georgie. "What are you laughing at?" Jason yawned and put his left little finger in his left ear and twisted it back and forth.

"Why son, your hair is standing up straight and the bottom of your pjs are at your knees; you do look comical," mentioned Jan Vance to her son.

Jason, a freckle-faced blue-eyed curly strawberry blonde, but today his hair was straight up. He then turned and laughed at his sister; her hair was straight up too. Heather and Jason were fraternal twins, flu had kept them home. They laughed at each other and noticed other laughter, and it was not their mother's. They both looked at their mother. "What's that floating in the towel?" they asked.

"It's something your dad brought home; his name is Georgie," she unwrapped him again.

Jason put his arm beside Georgie's arm and said, "Why is his skin so different than mine?"

"Because there are many different races in the world and we are just one of them," answered Jan Vance.

Georgie began laughing. Heather asked, "What is he laughing at, he is the one that looks funny and he kinda looks like Johnny."

A frown came over Georgie's face and he replied, "I'm Georgie, I'm just Georgie, and besides, I'm hungry; may I use your left breast?"

Jan Vance turned somewhat red, her freckles turned darker and her eyes lit up. "Certainly not, I'll get some warm milk."

"I haven't had warmed milk since I was a baby," replied Georgie.

"You are a baby," exclaimed Jan Vance.

Georgie frowned and stuck his finger in his mouth and pulled it out and said, "I feel a buildup!"

"What do you mean a buildup?" asked Heather. Buzz, bang, lightning came out of the finger that was in Georgie's mouth. A sliver-green streak was sent to the ceiling.

"Ma, there's a hole in the ceiling! Georgie put it there, I didn't," said a squeaky voice from Jason, a changing voice.

Mrs. Vance came back with a heated beer bottle with milk and a nipple; with a laugh Georgie said this was my favorite beer, he grabbed onto the bottle and sucked the bottle dry and burped. "Georgie, is there any chance you can contain the lightning bolts because it's cold out and we don't want to live in a cold sponge," announced Mrs. Vance while she looked at the ceiling where the lightning bolts had gone through the ceiling insulation and the roof, the asphalt shingles on fire.

There was banging on the front door as though someone was trying to smash through. "It's Joyce from across the street," she opened the door.

"I called the fire department; your house is on fire!"

Mrs. Vance raced to Jason's room and placed Georgie on the bed and said to Georgie, "If anyone sees you, they will place you in a freak show so hide under the blanket. Don't make a sound." She ran out of Jason's room, tripped and fell, got up and fell back down while trying to put her slipper on, then rushed to the kitchen, grabbed the fire extinguisher, and ran to the front door, saw the fireman hosing down the roof; she ran back to the kitchen, grabbed a large pot, stuck the fire extinguisher in the pot, put it under the hole in the ceiling, grabbed the extinguisher, and ran back outside to watch the fireman, making sure no fireman came into the house.

Totally exhausted, Mrs. Vance breathing hard stood in front of the door blocking it. All the while Joyce rattled on about getting the kids out of the house before it burns down. Out of breath, Jan said, "My house is not burning down and no to getting the kids out of the house." Jan stopped the fireman trying to break her grip on the doorknob with a bang on the fireman's leg with the fire extinguisher. "You can't go in, my kids are asleep, the fire is out on the roof," she put down the kitchen fire extinguisher.

A fireman on the roof said, "I'm going to cut a bigger hole in the roof!"

"Don't you dare cut a bigger hole in the roof," screamed Mrs. Vance. "It was just a minor lightning strike."

"A what?" said the puzzled fireman.

"I'm sorry, I just coughed," muttered Jan. "Get off the roof and get back to the fire station," she yelled.

"Yes Mrs. what's your name, we will," said the fireman on the roof.

Jan Vance picked up the kitchen fire extinguisher and slammed the front door. Joyce stood there with her mouth open. "Well, I never," and walked slowly back across the street mumbling to herself.

Jan ran to the kitchen to put the fire extinguisher back, kicked over the pot with her bare foot, and screamed, "Ouch." The pot she left under the water pouring from the roof, ran back and got a bigger pot from the kitchen while being drenched. Then ran to Jason's bedroom with one foot wet, clothes and hair soaked, to get Georgie while Jason and Heather were standing in the front room, scratching their behinds and wondering what was going on, half asleep.

Chapter 8
Indian Boys

Victor Vance dropped off Johnny Two Buck at his house, as he did every school day. His family was from the Zuni tribe but did not choose to live on the reservation because of the distance between work and the reservation. Mr. Two Buck was the artist in residence at the local college and performing the tasks his ancestors had done for thousands of years. Johnny was an excellent example of a Zuni; his workmanship was absolutely spectacular as was his father's and mother's.

Mr. Vance and Johnny had talked about the big question of whether his mother and father would like another child, who looked exactly like Johnny, at home; the answer they came up with was that Georgie was a clone. He didn't have the mind of a Zuni Indian, after finding out what Georgie had done at school to their son. Mr. and Mrs. Two Buck listened to Johnny; he divulged that Georgie could be dangerous. "He has a silver-green light that he can project at any time, he singed my shirt in back that I didn't see until I took it off."

They thought the real question was who will keep Georgie as he grew and matured. They decided for good or bad, Victor and his wife would interrogate him first to find out whether he will have a stable personality.

"I will call you, Johnny, as soon as I find out more about this infant, Georgie. He seems to have qualities beyond the norm. I and my wife will spend time with Georgie to find if he can handle normal family life. After, say, a week or two we'll express our thoughts with your family." Mr. Vance closed the door of the car, he had another thought and rolled down the window and said, "Can you keep a secret for a day about Georgie?"

"I'll try," replied Johnny.

"Don't tell anyone, even your mother and father, that Georgie came out of a five-gallon vat."

Victor Vance drove to his house thinking how many kids can keep a secret for more than twenty minutes, especially his kids; they had probably blabbed to the neighborhood kids. Sure enough, Mr. Vance pulled into the driveway and Jason and Heather had the kid next door on the ground yelling, "You're crazy, we have a younger brother; he is just one month old!"

The kid was on his back and said, "No, you don't; your mother hasn't had the big belly!"

Victor Vance slammed the car door so hard that the kids heard it, because they had paid no attention to the car pulling up, they just kept screaming at the top of their lungs. Even the door slamming didn't stop their yelling. Mr. Vance walked over and yanked them apart and calmly spoke to his kids, "Get in the house now!"

"But Dad, Jimmy doesn't believe we have a little brother that's silver-green and shoots lightning from his fingers!"

"What, no thunder with the lightning, that's ridiculous," Victor said. "He's just yellow with meningitis; now get into the house!"

Jason and Heather knew if he said it again, their fannies would be red in a matter of minutes, consequences came in a hurry when Victor Vance showed anger, so they rushed into the house. Mr. Vance took Jimmy by the hand, took him next door and rang the bell so that Mrs. Bolton wouldn't think that it was okay to hold Jimmy down and scream at him, he wanted to soothe any hard feelings. The door opened slowly because Mrs. Bolton had a bowl in her hands and a whisk beating up some egg whites.

"What has Jimmy done now?"

"Oh, he hasn't done anything wrong, my kids and your kid had a disagreement and my kids looked like they were getting violent so I brought Jimmy home; bye."

"Oh okay," replied Mrs. Bolton.

"No hard feelings, Jimmy?"

"No Mr. Vance."

Victor Vance walked into his house. Mrs. Vance had both Heather and Jason sitting on chairs, again explaining the situation. "He'll be taunted as a freak as you taunted Jimmy next door. People will never, never allow Georgie to have a normal life of any kind."

With a chattering upper lip, Jason said, "Dad, we are both sorry; we'll try to keep our mouths shut."

Heather Vance said with tears in her eyes said, "Sorry-sorry, Dad."

Victor Vance hugged his daughter and mentioned, "He will be hard to get used to." As he cuddled Heather and kissed them both, "Don't just try keeping your mouths shut, keep them shut or something bad will happen to Georgie and the only way we can stop it is by never saying a word about his existence until we know all there is to know about Georgie. If he is to have a somewhat normal life, or will he turn bad."

A long thin silver-green light slowly crept just above the floor from Jason's bedroom. The family knew that Georgie was listening to their conversation as they stepped into the bedroom, careful not to step on the silver-green light. Somehow, they thought it was part of Georgie's being. Georgie was now standing on the bed but still floating vertically, he looked like he was standing, this startled the entire family as they entered the bedroom.

Jason said, "Why are you still floating?" Jason moved closer to the bed.

"I fear that I might start another fire in this beautiful house and I don't want to do that."

"Georgie, I want you to know that we mean you no harm." Jason and Heather shook their heads, meaning they would keep his extraordinary gifts secret. "All of us want you to be our second son, we hope you will trust us and we will help you in every way," responded Victor.

"So far you have been very nice to me," replied Georgie. "I come from a background of distrust and deceit. Only if I can overcome fear and distrust of you and other people," explained Georgie.

Mr. Vance left the room for a minute and came back with a clipboard, paper and pencil and asked, "Georgie, since you have a memory of another life and you can verbalize, can you write your name and street address?"

"Maybe," he answered. Victor gave him the clipboard with paper and pencil, he held the pencil okay but couldn't write legibly then said, "I never learned to write."

"Boy, you can sure tell you're a school teacher because in my neighborhood, if someone asked this question and wrote it down, they'd ask how did you get fucked up."

Jason and Heather jumped back at the word. "Wow Dad, he sure knows words we didn't know." Jason had his fingers crossed behind his back.

37

Georgie was trying to answer all their questions so he continued, "I was born with a speech impediment, but my mother at first thought it wasn't true, until I was old enough to speak and of course, I couldn't, I could drool and grunt. My brother never ever let up teasing and bullying me and worst of all, physically abused me with a constant stream of beatings away from mother's eyes. She saw the bruises but thought I was handicapped neurologically and had fallen or tripped. She thought under the barrage of profanities and abuse that my brother loved me and that if anything happened to her, he would take care of me. He killed me by running me over with his truck."

The Vance family noticed leaves, very tiny ones, emerging from his skin, but smoldering and turning to ash and falling onto the bedspread but the ash had not cooled; the bedspread on the bed was a flower design with a red-orange background, gold flowers big and small and very pale green leaves, and it was turning brown being scorched by the falling ash still hot.

"Georgie, can you stop the burning permanently?"

"I am not sure but I will try right now, Mr. Vance."

"Call me Dad and if you don't mind, I will call you son and Georgie, of course." Talking about his brother who killed him, his skin changed to silver-green; when talking about his mother, his skin was normal. When his emotions took over, he began to weep, his tears rolled down his cheeks in a normal fashion, but left streaks on his face. His face silver-green where the tears rolled down his cheeks, the rest of his face looked normal.

"My brother, you can well imagine, is constantly in trouble with the authorities and constantly dealing in illegal substances." The top sheet on the bed now had holes in it and was completely brown with steam rising from it as the tears hit the hot spots on the bedspread. While this discussion was taking place, his hair turned from jet black to white and black again.

Mr. Vance interrupted Georgie's description of his previous life, "Do you think you can clear your mind?" Georgie nodded as the last tear fell onto the bedspread but this time it just turned the spot on the bedspread silver-green and Georgie turned to a normal skin color. "That's good, Georgie, don't think of anything negative. I want to put you into the tub, you're rank, do you like hot and spicy?"

"I don't know what that is because my only watering was hosed down every night in cold water."

"Jan, where are the rubber gloves, dear? I'll need them to give Georgie a bath," requested Victor Vance. The family had misgivings about giving Georgie a bath after he put a hole in the ceiling of the living room, with a flick of the wrist.

Mr. Vance asked Georgie, "Have you ever had a bath?"

"Which life?"

"Your first life," replied Mr. Vance.

"Yes, the kitchen sinks twice. I was mostly hosed down. Not once did I have a chance of peace and quiet while taking a bath. Always had wet clothes to put on. Since I am in this baby body, I assume you will have to wash me Mr. Vance… Dad."

"Yes Georgie."

Chapter 9
Bath with Rubber Gloves

Mrs. Vance was back with the rubber gloves. Georgie held his arms up to be carried while Mr. Vance put the protective rubber gloves on. "Do you think, Georgie, that we can make it to the bathroom without putting a hole through a wall?" asked Mr. Vance.

"I'm new at this life too, Mr. Vance." Victor's hands were starting to sizzle.

"Georgie, turn off the heat, my hands will blister in seconds if you don't shut the heat down."

"I am thinking cool and I'll try to keep the lightning bolts to a minimum." The passage to the bathroom was uneventful.

"That's better, Georgie, I wasn't sure we'd make it to the bathtub." Georgie and Mr. Vance's conversation entering the bathroom was one-sided. "Georgie, after your bath I'm taking you to my classroom and I'm going to make sandals so that you'll be protected from static electricity." Mr. Vance ran the bath water hoping against hope that he didn't get a big shock. Mr. Vance asked Georgie, "Do you have a way of knowing when you're giving off a bolt?" Before Georgie could say a word, he sneezed and blew orchid leaves across Mr. Vance's face and the wall of the bathroom. "Was that mucus you hit me with, Georgie? It struck Dad across his forehead!"

"No, that is a sneeze, that's snot." Georgie put his left index finger on his left nostril and blew through his other and hit Mr. Vance across the chin and mouth with a high viscosity silver mucus. Victor looked in the medicine chest mirror and it appeared his own skin looked like a mask of silver-green.

"Georgie, this isn't Halloween," and they both laughed, Georgie laughed a lot. Dripping with snot, Mr. Vance put some of Heather's bubble bath in the water, while Mr. Vance wiped his face with a towel. He placed Georgie in the water and somehow, Georgie flung a stream of bubbles across the rest of Mr. Vince's uncovered face.

At home with his mother and brother, he had never laughed; he didn't know happiness existed and with the friendliness of the Vances, Georgie felt safe and secure to laugh for the first time. Georgie laughed more; Mr. Vance had his head under the water faucet of the sink. "Only so much is funny, Georgie." Mr. Vance wiped his face with a towel then snapped Georgie with it.

Georgie stopped laughing when the soap got in his eyes. "Georgie, you're not supposed to be smart at your age," he wiped Georgie's eyes with a slight hint of malicious intent.

"Ouch, that hurt my face," but Mr. Vance threw the towel over Georgie's face to break his concentration.

Victor Vance snatched Georgie out of the tub, his hands under his armpits that set off a chain reaction. A high-pitched laugh, a low-pitched laugh, several giggles, a snort then a lightning bolt that put a hole in the bathroom ceiling sending down debris that whitened Mr. Vance's hair and lit up Georgie into laughter again.

"Georgie, I may have to keep you in the dog kennel if you keep burning holes in the house!" Georgie, still an infant in his new form, could not resist using these new powers that came to him just thinking about them. Suddenly, it occurred to Georgie that he needed to walk because people would pick up on his levitation and moving through the air without touching the ground. Mr. Vance turned his back on Georgie. Georgie slipped into the hallway and into Jason's bedroom again without anyone seeing him. The noise created by the hole in the bathroom ceiling had everyone running from the front room.

"Well Dad, this doesn't go all the way to the roof like the other one."

"Dad, your hair sure turned color," remarked Jason with a smirk on his face. Mr. Vance began rubbing his face in frustration. Mrs. Vance grabbed him and put his head under the cold-water faucet. Heather and Jason realized that the silver-green brat had escaped. Mr. Vance splashed through the bathtub, getting his shirt wet and covering him in suds from the bath, the bubbles were so high it took several seconds to find he wasn't in the bathroom.

"Do you mean that kid is not under all the foam and bubbles?" said Mr. Vance, still wiping his head with a towel. Heather and Jason laughed then looked out the bathroom door and there he was going into the kitchen. The children scrambled into the kitchen, they heard the refrigerator door slam closed and things being dropped.

As they rounded the corner, there was no Georgie. "He must be in the frig," as he spoke, Jason opened the door. There was Georgie trying to unscrew a cap on one of Dad's beer bottles. "Georgie, you can't drink that, you're not twenty-one, babies drink milk," as Jason stared at Georgie.

Heather wrenched the bottle out of Georgie's hands, but not without a shock. Heather screamed in pain and pulled back and again screamed. "You little freak, give me that." By that time, Jason grabbed the bottle with both hands, while Georgie somehow controlled the bottle with an unseen control of his own. Heather got her hand back in the struggle. Here were two kids trying to take a beer bottle from a baby and the baby was winning without touching the bottle.

Mr. Vance came around the corner with a determined look on his face, matted hair, torn shirt, ripped pants slipped below his belly button, one shoe filled with water and squishing when he walked. His other foot was halfway out of his left shoe and his tie was twisted and resting on his back where Mrs. Vance had twisted it when she stuck Mr. Vance's head under the faucet. The top of his shirt was wet and bothering him because the cold water was dripping down his chest.

"Georgie, give me that bottle this minute," demanded Mr. Vance. Unfortunately, the bottle was made of glass and it bounced off Mr. Vance's head and knocked him to the floor without breaking his head or the bottle. While he was on the floor, Mr. Vance remembered he put an extension cord in the bottom drawer. The extension cord was a twelve-footer; while Jason and Heather had hold of one foot each of Georgie, Mr. Vance tied a slipknot in the cord and threw it around Georgie. It circled Georgie's chest and arms.

Mr. Vance crawled backwards while getting up, he pulled Georgie to Jason's bedroom and tied the extension cord to the bed post. He then wrapped the cord around the bedpost until Georgie came in the doorway with Jason and Heather still holding on to his feet. Mrs. Vance brought a baby bottle of warm milk. She had found the bottle behind some old dishes on the very top shelf in the kitchen cabinet.

Georgie dropped the beer and grabbed the baby bottle without sparking or giving Mrs. Vance a shock; even so, she jumped back knocking Jason to the floor. "Georgie, we can't go on like this, either you behave or you are going to Juvenile Hall, do you understand?"

"I'm partly sorry but this body and power is electrifying, Mr. Vance, I just want to show off so bad. The best thing is for me to talk coherently so everyone understands me."

"Georgie, you are destroying the house, our patience, and exhausting our family."

While Jason got up from the floor with tears in his eyes, Georgie drank the milk. His coloring changed from silver-green to normal while drinking the milk. He seemed longer as he finished the milk. Georgie then dropped the baby bottle, it bounced on the floor, bounced back to the mattress, Georgie was asleep. The Vance family silently walked out of Jason's bedroom but Mr. Vance went back in and tied Georgie securely to the bedposts. Then Mr. Vance asked his family to come into the living room and have a family meeting quietly.

He said to Jason and Heather in a whisper, "Do you think you can help me and your mother take care of this makeshift, unruly, gifted child?"

"Gee Dad, I don't know," Jason said.

"Maybe if he uses his strength on us to burn us with that sliver-green beam of light; that hurt us with the beer bottle, but we held on," said Jason and Heather.

"Sure looks like Johnny Two Buck, only smaller!"

"He is Johnny," said Daddy Vance in a low voice.

"What?" Heather jumped. Daddy Vance clamped his hand over his daughter's mouth with little pressure. She said, "But what happened to his skin, a clone should look identical?"

"What are the green things hanging out of his skin?" a questioning Mrs. Vance asked.

"Jan, I don't think he is a clone, he is something else."

"This business of floating seemingly, no gravity holding him down like the rest of us; what's that?" barked Jason.

"Hold it down, everyone, let me tell the truth and how it came about and how Georgie was born," said Mr. Vance as calmly as he could. "I'll start with births. There are two parents involved in the birth of a child. Barring that some invertebrate animals and plants give birth, budding is actually a kind of cloning and then there is no such thing as human cloning from DNA. Keep this a secret.

Georgie is the product of two different ones from a parasitic plant, now this will grow on any kind of nourishment.

"Georgie is an impossible combination caused by the plating solution. Somehow my makeshift plating solution contributed about ninety-percent to his birth. Johnny contributed a piece of skin of his left thumb, that's five-percent and an orchid contributed five-percent. Now how this happened over the president's holidays, I have no idea except that the chemical qualities of the plating solution promoted organic life and for some reason, an entity wanted this to happen.

"Oh God, why did I say that I keep the chemical formula in my desk drawer at school; what if someone finds it!"

"Vic, you keep rattling on but what are we going to do with this child, this is crazy," Mrs. Vance emptied her soul.

"You always wanted another child; here's your chance!"

Jason and Heather looked at their mother as she puzzled it out loud. "What about Johnny's family? That complicates the adoption."

"What adoption, he came out of a five-gallon vat of homemade plating solution!"

"Dad," said Jason, "let's keep him; I can play cops and robbers with him and I'll bet he'll be top notch in cops and robber games!"

"What do you mean? One shot from his finger and he could kill you, Jason!"

"Oh yea, I never thought of that but we could win against other kids."

Mr. Vance glared at his son for a moment before he spoke again, "First of all, this is reality not some dumb game you want to play," still staring at Jason.

Jason was now cringing after what he said and seeing the annoyance in his dad's eyes. "Johnny said to me he looks Zuni, but he doesn't have a Zuni brain and his mom and dad would have trouble with him floating, electrical charges flying around their heads."

Mr. Vance pounded his fist quietly on the coffee table and said in a low voice, "I'll go over to Mr. and Mrs. Two Buck's house and talk to them as soon as I make Georgie some car tire sandals at school."

In 1979, California still hadn't passed a law that car tires had to have steel cords. Some tires being sold still had nylon cords. Sandals made from nylon cord tires will last a very long time except on Georgie, he probably would have to make a new pair every day, thought Mr. Vance, *how will I keep up*. "I'll need everyone to come with me to care for Georgie and see that he doesn't get out of control."

The drive to the school was uneventful, Georgie stayed wrapped in his blanket and in Mrs. Vance's arms with a baby pacifier stuck in his mouth. The only thing mentioned was from Mrs. Vance that Georgie seemed to be getting heavier. Heather and Jason were still thinking about the stare that their dad gave after Jason had talked about cops and robbers. They turned into the school parking lot. Mr. Vance asked Jason to unlock the gate and the classroom door, he handed him the keys. Heather had to open the car door and help her mother out with Georgie.

Mrs. Vance complained, "His weight has changed more, he seems larger." Mr. Vance came around to the passenger side and took Georgie from his wife.

Chapter 10
Crafts

Mr. Vance worked in the room of his choice because in the early years of the school, he had been asked to design the room. The original part of the school was finished in 1967. But Mr. Vance's room was completed in 1969 and it was a room especially for art and science. Everyone thought it was a weird combination but also thought there was just a fuzzy line between the arts and sciences; after all, many of the artists had to create chemicals and equipment used in other industries today.

Mr. Vance grabbed white paper from his desk. He walked to the back of the room where the band saw was located. Victor Vance intended to outline Georgie's feet by pressing the paper around Georgie's feet and adding a half of an inch all around but Georgie had other plans; he burned the paper to his foot size. Jason had been holding Georgie but dropped him as the flames engulfed everything; only the paper under Georgie's foot was not burned.

"Well, I wish this happened in class." Mr. Vance stomped out the flames on the cement floor. Georgie had left the space between his toes on the paper; amazing, Mr. Vance thought it a perfect burn and a perfect pattern. He picked up the jagged footprints from the floor, traced his foot patterns onto a piece of rubber tire with a piece of chalk. He went to cut out the rubber shoe bottoms on the band saw. He switched on the saw, it switched on Georgie.

He giggled and took off flying around the room as though tethered to a rope attached to the middle of the room, while Mr. Vance sawed the smelly old tire. Heather and Jason began giggling and chasing Georgie around the room. Mr. Vance cut out strips of leather. Leather inserts to cover the rubber tire sandal soles. He put quick drying glue on the rubber to complete the sandal bottoms. He reached over to the cabinet to the right of the band saw and took out buckles, rivets, and equipment to secure the rivets.

After finishing up the sandals, without looking, Mr. Vance slyly jumped up and grabbed the circling Georgie, who immediately crashed to the floor. Heather and Jason couldn't stop their forward momentum and bumped into Mr. Vance, tripping over Georgie and sprawling them onto the floor.

"Clean up on aisle 6," blurted Victor Vance.

Georgie laughed but the Vance kids wobbled and hobbled, some aches and pains slowed their enthusiasm. Several groans were heard but no crying, while Mr. Vance picked up the sandals from the band saw table and put the right one on Georgie. But as Mr. Vance recovered from the collision with Georgie, he asked his wife to pick up Jason and Heather, who now were sitting on the cement floor, while he put a stainless-steel cable between the leather and rubber at the heel of the left sandal so that it will drag on the floor to dissipate the static electricity.

Mr. Vance bent the cable in the middle of its twenty-inch length then put the sandal on Georgie, he then put Georgie on his feet, immediately Georgie dimmed lights and turned to normal coloring.

"Dad, how did you know to stick the wire in Georgie's sandal?" inquired Heather.

"I simply grounded him to the cement floor with the cable dragging and it eliminated the static buildup." Suddenly, Georgie took his first step; the next step was faster, the next even faster; the next equivalent to running.

Mr. Vance yelled, "Slow down, Georgie." Mr. Vance took one big leap and caught Georgie in his arms. "The cable is working properly, Georgie didn't shock me."

Georgie stayed a normal skin color. He giggled, Mr. Vance tickled him and they both laughed but Mr. Vance warned Georgie that there were many sharp corners in the classroom and if he got hurt, he didn't know how to repair him. Georgie laughed with a bubbly sort of attitude and gashed himself on the end of a steel table. Up popped leaves that covered the wound then they disappeared and Georgie turned to normal skin color.

Mr. Vance and family stood staring at Georgie still in Mr. Vance's arms. Georgie was now at three foot tall and growing. "Don't scare us like that," said a frightened Mrs. Jan Vance.

Heather and Jason were still staring at where the wound was located on Georgie's arm. Jason said, "How did you do that? Superman has everything bounce off him and Wonder Woman uses bracelets to ward off oncoming danger. Vampires only die when someone pounds a wooden stake in their heart. Georgie uses an eight-second heel job, his defense against unknown perils."

"I don't know how I did it," answered Georgie as he jumped on Victor's shoulders.

"Mom, Dad, his lips didn't move and I could hear what he is saying," complained the shocked Heather.

"Don't worry, children, he likes you; he won't shock while he has the sandals on his feet. We need to get out of here," said Mr. Vance while taking Georgie off his shoulders and standing him on the floor. "When he walks, make sure that the stainless-steel cable drags on a surface."

Then with some concern, Victor Vance thought that Georgie might pick up static electricity from friction with the air; *no, don't think it*. Mr. Vance had to stoop and hold Georgie's hand to keep the stainless-steel cable on the ground going to the car. He dragged the cable on the asphalt for a final second before placing Georgie beside himself. "We'll go over to the Two Bucks and ask them if they want their unexpected son."

Georgie began to float and Mr. Vance held him down on the seat with his right hand while driving. "Jason, son, hold the cable to the dashboard, no not under it, against the dashboard."

The Two Bucks lived on Cherry lawn street. It was a quiet Saturday afternoon as they pulled into the Two Bucks' driveway. Winnie opened the house door and waved as the Vance family opened the car doors. Heather and Jason ran to the door and raced to the playroom to get their favorite toys at their good friend's house. Mr. Vance took Georgie's hand, making sure the cable dragged on the ground so that the introduction of the unexpected son wasn't a shocking one, which had happened at the Vances' house, and to make sure there were no holes in the roof!

Winnie Two Buck was tentative at first. Johnny had told her what happened in the classroom and she had thought he had made up the story. She put the thought of making a twin in the category of impossible, laughed politely at her son's exaggeration. But Mr. Vance approached her with an Indian child, with homemade tire sandals that were too small with something hanging and dragging on the ground from the left sandal; she became threatened and nervous in the prospect of seeing an impossibility come into her house. It was like an Indian legend brought up by a mystical ceremony and hallucination induced by sleep deprivation and Paiute smoke inhalation.

The fear of the unknown struck into her, she was ready to flee. Vic, seeing her consternation, took her hand and said, "I will introduce you to Georgie."

"Wait, Ed is in the shower and he'll be right out."

Suddenly, there was a silver-green light streak across the room to the toy room. Georgie's hand slipped from Victor Vance's, a blur escaped and the light vaporized. Lisa Two Buck leaped from the door and hardly took a step and ended up in her bedroom, but no sooner in, she was out, her arms wrapped around Ed. "There's a malevolent spirit in the house and Vic let it in!"

Johnny yelled out, "Mom, Dad, come into the toy room and see Georgie!"

Mr. Two Buck followed by his wife then Vic and Mrs. Vance peeked around the door. Winnie Two Buck shrank back and screamed, "Which one is my son?"

Victor Vance grabbed Winnie whose anxiety level skyrocketed. Vic said in a calming manner, "You should know which one is your son, he's the taller of the two!"

"There's no difference in size," answered Winnie Two Buck.

Victor Vance stared at her for a moment and looked in the room and turned wide eyed in disbelief and stammered, "That can't be!" The tire sandals had ripped apart and were in the hands of Georgie. Dumbfounded, they both held onto each other.

Ed had been drying his hair and asked, "What happened?"

"They are both the same size! When that person or whatever his name is, Georgie, the one that came in this house small, now the same size as Johnny," cried a baffled Victor Vance.

Georgie spoke, "The cable dragging was stunting my growth."

Victor Vance said to Georgie, "Are you going to be ten feet tall in another day?"

Georgie looked at both the Vances and the Two Bucks and replied, "Don't think so, I think I am as tall now as I was in my other life."

"Other life!" Mrs. Two Buck fainted and Vic and Ed grabbed onto Winnie and laid her on the couch in their family room.

"Georgie," asked Mr. Vance, "would you and Heather and Jason step out of the room please?"

Mrs. Two Buck looked around the room. "The evil spirit vanishes?"

"No, he is in your front room," as she got up.

All four stood motionless, staring at each other, Mrs. Vance dropped to her knees, holding her head. "How can that be; just yesterday he was a baby!" Stressed out, she fell on the floor. Mr. Vance rushed to pick her up, thinking she had injured herself. Jan Vance babbled, "We couldn't handle him just yesterday when he was a baby, how are we going to control him now!"

But as she completed the sentence, Georgie was on the other side of her; Mr. Vance and Georgie helped Jan Vance up. "You're as tall as Johnny or are you Johnny?"

"No, I'm Georgie," he held Mrs. Vance's hand. He could see the fear in her eyes. "I realize I'm a freak. I should not be alive! I am not your other son, Mr. and Mrs. Two Buck, but just a replica, a mirrored being and a sudden shock, however, I will try to please the Vance and Two Buck family.

"Since my body has Indian heritage and the source of my genetics. My brain is from another source and another race, please forgive me if I have caused you pain?"

"You are a benevolent spirit, not what I had imagined," Mrs. Two Buck said to Georgie. "I have only one son, I do not want more."

Chapter 11
Amazing

On the way home, Georgie sat between Jason and Heather, he was now equal in size. It had been just an hour or so ago they had tickled his feet and said baby words to him, now they sat looking up at him amazed at his size and at his verbal expression that no longer sounded immature.

Mr. Vance said, "Hold onto the left sandal, it has the steel cable."

Heather opened the backdoor on the left of the car and placed the cable in the door jamb. The shimmer of silver-green glow diminished. Georgie, who sat between them with normal skin and complexion, said, "I am sorry I caused so much trouble at your friend's house, Mr. Vance."

"Don't worry, Georgie, as the days pass and Johnny talks about you, they will accept you."

Their feeling toward Georgie was love as a baby, but their feelings now with his spurt in size, intelligence, this would upset child of any age. It was almost as if he was an imaginary person or that he had been pumped up like a balloon. None of this was true, he was a real human being with real feelings and real thoughts from his previous life.

Heather and Jason couldn't comprehend nor could Mr. and Mrs. Vance. Nevertheless, they were going to incorporate him into their lives without questions, without answers. This mind-boggling transformation from baby to juvenile in the matter of one day had the entire family staring to the point of embarrassment. Georgie responded to their stares, "What's up, I'm getting serious looks that I don't understand. Why do you all have unbelievable scans of my body? When you have seen it many times in Johnny?"

Mr. Vance kept driving and trying to keep the car on the road replied, "We are thinking that you may disappear tomorrow or you may be ten feet tall. How do we know how to plan your future?"

Georgie looked at everyone for a moment and suggested, "Please do plan my future, I will not grow ten feet tall, I will grow as Johnny grows; after all, my genetics are his genetics with a few discrepancies that came from the plant and the plating solution."

Mrs. Vance turned and looked at Georgie from the front seat and replied, "That's the problem, Georgie, this growth spurt has unnerved us and the Two Buck family. We don't have a stable situation; the whole family and I may seem a little frightened and intimidated by your actions and thinking."

"My old life wasn't a life. It was constant terror, humiliation from my brother because I had a speech impediment and he presumed me dumb. The beatings I took, my mother couldn't help as she was too busy trying to make ends meet, she had no control over my brother and I. Constant fear reigned over my head and into my soul, I had no alternative but to endure the whims of my brother.

"Now, I'm free and happy, I thank you, Mr. Vance, for inventing non-toxic plating solution and not throwing it away when it became contaminated. I just wouldn't be here. Speaking flawlessly, not stuttering when talking allows me to speak clearly and precisely."

The Vances were spellbound, just yesterday he had fits of screaming and annoying behavior and today he sounded like Einstein. Everyone had thought the word chaos was the order of the day, instead refinement and order were the words. Until Georgie's left sandal fell off and a streak of silver-green light caromed off the back window of the car and cut a swatch across Mr. Vance's hair. Georgie's left index finger had been pointed at the back window as he hiccupped and that set off the charge.

The stench quickly had everyone in the car holding their nose and rolling down the windows to clear the air. Mr. Vance turned and looked at Georgie, revealing a reverse Mohawk haircut. Georgie hurriedly put on the sandal making sure the cable was in the car door jamb but again, sending a horrible smell through the car again from the rubber sandal, his fingers burned while putting it on.

Georgie changed from silver-green to normal skin color. Everyone held their nose as they pulled into the Vance driveway; everyone then rushed from the car, leaving the doors open, coughing and sputtering; even Georgie's eyes were watering while checking to make sure the cable was on the ground. Mr.

Vance climbed out of the car and went straight to the back window of the car to check the black smudge and said, "There's no hole in the glass."

He reached around and put his knee on the backseat and with a handkerchief cleaned off the smudge, feeling a slight dibbling of the glass. His wife trying to hold back a smirk and laughter, blurted out, "Your hair! I'm going to have to trim it, you'll set a trend with the first non-bald bald guy at work."

Victor Vance moved to the side mirror on the driver's side and stared at himself and shook his head in disgust. Mrs. Vance responded, "Come inside and I'll trim your hair up."

"You mean buzz it all off!"

Mr. Vance sat in a chair with an old shirt wrapped around him, staring in a hand mirror while Mrs. Vance buzzed his head. Adding insult to injury, she put shaving cream on his head and finished the job with a safety razor. But the purpose was to wash off the silver-green line that ran from his forehead to the back of his skull. Mrs. Vance stared at Mr. Vance's head for several moments and choked and coughed and babbled, "It'll flake off with age," as Mr. Vance rubbed his head with a towel then with soap and water and a washcloth but nothing helped.

"Boy, I'm going to be the butt of jokes." Then he realized, "What if this trauma to my scalp killed the hair follicles and I'll have a reverse Mohawk the rest of my life? I'll just have to wear a hat to work," pondered Mr. Vance.

Mrs. Vance picked up a magnified glass and intently studies the line and said, "It looks like a tattoo!" Mr. Vance looked at his strawberry blond hair all around him, not on his head but on the floor, and a silver green line going from his forehead to his neck in back. Heavily freckled and with a pale complexion and green eyes, Mr. Vance could play a Bob Hope character with the ski nose.

Georgie walked into the room with a princely step, with his chest out and stomach in. He swaggered over to Mr. Vance, wiped his left index finger over the silver-green line, and it disappeared. Georgie said, "Whoops, I missed a spot in the back." He touched the back of Mr. Vance's head and it dissolved.

Mr. Vance whirled the hand mirror around his now very red face and scalp and cried, "How did you do that!"

"I don't know. I think it's a magnetic thing," announced Georgie.

The smoldering ember subsided as Mr. Vance's blood pressure went down and calmness swept over his face. Victor Vance thought he had one problem solved somewhat. "Now I'll have to wear a hat to school so the kids don't quiz me on what happened to my hair."

Chapter 12
School

Mr. Vance had called the night before and asked Ed Two-Buck and his wife Winnie to come to school with Johnny so that they could enroll Georgie. "We could have him in classes with Johnny and he could show him the ropes if that's alright with you, Ed?"

Victor and Ed made up a story to tell the counselor and the principal. The counselor spoke first, "This is a funny time of the year to change schools; where did you come from?"

Georgie was about to speak when Mr. Two-Buck mentioned, "Georgie is a timid one so we left him on the reservation with his grandparents so that the culture change wouldn't intimidate him. Now that we think he has mastered the differences—"

"What's that smell?" the counselor asked.

Georgie had stuck a peace-pipe under his shirt that he had taken from Mr. Two-Buck's car and some tobacco and lit it and now smoldered under the back of his plaid woolen jacket-shirt. "Georgie, son, the school district doesn't allow smoking on campus," said the counselor in no uncertain terms.

"I understand, sir," as Georgie slowly backed up until he was beside Johnny and slipped the pipe to Johnny. Johnny immediately ran from the office to his locker, knocking the ashes from the peace-pipe. He slammed the locker door shut before anyone could see what it was and ran back to the office and sat as though nothing had happened.

"What is that smell?" the counselor asked again.

Mr. Vance said, "Oh that's essence of Zuni incense in the jacket that came from the reservation."

"Oh, oh, I thought something was burning."

"No there's nothing wrong, just a typical Zuni essence," said Ed Two-Buck.

The counselor paused for a moment and remarked, "Georgie looks just like Johnny."

"Yes, they are identical twins; they were four years old when I took the job at the university."

"I see," said the counselor. "And your address is his?"

"No, he is staying with Mr. Vance."

"And why is that?"

"Because we don't have another bedroom."

"What's wrong with doubling up with Johnny?"

Mr. Two-Buck didn't anticipate the question and stammered, "I thought it would be best."

Mrs. Two Buck quick-wittedly said, "They fought a lot when they were on the reservation."

"I see," said the counselor. "But you do want them in the same classes?"

"Yes of course, but we don't want them together at home," answered Mr. Two Buck.

"Here's his schedule and I hope you enjoy your education, Georgie, at our school."

"I'm sure I will," as a silver-green color flashed across his face.

"What's that on your face?" asked the counselor politely.

"Oh, that's one of the things they fought over as four-year-olds," answered Mrs. Two-Buck.

Mr. and Mrs. Two-Buck and Mr. and Mrs. Vance whisked the boys out of the counselor's office before any more questions were asked. The counselor looked out the door of the office, scratching his head with a puzzled look on his face. "Georgie, come to C5 and get your new sandals," mentioned Victor Vance. "Wow Georgie, do not strut like that at school. Kids pick up on differences and exploit them in fun but sometimes kids will turn vicious and create situations that cause serious trouble in your life and theirs," explained Victor Vance as he gave Georgie his new sandals.

"Don't worry, Dad, I will not intentionally cause trouble under any circumstances."

Johnny tugged at Georgie's arm; the bell would ring in five minutes. "Hurry, we'll be late to D-5, our English class."

As they ran, the campus guard told them to walk, they did as they were requested, the boys walked into English class. "Take your class schedule up to the teacher, her name is Miss Bloom."

Miss Bloom quickly wrote his name in the class attendance book and gave Georgie a seat between two girls in the middle of the classroom. The girl on his left kept combing her hair with a mirror hidden in her English book and the girl on the right was putting on makeup secretly, using the same trick with the English book. The teacher Miss Bloom asked the class, "When do you use the verb to be, is, and are in a sentence?"

Georgie and Johnny were the only ones that raised their hands. The girls beside Georgie never looked up; they both stared at their mirrors oblivious of their classmates and class participation. Narcissism seemed to be the only thing on their minds. "By the way, this is our new student, George Two Buck, Johnny's twin; he has been living on the reservation with his grandparents. He likes to be called Georgie. Georgie, would you answer the question?" requested Miss Bloom.

"Is is singular and are is plural," replied Georgie. Georgie noticed the girls still hadn't looked up. So, he pointed his right index finger at the girl on the right and slowly greened her mirror. The girl on the left, he changed his approach, Georgie created a green streak in her hair.

The girls chirped simultaneously, "My mirror! My hair!" and tried to rub it out and found that it did not rub off but in turn wouldn't come off their hands. Stained like a grass stain, they both raised their soiled hands to go to the restroom. Miss Bloom thought they were going to add something valuable to the classroom discussion but Georgie immediately eliminated the stains as they said, "There's green stains on me!"

Miss Bloom answered, "Where?"

The girl putting on the make-up raised her mirror and said, "See!" then turned red and blushed through her very thick make-up, realizing the mirror was now clean. Miss Bloom came roaring down the aisle and picked up the mirrors but didn't take the make-up or comb and said, "See me after class."

As Johnny and Georgie walked out of class at the bell, Georgie mentioned, "The school I went to in the slum area, students never got into trouble because the teachers were too afraid that the students would retaliate, and they did at times."

"Really," remarked Johnny, "and how did they handle the situation when it came up?"

"They didn't, the administration let the teachers involved fend for themselves which created chaos and no one was taught any subject matter in the class. If they weren't the toughest in the class, you walked softly and didn't carry a big stick because if the teacher did anything to get on the bad side of a student, good students would protect the teacher in the classroom but the teacher that caused the disagreement, the bad student would catch you in the hallway and rip you apart with a knife."

"If the two girls you got into trouble were to find out that you were the one that caused the situation, they'll come at you with fifteen of their friends and punch your lights out. They are the queens of the campus."

"I've been the center of beatings and survived. I hope my access to unusual behaviors will help in my defense," replied Georgie.

"I'm sure they will. Our next class is math, something they never taught on the reservation until recently. Our Mr. Clancy's face looks like a prune and his glasses are too big and magnify his eyes to the point you feel you have the blue and red spectacles for three-dimensional viewing. I don't mean to belittle him," Johnny remarked politely.

"Johnny, you'd have never lasted very long where I really come from, they would've hanged you by your legs and used you for a punching bag," Georgie conveyed his first opinion of Johnny.

"You think it?" answered Johnny.

"I think it," replied Georgie. Johnny sat in his seat.

Chapter 13
Classes

Georgie placed his class schedule on Mr. Clancy's desk. Mr. Clancy was writing Math problems on the chalkboard and didn't notice the newcomer so Georgie waited patiently at Mr. Clancy's desk while he finished writing the problems on the board. Just as the tardy bell rang, the two girls rattled him with their unusual skill, they popped through the door. Beth and Babs stood at Mr. Clancy's desk too.

Mr. Clancy wiggled his nose like a rabbit gnawing on a carrot and said, "Thank you for making it to class on time but you're not seated."

The girls ignored Mr. Clancy's request and boxed in Georgie. Suddenly, they both pulled out from their backpacks permanent markers and struck Georgie on his cheeks and scampered to their desks as the rest of the class broke out in laughter. Mr. Clancy had glanced to the side from the chalkboard and turned to face Georgie and requested, "Johnny, why do you have war paint on?"

The class laughed! "I'm not Johnny, I'm Georgie," he answered. "Here's my class schedule."

"Well, if you're not Johnny, where's Johnny," giving a soccer announcer's impersonation—where's Jooooohnny. The class laughed again. Mr. Clancy did a subtle dance with pride in admiration of his impersonation. He then said, "If you're not Johnny, who are you and why are you wearing war paint?" asked Mr. Clancy, twitching as his big glasses moved down his nose.

Georgie asked, "Why are you twitching like that?"

"Because I'm going to be in a dance contest next week!" Mr. Clancy put Georgie Two Buck on his class-seating chart.

"My name is not Two Buck, it is Georgie Vance; erase that now and put Vance!"

"You're between Babs and Beth," answered Mr. Clancy.

"Do you think that's a good idea; they marked my face," a slight silver-green color crossed Georgie's face and the black marks vanished as Mr. Clancy stared in disbelief.

"So you and Johnny are brothers?"

"Yes."

"Those lovely girls didn't mark your face."

"No sir, Mr. Clancy!" Georgie sighed and turned to go to his assigned seat but turned back to get his class schedule and his appearance slowly discolored as he sat down; he looked at his right hand and noticed the color change.

Quickly, he concentrated on his normal color. The girls looked at him with impish smiles and Beth whispered, "We'll get you later."

Georgie thought maybe the suburbs were as bad as the intercity, only they were subtle and secretly dangerous. He thought to himself, *Would they try to have me run over in a fancy suburban truck, not a funky twenty-year-old Japanese crumbled and ratted out truck*? His body was still trying to turn silver and green and Johnny signaled from his seat that he was turning color; *look at your hands and concentrate harder*, Johnny thought.

Georgie gritted his teeth and slowly his in between color of a mixture of silver-green and normal faded to normal. He was helped by Mr. Clancy, the only teacher wearing an expensive suit and tie and undulating as though he was on the dance floor learning a new move; his movements and rhythm fell on deaf ears because this was a high-end math class and they were all tight asses except Johnny and himself.

Beth and Babs seemed to be his heart's desire and not high-end math students. As he danced, his eyes were on the girls. Georgie saw dances at the dance hall, actually it was a bar and grill, while he was picking scraps of food from the garbage but Mr. Clancy began to look like a bird of prey seeking sustenance from an unsuspecting victim. The girls ate up the attention and inspired Mr. Clancy to greater flattery.

The girls were competent and could answer the hardest question; maybe, just maybe, he respected them for their minds. He thought, *Do you think that's possible*? As the bell rang, Babs and Beth were beside him in the commotion of class dismissal and marked Georgie's face not once but twice each and giggled and said in unison, "Take that!" and ran out the door.

Johnny jumped over a row of desks and pointed at Georgie's face and erupted with, "Look at Georgie's face, Mr. Clancy; do you think he did that to himself?"

"I can't imagine who did that," answered Mr. Clancy.

"Sticking up for your favorites, Mr. Clancy," muttered Johnny.

When Mr. Clancy turned to look at Georgie, the permanent pen marks had disappeared. "How did you do that?" demanded Mr. Clancy.

"Do what?" replied Georgie.

Johnny and his brother the clone escaped into the hallway; hearing giggling, they turned, Babs and Beth are peeking out the next door down, Johnny and Georgie turned in the other direction with deadpan faces but Georgie swiftly moved his arms backward and shot orchid leaves that splattered them with a resounding loving kiss with their mouths open and of course, a choking sound came from the door down the hall.

"The girls are mildly deluded in the head, thinking they got away with something without penalty," cracked Johnny.

"I know the type; they'll be back for revenge," Georgie reacted. "Seriously."

The schedule said Mr. Vance's class next then lunch. Johnny laughed as he looked up from the schedule and said, "You're going to see how crazy people act when they are without breakfast and ate candy with lots of sugar turn fanatic anticipating lunch," Johnny soberly said.

"What do you mean? I always missed breakfast and I was never crazy; maybe a little nutty and had some fights but never killed anyone," remarked Georgie.

Johnny stared at Georgie for a while, suddenly judging Georgie. *No, I better not*, thought Johnny, *he hasn't done anything wrong*. Johnny tripped as they walked down the hallway to C5 Mr. Vance's room. Georgie caught him and said, "We both had breakfast so I won't let the crowd hysteria bother me, Johnny."

"Don't let the pandemonium overtake you and join them," demanded Johnny.

"It's my first day and we already hit a snag. I don't want to hit anyone especially with Mr. Vance as my dad," Georgie replied calmly.

Georgie had never really seen Mr. Vance's room, only from a cocoon that he was developed in and it was a short time in the room but mostly in a cabinet. He remembered how comfortable it was in that five-gallon vat of solution. As

Georgie stepped into the room with Johnny, he could see why everyone loved the room, well, most everyone. Posters on the ceiling and on the cabinets of children's favorites from old and new stories that helped keep children in a child's world.

Mr. Vance had a video camera on a tripod pointed at the floor with a background of the ocean on an eighteen by forty-eight-inch background. It was two pieces of school-sized paper for artwork taped together. The paper ocean had a slit in it so that sharks' fins made famous by the movie *Jaws* could stick out from the ocean seen on the paper without seeing the body as it appeared in the movie but rather than eating people, the shark trimmed fingernails. The sharks doing the trimming, of course, in animation and a real finger.

"Well, you'll see after Mr. Vance takes attendance and gets the class underway," announced Johnny.

Mr. Vance said, "Is everyone here and is everyone happy?"

And every student said, "Yes."

Mr. Vance turned on the record player. "Our room is being attacked," the record player had the sound of an airplane machine gunning. Everyone went under the tables and waited until Mr. Vance lifted the needle from the record. Mr. Vance called Johnny to help with the animation process. Mr. Vance assigned a stool for Georgie beside Johnny but everyone sat on the floor around the paper ocean, trying not to get his or her feet wet, really not getting their shoes in the animation.

Georgie sat on the floor with the rest of the students and watched the process in action. "Before we get started, I want to introduce Johnny's twin brother Georgie. He came from a vast and mysterious unknown part of the world. The only other organism that has experienced this world is Dolly, a sheep in Scotland," described Mr. Vance. He then tried to cover up his mistake by saying, "That's just a joke."

Georgie laughed and said, "Turn silver and maybe a little green, Mr. Vance."

Mr. Vance put a serious look on his face and asked Johnny to come up and run the video camera while Patrick stood by and watched how the camera functioned so that he can have a chance to run it. Then Mr. Vance looked at Susan sitting on the floor in front of the paper ocean and explained, "Peter is going to put the shark with its mouth closed in the slit in the paper with its dorsal fin sticking out of the slit and he'll move the shark from left to right at three-quarter of an inch at a time while Johnny turns the camera off and on; this will create the illusion that the shark is moving through the water.

"As you can see, I'm holding up four sharks drawn with its mouth and body in different positions and the shark is drawn on both sides so that it can move left to right and right to left and after the shark gets to the center, Susan will put her right index finger out and the shark will jump out of the water and trim your fingernail using all the sharks with mouths opened and closed and their tails twitching.

"Susan, change fingers and Peter will have the shark move from finger to finger as though he is trimming them and of course, your thumb," Mr. Vance took a deep breath.

Johnny, running the camera, rewound the tape and the show was on. After three minutes that took forty minutes to tape, all laughed and giggled and said, "Let's see it backwards," as the warning bell rang for cleanup. The class didn't have anything to clean up so the three-minute tape was run backward before the class was over.

Chapter 14
Lunch Time

Johnny waited for Georgie to leave the classroom because of the rush of students exiting; he was the last one out. The other students bolted to the cafeteria along with the rest of the eighth-grade. Johnny looked at Georgie and asked, "Why are you so late getting out of class?"

"Mr. Vance asked me how am I getting along. I said fine except for the two girls marking my face and he asked me where are the marks? I made them reappear and he asked me how did I do that and I said, 'I just turned my skin over'."

The hustle and bustle and the noise of the rushing students blotted out the rest of what Georgie said in the mayhem of lunchtime. Johnny pushed Georgie to make sure they kept their spot in line, several girls kept trying to push past them out of line. A voice rang out and enunciated clearly, "Gentleman, let the girls go first."

Johnny replied, "Yes Miss Syndly," and under his breath he said, "Witch!"

"What did you say, young man?" demanded Miss Syndly.

"I said we should hitch ourselves to the girls all the time, Miss Syndly!"

Miss Syndly stared at Johnny and Georgie and pointed, "When did you get a twin brother?" as her sunken left eye twitched on her leathery face with many wrinkles, her hair dyed blond.

"She must have been an extreme sunbather in her youth," mentioned Georgie.

"I didn't know you had a twin, Johnny?"

"Yes, Georgie lived on the reservation with my grandparents but decided to come to the city, Miss Syndly." Johnny turned and said to Georgie, "Oh god, I hope they don't have peas today!"

Miss Syndly interjected, "Peas are nutritious, boys!"

Johnny crossed his fingers of his right hand behind his back as he picked up a warm tray from the pile and made sure Georgie did the same. Johnny said to himself *no peas no peas* as he tightened his grip on his crossed fingers while the girls in front of them argued over what to eat—chicken or hamburgers—which was better for their complexion. One girl screamed at the other. Johnny said, "Lunch time is not forever, girls."

The four girls put their hands on their hips, made funny faces by pushing their noses up with their left index fingers and pulling down on their faces with their right index fingers and their middle finger and saying, "Buzz off!" at the same time.

Georgie answered with, "You girls must take lessons from a female goat!"

The girls turned red but by this time, the entire line started yelling, "Let's go, dopes."

The same girls had done this before and Miss Syndly must have been in the same situation many times in her long experience, a hundred years ago, because she ran over and said, "The girls have a perfect right to choose!"

The girls then stuck their tongues out at the entire line. The four girls finally decided on chicken, bread, and peaches for their complexion. Johnny and Georgie shuffled forward with their trays, asking for chicken, and Miss Syndly interjected, "Give those two chicken, peas and bread; oh and Brussels sprouts!"

Johnny turned and gave Miss Syndly a dirty look but Georgie was happy to eat anything. In his previous life, his food came from a garbage can at the back of a restaurant. Georgie responded with, "Thank you, Miss Syndly, for the peas."

Johnny turned and gave Georgie a strange look. Miss Syndly said, "You deserve the back end of the chicken and peas, Johnny," with a hideous smile on her wrinkled face. She then followed Johnny and Georgie to their seats then she rubbed her hands together in anticipation of the horrible event coming up. She kept saying, "Eat your peas!"

Georgie gobbled everything in a matter of seconds with his left hand and while Miss Syndly looked amazed, with his right pinky, burned Johnny's peas and Brussels sprouts to a crisp. Miss Syndly sat down beside Johnny and muttered, "Finish your peas and Brussels sprouts." She grabbed her left foot, took off her shoe and then her right shoe, rubbed the bunions and corns. Groaned, "Heaven give me strength," and smiled at Georgie for thanking her.

Alas, the tray made of fiberglass caught fire from Georgie burning Johnny's vegetables. Miss Syndly screamed and jumped up and yelled, "Fire," and everyone ran for the exits. Miss Syndly was caught between the students running for the east and west exits; consequently, she began to twirl and knocked by the students became dizzy and fell to the floor, yelling peas and Brussels sprouts. Johnny took his tray and ran for the dumpster outside of the teacher's room through the cafeteria kitchen and threw the tray some distance from the dumpster.

Just at that second Mr. Ritz the science teacher alias cracker man came around the corner with a cigarette in his hand, the tray hit Mr. Ritz's hand as he was throwing his prohibited butt into the trash and he fell and hit his head on the sidewalk and was dazed. Miss Syndly had gotten up from the floor in the cafeteria and followed Johnny to the dumpster, but her feet were hurting so much she was walking on her heels, trying to keep from aggravating her bunions.

Johnny was standing in front of Mr. Ritz sprawled in a sexual position. Johnny stepped aside and Miss Syndly tripped and fell on top of Mr. Ritz. Miss Syndly was unable to get up because Mr. Ritz put his arms around her and giving her pelvic thrusts was laughing uncontrollably. While the fire was blazing up a storm in the dumpster, the principal came running up with a fire extinguisher and put out the fire.

Mrs. Buckwith said, "Good heavens, what are you doing to Miss Syndly? I want you both in my office immediately! I've never seen such a thing on campus!"

Mr. Ritz, still lying on the sidewalk, felt warmth on his chest, pulled out his cigarette pack and tiny notebook; they were smoldering and he found a hole in the notebook; he threw the cigarettes in the dumpster fire and put the tiny notebook back in his shirt pocket.

Johnny had already faded into the background and returned to the cafeteria finding Georgie walking through the now empty cafeteria, picking up hamburgers. "Hey, wait for me, where are you going?"

"Into the bushes by Dad's room to eat the hamburgers."

"Don't take the tray to the bushes; grab some napkins and wrap three hamburgers at a time. How many hamburgers do you have, Georgie?"

"I have six, want one, Johnny?"

"Yes of course, Georgie." They looked out and saw Mrs. Buckwith had grabbed Mr. Ritz's left ear and Miss Syndly's right ear and proceeded to take them to her office.

Johnny looked at Georgie through the leaves and branches of the bushes and Georgie said, "I'm sorry I caused such a mess in the cafeteria. I only meant to get rid of the food you disliked!"

"I know you were just trying to help me but you can't do things like that and expect to live a normal life." While they were eating the hamburgers, Johnny said between gulps, "People will pick up on your exceptional behavior and soon students and the whole world will be egging you on to do tricks and abnormal things. You'll never be able to sleep, strangers will be knocking on Mr. Vance' s front door, back door, the windows until they drive Mr. Vance's family and you out of your minds!"

Reality set in on Georgie. "I thought this would be fun; now I find it can truly cause trouble for our families and I'll be called a freak for the rest of my life.

Chapter 15
Garbage Smell

Mr. Ritz alias the cracker man, a science teacher, an aroma invaded the office like a cannon blowing a hole in the building; it permeated the office, the principal and Miss Syndly both were holding their noses and the principal screamed in a squeaky high-pitched almost inaudible voice. "Mr. Ritz, no wonder you were by the dumpster, you smell like garbage; were you in the dumpster?"

Mr. Ritz hesitated and had a pleading look on his face and said, "Yes, my cigarette pack caught on fire," he showed the hole in his shirt pocket, "a silver-green light came through the wall of the cafeteria building and hit my pocket, knocked me partly in the dumpster and then on the ground. As it hit, it disappeared."

The phone rang, it was the cafeteria manager Alice. "There is a hole in the pots and pans hanging up on the south wall and there is a tiny hole through the brick wall, you can see the dumpster through the hole. The dumpster is on fire again. I called the fire department."

"Thanks Alice," the principal hung up the phone. Alice thought it strange that she would hang up like that. "What about the flask in your back pants pocket?" demanded the principal, still smarting from Mr. Ritz's aroma.

He turned around and said, "See," slightly staggering.

Mrs. (bitch witch) Buckwith, the principal, walked over to the big potted plant and took the flask out of the dirt that partly covered it. Mr. Ritz didn't have time to completely cover the flask. She stared at Mr. Ritz and said, "This is serious, Mr. Ritz, drinking on a public-school campus."

"That's not mine," insisted Mr. Ritz.

Mrs. Buckwith turned the flask over. "There's an inscription on the flask," and she read it out loud, "To our favorite principal REGINA BUCKWITH.

"I told you it's not mine," said the cracker man, just mildly slurring his words and wobbling slightly with a greasy smile on his face.

The principal's eyes grew large. She gnashed her teeth just about to hit Mr. Ritz in the face with a right hook, when Miss Syndly yelled out, "You drunken fool! Mrs. Buckwith, you are accusing Mr. Ritz of drinking on the job when it's your flask, well I never!"

The entire office staff heard the tirade and all the secretaries ran to the principal's office windows. There, two women swinging on each other but missing. Mr. Ritz was taking all the blows. The cracker man felt no pain; in fact, he was laughing and said, "I'm going to send you girls to the office!"

Miss Syndly grabbed the flask sitting on the principal's desk and walked out of the office. The cracker man muttered to the secretaries, with their mouths wide open, "Better watch those two when they get together, break it up as fast as you can; they may hurt their reputations as the nastiest drunks on campus. They hit like powder puffs."

The cracker man jauntily strolled out of the administration-building door. His head did bang into the door when he tried to open it. One secretary came running out of the principal's office with a bloody nose gasping, "Damn powder puff punched my eye, my nose!" It seemed that the fighting was not over the flask so much but the position of principal. Miss Syndly had seniority over Mrs. Buckwith and felt irritated that bitch witch got the job. The women lay exhausted on the floor.

Johnny and Georgie came out of the bushes and wiped their faces with napkins that came from the cafeteria. Why were a crowd of students are peering into the principal's office windows? Johnny and Georgie pushed their way through the crowd and saw the principal, now sitting up screaming. The bell for the next class rang' no one dispersed, as though they were stuck to the cement and some noses bent on the window glass, but slowly the yard guards kept repeating, "Time to go to class or lunch."

So, Johnny and Georgie turned to go to their classroom E6. Johnny whispered to Georgie, "We are going to Mr. Ritz's science class." Of course, Johnny and Georgie didn't mention the scene at the dumpster or what took place in the principal's office as Georgie and Johnny walked into Mr. Ritz's classroom. Georgie saw familiar faces, Babs and Beth, nonchalantly sitting, putting on makeup and eyeing Mr. Ritz knowing if they gave him sexy salutations with their glances, they would get an "A" for the day. Their expressions went from contrived benevolent to malevolent when they saw Georgie standing at Mr. Ritz's desk waiting for Mr. Ritz to sign him into his class and initial his class schedule and put him on the classroom seating-chart.

Mr. Ritz looked at the piece of paper and shuddered. "Aren't you already in this class?"

"No!" Johnny walked from his seat in the back of the room and said, "This is my twin brother, Georgie."

Mr. Ritz looked back and forth and replied, "Boy, Indians sure look alike!"

"We should, we are identical twins," Johnny remarked.

"I can tell you're twins, don't you think I know that?" Mr. Ritz scribbled his name on the schedule and Georgie's name on the seating chart and assigned him to a seat beside his brother. Instantly, Mr. Ritz began talking about his incident that happened at lunch. He went on to say, "I was standing by the dumpster talking to the custodian when I had a sudden feeling in my chest. I looked down and I see a hole in my shirt pocket! I had this 6 by 3-inch spiral notebook in my chest pocket of my shirt and it is smoldering.

"The notebook had a hole in it but not all the way through, now how do you suppose that happened?" as he pointed to the hole in his shirt and held up the notebook.

One of the boyfriends of Babs and Beth raised his hand and Mr. Ritz said, "Yes Peter."

"One of your lit cigarette's ashes fell into your pocket," remarked Peter.

"No that is not what happened because I saw a hole in the cafeteria's kitchen wall and I saw a flash of silver-green light then it disappeared," replied the cracker-man, analyzing the sequence of events. "How do you suppose that hole occurred?" as Mr. Ritz went on.

Johnny and Georgie flashed a quick look at each other, their eyes having a guilty glare. Georgie had a tinge of silver-green across his face. Johnny, as he saw Georgie's face turn color, motioned with his hand across his face. Georgie nodded and wiped the silver-green off his face.

Mr. Ritz picked up on it; while he had a silly nickname, he was no fool and asked Johnny, "Do you have anything to say?"

"Yes, I have, Mr. Ritz, I think it was a micrometeorite. Or I saw a glint of something but thought it came from Miss Syndly's feet when she took her shoes off; it was some kind of an entity escaping from that horrid silver-green odor such as a pleading for mercy flea," answered Johnny.

Mr. Ritz laughed and so did the class but Georgie's face had no hint of laughter, it suddenly struck him: *terror of all terrors, he had almost killed Mr. Ritz. I'm not like my real brother, I'm a normal kind human being.* Georgie's face erupted into a cold sweat as the warning bell rang, it was the end of the school day, the students began talking to one another and Mr. Ritz knew that it was hopeless to get the students to concentrate on anything but leaving.

As soon as that final bell rang, they were like phantoms that dissolve without a trace. Johnny and Georgie were left standing alone as the last bell rang, even Ritz cracker was the first person usually to leave, was lagging behind the students when suddenly the detestable Miss Syndly rushed through the door of Mr. Ritz's room and said, "Don't you tell anyone what you saw!"

Johnny covered his mouth to prevent from laughing; he was thinking that nearly the whole student body saw what happened in the principal's office and crisply answered, "Everyone saw!"

"You two boys stay here. Are you talking about the office incident?" Miss Syndly narrowed her eyes, twisted her mouth, and whispered, "I mean taking my shoes off in the cafeteria."

Again, Johnny put his hand over his mouth so that it would prevent him from laughing directly into Miss Syndly's face, he turned away. But Georgie had beads of sweat pouring down his face. Miss Syndly demanded that they go to the principal's office that very minute, Georgie didn't know what to do but took off his neckerchief from around his neck and wiped his face. Miss Syndly sensed something was wrong. She herded Johnny and Georgie to the office.

The principal was still on the floor of her office yelling, "I'm not an alcoholic and that flask is not mine! I deserved the job."

Johnny and Georgie stood wide-eyed as two secretaries picked Mrs. Buckwith off the floor saying, "You have a great right hook; come and look at Betty's nose, I think it is broken."

"Oh my god, did I do that?"

"Yes," said the secretaries.

But before the principal could look at Betty's nose, Miss Syndly who was now back at the office insisted that the principal hear the two boys' story of what happened in the cafeteria. Depressed and defrocked of her composure, she tried to listen to their story but just staggered and rubbed her eyes, trying to keep the tears back when Miss Syndly began shouting, the principal staggered again almost falling to the floor.

She always had a nondescript look on her face but had an agonizing frown now as abused from the ever pugnacious, combative mouth of the hated Miss Syndly. Beaten down and pushed into a corner of her office by her vicious assistant principal. The beleaguered Mrs. Buckwith almost collapsed but a twitch developed in the principal's right eye then a cataclysmic convulsion burst through her depressed demeanor. The principal stood straight up, even put her high heels back on, which she had taken off, this made her tower over Miss Syndly, she walked to her desk and grabbed a tissue from the box, wiped her eyes and blew her nose, determined not to cry again with Miss Syndly is almost on her back.

"I am not to blame for this accident that happened to Mr. Ritz. I didn't take my shoes off in front of everyone," said stinky Miss Syndly to the principal.

The principal was a beautiful and charming young woman that allowed her to progress up the ladder in education through enticing others in administrated positions with her charms and looks, she mesmerized the school board.

After a meeting in the superintendent's office, she gave him a polite hint about going to dinner; he mentioned he had a reservation at a restaurant and he would add another person to it; it wouldn't be any trouble. The superintendent got out of his chair, walked around his desk, and kissed Miss Buckwith.

Several meetings later in his office on educational subjects and several dinners cater, the superintendent asked her to hit the sack with him but she refused so he had made her principal feeling the extra pay and not having to take care of the dirty work as assistant Principal last year. Assigned Miss Syndly from her classes to assistant Principal. As Principal, this would put her in the mood besides, he would see her at the meetings in his office more often, he would have a juicy target to shoot for.

Mrs. Buckwith had a reasonable moral code, but was relinquishing part of it as she let loose on her conniving assistant principal, "Get the hell out of my office!" As the harsh words permeated the administration building and slammed into the secretary's frontal lobes, the two top officials were nose to nose in a situation that would make anyone blink but Miss Syndly, stinky, stayed nose to nose and didn't twitch.

The battle-hardened stinky that had many such encounters in the years past as an assistant principal before. The superintendent kept Miss Syndly around because she always had the students in line; nothing got past her. Georgie turned away, Johnny's jaw dropped and stared at the two women, thinking *what are we doing here?* "Where is Mr. Ritz?"

"I don't know," answered Miss Syndly.

Neither one blinked. Miss Syndly, the elder staff member, never backed down; she had a constitution of steel, mayhem and ferocity of a wolverine, almost snarled but kept her cool as she always did. Mrs. Buckwith yelled again, "You miserable dried-up prune, get the hell out of my office!"

Not flinching and not batting a brownie, Miss Syndly said, "Eat your peas, you dumb bitch!"

"Now that we settled that! Let's hear what the boys have to say, Miss Syndly." Still nose-to-nose, the principal crisply asked Johnny, "Talk!"

"Mr. Ritz left before the final bell."

Mrs. Buckwith went on gazing daggers at her assistant principal. "Peas, is it!"

"Yes," asserted stinky the dried-up prune.

"Johnny, what happened in the cafeteria?" as the principal took off one of her high heel shoes, holding it in a threatening fashion at Miss Syndly. Testily, Miss Syndly just stared. Ah, Miss Syndly became light-headed. She began twirling around and fell on the floor. Gritting her teeth and lying rigid on the floor. The principal thinking now she'd gotten the stinky prune right where she wanted her. "How did the fire start?"

"I don't know; it must have been someone's intensity or spontaneous combustion," answered Johnny.

"Some kid with matches," injected Miss Syndly now limping and scratching her crotch.

"Shut up; go on, Johnny," said Principal Buckwith.

"Then everyone thought the fire started by a chemical reaction of the peas and Brussels sprouts hitting the paper tray. Georgie and I were the only ones that had peas and Brussels sprouts."

"How did that happen?"

"Miss Syndly forced them on us. Then when we sat down at the table, the fire started. Miss Syndly took off her shoes and we didn't know where Mr. Ritz was!"

Now the red-faced wolverine reiterated, "I did not take off my shoes!"

"Then where did the sudden horrible smell come from?" asked Johnny.

"It came from the vegetables burning," insisted Miss Syndly, now sitting cross-legged on the floor.

Victor Vance opened the principal's door asking, "Why is the secretary lying on the desk holding a wet tissue on her nose?"

Miss Syndly turned toward Victor and he saw something serious was going on; he said, "Let's go home, boys."

The two women, one still on the floor, didn't say a word; apparently, they had run out of gas. The last word they heard as they walked out of the office, "I'm sorry," not knowing who said it.

"Was it hot in there?" whispered Mr. Vance. He picked up the wet tissue from Margaret's nose. "Who did it?"

"The principal," said Kim, the other secretary.

"Um," replied Mr. Vance as he pushed the boys out the administration-building door.

Chapter 16
Tension

The car was agonizingly quiet. Mr. Vance didn't say a word until halfway to Johnny's home. "I can understand that both of you are unnerved, especially you, Georgie." Both Johnny and Georgie glanced at Mr. Vance and looked away and said nothing for several seconds.

Georgie mumbled almost incoherently, "I almost killed Mr. Ritz!"

"Say that again? I heard killed," asked Mr. Vance. "And by the way, call me Dad if that's OK with you."

Georgie muttered, "Yes."

"Kill, that's a very harsh word, Georgie."

Georgie hesitated for a moment, "That silver-green light I can flash; if I use it while I'm laughing or fooling around it is harmless but if something sets me off, for instance Miss Syndly, I think it can be lethal. I burned up Johnny's peas and Brussels sprouts, that Miss Syndly made us take, not realizing that the tray is made of paper; it scared me and I jumped in kind of a fright and I shot a silver-green light accidentally and I didn't know what happened until we got to Mr. Ritz's class.

"He told us he was standing by the garbage dumpster when something hit his shirt pocket where his heart is and pushed him backwards, he felt something in his pocket and pulled out a little spiral notebook. Johnny says he was probably smoking a cigarette and the notebook was behind the pack; he never mentioned the cigarettes but there was a fire in the dumpster and a hole in the brick wall of the cafeteria kitchen. Johnny told them that it was a micrometeorite but I know it wasn't."

Mr. Vance stared out the windshield at the oncoming traffic and quietly said, "Who would believe that this is going to turn my hair gray?"

"I'm sorry Dad, but I thought it would be easier in the suburbs; now, I see things are no different."

"The only thing I can say is do not get excited until you can control that ray, Georgie," Mr. Vance expanded on Georgie's statement; "There are just different kinds of turfs to fight over; don't let it be a negative one."

Georgie responded, "I just couldn't figure out why the two ladies were screaming at each other, until now, that I think about it."

"You see, there is competition everywhere. The situation you came from, most of the competition is settled physically or with weapons; here it is mostly settled by words or devious deeds but things can come to blows. They never tell the higher echelon about the quarrels unless it'll give them rewards," Mr. Vance pontificated.

Georgie's demeanor didn't change, he expressed anxiety. "Again, I thought school here is a cinch but I didn't think two egotistical girls would put us in trouble with their interchangeable boyfriends."

"You mean Beth and Babs and Peter and Paul?" Mr. Vance stopped at a stoplight and turned on his left turn signal, they were at Johnny's home just down the street three houses on the right.

Johnny opened the right rear door and said, "I'll see you both at school tomorrow. I hope the day goes better than your first day at school, Georgie."

Georgie made sure his stainless-steel cable was tucked into the door jamb. "I'm going to try to be as normal as possible but I'm not sure I can handle further interrogation from Miss Syndly about her embarrassment and I want to have lunch outside if it's not raining. What about Mr. Ritz?" Georgie looked and smiled at Dad Vance.

"He'll probably come T.W.I.!"

"What does that mean?" asked Georgie.

"It means teaching while intoxicated," Victor Vance said but didn't say another word.

Jan Vance asked Georgie as he came through the front door, "Do you have any homework that you need help with?"

"I do have some homework but I think I can manage," answered Georgie.

Heather and Jason wanted to talk to Georgie but he went right to his room and closed the door. "Heather and Jason," reported Vince, "he's upset, give him time to recover. He had incidents with four students, one teacher and the asst. principal and the principal. One secretary had a bloody nose, possibly broken," Mr. Vance divulged.

"Wow, heavy first day!" exclaimed Heather.

"Yes, it seems implausible he had trouble on the first day. I hope that he fits in at the school without any more trouble. Miss Syndly is always strange and a master of deceit," Mr. Vance mentioned with some dejection.

"What should we do?" asked Jason.

"Try to keep his mind off the incident and keep him as happy as possible. He told Johnny and I about his previous life and it wasn't pretty, this problem is a serious one and it's not going to go away," said Victor Vance.

Mrs. Vance looked very concerned and commented, "It doesn't have something to do with Mr. Ritz?"

"Partly," Vic replied.

Georgie came into the front room and said, "There could be something else brewing at school other than Miss Syndly. A boy named Cal Smith enrolled at the school while Miss Syndly and Mrs. Buckwith were fighting in the office. He is very muscular looking, he must take some sort of pill, he showed his schedule and acted like a heavyweight boxer, when I told him where D5 is located."

Chapter 17
Nightmare

Georgie opened his math book as he sat on his bed. He had written the assignment on lined paper, it said page 42, complete all problems. He noticed every time he thought of Mr. Ritz and the hole in the spiral notebook he shuddered and silver-greened the wall whenever his right index finger was pointed at the wall. Quickly, he would try to wipe the spots off but no use; the silver-green light had scarred the wall with a dirty silver-green smudge and he couldn't wipe it off. He fell back on his bed closing his eyes as tears flowed, he caught them before they hit the pillow and suddenly, he felt that his brother was chasing him.

He sees him driving that crummy little truck, it looked like it went through a meat grinder twenty years ago. It sputtered, clunked and emanated horrible noises. His brother Joey began knocking down and scattering men in front of the liquor store, he is chasing me. Georgie's body began levitating off the bed I don't want to be caught, Georgie plunged into another group of men waiting to be picked up for day jobs but Joey kept coming in his battered piece of scrap, scattering the men.

Georgie turned and he could see through the dirty windshield, Georgie ran behind a telephone pole. He said to himself that isn't how it went. There is a screeching of tires and Joey is directly facing his brother now, Georgie is all alone in the parking lot nowhere to hide. Through the windshield Georgie can see his brother's face with a look, I've got you now. Georgie screams!

The scream was heard throughout the Vance house. The Vance family jumped up from whatever they were doing instantly. Mr. Vance was the first to reach Georgie's bedroom door, it was locked! Mr. Vance and Jason hit the door and broke the latch. The family rushed in and found no Georgie on his bed, just his math book.

A moan penetrated their anxiety, it was muffled and hard to distinguish where it came from, again a moan. They looked up, Georgie's head was stuck in the ceiling and his right foot stuck in the dry wall too. Mr. Vance grabbed his left foot and pulled him down with a resounding bounce on the bed, knocking his math book high in the air with Heather catching the book in flight and Jason grabbing Georgie's right arm so that Georgie wouldn't bounce off the bed and on the floor.

But Georgie ripped his arm and leg away and landed on the floor feet first. Covered with dust from the dry wall and sweat that held the dust on his body. The entire Vance family jumped back, not only did the dust turn brown, but Georgie was sparking. Georgie spoke, "Wait until I calm down, I had a terrible nightmare."

Georgie commanded himself to divest from this terror and slowly, he turned to his normal color. Wide-eyed and frightened, the Vance family stared in amazement and fear, then Mrs. Vance said, "Are you all right, are we alright?"

With a frown, Georgie replied, "I hope that never happens again."

But it did that night. This time it wasn't quite so severe, Georgie was fighting back by trying to change the nightmare as it occurred. Finally, after several nights it diminished to the point when the nightmare started, Georgie could cut it off immediately. After enabling himself to control his dreams, Georgie helped repair his room.

Chapter 18
Thoughts

Dawn had Georgie up early, the sun peeked through the window because Georgie didn't pull the shades down or pull the drapes closed before he fell asleep, the reason was he didn't have that paraphernalia in his other life, drapes and shades.

In his mother's dark dank cellar apartment, no light came in the windows. The alley window if it was open when raining, cars passing through the alley splashed water on his bed. The windows were now broken out. There was no need for him to pull down shades. He thought, *I would remember nights of nightmares. While I'm awake early, I have time to finish my homework.* He never did anything of the sort in his other life.

The Vances had replaced his dirty sheets and blankets; they couldn't let a child of theirs sleep in dirty linen even though they had only known him for two weeks and were completely shaken at his growth and surprised at his sudden stop at the same size of Johnny.

Georgie's astonishing IQ, the entire Vance family thought for someone that came from a horrible background would be so smart. Mrs. Vance yelled up the stairs to the bedrooms, "Breakfast is ready!"

Georgie stared at the ceiling as the voice of Mrs. Vance rang out. He took his homework and books and met Heather and Jason running down the steps to the kitchen. "Last one to the kitchen is a rotten egg," Heather's voice blasting the whole household.

Dad was in the living room and Mom had gone to the bathroom when Heather yelled it out. Georgie jumped from the highest step to the kitchen door. "Hey, no fair," the Vance family yelled in unison.

"What took you so long?" announced Georgie while sitting at the kitchen table.

"How did you do that?" asked the new dad.

"I don't know. I just thought of it and it happened," as Georgie buttered a piece of toast.

Victor Vance raised his eyebrows and said, "Anything else you want to tell us?"

"The only thing I can tell you is I don't want to have that nightmare again and I don't want to see that principal and that Asst. principal. One thing, the aggressiveness of those two ladies is almost as bad as the drive-by shootings I have seen when I lived in the alley with my mother. My nightmares are caused by my brother, he is the culprit in most of them."

"Let's not talk about such matters at the breakfast table," commanded Jan Vance. Georgie then thought of the hiding places where his brother stored his weapons but didn't mention it to his adopted family. The cruelty, degradation and weapons he wanted to put out of his mind.

Victor Vance and family were trying to put nightmares out of Georgie's mind and dreams. Mr. Vance got up from the table and whimsically said, "Is everyone happy?" and started to dance around the table and turn on the bubble machine. Then pranced out the door to the garage to warm up the car singing an Elvis tune.

Victor Vance tried to play the Elvis tune with the horn on the car horn but it didn't work. He pushed the automatic garage door switch. Mom Vance announced, "OK kids, to the car."

Jason and Heather were fraternal twins and were blue-eyed and a grade ahead of Johnny and Georgie. In the car, the conversation revolved around the differences between identical twins and fraternal twins, which was one sperm one egg split and two sperm two eggs but Georgie was a clone not an identical twin. The appearance of silver-green skin and green leaves protruding from Georgie's body were due to his inception. Heather asked, "Can you place the leaves anywhere on your body?"

"I don't know. I never tried to place them. I just think leaves and they squirt out. Skin color is a nuisance. If I stay calm, I have normal skin color," responded Georgie.

Just then Georgie squirted leaves out his ears and got Jason and Heather laughing, then swinging at falling leaves. "Well, try to place the leaves on your right index finger," responded Jason.

Georgie's face changed from normal skin color to silver-green and back again. Emerging from the finger, green leaves, "What kind of leaves are those, Mr. Vance, I mean Dad?" asked Georgie.

Victor turned around and said to the kids, "They're from an orchid, I don't remember the genus."

"Wow, that's neat," Heather remarked.

"I did know I had leaves coming out of my body but I didn't know that I could control their placement." As Georgie stuck his finger out of the car and peppered a telephone post. "How did you know, Jason? I didn't know."

"On the ceiling when you had the nightmare, there were leaves on the ceiling in the corner of the room," Jason said contemplatively.

Victor Vance stopped the car in front of the school and let his children out. He then drove his car to the parking lot and walked to his classroom that had been built a number of years later after the main buildings were built and was of his own design.

Miss Syndly immediately came out of the faculty lunch room after peeking out the window of the door, then calmly walked over and asked Johnny and Georgie to come to her office. She had been at the window making sure Victor Vance had driven away to the parking lot. Miss Syndly smiled at everyone as she escorted the two boys to her office, even at the secretary that had a large bandage on her nose from the missed punch intended for Miss Syndly. Jason and Heather followed them in the office-building door.

Miss Syndly turned around and said to Heather and Jason, "Don't follow us into the building," then shut her office door in their faces. Miss Syndly quietly walked around to her chair and sat down; she wasn't as well-groomed as the day before. She had been obviously concerned about the incident in the principal's office the day before and she was mulling in her mind where did the flask go and who had it. If she could find it, with that inscription, she could show it to the school board and possibly get back at Mrs. Buckwith and put a dent in the high esteem the superintendent held her in and get her fired.

She could take over the principal's position at the school. The position she rightly deserved in Miss Syndly's mind. She had the boys sit down in front of her desk and immediately said, "Where is the funny little bottle that was in Mrs. Buckwith office?"

Georgie looked at her and said, "Don't you mean the flask with the inscription that incriminates Mrs. Buckwith?"

Miss Syndly cleared her throat twice and coughed, thinking that the little S.O.B. of an Indian was smarter than she thought. Before she could speak, Johnny reminded her that the flask was originally in Mr. Ritz's pocket. Johnny said, "I saw him dig a hole in the big flowerpot with his left hand, then slip the flask out of his pocket and try to cover it up in the dirt while standing straight, looking at Mrs. Buckwith fidget at her desk. So why don't you ask him where it is, not us?"

"Okay, you're dismissed," as Miss Syndly held up her right arm and flicked her fingers at the door of her office. She stared at them through the glass of her office window as they turned the corner to go out the administration-building door.

Georgie turned to Johnny and said, "The morning is not starting out bright and cheery."

Standing in front of them were Babs, Beth, Peter, and Paul. "I see you have been talking to the asst. principal. What were you talking about?" demanded Beth.

"Nothing about you four," answered Johnny.

Just as Peter and Paul stepped forward to apply bodily harm to the Indians, Miss Syndly walked out the door and said, "What are you two lovely girls doing here, you're usually holding court on the quad steps and prancing."

"We have never seen identical twin Indians before and we wanted to get to know them better," said Beth, and the three nodded their heads in agreement.

Miss Syndly snapped crisply and spoke, "Come with me, boys."

"Oh, are they in trouble, Miss Syndly?" asked Babs hoping to get a few digs in if they were in trouble as she revolved her shapely rear.

"None of your business," quipped Miss Syndly. She, Miss Syndly, hated anything beautiful and with boyfriends that drooled over them. Wiggling her head back and forth thinking that Mrs. Buckwith loved the two girls, the student body made them co-presidents of the eight-grade class. They called her stinky because she kept taking her shoes off at inappropriate times, stinky alias Miss Syndly babbled, "Come along quickly, I have no time to lose," thinking of her principal-ship close at hand.

Mr. Ritz's room E6 was a room that faced the street so the cracker-man can run out to his car to sip a nip and puff and suck on a breath freshener between classes. As they turned the corner to his room E6, they saw a flash as Mr. Ritz slipped quickly into his room. He swiftly sat in his desk chair and sat as though he had been sitting for a long time and looking over and grading papers. He looked up with a smile, as always with indifferent intensity behind his smooth but devious behavior; this time he was thinking, *What the fuck do you want, you old stinky bitch*? Somehow Georgie could feel the ungraceful salutations to Miss Syndly. Looking down at Mr. Ritz, she said, "Do you know where the bottle is, Mr. Ritz?"

"What bottle?" replied Mr. Ritz.

She lowered her head to his ear, "The flask," as students began filing in the room.

"Oh, the flask with the orange juice in it?" Miss Syndly turned red with rage and Mr. Ritz's face turned red because of his big fat lie. Mr. Ritz blinked his eyes twice and replied, "Did you ask the boys or Mrs. Buckwith?"

"I know it has her name on the bottle," reported Miss Syndly.

Mr. Ritz asked Miss Syndly, "I have a class to run; can we curtail this conversation, we're here for the kids' education," he said in a whisper.

Miss Syndly turned back from walking out the door as the students were coming and gave Mr. Ritz a most vicious look. Mr. Ritz stood up and said, "Hurry to your seats as we always do. I have a special lesson that you all will like."

Miss Syndly put her hands on her hips, burned for a moment, rolled her eyes, and muttered, "Come boys, you have to make it to class before the tardy bell rings." She took a pencil from her ear and pulled out passes from her pocket and wrote out a pass for each. Miss Syndly walked to the administration building and nodded to the secretaries and closed the door to her office. She sat down and bumped a pencil off her desk blotter thinking what to do to get the job she always cherished.

She looked around her office for a moment, looked in her desk drawer, stared at her pencils and pens then her eyes widened then squinted as she remembered that hidden under the perfectly placed decorative paper neatly placed in her desk drawer. All she had in the drawer stood at attention as though she had a connection with the military. She hesitated then took everything out of the drawer and pulled up the decorative paper and said to herself, *Where is it?* Then she pointed to her head in the German fashion with her right index finger and replied to herself "dummy, it's on the underside of the middle desk drawer; well, I had to take everything out anyway."

Because of her arthritic back, she just reached under and pulled it out. She pulled the drawer out, turned it over and there it was—the slim-Jim or otherwise known as a free car, a way to break into a car. She took it from a boy that they had sent to Juvenile Hall. Miss Syndly looked at her wristwatch and determined she had twenty-five minutes to break into Mr. Ritz's car. She thought to herself, *I can do this in five minutes*. Miss Syndly shoved the slim-Jim between her breasts and giggled as it slipped through her bra; it was cold on her skin.

She sat thinking of a plan of attack. *Hell, I'll do it and get it over quickly and put Mrs. Buckwith, bitch witch, on the defense and smash this immoral relationship between Mrs. Buckwith and the superintendent.* She, stinky, will convince the board of education. She will convince the board that she was the right person for the job as principal and that her thirty years of work and sweat, she deserved the job. She looked at her watch again and said out loud, "I better get started if I'm going to recover that flask."

She got up from her chair with her back mildly resisting the upright position. Putting her right hand on her back pushing forward and sticking her chin out, she marched through the door of her office and out the administration building door. There in front of her were two boys one with a tank top on with bulging muscles. This was the eighth grade; how could a kid look like that? The other Hispanic kid with his right hand clenched, the boys were nose to nose, suddenly the Hispanic kid threw a punch and hit the other kid in the face and in his hand was a combination lock with his middle finger inserted into the steel U and the body of the lock in his fist.

The blow broke the muscular kid's nose and fractured his left cheekbone as the blow crossed from right to left. Georgie flashed between the kids, took the lock and broke the kid's middle finger to even the side. Blood gushing from his face, the muscular kid swung wildly at the other kid and hit the kid in the face. Blood flying through the air, spattering Miss Syndly's pant suit and face; she jumped between the two brawling boys.

They tossed her aside like so much trash. The principal saw the terrifying fight through the window of her office and called the police. Fortunately, a patrol car turned the corner from Commercial Blvd to Burton Street where the school was located. The police dispatcher quickly relayed the call for help. Miss Syndly was lying on the cement, the principal ran out the door to prove her persuasiveness and control was superior to Miss Syndly's techniques.

While the two policemen jumped from the patrol car and ran to the bloody scene, they found Mrs. Buckwith on the ground bleeding. Miss Syndly believed this was her chance to get that flask and had left the fight. Miss Syndly had a few scrapes on her arms but that was not going to stop her from continuing the search for the flask. A crowd of students were accumulating. Mr. Ritz came and saw the fight and helped manage the crowd.

Slowly, Miss Syndly, stinky, backed away from the growing throng and ran through the gate in front of the school which was closed at night to the street; passing the patrol car and running past several other cars to Mr. Ritz's car. She pulled the slim-Jim from her bra, cutting the cloth between the two cups and allowing her breasts to flop down and flatten from their usual perky position. She pushed them up but no use. "Oh, let them out." She set to work with the slim-Jim, pushing it between the rubber and the glass, getting blood on the glass from the scrapes on her hands. She pushed the slim-Jim up and down. She can't find the latch, once again she pulled the slim-jim up and down several times.

"Ah shit!" Stinky fell exhausted against the car; her right pocket on her pant suit caught the car door handle; she rolled to her left, her pant suit pocket opened the door. "Ah shit, it wasn't locked!" Miss Syndly heard the chicken cackle laugh of Mr. Ritz; she looked up. There he was, talking to Mr. Johnson, they were coming toward the car; she was caught! Slowly, she bent down. Her arthritic back cracked, it kicked in and it took a while to get under the car slowly and painfully she made it on her stomach and crept under the car. She thought rigor mortise had set in as she dragged her left foot under, just as Mr. Ritz got in the driver's door and sat down, pushing Stinky's face to the asphalt and grime of the road.

Mr. Johnson, a heavyweight, took a seat in the sports car, and really dropped on Miss Syndly. Usually, she screamed at this point but realized she'd be the butt of jokes and conversation around the school for the next year. Gasping for air, she lifted her head off the terrible smelling asphalt, hit her head on the underside of the car, moaned, planted the left side of her face in the disgusting scum on the road. At that moment, her fanny pack and the seat of her pants caught on a burr on the muffler. She tried to concentrate, focus and saw two pairs of legs leaving the car.

A sigh of relief, she made an effort to crawl from under the car, hitting her head once again. Planting the right side of her face in the repulsive smut. Stinky can't move, she struggled and heard a long-extended rip and a sudden pain in her left butt cheek, finally she forced herself from under the car and rose from the filth, pulled her fanny pack to the front, saw that her pack had opened her Tampax and her adult snuggie lay under the car, she wasn't about to crawl under again. Miss Syndly opened the driver's side door.

On the seat was the flask, she put it in her back pocket. Her back pocket was also partly ripped out and the flask fell to the grass silently as she walked to her office to freshen up, but halfway there, she realized the flask was gone by patting her backside and putting her hand through the pocket and out the bottom. Noticing her blouse was dirty, she extends her left hand to her face as though she was stretching her nose, but as she looked at her fingers, they were as dirty as hell.

By this time, kids were pointing fingers at her, laughing at Miss Syndly. She ignored them and turned around, keeping her body between the staring, laughing eyes and picked the flask off the grass, slipped it into the front pocket of her pants; now she looked like a man that put two folded up socks in his pants. Miss Syndly put her nose in the air and proceeded to her office as though she was some flamboyant model wiggling her ass like a celebrity. Gracing the field of onlookers, the secretaries smirked at the asst. principal.

Miss Syndly walked into the administration building to her office with her left butt cheek hanging out. Miss Syndly looked in her desk mirror seeing that her face was filthy she went to the closet, got out a pair of slacks and blouse and proceeded to the lady's room.

Holding the flask under her slacks, she opened the restroom door with her left hand and locked it with her right. Sitting on the toilet and washing her face, Miss Syndly imagined herself in front of the school board expressing her devious opinion of Mrs. Buckwith and Mr. Jack O'Connor, the superintendent. *I'll get that womanizing bastard that leaves me out and Mrs. Buckwith in*. Still imagining sex with the superintendent, she walked out of the restroom with the paper toilet protector attached to her backside, protruding out of her slacks.

Her feet were hurting as the dream carried on, two large feet emerged in the daydream, she grumbled, straightened her slacks, then took out a mirror from her desk and was disgusted at her looks in the mirror. Her feet attack her, foot pain engulfed her as she sat down at her desk; the slacks, when she pulled the paper toilet protector out, gave her a wedgie. She threw the toilet protector in the trash can by her desk. Straightened her panties and said to herself, *It happens every time*, grumbled "shit."

Miss Syndly pondered a moment then looked down, opened the bottom drawer, pulled out her T.V. special foot massager, opened the top side desk drawer, picked up the Boric acid, poured it into the liquid in the massager, turned it on, flopped off her shoes, put those big bunion feet into the undulating fluid, and said, "Ah."

Chapter 19
Anger

Gazing at the periodic table that decorated the science classroom, Georgie was still concerned about the silver-green light that almost killed Mr. Ritz. He can't help but think that whether he liked it or not, he had responsibility and no matter what he does, he will never point his finger in anger again. He looked at Johnny now, his twin brother, same genetic material; his body was made up the same, but not the same brain. How could that happen as he patted his almost genetic twin on the shoulder and said, "Thank you."

Puzzled, Johnny looked at Georgie and said, "What?"

"I was just thinking if it hadn't been for you, I wouldn't be sitting here now."

Johnny's eyes opened wide then rolled around in their sockets, his mouth twitched twice and muttered in a stuttered voice, "It was an accident, you are an accident, a quirk of fate."

"No, I was dead. I saw myself on the ground crushed by my brother's car," Georgie's voice ended in a whisper.

The class had started, Mr. Ritz began rollcall. Babs hit Georgie with a paper wad and it hurt. She was only two desks away. Georgie never looked her way remembering he just made a promise never do anything in anger. It was tempting in Bab's case. Mr. Ritz opened the lesson in astronomy that everyone had read the chapter for homework supposedly the night before. He asked, "Beth Patterson, what speed does the Earth move in its orbit?"

Beth's eyes sparkled and in her extroverted capricious way said, "The speed limit," she said.

"And pray what is that?"

"Sixty-five miles an hour + or −."

Everyone roared with laughter and even Mr. Ritz cracked up and slipped on the floor and sat holding his sides. The entire class stood up to see Mr. Ritz spinning around like he was break dancing while Beth bowed first to the front of the room and then to the right side, then to the back, then to the left and proceeded to go into a cheerleader routine.

Mr. Ritz stood up and said to the class, "If anyone can give me the correct answer, I'll let you go early."

Johnny raised his hand and Mr. Ritz said, "Yes Johnny."

"Sixty-eight thousand miles per hour, plus or minus."

Thinking he needed a drink after that one, he yelled, "You are outta here," thundered Mr. Ritz still smiling and thrusting his right arm into the air and everyone was out of the classroom except one girl.

Mr. Ritz had the door locked and was jogging to his car as a girl yelled at him, "Come back!" Her dress was caught in the classroom door.

"I guess I was a little too quick, sorry."

Misty put her books in her left hand and with her right hand straightened her dress. She left in a huff; she was a straight arrow. Mr. Ritz laughed as he went to his car anticipating that drink, when he looked in the driver side window but didn't see the flask and there was brown stuff on the driver's side window.

Chapter 20
Aggression

Johnny and Georgie were walking toward the lunchroom to get a snack when Beth and Babs jumped in front of them hand in hand with their boyfriends. Paul, the bigger of the two, said to Johnny, "Why are you making fun of Beth?"

"I didn't, I just answered the question," announced Johnny.

"Look, you little pipsqueak of an Indian, I'm going to rearrange your brain if you do that again!"

Johnny and Georgie began walking away with Paul and Peter right behind them, Paul grabbed Johnny's right shoulder. Georgie turned like lightning, twisted Paul's right arm behind his back and with his left fist closed except his index finger extended, he shot orchid leaves into Paul's face, covering his eyes; he let go of Johnny. Georgie grabbed Johnny and quickly glided around the corner into the lunchroom. "Hey it worked," said Georgie.

"What worked?"

"The leaves at the end of my index finger thing."

"Oh, that thing," replied Johnny.

"Oh, damn, I used my index finger, at least I didn't do it in anger."

Not knowing what the hell he was talking about, Johnny looked puzzled until the girls and their boyfriends came in the lunchroom door still pulling leaves off his face with the help of Babs, Beth, and Peter. One of the cafeteria workers came out with a broom and handed it to Paul to clean up the mess of leaves. Paul slammed the broom to the floor.

Just as Miss Syndly gingerly walked through the opposite cafeteria door and stared menacingly at Paul and he instantly rethought what he had done and picked up the broom and swept the leaves into a dustpan. Miss Syndly, standing beside Paul, the boy towering over Stinky, she said, "You wouldn't want garbage duty again, would you?"

"No Miss Syndly."

"You wouldn't want me to call your parents, would you?"

"No Miss Syndly."

"You and your friends sit down at the table in five minutes or I'll assign you all to garbage duty," she remarked with ferocity in her voice. Walking away, Miss Syndly sat down at a table between Johnny and Georgie and the girls that think they were Venus in Goddess form. While Miss Syndly had a big ego, she kept it under cover, until she was not getting her way. Suddenly, she stood up and shouted, "Who let you out early?"

The girls knew if they didn't give a straight answer, Miss Syndly would put them on garbage duty. That was when they saw leaves coming out of her slacks in the back and the girls began laughing. "What are you laughing at?" said Miss Syndly crisply. "Once again, who let you out early?"

"Mr. Ritz, the cracker man, Miss Syndly, he said he needed a cigarette and some comfort."

"I believe the name is Southern Comfort," said Miss Syndly. "You better be right," she finally discovered the leaves that Georgie shot in her back pocket because she had a funny itch, ripped it out of the pocket, a roar inundated the lunchroom as the leaves hit the floor of the lunchroom. As Miss Syndly tussled with the leaves and her dress pants, she said, "Did he say that?"

"Well, Mr. Ritz didn't come out and say cigarette exactly, Miss Syndly."

The asst. principal with brown eyes blazing, stomped out of the cafeteria going straight to Mr. Ritz's room. But by the time Miss Syndly got out of the cafeteria, her feet were killing her, she began limping. One of her snitches, spies, walked up to her and said, "You have leaves hanging out of your slacks."

She felt in between her slacks and blouse. "Oh no, I didn't get them all," instead of emptying the leaves, she quickly pushed the rest inside her pants.

Miss Syndly was in the middle of the quad dripping leaves out of her slacks. Slowly, oh so slowly, she made it to Mr. Ritz's room; she slammed open the door, it banged into the wall of the classroom, but there was no one in the room.

Chapter 21
Unconscious Moving

"How did we get into the lunchroom?" asked Johnny.

"I just scooted us in and I emptied a load of leaves in Miss Syndly's backside," replied Georgie. Georgie didn't want to answer any more questions, about what he had done because he himself really didn't know how it had happened. He went up to the cashier and took a chocolate bar with almonds out of the rack and paid for it. The cashier smiled she returned his change of a dollar. Johnny, right behind him, bought a peanut candy bar and said right in front of the cashier, "When did you know you could fly?"

The cashier gave a strange look and laughed and reported, "Do you think you're an Indian bird that can change into a human?"

"I don't know. I never tried it, I'm new at this Indian stuff."

The cashier began laughing even harder and answered, "Fun is fun, let's get off the subject."

The lunch bell rang for the seventh grade. While this conversation was going on, the ears of Beth, Babs, Peter, and Paul were recording the conversation between the cashier and the two Indians. "That's impossible," Babs whispered to her friends. "They are quick, maybe I should ask them if they want to play in the upcoming baseball season."

But the conversation stalled when Miss Syndly came back to the lunchroom with a poster that said please wipe your feet before coming into the cafeteria. Actually, she had two posters, one for the east and the west door. But between her bunions and toilet paper protector, her stride looked like two hips and knee operations happened at the same time. Lunging forward stiff-legged, Miss Syndly crossed the cafeteria and walked out putting up posters. She gyrated awkwardly as though something was irritating her. She slowly painfully walked toward Mr. Ritz's room while voices all around her were saying, "Hello Miss Syndly."

She nodded her head and a smile made from years of practice of concealing her distaste of children, practice in front of a mirror to get it exact so few of the students knew her real demeanor. She always preyed on their frailties and their naive ties to childhood. She turned the corner to Mr. Ritz's room again, she saw Mr. Ritz down at his car with both doors open, searching for something. Knowing full well what he was looking for, Miss Syndly asked, "What are you looking for?"

"Oh, I'm not looking, I'm…cleaning the seat of my car," he grabbed a bag from the seat and began stuffing papers and cigarette boxes into the bag. He crunched the Marlboro hard packs as he threw them in the bag. His animosity toward Miss Syndly never showed, but she knew it was hidden among his thoughts.

"Why did you let your class out early?" she asked in a pleasant tone.

"Well, they answered all the questions, that was the end of my lesson plan," quipped Mr. Ritz.

"Tomorrow make it longer, put a copy of it in my box."

Mr. Ritz's eyes narrowed, "I see you forgot something in the restroom, Miss Syndly," part of the paper toilet cover had inched its way out of her panties.

Miss Syndly stuck her nose in the air and said, "Well," she turned and marched away.

Mr. Ritz's thin lips turned up at the corners knowing he got the last dig in, but changed quickly as he said, "Where is that god damn flask? That stinky ass bitch must have it!"

Lunchtime went on, more and more debris hit Johnny and Georgie, it was to the point of having to leave the lunchroom, but as they exited Miss Syndly came from the restroom where she felt funny on her lower cheeks and gave her panties the once over for anymore protector paper, she crushed it into a ball of sorts and threw it in the trash can. Immediately rushed over to the lunchroom, grabbed Johnny and Georgie, "Why are you leaving the cafeteria. it's drizzling outside?"

Johnny pulled a paper wad from his hair and replied, "This!"

The foursome of harassers scurried out the west door when Miss Syndly came in the east door of the lunchroom. There was mumbling from the west door as Beth, Babs, Peter peering over Paul's left shoulder, Paul announced, "I'll get those Indian snitches!"

Miss Syndly seemed supremely in command as she walked as though her feet didn't hurt; she almost pranced into the cafeteria. She took the paper wad in her hand and quipped, "Are the pranks getting out of hand, boys?"

Johnny looked at her and thought, *Why is she taking interest in us? She must have found the flask in Mr. Ritz's car and thinks she has the principal job sewed up.*

In a very diplomatic way, she said, "I'll have to talk to the co-presidents of the class and friends of the new execution of rules behavior and the consequences if not followed." Miss Syndly gripping the paper wad in her right hand began walking through the cafeteria as though she had been crowned queen and was inspecting her subjects.

Chapter 22

The boys, as they left the cafeteria, jumped a big puddle and zigzagged through the crowd of students standing under the covered area of the campus and made their way toward Dad's room. Georgie had a question of his gestation period and the knobby inverted skin between his two nipples on his chest. Johnny was trying to explain as they were now under the overhang of the roof of the "C" wing building dodging two eighth-graders trying to splash them from a puddle that had developed on the cracked sidewalk where the tree had lifted it.

Two seventh-graders stood under the down spout slightly detached from the rain gutter; they were rotating around so they can get completely soaked and plead they have to go home and change clothes to their counselors and miss the rest of the school day. Georgie looked at Johnny, "Is that the way they get out of school for the rest of the day?"

"Yes, they probably have a test in their next class which they didn't study for, this is an easy out."

"The school I went before my transition, we didn't go home; we just hung out in front of the liquor store with the rest of the bums," replied Georgie.

"Didn't the men try to hit you up for your money?"

"They wouldn't dare touch me or my friends because my brother is a mean son-of-a-bitch; he stands six-foot-six and weighs two hundred fifty pounds or more and has an automatic rifle in his pickup truck, the poor bastards have all been harassed by my brother and even though he hated me as much as he hated them, he would kill any one if they touched me, just for the pleasure."

"You mean kill them?" asked Johnny.

Georgie nodded his head in a yes, "I saw him shoot and kill for money several times, you have to remember I couldn't speak so he took me along sometimes when my mother insisted and sometimes, he'd dump me at the liquor store; then I knew he was going to meet a girl."

Johnny, stunned by the information, stopped and stared at Georgie as he walked into Mr. Vance's room. Slowly Johnny collected his thoughts and caught the door before it closed and slipped into room C5. Mr. Vance was at his desk eating his lunch when Georgie said, "Dad."

"Yes son," replied Mr. Vance.

Georgie raised his shirt and asked, "What is this knobby thing here between my nipples?"

Victor Vance studied it for a moment and thought to himself, *Does he really want to know or is it just an annoyance and he wants to get rid of it?* Then he replied, "It's a clone thing."

"I really want to know what it is," Georgie asked politely.

Victor put down his iced green tea and left his sandwich of skinless turkey, lettuce and tomatoes with crushed sesame paste and pickled bell peppers sauce, an Indian delight that Johnny's mother made. He got up from the desk and walked back to the cabinet where the plating solution was stored and grabbed the handle and opened the door; a silvery-green light sputtered and went out. Victor looked at Johnny and quickly muttered, "Johnny, you didn't spit in this solution, or cough or drop a tear?"

"The first day back to school which was yesterday, I tried to pick up the clone pail using my injured thumb and it was painful, maybe a tear rolled down my cheek and fell in the solution."

"But this isn't the five-gallon container that Georgie was created in and born in; this is the fresh solution," answered Victor Vance. For a moment all three stood perplexed as they saw in the solution a silvery cocoon shaped egg but this time it was transparent with a green overtone.

"What is that in the egg cocoon?" asked Georgie.

Victor Vance went to his desk and from his desk drawer he pulled out a magnifying glass and took it back to the cabinet and peered into the cocoon shaped egg with its green glow and studied it for several seconds then handed the magnifying glass to Johnny; he studied it and said, "The pain was so severe I didn't notice that I dropped a tear in the container but I did cry and my cheeks were wet."

"It looks to me as if it is part of your anatomy, Johnny," suggested Victor Vance.

"What part is that?" answered Johnny.

"I think it is a tear duct and gland."

"What is that stringy thing hanging from it?"

"That's a tear duct leading to your eye that flushes your eye," remarked Mr. Vance.

Georgie being unfamiliar with human anatomy was quiet as the conversation went on. Georgie said, "Does that mean we can make parts of the body?"

Stunned at the thought Victor Vance and Johnny recoiled as though bitten by snakes, their eyes widened and took deep breaths and slowly nodded their heads. Mr. Vance muttered, "Maybe, but let's not pursue it any further." He took the cover off the silver-green container that Georgie was cloned in and said, "See, this tub is three-quarters up the cocoon-egg shape?"

Georgie noticed how pliable it was, bending it up and down. "That was your umbilical cord that brought air to your brain and body but didn't bring you food. I cut it off with scissors. It's something of a mystery. How long does a butterfly stay in a cocoon under favorable conditions and not eat and yet come out a marvelous beauty? This is your birthplace and it took only three days of gestation and how fast you grew in one week."

Georgie stared back at the umbilical cord and said, "I don't remember a thing about it."

"No one remembers their birth," answered Johnny.

Georgie looked at his stepdad and said, "Dad, I just want to be a normal kid now that I'm not speech impaired! I do want to see my real mother again."

"Do you think you can find your way there?" asked Victor.

"I only know my way to Johnny's house, your house and the school," replied Georgie.

"Son, you live in Sonoma County in the state of California between Cotati and Sebastopol."

"I remember that I lived in a basement apartment in an alley behind a restaurant and a garbage dumpster with rats. It is a very crowded area. At night you hear an occasional shot and screams. My mother and I huddled together in fear of a stray bullet passing through the windows so we always huddled below the windows in the safety of the concert walls and bricks with the mattress on forklift pallets above the damp green floor.

"On the weekends, several men blocked off the street in front of the restaurant and the ladies in the area would stand on the street in their prettiest clothes waving at the men with red lights aglow. The same men that blocked off the streets had vendor carts that they wheeled up and down the street selling hot dogs, homemade pie. They scooped the beer out of galvanized five-gallon dishpan inserted in the carts with covers over the beer and hot dogs and other foods. The hot dog steamers were heated with propane tanks in front of the carts leading to a burner. On top of the burner a pot filled with water and dogs, the aroma is very enticing when your stomach is growling.

"Other guys sold lemonade, beer and popcorn and probably drugs. The carts were made at a cabinet shop at the other end of the street. I'm not sure my mother told me what town or city it was; all I know is that I hated the place and the people around me, especially my brother. My mother is the only one I trusted. My brother had a separate bed in the kitchen near the door.

"In the summer time, it was hot and sticky and you couldn't sleep. The wooden screen door would creak and groan when users came to buy their little rocks or the bang of the door. Smashing into the wall when my brother threw the person out because he or she didn't have the money. Then came the whimpering or swearing," moaned Georgie.

Victor Vance and Johnny Two Buck stood bewildered and astounded at the ramblings of Georgie. Pausing for just a moment, Georgie's face and twisted mouth began to move his lips, crinkled, his eyes rolled up in his head and he went limp. Johnny and Mr. Vance caught him before he hit the concrete floor and pulled him over to a chair. "Dad, I don't feel so good," Georgie said with a heavy breath. Georgie began turning silver-green, suddenly he shot up to the ceiling, his body image burned onto the false ceiling and it dropped away, falling on Johnny.

Victor Vance took a towel from a cabinet and to the sink to wet down a towel. Coming back, he ran into the remnants of the burning ceiling. Victor Vance had to use the wet towel on Johnny first, putting out the flames then, as Georgie came floating down and landed back on the chair, he used the wet towel to put out the flames on Georgie and stamped out the parts of the ceiling that landed on the floor.

Victor Vance then ran to the phone and called the office and said, "Call the fire department and an ambulance and send them to room C5, and hurry." Smoke began pouring out the classroom door and a crowd pushed their way into the classroom; luckily, Georgie turned back to normal color. Victor pushed the students back out of the room and locked the classroom door after the smoke had cleared. He quickly went past the sink to the door leading to the patio and opened it to let the smoke out.

He ran back to Johnny and Georgie. Johnny looked a little worse for wear with burn holes in his clothes but was all right. Georgie was breathing heavily and had a normal color but unconscious. The drone of sirens, barely heard over the crowd of students' babble outside the front door of the classroom. The belching of whistles and sirens grew to a deafening roar as the fire truck and ambulance entered the school parking lot and to the first classroom through the gate and stopped at room C5.

The paramedics were shouting, "Out of the way please!"; the cacophony of students outside the room filled the room along with the smoke. Mr. Vance rushed to the door and unlocked it before the firemen smashed it in. Johnny and Mr. Vance had tried to put out the fire. The first paramedic came through the door and asked, "Where is the patient?"

The other men extinguished the fire. "Over here on the chair," Mr. Vance pointed toward Georgie. Just as the paramedic made it to Georgie, another fireman came through the door asking, "Where is the fire?"

"The men before you put it out, but there are some smoldering ceiling tiles on the floor," as Victor Vance was holding back the surging students who came in when the last fireman opened the door. Looking up at the ceiling, the fireman asked and responded, "That's a funny damn hole in the ceiling. How did the fire start? I see no electrical wires there."

"I'm not sure," said a hesitant Victor Vance.

The paramedic called on his two-way radio to another paramedic to bring in a stretcher. Mr. Vance was still at the door holding back the students, "Let the paramedic in and no, you can't come in," he said in a forceful voice.

Georgie's heartbeat went bump-bump-bump and not bump-bump as the paramedic pressed his cold stethoscope to Georgie's chest and to his ears, "Maybe this kid has an extra heart chamber." Another paramedic wheeling a stretcher in stopped beside Georgie's chair; they went to grab Georgie but Georgie whirled in the air and landed on the stretcher.

The first paramedic with the stethoscope in his ears squeaked, "How did he do that?"

Both paramedics looked at Victor Vance and he shrugged his shoulders and said, "Maybe he knew that's where he is supposed to be." Victor Vance was still at the door of his classroom holding the students back, and heard two voices calling "Dad"; he looked past the crowd and yelled, "Let them through!"

"What happened, Dad?" said Heather and Jason Vance.

"Georgie had some kind of convulsion and hit the ceiling, setting it on fire," their father answered.

Jason said, "Oh yes, like at the house." Victor nodded to his children as the two paramedics wheeled Georgie out of the room through the crowd and into the ambulance with at least a thousand kids behind the paramedics.

Chapter 23

As the orderlies of the hospital took Georgie from the paramedics, they noticed leaves on the gurney; the orderly threw them on the floor. But near the left hand of Georgie, more leaves appeared. Puzzled, the orderly studied a leaf while he pushed Georgie toward the E.R. But the nurse in charge demanded to know what the orderly was doing with leaves. He said, "These leaves appeared on the gurney from this patient's left hand. Odd-shaped leaves."

"Nonsense, it can't happen," the E.R. nurse responded and pushed him aside and wheeled Georgie to the examining room. While the leaves appeared, Victor had been just as surprised and said, "They must have fallen off a tree when we rushed in with Georgie."

Heather, Jason, and Johnny nodded in agreement. The E.R. nurse ignored everyone and moved Georgie through examining room to critical care. The doctor was in the E.R. when the nurse abruptly screeched, "Tie this creature down! I think he swallowed an electric eel." She pulled her hand away from Georgie's body and fell to her knees; her lips pulsed as though she was trying to say something else.

The doctor and the orderly were standing on the other side of the gurney and only saw her fall. The orderly came around the front of the gurney but Victor Vance was right behind the nurse and picked her up, concealing her body from the orderly; she had a silver-green tinge on her lips. Her lips kept moving and finally the words, "Eel electric," her eyes fluttered, her skin turned normal, and she said, "What are you doing holding me?" as she awkwardly took a step away from Victor toward the orderly.

Georgie was now breathing normally and marginally alert, muttered, "Where am I?"

The nurse announced to Georgie, "Don't you worry, the doctor and I will get that electric eel out of you." She then stuck a tube into Georgie's mouth and down his esophagus to his stomach to catch that horrible eel.

His Indian eyes showed distress and alarm when she forced a tube up his rectum, she then said, "I have that bastard trapped now!" With her right hand on the tube in his rectum and her left on the tube in his throat, Georgie appealed to the doctor with gestures, "GET THIS WOMAN AWAY FROM ME," and ripped the tubes from his body!

The doctor, wide-eyed from what just occurred and the nurse with her nose in the air saying, "NURSE CRATCHIT will visit you, Indian," and left the ER!

The doctor responded, "How can I help you, son?" He held in his hand a sphygmomanometer ready to take Georgie's blood pressure.

Georgie asked, "Aaa, what's up, Doc? What's that?"

"It's to take your blood pressure if that's okay with you," the Doctor asked politely.

Georgie tried to move his left arm but noticed he was strapped to the gurney. Georgie looked up at the Doctor and said, "Why do I have restraints?"

"The nurse thought you are violent."

"I'm not nuts; about her electric eel assumption, that's crazy. I've never seen one in my life."

Victor Vance didn't know what to say; he noticed two new leaves on the gurney and tried to hide them. The doctor asked, "May I see the leaves?" He studied them for a moment and quipped, "Yes, I know this variety of orchid. I have grown them in my hothouse. Where did these leaves come from?"

Heather and Jason tugged their dad's arms; he turned and looked at them and said, "They'll never be able to treat him if they don't know."

"Dad, no one will believe you," replied Jason.

"Is there anything wrong?" asked the doctor.

"Yes and no," replied Victor.

"What do you mean?" answered the doctor.

"The incredulity of what I'm going to say is one hundred percent true, doctor. Georgie Vance is a clone!"

"You mean he is a twin to that boy standing behind your son and daughter?" the doctor responded with a puzzled look.

"It was a totally unknown birth that happened over the president's holidays," muttered Victor Vance.

"You mean someone you know had a baby out of wedlock?"

"No, the only one involved is Johnny the boy you asked about earlier. He was born on February twenty-fifth of this year," struggled Victor with the unbelievable information.

"Sir, I do not understand anything you said. This boy looks to be the same size as the other boy."

"I'm telling you they are not twins but he is a clone from Johnny and grew in a matter of weeks to equal the height of Johnny."

The doctor was really puzzled and said, "Nothing you have said makes sense or is possible."

"Johnny, come up here and show the doctor your scar on your thumb."

"Yes, I see the new skin; what of it?"

"That's the portion of genetic material that created Georgie and genetic material from an orchid. He can create leaves at will, they seem to come out of his fingertips."

"You're telling me that orchid cells are living in a human body?" whispered the doctor.

"Yes, I feel the attacks are caused by the chloroplasts in his bloodstream."

Chapter 24

Off in the distance, a commotion…someone yelling, "Put it out!" A fire at the other end of the ER! Just as Victor Vance was about to tell the most extraordinary tale, that of the silver-green light that was destructive when not under control. Victor pushed Georgie on the shoulder and said, "Watch the light. I think you set a fire at the other end of the room."

The doctor, amazed at these preposterous statements a teacher was making about two children, and he expected him to believe! "Sir, you are sick and should be tested by a psychiatrist to see if you're suitable for teaching."

Victor Vance took the admit papers from the clipboard and said to Georgie, "Burn a hole through the papers to show this non-believer."

"But Dad, I'm strapped down."

"Break the strap on your right hand."

"I'm trying to cooperate with the medical personnel."

"Now is not the time to be completely cooperative, son." Georgie nodded, turned a little silver-green and muscled the strap until it succumbed. The doctor jumped back and marveled in fear that this relatively small kid had so much strength. The doctor had bumped the gurney so Georgie turned his head and politely said, "Sir, I hope I didn't unnerve you and I'll try to just burn a tiny hole in the paper."

The doctor said Yes with his lips but didn't make a sound, there was a clattering sound below the doctor's waist. Georgie raised his right hand to the paper that Victor was holding and in a flash, the paper was burning in the center. Victor rushed over to the sink and turned on the cold water and threw the burning paper into the sink. The doctor sat down on a stool and rubbed his eyes with both hands. "Let's go for an M.R.I. and I'm sorry about what I said, Mr. Vance. Help me push Georgie to the imagining room."

Silence enveloped the six until they were halfway there and passed the nurse's desk. "Call the imagining room and tell them I'm coming with a patient," the doctor requested.

Georgie laid quietly until the door of the imagining room opened, his old language hit his lips, "What the hell is that big thing?"

"It has no outward effects on your body, we're just going to look in your head," replied the smiling doctor.

They had pushed Georgie halfway into the body covering machine when Georgie broke the strap around his chest and cried out, "Are you sure this thing isn't going to eat me?"

Laughing, the doctor answered, "No son, the machine will take photographs of your veins and arteries."

The imaging tech girl pressed a button six times as the upper part of the image moved from head to foot. "It's all over," as the image tech pulled Georgie from the clutches of the light tan giant contraption, by the medical imager.

Georgie, lying on the gurney, asked, "May I get up now?" going back to polite language. The doctor nodded and Jason untied the strap just above his knees and Heather released the strap around his feet and left hand.

Johnny spoke up, "Can we take him home now?"

"Are you sure you're not identical twins?" as the doctor scratched his head in wonder. "You can't go home until the pictures are looked at by a specialist." At that moment the door abruptly opened, the specialist came in with the x-rays and put them on a light enhancer attached to the wall. The enhancer was four by five feet. First, he put the feet up then the legs to the knees, the thighs, abdominal area, chest, neck, and head all looked normal until magnified. The blood flow in smaller arteries in the brain had bubble-like structures that seemed immobile.

"I fear the leaves have invaded his brain and cut off the blood supply," said the specialist. Just as he made the statement, the image tech put another x-ray of Georgie's brain on the light enhancer, the bubbles had not moved from their position but turned over, up was now down and stayed at the same location. The tech put up another x-ray with the same bubble in the same location, again twisted.

Georgie fell back on the gurney in the prone position and the doctor said, "Push him back in the M.R.I. and take six more x-rays of his head."

As the specialist hung up the new x-rays, the bubble appeared to bounce up and down. "That's how a chloroplast behaves," remarked the doctor. The six x-rays were two seconds apart and showed the movement of the chloroplasts. "This establishes that the orchid is a parasite and is alive and well in your veins and arteries. Furthermore, that is what gives Georgie strength and energy and what gives Georgie the blackouts. I still can't believe what I'm seeing," pondered the doctor; the tech and the specialist came to the same conclusion. "I have no clue how to help Georgie. I could put it on the agenda of the board of directors?"

"Doctor, Georgie does not want to spend his life being pushed and probed by doctors and scientist checking his orifices every other day and confined to some institution. What if they locked him up because they think he is too dangerous to walk around free just because of his background?" Victor Vance said astutely.

The doctor paused for a moment and suggested, "If the chloroplasts don't kill him by shutting off the oxygen to his brain, they might plug up his heart if too many collect there at one time."

Victor pondered for a moment and asked, "Will the chloroplasts stay the same size throughout his life?"

"There's a possibility that they won't grow any bigger and if maturity in his case, his veins and arteries, will enlarge as he moves into adulthood, he may live a long life."

Chapter 25

Georgie had the promise of the three doctors, med tech, and specialist that they would not reveal his secret to anyone and as proof they gave him all the x-rays and put them in his hot little hand in a big brown envelope along with admission forms.

By touching Georgie, it shocked the doctor and he said in pure Jack Benny, "Now cut that out."

The Vance family and Johnny continued to laugh and push the wheelchair that hadn't touched a wheel on the floor of the hospital since Georgie sat down. The attendant that followed them out, to recover the wheelchair, never noticed it until Georgie floated off the wheelchair and it crashed into a pole. "I hope you stay well," as he took possession of the wheelchair, possibly never realizing what he saw.

The doctor stood staring out the door when the attendant pushing the wheelchair said, "Something strange about that kid."

"You'll never know," replied the doctor as he picked up his violin, played the Jack Benny theme song.

The attendant muttered, "I wish you'd get that thing fixed or stop playing it. That banjo squeaks."

"I'll have you know this is a Stradivarius," the doctor cried in anguish and gritting his teeth.

"I thought Stradivarius was a ruler of Rome like that guy that watched Rome burn," mentioned the attendant.

Chapter 26

"The Vice Principal, Miss Syndly, watched the rest of your classes, Mr. Vance; I hope the child is okay?" replied the principal.

"He's fine, he's coming through the door now," but as Victor Vance said that, both Georgie and Johnny came through the door at the same time, confusing the principal. The secretaries and the nurse rushed to the side of the boys and politely asked what had happened and was there anything they could do to help? Everyone in the administration building was always kind except Miss Syndly and Marsha, one of the counselors.

Georgie said, "I'm Johnny," and of course, vice versa as the boys smiled at each other.

Everyone gathered around Johnny and asked, "What happened to you?"

"I had a brain freeze," calculating the real seriousness of the situation. The secretaries thought to themselves, too much stress, and the nurse thought Petite Mall. They caressed Johnny while Georgie stood back and laughed at the nonsense going on. After shocking the doctor, Georgie realized that if he was careful, he can control the silver-green light without hurting other students. But just as he thought of shooting everyone in the ass, Heather and Jason walked in and grabbed Georgie's arms; he missed, fired, and hit the light fixture on the ceiling, hanging by its electrical wire dust and plastic particles lightly rained on the group, enough so that everyone looked up with a puzzled frown, especially on the vice-principal and principal's faces.

The principal remarked, "Things of this sort have been happening all around the school but stopped until now." She then turned to Mr. Vance, "Do you have any idea how things like this happen?"

Victor grappled for a minute on what to say and answered, "They must be things improperly installed."

Johnny and Georgie had shit-eating grins on their faces. Heather and Jason were looking at the ceiling as though completely surprised. Miss Syndly, slipping off one shoe and then the other and putting them back on, while they were thinking stinky, offered, "Funny we have defective pans in the kitchen and defective brick walls with cleanly cut and precise holes and funny looking leaves on faces in the cafeteria."

Obviously, the Vance family and Johnny said goodbyes and quickly left the school premise in the car, while Victor Vance thought that the pressure was slowly building and if Georgie wasn't more discreet with his abilities, well, he hated to think what will become of them all. Through the fog of Dad's thinking, a voice rang out, "Dad, you're going to go through a red light!"

"What?" he answered.

"Slam on the brakes!" screamed Heather. The passenger side door ripped open, a rush of air pushed Johnny and Heather back in their seats. The car seemed to go out of control. The smell of burning rubber began to permeate the interior. Horns created a cacophony. Tires still moving on pavement roared their resistance. Wheel covers flew from contorted rims. Screams from the Vance family car erupted into a maelstrom.

Spectacularly, the car began to move backward from the intersection, allowing the others to pass through without a collision; all that was left was the stench and skid marks of the rubber. Silence came over the family, then gasping for air gained prominence in the car.

"What happened? I thought we were dead," cried Heather.

But outside of the opened car door came a voice of agony saying, "Let us all go home!"

Victor, now berating himself, looked out the open passenger door and there was Georgie lying on his back with his feet in the air, shoes smoldering without the soles of his shoes, the tops of his sneakers were there but the bottoms were gone, white skid marks along the black of the tires. Victor and Jason released their seatbelts and jumped out of the car to help Georgie but by the time they lifted him off the concrete and to his feet, supporting him so that his feet wouldn't hit the hot road, Georgie put his feet directly on the surface and walked to the car; of course, his feet were bare except for the tops. His skin had replenished itself in a matter of seconds.

As Georgie got back into the car, he pulled his shoe tops to the middle of his shins. Victor Vance looked at Georgie and smiled and remarked, "If I didn't feel so foolish, I'd laugh."

Nothing else was said until Victor Vance let Johnny out of the car in his parents' driveway. "I hope the rest of the day and night go smoother."

Johnny waved but said nothing and tried to smile as he trudged through the door of his parents' house. "Dad, that's the second time this week we were nearly in an accident," reported Jason.

"Yes, so many things have happened; my mind has been preoccupied," admitted Mr. Vance.

"All because of me," answered Georgie. "I'm really sorry but if you knew that you were dead and saw yourself dead and yet you're alive and have extraordinary senses that have stunned you and qualities nearly beyond control at this moment. If growing up isn't hard enough, but with my condition keeping these qualities under wraps and suppressing constant thoughts of what I can do are emotionally unsettling.

"I want to try things that no ordinary kid would even think of. It's so enticing and compelling that so many nos to myself absolutely blows my rational thoughts. Just like stopping the car and pulling it back from harm's way. I did it as a reflex and my feet hurt because of the friction at that moment, something I would never have done as the other Georgie besides Johnny and the rest of you are my family now and I want to keep you safe."

Chapter 27

At supper, Mr. Vance asked his wife, "Why is the coffee cold?"

"It's left over from the parents' meeting at the school and so are the sandwiches for supper."

"Yes, you took over the meeting; the ambulance picking up Georgie everyone left the meeting to see the commotion created by Georgie's collapse and ride. By the way, Georgie, what happened?"

"Well mom, before I say anything about this afternoon, I'd like to warm up Dad's coffee," Georgie pointed his right index finger at Victor Vance's coffee and a silver-green light slowly appeared and delicately produced a swirling motion until a minuscule amount of steam rose from the mug.

"Hey Georgie, that's a great idea for an invention; a sort of oven that has a timer on it and it cooks in seconds instead of the usual oven time," Victor Vance mentioned enthusiastically. Dad put sugar and cream and took a drink. "Perfect, Georgie, perfect! Now if you could keep the chloroplasts under control like the silver-green light, your special qualities will be completely unnoticeable."

Georgie nodded his head as he finished swallowing a bit of ham and cheese sandwich and said, "It took me a while to control the silver-green light and you can see I have complete control over it. But if I get excited, I feel my arteries and veins contract, at least I think they do, and that's the problem."

As the family finished dinner and the children washed the dishes. Heather washing and Jason and Georgie drying, the experience took on new meaning. Georgie showed speed with his dishtowel and didn't have to use the kitchen ladder to put away dishes; he merely glided to the top shelves and placed the dishes carefully, rearranging them so that they looked neat and in precise order. He had a dishtowel on his shoulder as he did in his mother's kitchen, except he was on a kitchen ladder in the basement when a Mac 45 machine pistol fired and plastered the room just under where he was standing on the ladder.

Tearing the step below to shreds caused him to fall, catching the counter with his right foot and flipping him before he hit the floor on his back on to a mass of shredded slivers of wood. All this time he had his eyes closed, the concussion hitting the floor jarred his eyes open, seeing the debris swirling around the kitchen, he closed them all the time thinking in his callous way another dissatisfied customer of his notorious brother the drug dealer.

Georgie dropped to the floor with a loud thump and yelled out, "That was a godawful experience," he quipped, looking up at the light illuminating the kitchen. "There's a fly on the light globe." Slowly, Georgie rose up in a sitting position, raised his right index finger, and let the silver-green light ray strike the fly. It dropped to the floor. "Boy, I wish I could have done that to the Mac45 shooter," remarked Georgie in a forceful tone.

Mr. and Mrs. Vance came running into the kitchen as Georgie jumped on his feet first on the kitchen floor doing the twist and making his own music courtesy of Fats Checker, no…"Fats Domino" and "Chubby Checker".

"Oh, I get the guys mixed up."

Everyone stared at Georgie but Mr. and Mrs. Vance had an angry scowl on their faces. "Didn't we just come from the hospital," he looked at his watch, "two hours ago?" Mr. Vance using his spitting technique, when students become almost incorrigible, he usually expectorated at them unintentionally, which seemed to bring them back to consciousness but Georgie was another matter, being in much more difficult situations, he didn't think anything would work.

Georgie did have common sense on his side but with these new qualities, Mr. and Mrs. Vance thought they might push him over the edge. "Georgie, NO MORE SPECIAL QUALITIES IN THE HOUSE, get the step stool out to put the dishes on the higher shelves," announced Mrs. Vance.

Georgie, realizing this was the first time the Vances had lost patience, said, "I will do what you ask as you see me as somewhat uncontrollable, I see myself as uncontrollable too, I only lived in this body for a short time and it took time to get used to it as well as the sudden sensations of power and then finding I really do have the ability to do these unusual pranks." Georgie realized that he had upset and befuddled the Vance family to the point of admitting failure of placing him in the family as a member in good standing.

How can I make it up to them? he thought. The Vances were so different from his real genetic family. *Can I truly fit in this very close and loving couple and their two children?* Jason taped him on the shoulder and pleaded, "Come back from wherever you are, Georgie."

"I was just thinking I don't fit in with you guys or the Two Bucks' family I should probably leave and go back to my old neighborhood, if I knew where it is, Mr. Vance, I mean Dad!"

Everyone looked at Georgie knowing that he meant what he said. Mrs. Vance walked over to Georgie and hugged him and replied, "Vic and I only thought of the house and its contents. You have an ability with the wave of a finger to obliterate anything at will; we know you don't do it on purpose but it can happen if you're not careful. We don't want you to leave; we just want you to be more careful and think before you proceed with anything in the house."

Chapter 28

Several weeks passed with Georgie and Johnny avoiding any conflicts on campus with the Bobbsey Twins and their boyfriends, Peter and Paul, and their teachers, the vice principal, and principal. Mr. Ritz was always bothersome; he came up with some old Hollywood style talk of Indians; he would say "how" are you or me need "wampum", don't you?" Sometimes he left the Indian teas out and said to the class, "Me Tarzan you Jean or Jane," and he seriously believed he was wonderful.

While many envied teachers' time off, they did not realize the psychological toll it took after several years of teaching, especially if you're not exactly suited for the profession. Mr. Ritz meant well, but once he went off on a tangent, he was unable to stop. So, something had to happen such as a block in his thinking.

Johnny and Georgie sat down in Victor Vance's room C5 after school and began talking how to get him off the Indian teas. Dad Vance was in the administration building talking about school textbooks with the secretaries. Johnny and Georgie decided on two plans—ask Dad to speak with Mr. Ritz and politely ask him to cut out the Indian wisecracks. Plan number two: scare him out of his wits with Georgie's special qualities.

Victor Vance's talk with Mr. Ritz went well and Mr. Ritz took the hint that the boys didn't appreciate his quips of Hollywood Indian life. So, Mr. Ritz's jokes and laughs came to an end but only for three weeks. Then, ever so slowly, he couldn't help himself, he needed laughs. On a Monday into the class, he said, "Where do you sell your old feathers, I need some for my hat?" He answered out loud, "In your beaver wigum joint, you two aren't married, are you?" Of course, his offensive remark was over everyone's head. All the students sort of frowned as he laughed at his inane jeer.

The fifty minutes were over and Mr. Ritz was the first out the door and to his car. It almost seemed he left the window open so he could slip right in his car with a cigarette in his mouth, lit. Mr. Ritz, cracker man, had some amazing skills such as flipping a cigarette in the air while opening the car door catching it in his mouth! Wouldn't you know it; by the time Johnny and Georgie went out the door, Beth and Babs had their boyfriends looking like Lurches on the Addams' Family. "Well, hello," said Johnny.

Georgie erupted with, "Are you going to click your fingers and say in a deep brackish crackling voice, 'Georgie eat bugs'!"

That enraged Peter and Paul, they puffed themselves up like roosters ready to square off. The girls said, "Hey dummies, he insulted himself." While this added to the noise and confusion at the door of Mr. Ritz's room, Beth, Babs, Paul, and Peter meant to be there just to intimidate the Indians. Georgie put his arm around Johnny and whisk him around the corner that exposed them to the main street in front of the school and Mr. Ritz's car where he was smoking a cigarette and taking a swig of booze from a flask. He saw the boys turn the corner from his right eye's peripheral vision. He brushed away the smoke from the window that he had rolled up. He saw the two girls and their boyfriends run around the corner, he then looked back at the Indians and thought, *Boy, they are in trouble now*, but the Indians were gone.

The four looked surprised, no Johnny and Georgie, they looked behind the bushes then knelt down to look under the cars—GONE. The administration-building roof was solid and easy to walk on; actually, they were on all fours so no one could see them; they couldn't get off the roof because the tardy bell hadn't rung. The campus quad crowded with students, they would be seen jumping off the administration-building and they had caused a big scene the other day and now this; Miss Syndly would be right on Victor Vance's rear for good.

Johnny and Georgie's next class was math and the girls will be making their way to Mr. O'Neill's class. The tardy bell rang and there was a blur on the campus quad as the students ran, trying to stay out of the grasp of stinky Miss Syndly. She was running across campus, her eyes staring straight forward on room D5 door where two students were lingering; ten more steps and she'd have them corralled.

The students looked up and Miss Syndly was on them; no escape was possible although her feet always hurt, she was still fast on her stinky barking dogs. As Miss Syndly herded the two into her office, the Administration building door swung closed, the campus quad was deserted. "When we jump down, you'll have an ankle sprain and we'll get a note from the nurse," suggested Georgie.

Georgie planned to drop in front of the administration door because it had no window. As they gently descended, the door swung open and smashed into Georgie. A head came out from behind the door and said, "Mr. O'Neil called and you two are not in class," the boys noticed stinky the Veep had one shoe in her hand.

"I sprained my ankle, Miss Syndly," Johnny looked at her shoe and said, "Did you hurt your foot?"

She didn't take the avoidance question to pull her off the tardy and try to gain sympathy from her. "Get in my office; I'll get the nurse," as she came in her office behind them.

Georgie helping Johnny to a seat while Miss Syndly picked up the phone and asked the nurse to come over. Miss Syndly began talking in an incoherent mumble as she massaged her right foot. The nurse came in the office, Miss Syndly asked in a commanding and domineering intensity, "Did you bring your medical kit, of course you didn't; go get it! My feet are killing me; this foot ailment is not fun!"

The completely upset nurse ran to her office and ran back faster than Georgie if that was possible; she completely ignored Johnny's sprain. First, she rubbed Miss Syndly's foot in the kneeling position for five minutes then sprayed it. Miss Syndly took off her other shoe and the nurse sprayed the other foot right through the sock. Apparently, the nurse had done this treatment many times.

Georgie helped Johnny up off the chair still deploying sympathy tactics as Johnny winced and cleared his throat with a slight gargle and then an, "Oh."

"Sit down, you two, I'm not finished with you," said Miss Syndly sharply. Johnny gave it a big act sitting back down keeping his right foot from hitting the floor. Miss Syndly looked at the nurse and spewed out, "Go tape the boy's ankle now."

The nurse quickly turned to Johnny and had the tape ready to tape over the sock. But Johnny nimbly pulled his shoe and sock off the nurse was somewhat trembling as though she had been verbally threatened often.

"Okay, you may leave now, nurse," stinky Syndly said malevolently. "And close the door, nurse." Miss Syndly stared at Johnny and Georgie for a moment and then said, "How can I tell you apart?"

Silence and hesitation before Georgie spoke after watching the treatment Miss Syndly gave the nurse, "I'm Georgie," looking at Johnny's ankle.

"You mean George?"

"No, my name on my birth certificate is Georgie and on Johnny's birth certificate is Johnny."

"So, I still can't tell you apart."

"You never will physically, only with the clothes we are wearing."

"No moles or scars?"

"Moles, no scars, not so far," answered Johnny. Johnny raised up his hand touched his right incisor tooth and replied, "I have a slight chip right here," as he hobbled over toward Miss Syndly's desk.

"That's close enough, go back to your chair." She then stared again, apparently thinking what to say next because she hadn't caught them doing anything wrong. She then looked at their shoes and asked, "Why do you have adobe mud on your shoes?"

"Miss Syndly, the school is built on adobe mud!"

"Yes, but don't you two use the sidewalks?"

She was trying to start an argument, thought Georgie. "Johnny was pushed and sprained his ankle."

"Who pushed him?"

"It was a group of students, mostly girls doing their lunch tirades at one another; the seventh-grade girls get in a seventh-grade girl physical frenzy; they weren't fighting they were pushing one another and running into the girls' lavatory and screaming as loud as they can. That's when Beth and Babs came running out of the lavatory and accidentally bumped Johnny, his right foot slipped off the cement sidewalk and twisted his ankle, also he picked up slivers from Mr. Aslin's fence."

Georgie in his old life had heard a lot of disinformation from his brother and would lay some on Miss Syndly and the girls that disliked them. "Do you mean our co-presidents of the seventh-grade class are delinquents that can't be trusted; they are the best students in the seventh grade."

Georgie knew that the disinformation wouldn't sink in at first for Miss Syndly but all the students on campus knew what they were like except the teachers and the administration. This could spell doom for girls and their enforcers, the Lurch brothers' grip on the faculty of the school. Georgie and Johnny put on a very effective appearance of concern and it seemed to be soaking into Miss Syndly's consciousness but there was a big IF when the girls saw Miss Syndly and gave their side of the disinformation (lying with a purpose).

Will Miss Syndly be buffaloed, snowed and brainwashed with the glitz and glitter of their beauty and devious personalities into thinking these darling girls were driven by the purest white snow or the grime of the street? Of course, the answer was maybe for both. But Miss Syndly was no fool. Beth and Bab's essences of bubbliness may wear thin if Georgie and Johnny expose them to the school inmates. "I want you boys not to cause any trouble, we have our share and I still can't figure out how the hole got in the wall of the cafeteria kitchen and the hole in the exhibit case in room C5, do you?" pondered Miss Syndly.

"I'm sure Mr. Vance has told you that when a projectile hits glass, it goes in perfectly round and comes through and shatters the inside?"

"No, he hasn't, Miss Syndly," answered Johnny.

But Georgie had seen the capability of a bullet; in fact he knew that there are many types and an enormous number of guns. His brother was not only a drug dealer but also a killer to boot. The hunger for money and power transforms people and especially his brother into a monster of horrid, unspeakable qualities of brutality and terror. You can tell Miss Syndly was still mulling around all unusual happenings that tortured the brain of stinky the asst. principal. She finally let them go, not knowing they two were totally responsible for most of her problems and of course, the crazy Mr. Ritz. Another item that would soon come up. Power had corrupted Peter and Paul and the crazed Bobbsey twins absolutely, be it ever so small amount of power; it corrupts absolutely with a sexual innuendo thrown in until it's discovered, and that was what Beth and Babs had over Peter and Paul.

Chapter 29

Miss Syndly sat back in her chair for a moment and then put her right leg on the desk. She didn't have to take her shoe off because if she sat down for more than several seconds, the shoes automatically come off as though sitting induced the action. "Somehow, those boys have something to do with the strange incidents. Whoever heard of leaves in the face?" She dropped her right leg, wiggling her toes.

As she lifted her left leg, she pulled out a book from her right desk drawer. The title: "Take the Facts and Deduce" by the author of the "Life and Times of Basil Rathbone and Nigel Bruce". The book came with a pipe and hat. Stinky only used them for inspiration. The greatest detective in the world, she thought as she put the hat on and the pipe in her mouth, was the person that can deduce not seduce, gee, that was enjoyable too. *Never mind that, I just need the facts. All I need is the facts, man, no, that's another detective.*

The two Indians were in the lunchroom at the time when the leaves hit the face of Paul and the two Indians were in the lunchroom when the hole occurred in the pots and pans and in the kitchen wall, almost hitting that drunken Mr. Ritz. What else do I know about the incidents, nothing, and two hundred other students and teachers were in the lunchroom.

A moment of silence hit this unrelenting and undaunted brain. "Fuck, I don't know anything," she threw her thinking hat across her office and bit off part of the stem of her thinking pipe, she threw the pipe and spit the stem in the trash alongside of her desk! Miss Syndly then took a brown paper bag out of the right-hand drawer while staring at the ceiling, unscrewed the cap and gulped down a big swig and blew a fart and said, "What a relief." Then she thought, was the drink of Southern Comfort or the fart the relief?

D5 door was closed and with no note from Miss Syndly, how would Mr. O'Neil handle their interrupting presence, but he just waved them in as they peeked through the door. Johnny smiled as he pulled the door open and walked through, Georgie followed. Beth jumped from her seat and explained to Mr. O'Neil, "They don't have a note."

"That's okay, Beth, I saw them in Miss Syndly's office and you know how she gets if you quiz her about something," said the gyrating fancy suit Mr. O'Neil with the pointer stick in his hand pointing at a math problem on the chalkboard.

"But that's not fair," Beth pouted.

"Quiet down, you're ruining my rhythm," he requested. The boys took their seats but not without ferocious glares from Beth and Babs. You could tell they thought they were the only ones that could get away with breaking school rules. Johnny and Georgie had gotten their math books from their backpacks as they sat down at their desks. "What is the answer to problem number five?" asked Mr. O'Neil.

Johnny raised his hand immediately and said, "Two and five sixteenth of an inch. Mr. O'Neil, I have a question for you: why is the U.S. still on the Standard Measurement system while the rest of the world is on metric?"

He looked at Johnny for a moment and responded, "How many in the class know that, raise your hands!" He looked left and right—no hands. "Johnny, it all stems from the pilgrims and an English king. They measured from the king's nose to his fingertip, it was thirty-six inches or one yard. That has stuck to this day in this country and not in the United Kingdom where the measurement took place."

The bell rang, everyone jumped up and headed toward the door. Mr. O'Neil's last word, he had his mouth open, Babs threw a paper wad that landed in Mr. McNeil's mouth; of course, he didn't know who delivered the paper wad. You could hear her mumble, "That will teach him for giving us a boring lesson," as she preened her hair and ran out the door right into the arms of Peter Lurch number one.

Miss Syndly, watching the classes passing, spied an embrace of a boy and girl and immediately sped with alacrity saying, "Ouch and damn feet. Babs, Paul, you know there's no embracing on campus, I'll see you both for clean-up after school!"

"But Miss Syndly, aren't I your goddaughter?"

"Yes, what of it."

"What will mommy have to say?"

"You better call her and Paul, you do the same with your mother." Miss Syndly knew she had to be tough and sped away from further conversation. The board of education and the superintendent will surely know she was a real disciplinarian when she kept her own goddaughter after school for behavior correction.

The principal quietly exited the superintendent's office with a smile on her face after their happy entanglement. Rushing back knowing that she had thoroughly convinced the superintendent that there was no other man in her life; just he and her husband. She knew she could satisfy both of them and the flask on campus was erroneous. As she got into her car, she noticed some odd colors in the bushes then she said to herself that couldn't be, she wouldn't stoop that low and drove away.

Miss Syndly had parked her car past the entrance to the district office so Mrs. Buckwith wouldn't see her car. She came out of the bushes; her right foot had instant pain. She sat down on the curb and pulled her shoe off. A prickly burr had fallen in the back of her shoe. The grotesque scene unfolded of a sixty-year-old lady sitting on the curb with one foot in pain and red berries in her hair and dog poop on her other shoe, where the superintendent had walked his dog, her face twisted because of the repugnant smell.

With the flask in her lap, she turned to break a limb from the thorny bush behind her. The pain from the thorn made her scream and jump up, her stockinged foot hit the bottom of the foul-smelling footwear and she said, "Ah shit!" Nevertheless, she kept poking around in the bushes until she found a small branch suitable for cleaning her sneaker. She then hopped over to an outdoor faucet with the stick and began cleaning her shoe. She leaned against the building and took her sock off and mumbled, "I just bought these shoes last week and the socks the week before."

While trying to put her wet sock back on, two cars drove by, one was Mr. Ritz. "That cheap old hag must be doing her washing," as he puffed on a cigarette and sipped a glass of Southern Comfort. At that moment Miss Syndly, stinky, slipped and fell on the water-soaked ground that put the cracker man into hysterics and with his cigarette cough, the laugh almost killed him. Determined to make the superintendent's office and show him the flask with Mrs. Buckwith name on it, was do or die.

She put the flask between her breasts as she walked into the building, secretly belching under her coffee breath; she heard from the secretaries in the outer office, "What's that smell?" Some holding their noses and others holding their noses with tissues, some with long sleeves wrapped around their faces.

Miss Syndly came nagging and bragging, always with a frown and disgruntled look, denoting depression or school syndrome sort of a constant negative look and now this pestilent odor. They all thought when was this old stinky lady going to retire with her firecracker irritating personality that flooded the room she was in with odor and depression. The secretaries watched this bombastic piece of meanness and odor stomp by and all they can think of was fumigation. The next thought in the secretaries' minds was that some heavy-duty shit was gonna fly!

Chapter 30

Lying out on the grass in the backyard, Georgie found a broad grass blade and put it between his right and left thumbs as the other Georgie had done in his previous life, he blew holding the blade of grass tight between his thumbs, which made a fizzy sound. Heather and Jason had a kite trying to make it stay up after running around in the backyard several times and getting no cooperation from the wind; the kite crashed to the ground. "That's it, no more tries."

Breathing hard, Jason said to Heather, "Do you want to try it?" He began winding in the string.

"No, I guess not there's just not enough wind."

Georgie hadn't been watching or listening until his blade of grass broke. Georgie looked and said, "Hey, let me try. Hand me the kite." Georgie rose off the ground and landed on a chair.

Jason said, "Here's the string and run."

"Give me the kite; you unwind the string, Jason." Jason unwound four feet. "Now how is that going to work?" Georgie gave Jason a wild-eyed look and jumped to the top of the twenty-foot tree, holding the kite in his left hand and grabbing the top branch and instantly putting his feet on two lower branches.

Jason yelped, "Damn string burned my hand!"

Georgie immediately tumbled off the branch but threw the kite into the air. The string caught on his cowboy belt buckle. Jason and Heather watched in horror knowing there was nothing they could do to stop Georgie from crashing to the ground. But to try to catch him before he broke something.

He screamed, "Watch out!" Heather moved out of the way, Jason didn't. Georgie scraped Jason's nose with his right shoe, his left heel clipped his left foot.

Jason began hopping around, holding his left big toe. Georgie rebounded to the top of the tree while getting the string off his belt buckle. An air current picked up the kite but no one was holding the spool of string. This paper and wood contraption began to fly away. Jason and Heather chased the ball of string; Jason's toe had been forced into the soft sod but no damage. A slight limp didn't stop Jason from making a diving grab for the ball of string before it made it out of the yard.

Georgie bounded up to the kite and brought it back down. "Show off," Heather looked at Georgie with a frown on her face and said in a pleading way after saying a smarting sour rancid thing, "After all that work to get the kite up, now you bring it down?"

"Because I have a better idea; instead of sending the kite, why don't we go up?" said an enthusiastic Georgie.

"How do you mean?" they both asked.

"Heather, wrap your legs around my waist and arms around my back and neck as tight as you can." Georgie grabbed Heather at the wrists, bent his knees. Heather tightened her grip with her legs around Georgie. He pushed off the ground and they were higher than the tree. Georgie then came down lightly and said, "Jason, do you want a ride?"

"Of course, a new experience."

Georgie didn't get quite so high because Jason was heavier. This time down, Georgie landed on the garage roof. He had a thought. "Let's have some fun with Mom and Dad. Heather, you go in the house and get an umbrella and a long dress down to the ankles, Jason, you get the portable record player and the Mary Poppins' record," as he gradually and slowly came off the garage roof with Jason. Georgie put Jason on the ground running to get the music equipment.

When Heather came back, she also brought some lipstick and a feather stuck in a hat; she said, "You can be Mary Poppins, the English Indian nanny."

"Good thought, Heather," as he put on the dress, grabbed the umbrella and put on lipstick, a feather, Indian moccasins, as he rose higher and higher.

"Hey not so high, you're scaring us," explained Heather.

"Don't worry, get Mom and Dad and put on the record," yelled Georgie.

"Mom, Dad, come out to the backyard, Georgie wants to show you something," insisted Heather.

Mr. and Mrs. Vance came out of the back door into the yard. Jason put the record on. He had brought his drum set and with a little Indian background beat to a little sugar makes the medicine go down. Georgie descended as Mary

Poppins, the Indian nanny. Georgie pretended to be a conductor with his left hand and holding the umbrella in his right. Victor Vance said to his wife, "He sure has come around the far side of the mountain."

Just as they looked at each other in agreement, a sudden flash of light and a cracking sound took over the Mary Poppins descending. A very, very loud cracking sound and trembling of the ground, Mr. and Mrs. Vance looked up at Georgie, he had a screwed up look on his face and his feather fell out of his hat but the cracking sound kept persisting.

Jason stopped the drumming and turned off the record player and Georgie rushed toward the tree and turned to Mom and Dad. "I shot the tree mistakenly with the silver-green light!"

The Vances stood wide-eyed as Georgie floated down. Vic and Jan turned to one another, "There isn't any cracking in the Mary Poppins song when she floats down."

Apparently, they hadn't heard what Georgie said and suddenly the tree was leaning toward them and the house. Jan said, "What did Georgie say? The music was too loud!"

Vic looked at her then at the tree and cried out, "Get the hell out of the way!" He pushed his wife. Georgie dropped the umbrella and turned to the tree so it fell harmlessly to the ground, only smashing the record player.

Georgie landed in front of his mom and dad and with a pleading face said, "I'm sorry! I thought I had it under control!" Jason and Heather joined their parents in bewilderment as Georgie picked up the tree and carried it out of sight. He came back as quick as he had left, not bothering to explain anything. He proceeded to pull and cut up the stump and the roots with a handsaw from the neighbors' tool shed, he again disappeared holding the remains in his hands.

The laser-like silver-green light cut through to the earth, making a complete circle while Georgie stood motionless ten feet off the ground. The family walked over to the hole and peered in and Victor Vance kicked some dirt into the hole and muttered, "It won't be too hard to fill up," looking at his wife.

A voice said, "Watch out, it's heavy." It was Georgie. Dirt and fir needles begin to pummel the Vances then roots scraped by them. They staggered back from the hole as roots descended into the pit. They could only see hands on the side of the tree; a voice said. "I couldn't find a tree like the other one so I brought this fir tree."

Mrs. Vance asked, "Where did you put the other tree?"

"I put it in the hole I got this one out of the forest." Then he packed dirt around it, a heavy breathing kid with an Indian body and a brain from another race. Georgie set the tree down and began pushing more dirt into the roots while holding the tree. "Steady," he yelled. "I could use a little help."

Jason immediately ran into the garage and came back with two shovels. Then Victor Vance saw a hole through the tree, a hole big enough to put your hand in, nevertheless a hole. Dad looked at Georgie and moaned, "Oh no, do you think the tree will live?"

"I don't know, but that's the only way I could hold on to the tree while bringing it here, I had to complete the circuit, Dad," replied Georgie. Georgie tried to wipe off the sap but no use. It took two hours to complete the planting and two hours to get the sap off.

Jason and Heather, exhausted, sat down on the ground but their parents took the two chairs and Mrs. Vance said, "That is a mighty beat up and hardworking Indian maiden who was supposed to be a delight." Georgie stood there, the dress now dirty, ripped in several places and cuts on his hands and face as he hugged the tree bringing it to the yard. But as he stood there crumpled and dirty, the cuts slowly disappeared.

Chapter 31

The school board met once a month unless there was an emergency, a meeting can be called any time. This meeting was just the monthly meeting and everyone was jovial and polite. The principal of the junior high was laughing and talking with the board members, suddenly she broke into a beaming smile with anticipation of speaking to the superintendent, her lover. And of course, her other lover, a board member, her husband, she winked as he passed by while everyone was turned the other way. The smile quickly turned into a terrifying scowl as Miss Syndly walked in the room with a large handbag under her arm.

Mrs. Buckwith immediately excused herself and left the room. The superintendent began coughing and sneezing and got up and said, "I'll be back to answer any questions in just a moment." He put his handkerchief to his nose and left the room. He hurried down the school hall from the library to the teacher's room. There she sat with her hands over her pretty face accented with platinum blonde hair looking like Carol Lombard and Marilyn Monroe all wrapped into one. Suddenly, her husband burst into the room and both men said, "What's wrong?"

Actually, her husband said, "What happened?" This garbled their meaning.

"What the hell are you guys trying to say?" she took her hands off her face a snarl, a menacing gesture and then wrath of unspeakable hate vomited from her mouth, "That mother fuckin' son of a bitchin bastard," she really meant daughter of a bastard.

The two men said in unison, "What's terribly wrong?" The superintendent almost said lover but he held back because her husband was so much larger than he, except he was easily sexually persuaded.

Her husband asked, "Why are you so upset when Miss Syndly walked in the room?"

"Because she has factitious evidence that I have been drinking on campus."

"How could she get evidence like that?" pondered the superintendent thinking of his own interest having promoted her to principal.

Her husband said, "Well," having his hands out in a pleading position.

"Don Ritz had a flask which I caught him with trying to hide it in my big plant in my office," she explained.

"So what!" both men said in unison.

Her face rippled with a blush, she said, "You guys don't get it, didn't you hear what I said before; the flask has my name on it. That Don Ritz is smarter than you think. He personally had my name put on the flask so that if he is caught drinking on campus, he could claim other ownership."

"But you're the top authority, you can dispute that easily," the superintendent pontificated.

"Are you nuts, Syndly will display the flask here and now she will be the principal and I will be out!" The flask was on the conference table in front of the rest of the fourteen school board members, the flask! Miss Syndly standing in front of the conference table with one shoe off rubbing her foot against her shin and twitching with a horrible twisted smile on her face as the three—superintendent and Mr. and Mrs. Jack Buckwith—walked into the library.

Instantly, the president of the school board stood and said, "Mrs. Buckwith, address yourself to the school board."

Miss Syndly quickly put her shoe on and sat at the end of the big table. The superintendent took his place and the principal's husband sat down with his hand over his face and between his fingers, he looked at the flask; her name is in big letters. *To our favorite principal, RINGINA BUCKWITH* and down at the bottom, his name JACK. He scratched his nose with his pinky and stood up and blurted out, "I never gave her that," as he turned and looked at Miss Syndly!

Miss Syndly's smile turned her face into a happy face then she winked and thought, *I would like a piece of Jack!* The school president pounded the gavel and said, "We'll have order here, Mr. Buckwith, sit down please. Now Miss Syndly, you say you found this where?"

"I found it in a sock in Mrs. Buckwith's coat hanging on the coat rack in Mrs. Buckwith's office."

"How's that?"

"Mr. President, I walked into her office and put several documents on her desk to sign and turned around to walk out and clipped the coat with my elbow, it hurt. I stood there for a moment in pain, my left elbow slightly red, and thought to myself how did my elbow get that spot from hitting a coat? I reached into the pocket and pulled out a sock with the flask in it.

"Of course, I couldn't believe it at first, later I could smell the aroma of alcohol in the office, of course, I put the flask back."

The president paused for a moment and then asked, "What did you mean smelled the aroma later?"

"I came back later to pick up the documents and that's when the aroma hit me."

"So, you're insinuating that she had a drink from the flask after you found the flask?"

"Yes."

"Mrs. Buckwith, would you care to comment on any of these statements of Miss Syndly?" requested the president of the school board.

"Yes, I would, there is no truth to anything she has said and the flask is not mine and I will not stand for this vilification," demanded Regina Buckwith.

"How can you prove differently?" asked the board members.

"I can't, but with one exception—my husband," she turned and looked in his direction.

He stood up and said, "I have never seen that flask period," he announced.

"Nevertheless, I will have to suspend Regina Buckwith until there is a thorough investigation and you're suspended from your duties until notified. Miss Syndly, you will take over her duties."

Miss Syndly scratched her ass so everyone could see it, put on her shoes and stood up and said, "Yes sir," and sat down with a hideous gleam in her eyes.

Regina was a tough lady and felt like taking a couple of swings at the old bitch but kept it within herself knowing in the long view, things would right themselves. "Thank you, Mr. President, I will do as you say," said Regina Buckwith.

"Now can we go on with thoughts on the budget cuts," asked the President of the school board.

Chapter 32

Miss Syndly was outside directing traffic and had a grin that seemed to be vulcanized on her face and a gold tooth with a diamond embedded in it. The diamond sparkled when the sun hit it. She had shoes with springs in the heels when she walked, she pranced. Miss Syndly opened the door to the Lamborghini Contauch. Beth and Babs looked like Siamese twins before they rolled out of the car. Babs's mother responded, "Really darlings, we should bring the Rolls; you've broken my cigarette holder."

Miss Syndly helped the girls up off the ground; her tooth flashed its brilliance and Beth grabbed at it and said, "Where did you get that?"

"Oh, just a fashion statement," answered Miss Syndly.

The girls stood stone-faced thinking something had happened; something vague and deceptive so they played it cool and said, "We have to get to class, Miss Syndly, we'll see you later."

Babs' mom said, "Ta-ta," and released the clutch, stalled the car, and spewed out nastiness, "This fuckin' thing! I'll never learn to drive it." She then started it up and jerked her way off the school property.

Victor Vance let the children off in front of the school before driving to the teacher's parking lot. Johnny was waiting patiently at the front gate with Georgie, he said out of the side of his mouth, "Something is up with Miss Syndly, she never greets children at the turnaround, notice how she's dressed."

The glaring smile spread across a rather prudish face with makeup that accented her wrinkles and brilliant drizzling mouth. "What is that in her mouth, or teeth?" commented Georgie. "Johnny, were you up close to her?"

"Yes, she has on a necklace with diamonds and a ruby in the center, diamond earrings and a gold tooth on her left front tooth that has a diamond too, that is what sparkles."

Georgie looked past Miss Syndly's sparkle and murmured, "Here comes trouble."

Peter and Paul with tank tops, their eyes glued on Johnny and Georgie, Jason spoke up, "They must love themselves and have mirror mania."

"They are coming straight at us," muttered Johnny.

"Migrate toward Miss Syndly," Georgie answered back. All four began a nonchalant gait amidst the babble of the crowd arriving. Peter and Paul as they walked by formed the word chicken on their lips as they pushed and nudged students out of their way. Miss Syndly gave them a glare, it meant trouble. The intimidation factor that this woman had was as though she had an invisible baseball bat in hand and if a student didn't behave instantly, thunderous bruises will fall upon your shoulders.

Peter and Paul had seen the consequences in a fight in front of the administration building when a Hispanic boy of good size decided to take on the intimidator of the school who had threatened him earlier with a beating. The tank top muscular brute of a kid was again reading him off with four-letter words, well, maybe sentences. The Hispanic boy with a combination lock in the palm of his right hand and the u-bar around his middle finger slammed it into the brute's jaw.

The kid got six months in the Juvenile Correctional Center. So, Peter and Paul took over his position as brutes of the school. But tread lightly around Miss Syndly. As these thoughts crossed their minds, they saw Babs and Beth waving at them and turned away from the confrontation with Johnny and Georgie.

The two boys and the two girls walked into the administration building and there, on the signs, indicated principal and vice principal: Miss Syndly Principal and that darned English teacher that screwed up the party at the resort VP at the end of last year. Peter and Paul shook their head in disbelief. "Mrs. Buckwith is the nicest and the most understanding." They then asked the secretary, "What happened to the principal?"

"She has been reassigned to another school as a teacher," the chief secretary announced.

"That's quick," quipped the boys and the girls.

"That is quick," the secretary answered!

Heather walked in and asked the same question. Heather turned to her brother Jason and her closest friends with tears beginning to form and said, "I liked her very much!"

"That is thoughtful," replied Babs, Beth, Peter, and Paul.

"Now we have an old prune that thinks she's god's gift to education and a VP that doesn't know how to pick a good kid out from a Juvenile delinquent; this school is going to pot," cried Heather.

She whirled around and stormed out of the building. You could see the chief secretary had the same thoughts as she sat down dejected. The three boys, Jason, Johnny, and Georgie chased after Heather to try to calm her down; she was bitter to the point of telling off the old witch. They found her at her father's room, C5, before she opened the door.

"Mrs. Buckwith believed me when I said I didn't steal Samantha's mink scarf but I did know her combination on her locker. I don't know who else saw her not spin the lock's combination, until going home I saw Beth with the scarf. Beth did accuse me of stealing it earlier in the day. Mrs. Buckwith analyzed the situation and came up with the right answer. Miss Syndly picks out the closet person to her and persecutes them until they give her the answers, she wants to hear the right or wrong. Now we have two administrators that work the same way. That fat tub of lard and stinky prune face!"

"But you always called Mrs. Buckwith bitch witch?"

"But that was just a cover up, going along with the crowd to fit in. I've always liked her; she is a model of beauty and if I had her picture, I'd put her on my bedroom wall with the rest of the celebs I admire," cried Heather.

"God, I didn't know you felt that deep, Heath," said a surprised Georgie remarked. "This conversation is going nowhere; what we need is action. But we need to get to class before the tardy bell rings or we'll be in front of the force that will kill education."

Heather kept mumbling, "That gold tooth with the diamond in it; where did that come from? She must be able to take it out any time she wants." Jason and Heather faded into the crowd of scurrying students going to their classes. Johnny and Georgie made it to Mr. Ritz's class on time. The first annoying faces are Beth and Babs in a throng of smiling faces. Mr. Ritz had told a joke. Georgie looked at Johnny and whispered, "Don't they smile at anything!" As they sat down, a spit wad caromed off Georgie's head. Johnny and Georgie turned to see Peter and Paul's faces vacillating between ugly and hideous.

Mr. Ritz was still laughing at his joke and didn't notice the gob of wet paper on Georgie's head remembering the first action was never caught. Georgie just pulled the wad off the side of his head and didn't acknowledge in anyway the perfect paper wad to the head. He had suffered much worse in his previous life and he knew now wasn't the time to reply in kind. Peter and Paul pounded their fists on the desktops and grunted to get the Indian's attention. Mr. Ritz turned to see what the pounding was about and said, "Didn't I tell you not to pound on the desks last week?"

Johnny turned a little. "Now we're going to get the big con job."

"Oh Mr. Ritz, it was just a fly on my desk; I tried to capture it and of course, I would have released it outside as you have taught us."

"You smart lard, if you say another word there will be penitence to pay. What's that noise?"

"I just opened my book, Mr. Ritz," muttered Paul. Seeing he had the attention of the class, Mr. Ritz turned to the chalkboard and wrote down the pages to read and questions to answer.

Georgie turned; a slight silver-green light rippled over his face, orchid leaves popped out at his fingertips; it was a tiny flash, inconceivable, struck orchid leaves in the faces of both Peter and Paul. Hideous screams gripped the class in terror. The toughies shrieked and groaned to Mr. Ritz.

"Now what the hell?" The class jumped to their feet, the door slammed open; Miss Syndly had been listening on the PA system. She stepped into the room. Stinky dropped her right red crystal shoe and sneezed and blustered out, "Damn Juniper pollen!" Her gold tooth with the diamond flew through the air with the greatest of ease, bounced off the corner of the wall to the other side of the corner to the forehead of Mr. Ritz, cutting him and knocking him to the floor, probably put on. Just so happened, after striking Mr. Ritz, the tooth tumbled in the air and showed its brilliance around the room, dropped into the hand of Mr. Ritz, now behind his desk, the gold tooth in his right hand while the left pulled out a flask from his hip pocket and took a nip.

The nip was faster than Georgie's leaf strike on Peter and Paul. Mr. Ritz was amazingly quick with his flask nips and breath mint. The only thing that gave him away, he staggered getting up, but everyone thought it was from the blood dripping from his forehead. Cracker man was faster than a speeding gambler in Reno.

Miss Syndly ripped off a piece of her dress and tied it around Mr. Ritz's forehead. Mr. Ritz put on his glasses and thought what the hell she was doing; it was only a scratch, while nurse stinky wrapped that part of her dress. "There's an inscription on the back of the tooth: from stinky to Mr. Ritz with love." Miss Syndly turned her red crystal shoes around and demanded that Mr. Ritz give back her picturesque adjustable tooth, "Give me that!"

She hit Mr. Ritz on the back of his hand, the tooth flipped in the air, she grabbed it and turned to Peter and Paul and said, "To my office; why are you two wearing masks in class, this isn't Halloween." She pushed them out the door.

The class was now stunned, Mr. Ritz was talking with a western accent, "She must think she's in a B-western movie. Anyone got a feather for chief Ritz?"

The class saw a little bit of saliva drop from his lips. A girl sitting in a front seat cried out, "Mr. Ritz has a concussion from hitting the floor. Let's help him to the nurse's office."

The girl and two boys grabbed him and began to drag the not to sober Mr. Ritz. Breath mint breath spewing over the three would-be good Samaritans, the boy on the right said, "Gosh, that was a great catch, Mr. Ritz, how did you do that?"

Mr. Ritz pondered a moment with arms around the boys, the three girls were in his armpits, two girls under his right armpit, he replied, "Natural ability; I was a quarterback in high school," still expectorating, or in children terms, drooling. Just before reaching the administration building and the nurse's office, Mr. Ritz, alias the cracker man, straightened up and began walking on his own; he looked in the principal's office window and there was Mrs. Buckwith cleaning out her desk.

He tapped on the window, he waved, no response. The girl Samaritan turned and looked. "The whole class is following us."

Mr. Ritz hurried through the office door leaving the students behind, rushed into the principal's office locking the door and pulling down the shades. "Do you need a little more help?" he approached her with pelvic thrusts. Her demeanor changed, thinking he had heard her through the door and he wanted to console her but she could see he had something else in mind. "Come on baby, let the good times roll," he said as he approached undulating.

Her face twisted quickly in anger and she threw one ferocious kick, the cracker man sank slowly to the floor saying, "Not only did you get the right one and left one and the long thing!"

"The sack will come back, Mr. Ritz," explained Mrs. Buckwith. Cracker man groaned several times and slowly got up, she said, "The nurse's office is open, maybe she will satisfy you." Mrs. Buckwith giggled and laughingly remarked, "If that doesn't work, there is Miss Syndly."

Holding his scrotum in one hand and popping a breath mint in the other, Mr. Ritz said, "Thank you for your kindness," he unlocked and opened the door.

The Samaritans had pressed their noses against the door window but didn't hear what was going on. "Mr. Ritz," the girl said, "you look worse!"

"I am worse; hold me up and take me to the nurse's office, ladies and gentlemen." He really didn't want their help, he just wanted to get to the nurse. They walked by Miss Syndly's office; she was pulling leaves off the face of Paul leaving big red blotches. Don Ritz covered his face; he ran by Miss Syndly's office and through the open building door held open by students.

"What are you doing out of class?"

"I'm wounded, remember," pointing to his makeshift bandage with a bloodstain on his forehead. Mr. Ritz responded, "I got hit by a diamond studded tooth."

"A dressed-up tooth did it!" Mr. Ritz was standing with the outside door handle in his hand and two students holding him up. The twisted and prune-faced woman had her dressed up tooth in place and demanded, "Get back to class or I'll tell your wife what kind of person you really are!"

Something clicked because Ron Ritz was instantly sober, he remembered the right cross his wife had laid on him and almost broken his jaw. He turned around and freed his arms from the kids and blurted out, "Everyone, back to class, you green-faced guys too."

The rest of the students came out from behind the bushes and filed into his classroom. It was like a funeral parade, a New Orleans special. The two Indians lagged behind because Peter and Paul kept eyeing them. Miss Syndly kept saying, "Catch up, you two." The passing bell rang and everyone ran off. When Johnny and Georgie were across the quad, they could see Miss Syndly's diamond-studded tooth sparkle in the sunlight.

Chapter 33
Before 2nd Life Mother

Georgie, up early with slippers on and pajamas, walked out to the front of the house and got the newspaper for his dad and mother. Dad was at the breakfast table with ham and eggs and coffee. Mom was just sitting down and Heather and Jason had fixed their breakfast and made a big bowl with cereal for each—breakfast of the champions—and milk and dog food for Tanny. Dad was thumbing through the paper and read off some baseball scores that he knew the kids were interested in and some local high school baseball scores that Jason was really interested in, knowing next year they would be going to the high school.

Jason, hearing the score, got up from his chair and went over to Dad and said, "I can pitch as good as Mike Wiley," looking at the box statistics said, "I can pitch as good as him."

"Don't repeat yourself, son."

"I've already hit off him and I know I'll make the junior varsity in the ninth grade."

"I hope so, son," answered Dad. Victor Vance put down the paper and a page he left it on said in big headlines" "Massive fire kills ten people in a restaurant in Detroit".

Down in the column, it said the popular Joker in Spades Restaurant burned to the ground across the alley. The fierce fire destroyed the building behind the restaurant, an old building. Everyone escaped except one woman, last name Martin, was in the Detroit general hospital. Georgie's face started to turn silver-green; he said, "This woman in the paper is my mother. So, I lived in Detroit and didn't know it."

"Are you sure, Georgie?"

"My last name was Martin and that is the name of the restaurant because the cleanup boy that beat the tar out of me when I was young, had the blazoned logo on his shirt." Georgie kept quiet until he got to school.

Georgie said, "Dad, I need to know if that lady in the paper is my mother."

As they got to the parking lot and walking to Victor Vance's classroom, Vic finally answered Georgie, "We can call Detroit General Hospital when we get home, Georgie. If she is seriously injured, she probably can't talk right now. She might be in the burn unit or resting from smoke inhalation and has an oxygen mask on and can't talk. So, let's wait until we get home before we call, Georgie."

"I guess you're right, Dad."

"Heather, Jason, and Georgie, get to class," as Mr. Vance opened the door to C5 to get ready for the onslaught of hopefully happy students. The day went calmly for Georgie. Babs and Beth weren't at school. Peter and Paul seemed down for some reason. They had their usual Levi's, white tee shirt with the school colors red and white cardigan sweaters on. They weren't trying to punch anyone or hassle anyone for money. They were just down in the face. Even though something was bothering them, Georgie stayed away from the two boys that constantly harassed him and Johnny; he couldn't stop thinking about his mother in Detroit.

The school day for Georgie lingered on and on until the final class with Dad in C5. Johnny, Georgie, Jason, and Heather piled into the car waiting for Victor Vance. Jason had the key and started the engine. A half hour later, Victor Vance strolled slowly to the car carrying some science books. "Dad, what took you so long?"

"Well, I had to prepare for tomorrow's craft class and collect some books." Jason turned the engine back on and Dad Vance made it home as quickly as possible after dropping Johnny off. "Now we can make the call to the Detroit hospital, Georgie."

Victor Vince dialed four, one, one and asked for the general hospital in Detroit. "You are connected, sir," responded the operator.

"Your phone, Georgie."

"Hello, I would like to speak with Joy Martin please."

"I'll connect you with her room."

"Hello, who is this?"

"This is your son, mother, I hope you're alright?"

"This is Joey."

"I don't want to speak to you," and hung up. Georgie looked dejected and depressed as he looked into Dad's face.

"Look, tomorrow is another day, Georgie."

"I want to sleep with Tanny tonight."

"She lets off a lot of gas at night, ask Jason, he knows."

"I don't care." Georgie settled into bed after eating a cookie and milk then brushing his teeth, Georgie said, "Tanny, jump into bed." She took the middle. Georgie pushed Tanny to the other side against the wall.

"Night." Mrs. Vance closed the door to Georgie's bedroom. Now that the kids were in bed, the Vances discussed Georgie's situation. Mrs. Vance put down her book and mentioned, "How can his mother recognize Georgie? He is a different person; he couldn't speak and he has a different skin coloring."

"The only way she can recognize him is what they did together," suggested Victor. A silver-green light came slowly down the hall. "Georgie, do you want to see your mother?" Through the light, a yes was voiced. "I'll take him to the airport."

Georgie emerges from his bedroom with Tanny at his side. "Can I take the dog with me?"

"No," said Dad. "Where did you get that suitcase?"

"It's Heather's from down the big hole. My clothes are in it along with some food I took out of the kitchen."

Victor looked at him amazed, "How did you get all this stuff that quick?"

"Jason and Heather packed it for me before I went to bed."

Victor turned to his wife, threw his hands up, and said, "Let's go, Georgie."

They jumped into the Vances' car. "Where is the airport?"

"It's over a big bridge, Georgie, The Richmond, San Rafael Double Decker bridge. You'll see a lot of the bay area."

"Gee, I would like to walk on top of the bridge and watch the sparkling lights." Georgie rolled down the window, jumped out and floated up to the top of the bridge then raced the length of the bridge and hopped back into the car.

Victor said nonchalantly, "How was it?"

"Nice, real nice, I wish you could come with me, Dad."

"What would both your mothers say to that trick?"

"No, Georgie no!"

"But mother, I can do it and I won't get hurt. They wouldn't let me run the bridge, Dad." Dad laughed at what Georgie said, a scared laugh.

They pulled into the airport and stopped at the Southwest gate. "Georgie, take care of the car while I run into the ticket desk and get a ticket to Detroit." Victor Vance scrambled out of the car and into the terminal, bought the two-hundred-and-ten-dollar ticket. Victor waved at Georgie to come in. Georgie opened the car door and ran into the terminal, while Victor ran toward the car. They met halfway; Dad handed Georgie the ticket and said, "As Jimmy Walker would have said, have a diamante trip."

Georgie was now on his own, he walked up to the ticket counter and said, "I have a ticket, now what do I do?"

The lady said after looking at the ticket, "First, young man, I will take you to the airplane gate." The lady talked to the attendant then turned to Georgie, "I want you to follow his directions. The lady on the plane will tell you where to sit and where to put your suitcase. I hope you will have a nice trip, young man."

"Thank you for your help."

The man took Georgie down the hallway to the plane, the man patted Georgie on the head, the stewardess took Georgie's hand and walked him to his seat, grabbed his suitcase and put it in the storage locker above his head. She fastened his safety belt. Georgie thought the seat was too hard so he floated just above the seat. The stewardess walked by and said, "You're taller."

Georgie kinda liked the stewardess so he lost his safety belt a little bit more. This time the stewardess plunked Georgie on top of the head, it shocked her a little, she held her hand and let out an ouch and gave Georgie a bedraggled look. Georgie purposely sank to the seat. After handing him a soda and lunch, she said, "You sunk to the seat, look out the window."

"I've never seen the top of the clouds before."

"The man in the window seat is asleep, yes and you can catch some zzes yourself, we have four hours to go and some minutes."

Georgie finished his soda and food, pushed up his tray, yawned and fell asleep. Since all that had happened after his new birth and now on an airplane to see his mother. His sleep was dreamy and positive. Suddenly, he felt something scraping on his head and something pulling on his right leg. Then heard, "Son, what is your name?"

Georgie looked down and said, "How did I get up here?"

The stewardess grabbed his other leg and of course, Georgie let her pull him back to his seat.

Georgie heard the screech of the tires and felt the bounce that woke him up. The stewardess asked, "Do you have someone waiting for you?"

"Yes, my mother, of course." Georgie made sure his return ticket was in back pocket. The stewardess got his bag and Georgie glided over everyone's head except two tall guys, he tapped them and politely asked them to duck. Georgie waved goodbye to the stewardess and the pilots. Dad had given him twenty-five dollars. He walked through the terminal thinking how to get to the hospital. The yellow cabs took people to the restaurant through the alley, he saw through the basement window.

He saw the rotating steps to the outside of the building. He could see yellow cabs through the windows sitting in front of the terminal. He grabbed his suitcase from the thing that goes around and scrambled out the door into a cab. "Sir, I want to go to the Detroit General Hospital."

The cabby turned around and said, "Do you have money?"

Trying to be polite said, "Yes sir." He nodded. Georgie memorized the way to the hospital. Grabbed his suitcase and went through the front door of the hospital.

The receptionist said, "What do you want, sonny?"

"I want to see my mother, Joy Martin. I think she is in the burn center."

"Sorry, they don't allow children into burn center."

"But I came all the way from California to see her."

"Well, didn't your dad come with you?"

"No. He is not my real dad."

"Didn't your stepdad come with you?"

"No, he is not my stepdad. He is my adopted father."

"Can we call him?"

"He is at work and I do not know the number at the school where he teaches."

That was enough; Georgie grabbed the sheet with all the patients' names on it. "Room ten on the second floor," and slammed the list on the desk as a silver-green streak rippled across Georgie's face, he raced up the steps to his mother's room. He walked into the triple patient room, he hovered and looked from above at the patients until he saw his mother; he said, "Mother, I'm here for you."

"Who is it?"

Georgie, not knowing how to answer, "Joey."

"Can't be, you hostile son-of-a-bitch. If I could see you, I'd swat you with a broom."

Georgie laughed, "No, your other son."

"Impossible, he is dead by the hand of his brother."

"Dad and the great force of the universe allowed me to survive."

"My other son couldn't speak, so you can't be him."

"You lock me in the closet, wash me down with the hose, your boyfriend used to beat me for breaking windows."

"Get the hell out of here, I saw Georgie's body with my own eyes."

Georgie, still hovering over his mother in bandages, heard the door open; he maneuvered himself to the ceiling, two nurses searched the room and asked Joy Martin if she had seen a boy.

"No, I can't see, you dumb broad, only a voice." Georgie's eyes began to fill.

Georgie made it back to the airport, went up to the ticket desk, and said, "I have a ticket to Oakland." He pulled out his ticket. "I want to go now, not tomorrow."

"We can do that," said the lady.

"At least someone is nice."

"Did you say something?"

"No," as he wiped the tears from his eyes.

Georgie ran across the top of the Richmond-San Rafael bridge for home. The door opened at the Vances, Jan looked up from reading the newspaper. "You're early, Dad's at the 'Back to School Night'."

"Nothing happened, couldn't recognize me and she couldn't see and, of course, she couldn't recognize my voice because at the time I didn't have a voice and she saw my body lying in front of Soft Stone Cafe."

Victor Vance opened the door to his house and heard his wife say, "Georgie is home. He is in bed."

Vic looked in Georgie's bedroom, he was asleep with Tanny.

Chapter 34
The Big Hole

Every year, Victor Vance took students and his family to the Grand Canyon on spring break. He began organizing the trip just after Martin Luther King's Jr. Holiday, a day of remembrance. This will be a tighter fit in the van with Georgie along so Jan and Vic decided to leave Jason and Heather with Janet's niece, Janis. They had gone the year before and they knew Janis had a pool and they talked to Janis on the phone; she said if they cleaned the pool three times while they were here, they can swim.

Mr. and Mrs. Vance were happy about the decision their children made. The prerequisites for going on the Grand Canyon trip were: The students must be familiar with large animals and not afraid of heights; a "C" average; no low citizenship grades; and a signature of a parent or guardian on the permission slip. The town of Cloverleaf was surrounded by a large rural area so many children had access to horses, mules, and donkeys. Georgie had no experience and Johnny had very little with large animals. They both had experience with heights, thought Mr. Vance as the passing bell rang.

Before Victor Vance let Johnny and Georgie out the door, he said to Johnny, "Ask your parents if you can go horseback riding this coming weekend."

"Okay Mr. Vance, I will as soon as I get home." The usual noise of passing engulfed them as they stepped out of C5. The constant screaming, laughter and profanities pervaded the campus and they made their way through the cacophonies that thundered the middle of the quad. There standing were Peter and Paul trying to impress the girls with their muscles as they posed in various positions, but without warning, Beth and Babs slapped them on the back of the head, while they were in a frontal pose gritting their teeth and flexing their biceps and making their nipples flip up and down that delighted the mostly feminine crowd.

The blows straightened them right up, the girls grabbed a handful of hair and pulled Peter and Paul away, screaming at them, "Don't you ever do that again," demanded the girls.

The boys pretended to walk away sheepishly but had their heads turned winking at the rest of the girls and they winked back. Johnny stopped for a moment and grabbed Georgie by the shoulder and said, "I saw a slight green tinge on their faces."

"Don't let your ego run away with you. Let's get to class," commented Johnny.

"What do you mean by that, Johnny? I was just commenting on the last blast of green."

"That's what I mean; stay away from arrogant comments; they'll twist your outlook on your new life."

"When did you become a philosopher? I'm already screwed up, I damn near killed Mr. Ritz with this damned ray that shoots out when I'm angry! I killed a tree and I don't know what I'll do with a horse. I've only seen a horse in a picture."

"I just don't want you to get a Peter and Paul attitude and become God's gift to the world."

Georgie stopped at the door D3, Mr. Clancy's math class, and glared at Johnny. "I don't understand all of this, it's crazy and I have no idea how it works and you jump all over me," said a slightly perplexed Georgie.

"I'm sorry but the things you've done unnerve me; you're doing them in my body and it scares me even though I haven't shown it."

The two walked into class, the tardy bell rang and Mr. Clancy blared out, "You both are tardy, the class policy is you must be in your seat when the bell rings."

Georgie turned around and asked Mr. Clancy, "Have you ever ridden a horse?"

"What does that have to do with math? Which one are you? I can't tell the two of you apart."

"I'm Georgie."

Mr. Clancy was quiet for a moment and reported, "I own an old fashion livery stable out by the Russian River called Clancy's Palace Livery."

Peter stood up, "Put their tardy down."

"Tardiness, Mr. Peter!"

"Well, it's like there is one too many of them, only one of me," with a superior turned up nose look.

"Sit down, Mr. Peter, you're filling the room with swell information and we'll soon have to get shovels to dig our way out. So, sit down!"

For the first time, Georgie and Johnny saw Mr. Clancy as a human being not some robot that teaches a subject that's only used infrequently in the lives of most working people. "Come out to the livery stable and we'll have a ball. Now let's get to the subject at hand. And I mean hand, as you may not know horses are measured in height by the measurement of hands. Some many, many years ago in ancient history, someone said my horse is bigger than your horse. Something bigger is always better and of course, it is not true."

Immediately, Paul stood up and replied, "I'm bigger and better," and sat down.

Mr. Clancy speared Paul with a look of disdain and said, "You're tedious and I suggest you raise your hand before you speak or you'll report to Saturday school!

"A hand in measurement is about eight inches," he wrote on the board in a scribbled sort of way. "In ancient times, measurement was haphazard and it cost many people their lives and the ruin of many structures. You see, architecture and engineering need exact measurements otherwise structures sometimes collapse and kill people and it still happens to this day. The hand measurement is a mere classic formality that kings used because most were illiterate and had scribes write all that had to be written."

Mr. Clancy wrote on the chalkboard: "Fifteen times eight hands 120 and twenty inches or ten feet to the shoulder, of course, this is oversized for most horses, with the exception of a Clydesdale."

Because Mr. Clancy went off on a tangent, the class became restless, Beth and Babs, Peter and Paul, begin making faces at each other. Mr. Clancy said, "Don't forget your homework assignment; write it down now because the bell is going to ring." As the bell rang, Johnny and Georgie got hit with paper wads but ignored them and went up to Mr. Clancy's desk and asked Mr. Clancy for an address at the Russian River.

He whipped out a business card from his desk without saying a word, Georgie nodded and Johnny said, "Thanks," and they left the room. Georgie turned slightly silver-green, a couple of students passing stared at them but moved on, scurrying to class.

Georgie remarked, "Boy, Mr. Clancy sure can blabber."

"Yes, but that's in class. I'll betcha he'll be different on a horse," answered Johnny. Both boys walked silently, thinking of the relief of not having the dominating egomaniacs in class with Mr. Vance.

Chapter 35

Mr. Vance and family drive to the Two Bucks and picked up Johnny, then to the Russian River and met Mr. Clancy in front of his livery stable, where he brought the six of them into the livery to find suitable rides. Heather fell in love with a palomino mare; Johnny and Georgie picked out the thoroughbreds thinking they had natural abilities and they should be able to ride the best with no trouble.

Mr. and Mrs. Vance went for sedate and easy riding and Jason thought of trying to ride the Clydesdale, the knights of old horse. Mrs. Clancy brought out water jugs for them while Mr. Clancy's three sons saddled the horses. Mr. Clancy began to speak and both Georgie and Johnny thought he would go into a long sermon on safety and they wouldn't get to ride for another hour but Mrs. Clancy came over and put her hand over his mouth and said, "You always get on a horse on the left side."

Georgie and Johnny looked at each other and Georgie picked up Johnny, moved to the left side of his horse and lifted him up in one swift move. Mr. and Mrs. Clancy's eyes widened at Georgie's physical prowess but Georgie paid no attention to their looks and ran toward his horse from behind and leaped, mounting by putting his hands on the horse's backside and landing on the saddle. Georgie overshot the saddle, grabbed the reins and flew over the head of the horse and was tumbling to the dirt floor but caught himself before he landed face first into the soft gelatinous feces of the Clydesdale.

Mr. Clancy grabbed Georgie as he fell and marveled how light he felt as he thought that he prevented him from serious injury and a broken neck of Superman. "Thank you for your help, Mr. Clancy."

"Which one are you?" he asked.

"I'm Georgie from the reservation and I live with Mr. Vance."

"I didn't know you two lived separately?"

"Yes, my mom and dad's place is small so I live with the Vances."

Georgie smiled and decided to mount as he was instructed from the left side of the horse. Mr. Clancy watched Georgie mount the horse, he noticed Georgie didn't use the saddle horn to throw himself up or the stirrup; it looked like a slow glide to Mr. Clancy, he yelled, "How did you do that?"

But Georgie was out the door and pretended not to hear the question. He knew there would be other questions, he thought best to get on with the ride. Mr. Clancy's eldest son Jack had stopped the family out in the corral. Georgie noticed Mr. Clancy stood outside of the livery stable door with a puzzled look on his face staring at Johnny and then at Georgie. Mr. Clancy said to himself they couldn't be identical twins; Georgie was physically strong and bright and Johnny tended to be a follower.

Jack Clancy said, "There is no turn signals or lights or gauges to fool with but sometimes they do burn gas every so often; don't be concerned, the horses are just letting off some methane. Now take the reins in your right hand and move the reins to the left and the horse will turn left and if you pull the reins to the right, the horse will move in that direction. If you pull back continuously, the horse will back up. Gently nudge the horse with your heels in the ribs; your mount will move faster.

"The thing that will surprise you as we finish the run and walk the horses, you will see the horses locate the livery stable and begin to gallop, because they want to get back for a drink and oats and of course, get rid of you." Jack Clancy turned his horse and yelled, "Wagon's hoe," and waved his right hand forward, he then turned to Mr. and Mrs. Vance and said, "I saw that on *Rawhide*. Clint, somebody always said it."

Then everything calmed as they moved deeper into the forest, they could hear the horses' hooves beating in rhythmic percussion on the trail and the Russian river meandering slowly past them as it makes its way to the Pacific Ocean. The horses constantly wanted to browse on the vegetation, everyone let the horses stop as the silence and the gurgling of the water crept into their consciousness.

Georgie became uncomfortable with the noiselessness surrounding him, the rustling of leaves and the waters gentle movement, its babbles glancing off pebbles and rocks in the riverbed, bursting the effervescent foam. Suddenly, Georgie felt dizzy and fell off his horse. Mrs. Vance screamed, "Stop!"

Jack Clancy looked back and announced, "No one get off their horse!" Feet thumped on the ground as everyone dismounted and Jack ended up holding the reins.

Georgie moaned and muttered, "The pain," and went limp as though he was dead. The family surrounded him in astonishment. Mr. and Mrs. Vance pushed Georgie into position for CPR. As Mr. Vance attempted, Georgie turned his head and murmured, "I thought I was run over by a truck! I heard bodies thumping against metal and screams of pain then the searing agony as my body is crushed by the battered pick up and my brother's head sticking out the window with a fierce glee written across his face as his wheels broke my ribs. The silence after death engulfed me and I thought I saw my dad again."

As Georgie's eyes began to focus, Georgie realized he was no longer on his horse and he arose slowly. Victor Vance whispered, "Don't get up like that, Jack will see it." Georgie eased himself back to the ground and grabbed a blade of grass and put it between his thumbs and blew. It made a horrible squeaking sound.

Jack laughed, "Come on, the horses are getting antsy, they'll be dragging me toward the barn soon. Remember, the left side."

Georgie dropped the grass and sprang up to mount but Mr. Vance grabbed his leg. Georgie's nose almost hit the mushy moss, "Get on normally, no fancy stuff," he insisted in a quiet tone.

Georgie put his foot in the stirrup and rose up with a smile. Jack being close to Georgie, now back on his horse, laughed and asked, "Georgie, how was your trip to the forest floor and back," thinking that Georgie fell off because he wasn't paying attention.

"Hallucinatory," as Georgie spun around in his saddle horn.

"Your trip certainly wasn't because of awkwardness."

"No, it was from my other life. Do you know this is the first time I've been close to a large animal?" Georgie said to himself, *I've said too much* and galloped off.

Puzzled, Jack looked at Mr. Vance and pondered, "What the hell does that mean—another life?"

Victor Vance shrugged his shoulders and replied, "On the reservation." thinking that Georgie had gone too far ahead knowing he came from a different kind of jungle and with no savvy of this one he was riding in and unfamiliar mode of transportation with the moods of a beast. Mr. Vance moved ahead quickly, finding Georgie's horse grazing without Georgie. He heard a voice say, "Holy smokes, I ain't never seen anything this tall in a tree!"

"Get down here before Jack sees you up there."

"What are these things called?"

"Sequoias or redwood trees."

Georgie swung on a branch, made a three sixty with twists and a back flip. It was an amazing acrobatic display as he descended toward his horse, it bolted. Georgie lay prone in the mushy moss digging his fingers into the ooze and mumbling something naughty. He tried to spring up to get on the horse before Jack came around the bend but the suction from the ooze gripped him, soaked him, pulled his shoes off and created a new hairstyle. The plastered look.

Jack launched into twisted laughter as he came around the bend. "You're black, not Indian with a green tinge," cackled Jack. The laughter picked up as the rest of the family came around the bend until a flash of black, green-silver and leaves flew by everyone and abruptly stopped on Jack's face.

A cackle rang out, "Now you're black too!"

Several seconds of quiet passed. Mr. and Mrs. Vance's facial expressions turned from horrified to calm. Mrs. Vance said, "Shall we continue our ride?"

"No." Jack turned his horse around and galloped toward his dad's livery stable. The rest of the horses turned and dashed back at a pace racehorses couldn't reach. Johnny and Heather were spitting leaves and fir needles, Jason and Mrs. Vance had scrapes on their legs and Mr. Vance had a small redwood tree pinecone stuck in his hair and was missing his hat. The horses pulled up right beside Jack who had his face in the water trough.

When he came out, he asked Georgie, "Have you seen a horse spit out water?"

Georgie jumped from his horse into the trough. That was it, the horses all had their tongues out trying to spit off the terrible tasting ooze and green stuff. Georgie pulled Jack into the water trough and dunked him. Mr. Clancy ran over with a grooming brush in hand and slapped the water with it and yelled, "I just cleaned this and now look at it!"

Jack jumped out and said, "He did it," pointing at Georgie, like a good little son but Georgie grabbed Mr. Clancy and threw him in. Mr. Clancy raised his head above the edge of the trough; he covered the faces of his sons. Mr. Vance and Jason turned away, holding the laughter. But Johnny broke into continuous belly-rolling screams and ha-ha… for several seconds. Mrs. Vance looked wide-eyed at the scene. The only things seen of Mr. Clancy were his white ten-gallon straw cowboy hat and two hands thrashing in black soup when Georgie dunked Mr. Clancy again.

Jack stood there in ultimate grime watching his dad flounder like flounders. His brothers rushed to help their dad out. Mr. Vance said to Mrs. Vance, "The ride went well! I hope the trip to the Grand Canyon goes better!"

Chapter 36

Lying in bed not being able to sleep, she jammed her cigarette into the ashtray and poured the rest of her coffee back into the coffee pot. Her cast iron gut can stand anything even at the age of sixty-eight. The bedroom reeked of stale cigarette butts. The walls were brown from nicotine. The windows were edged in smoke, kind of a frost pattern but with brown and gray translucent and opaque designs on the windows. She was so proud of herself; she had picked a fight with her niece who lived with her and verbally beat her into submission.

With one victory under her belt and after her smashing success at the school board meeting, she thought she would have a cigar before breakfast. In her modified voice due to cigarette and cigar consumption began singing as she took off her nightie which were men boxer shorts and a tee shirt that said, "Women's games have balls too"; she lit her cigar. She stepped into the shower humming and placing the ashtray on the bathtub edge, that stinky always carried with her at home. She pulled the shower curtain from back to front but as she started to turn on the water, she realized the Crook's Rum-soaked cigar, her status symbol while a great pleasure, was still in her mouth; she had to put it in the ashtray, oh well, she thought, at least the aroma will still be in the shower.

She continued to hum and then broke into song, her favorite, *The Battle Hymn of the Republic*. Miss Syndly especially liked the part of stamping out the wrath, to her that meant ridding education of corruption. She thought of herself as a teacher's teacher. Now she was in the position to change the world of education, of course she would start with her realm of influence, the school she was in charge… "I will straighten everything out at the school and then move into the higher echelons of education. I'll jump from principal to finance officer to asst. Then to superintendent then state superintendent."

She then reached out from behind the shower curtain and with her wet hand snatched the cigar from the tray then poked her head out of the shower curtain, drew in a lung full of smoke, put the cigar down, held her breath until back in the shower and released the aroma she loved. Stinky headed toward the garage; she remembered her unused coffee in the pot and reversed her course and picked up her dirty cup from the kitchen sink and proceeded to the bedroom with the pot of the coffee; she smelled the sugar and cream already left from the last time it was in her cup. Stinky gulped and poured more.

Of course, Miss Syndly had a special parking place now vacated by Mrs. Buckwith downgraded to the teacher's parking lot; she was subbing for the fat English teacher who took Stinky's place as asst principal. Mrs. Buckwith's books and papers sat outside her office in the hall. The secretaries were notified by phone that Miss Syndly was principal and Miss Yerkes, the fat English teacher, was the asst. principal. The secretaries sat back in their chairs thinking of the inhumanity to the teachers these two insidious creatures of darkness, Mr. Ritz notwithstanding, and the students of the school will be infected with for the rest of the year.

Miss Syndly stepped from her car; her red crystal shoes sparkled in the sunlight. Stood waving at the students in the front of the school as though she was on the red carpet and being interviewed by some master of ceremonies and she was up for an Oscar for a great performance at the school board meeting. With her nose in the air, she met Miss Yerkes at the administration building door; they pranced with noses pointed to the sky in an air of aristocratic nobility.

(Mark Twain had it right. Politicians, even school politicians, and diapers must be changed often, and for the same reason.)

The secretaries rolled their eyes in disgust but said nothing, knowing they could be fired at any time; besides, neither of two celebs acknowledged their existence. Yerkes and Stinky marched to their offices in step and made military turns and proceeded in humming the Battle hymn of the Republic. The head secretary with mouth open said, "Wow!"

"Times are going to be different."

Mrs. Buckwith walked through the door from the quad side. Her beautiful face looked not on the sad side but defiant. She gathered up her things in the hallway as the secretaries tried not to stare. Mrs. Buckwith asked, "Where is Miss Yerkes' room?" The head secretary ran her finger down the teacher room assignment sheet and replied, "Room D8" and looked up. Miss Yerkes was in charge of scheduling in the summer and assigned all the X students to herself.

So, you have five classes with the best-behaved kids in the school and some of the smartest. Yerkes will get outlandish things for her pet students. The two managed the trip to see the movie, *Showboat*. Yerkes classes were all girls.

Miss Syndly and Miss Yerkes took money from the student's movie fund. They didn't have money to buy tickets for all of the X students. They had to take money from their purses. 'Money, money!' was Miss Yerkes' motto. The ex-principal smiled, "Their flare for incompetence will rocket to every home in the neighborhood."

That startled the head secretary, she hadn't thought that Mrs. Buckwith will be vindictive if the charges against her were not true, she had reason to be. Dressed to the hilt as usual, the ex-principal trudged off to her new assignment. Quiet swept over the office as the secretaries thought over the possibilities of the consequences because of the changes in the administration.

A resounding collision with the administration office door of two bodies and Mr. Brown forcing the bodies through and into the office by the scruff of their necks said, "Miss Finch found them in the girls locker room with a ruler showing the girls what they got!"

"Sit down by Miss Yerkes' office door," demanded the head secretary. The two boys looked at each other then looked at the towering gym teacher and sat down on the floor. "No, on the chairs," as the massive Miss Yerkes came through the asst. principal door with a finger pointed at the boys and a sour look on her face.

The boys got up, one broke the ruler and threw it in the head secretary's wastebasket. Miss Syndly heard the commotion and stuck her head out the door of her office and almost skipped as though she was on the yellow brick road with her red crystal slippers and wicked wrinkled face, she then took off her left shoe and then her right and stinky was stinky.

As soon as the boys saw the hideous look, a sudden chill went through their bodies as Miss Syndly slipped her right hand back into her office holding a Styrofoam cup and poured the remaining coffee back into the pot then crushed the cup and threw it in front of the boys and said with a German accent, "What have these boys done?"

Miss Yerkes not knowing the techniques of Miss Syndly stepped back in uncertainty, she remembered the fiasco at the resort but this she never saw. Miss Syndly had put her shoes on and clicked her heels together. Mr. Brown abruptly lashed out with, "Caught in the girls locker room with no clothes on!"

"This will go hard on you," Miss Syndly motioned, then told them to come into her office. She sat them down in front of her desk then asked the attendance secretary to look up the boy's home phone and their parents' business numbers. The boys shuddered in their seats, the boy, Richard Brookston spoke up, the curly-haired blond, "We were only showing off!"

"That part of the anatomy is never shown off! It's called indecent exposure and this is a criminal offense!"

"Heck, we didn't know that," said an anguished Davis Blanton. The boys' eyes widened as their heads sank to their chests as Miss Syndly began dialing numbers and Miss Yerkes looked on. Mr. Brown realized he wasn't needed, besides Miss Syndly waved him off. The boys could hear the phone ring and wondered whose house it was. The answering message came on, Richard recognized it and a gleam of hope brightened his face and his head came off his chest as a gesture of defiance. He thought, *score one for me*. Miss Syndly hung up and began dialing another number. Richard and Davis heard a click and then a voice announced the company's name. Richard's head sunk back to his chest; it was his dad's workplace. "May I speak to Mr. Brookston please?"

Richard put his hands to his head. "Yes, this is him speaking."

"Richard has had some problems at school and I require your presence as soon as possible."

"Who is this?"

"I am Miss Syndly, the principal."

"What has he done?"

"I'd rather not tell you over the phone,"

"I can't come right away."

"I'll have the police escort him home, is your wife home?"

"No, she works."

"If you can't come, I'll send him to Juvenile Hall," announced Miss Syndly.

"I'll be there as soon as I can!"

"I'm going to assign him community service on his suspension."

Mr. Brookston didn't answer for another moment until the shock wore off. "Okay."

Davis began to shake and Richard bit his fingernails, Miss Syndly glowed. Miss Yerkes's tummy stuck out even farther than usual. The tummy moved side to side. Davis and Richard had never seen that before, Miss Yerkes had never been accustomed to extreme measures of discipline. She thought *money is money and I'll have to get over excellence.* Davis' mother came to school and said, "Send him to Juvenile Hall. I don't give a damn; he has been a pain in the ass!"

Mrs. Blanton slammed Miss Syndly's door and left. Immediately, stinky called the police to pick up Davis and have him transported. Richard's mouth fell open, the realization of something happening to them had never come true before. Teachers had always passed over their sexual behavior and brought it up with their parents but sending someone to Juvenile Hall for a prank seemed harsh to Richard.

"So Davis, have you been in trouble at school or in the neighborhood before?" asked Miss Syndly.

Davis knew it was a loaded question. He rolled his eyes and said, "Yes, once or twice."

Miss Syndly opened a vanilla folder and started counting, "One …mmm… fifteen times."

Davis slumped back in his chair as the principal picked up the phone and made the call. It seemed just an instant to Richard and police arrived and Davis was gone. A moment later, Richard's dad was sitting in Davis' chair and Miss Syndly came out with the story. Mr. Brookston gripped Richard's collar from behind and choked him while Miss Syndly's eyes brightened with pleasure and Miss Yerkes' belly twitched but kept saying money to herself, the word that calmed her down.

"Here is your son's community service assignment. The truant officer will oversee his assignment; he will introduce himself at your house this evening," said Miss Syndly in a polite and judicious manner. As the door closed behind Richard and his dad, Miss Yerkes moved quickly to the older woman, gripped her hand and whispered, "What a wonderful and decisive performance."

Stinky looked up from her desk and replied, "Yes, it was terrific, wasn't it?"

The girls involved in the incident, some were stressed out and upset, others didn't think it was funny but some who wanted to be sexually active and unskilled in the approach to the opposite sex were delighted in the display and kept their thoughts to themselves as the counselors tried to console the female gym class. The phones in the administration building rang off the hook for three days in a row before things quieted down.

The superintendent came over because he had gotten many calls and wanted to see if Miss Syndly and Miss Yerkes had taken care of the incident properly. Miss Syndly and Miss Yerkes thought, *Boy, would I like to see him measure it!* They simply said yes to everything and smiled longingly.

Three weeks later, after Davis got out of Juvenile Hall and Richard finished his community service, a funny thing happened at the school. The administration building went up in smoke. Miss Yerkes and Miss Syndly stood in front of the smoldering mess and said, "I knew the wiring was bad!"

The secretaries said the official cause of the fire was a malfunction of an electric time stamping machine on the counter. Years later, Richard admitted he put a paper clip in it and it shorted out. As the year went on, Miss Yerkes and Miss Syndly kept discipline low-key, the students settled down and watched the administration-building rise from the ashes.

Do you remember the boy who smashed the bully in the face with the combination lock? He was released from Juvenile Hall a year and a half later and heard of the fire and thought it was a good idea; so two years later, from the original burn, he torched the building. While the first fire was never blamed on a person, just the electric time stamp; the second burn down caused widespread concern from the school board and Miss Yerkes and Miss Syndly were reduced to teachers at an elementary school part time until they resigned.

But stinky Miss Syndly never gave up, she pursued a principal position for many years. The principal cause for not being hired was grinding and gnashing her teeth in front of the interviewer; the red crystal shoes were never seen again.

Chapter 37

I am getting ahead of myself. Saturday morning, the weekend prior to spring break, Mr. and Mrs. Vance met six students and their parents at the school parking lot. Mrs. Vance had rented a twelve-passenger van for a week. The maps were attained from an auto insurance agency. Student number one Homer Sampson a rather short crew cut kid with a funny laugh. Student number two Thor Majorkowski a big kid who was thin and was always eating chocolate bars.

Student number three Patty Pumpton a plump and tall child with a weight problem who went on a diet and lost thirty pounds so that she could make the weight limit of two hundred pounds. Student number four Tina Todd always laughing and giggling but always positive and told jokes. Student number five Denis Dalton nicknamed the brain with big ears and always a smile on his face and a funny hat with Holmes written on it.

Student number six Cactus Cathy Pointlander, her hair wasn't curly and wasn't straight in the sense of normal straight hair; it stuck straight out like a pincushion with hundreds of pins stuck in it.

Now the names may sound funny to your ear and a little lambsey divey but other students that applied were Ocean Moon and Groovey Polkas and Ding Whiplenut. None of these students had ever ridden a horse. When confronted with riding a horse, they politely declined with excuses such as, "I don't have riding boots and spurs and my mommy won't buy them for me and I want to wear them to school."

Ocean Moon said, "someone told me there were big rats in the Grand Canyon and if you kill them for me, I'll go. Will I see the moon over the ocean?" Jason and Heather happened to be in their dad's school room when the kid asked the question and they had to leave the room so they wouldn't embarrass their dad by laughing in his face.

"Another excuse for not riding a mule, they are funny looking horses therefore I don't ride funny looking horses," said another kid.

Those that were going turned over their permission slips to Mrs. Vance, kissed their parents and piled into the van. Everyone looked at one another and found that none of the so-called top students or the fashion conscience types had applied, just the adventurous ones. One mentally indescribable child. A student soon to be called a nut by the rest of the students and held in uncertain regard by the Vance family. He seemed to be singing to himself in very low voice.

Mrs. Vance turned from her front seat and asked, "Will you sing the song louder so that we can all join in?"

He immediately got up and acted as though he was conducting an orchestra. "The Wonderful Wizard That Will Transport us to the Wonderful Ground Below."

"Don't you mean "The Wonderful Wizard of Oz, Denis?"

"No, I made this for the mules that will carry us to our destination at the bottom of the Grand Canyon. "Denis swooped his hands once and continued, "Bright Angel and Kaibab are the main trails to one of the wonders of the world. Clank-clank go mules' feet on Bright Angel as we descend to one of the most beautiful creations in Oz, the land of our fathers. Peering down into the canyon on the mule sends shivers through and through while the mules graze on grass below the rim. The riders tremble and stare down at the canyon floor, two thousand feet below. Everyone looks away pretending they are at ease while the mules graze, until the wrangler begins down the descending trail, their steeds begin their clank…clank once again steel shoe against rock. "Tickety-tock don't crush the rock."

Denis turned to Mrs. Vance and said, "All together now," then to the rest of the canyon student crew singers. He announced, "Hi I'm Johnny Crash, that's what I do on my bike. I want to say cash but he's gone and I'm here, everyone sings: Down, down, round, round back and forth dust, dust endure we must trust, trust the mules we must!"

But after the third time round, everyone began "Row, row your boat." Denis gave the cut throat sign then screamed, "Knock it off!" Mrs. Vance asked Denis to sit down. Denis cringed, hammered his arm rest and pouted. Silence fell over the fidgety Grand Canyon riders of the purple sage until Mrs. Vance opened her brief case and pulled out pictures of the previous assault on the canyon. Heather and Jason passed the pictures quickly to the fidgety kids, something to keep their interest. The students hadn't been on an extended van ride and hadn't seen the canyon and dam before.

The first picture handed out was the Hoover Dam, to Patty, she said, "This isn't the Grand Canyon, what is it?"

"It's a dam on the Colorado River, the river that flows through the Grand Canyon and washed away the rock," replied Mrs. Vance.

Georgie, who had had very little schooling in his previous life, said, "Is that what it's called, I made something like this to prevent the rain water from running into the basement apartment I used to live in as a kid."

Thor and Patty turned and replied, "What do you mean? You're still a kid."

"I mean in a dream, I thought I built a dam of sorts." Mrs. Vance gave Georgie a funny look and shook her head no, Georgie nodded. Georgie looked at another picture and mistakenly thought it was the front of the restaurant he lived behind and suddenly thoughts, horrible thoughts, rushed back in his mind; he began to shudder and sweat and said, "I don't feel good, stop the van. I think I'm going to throw up."

Before Mr. Vance could stop the van, Georgie's eyes turned white, his head rotated left to right and right to left, his stomach muscles began to palpitate, his epiglottis flipped up and down like a yo-yo on a string. Georgie's hands crushed the armrests by the sliding door. A moment of silence. Georgie pivoted in his chair, Georgie's head rotated to the right and crashed through the window on the sliding door and let loose with some horrible black stuff, a Ralph of a giant magnitude. He pulled his head back, the van veered, and Georgie said, "Must have been something left over from the restaurant garbage can or it could have been the baking soda and vinegar mixture I drank this morning!"

In that instant of silence in the van, and Mr. Vance trying to keep control of the van, Georgie lunged through the window again, this time only his feet stayed in the van. Denis turned and replied, "Are you crazy; even Van Helsing wouldn't do that!"

Mrs. Vance's mind began spinning not literally but she thought it did, then words of trepidation crept out of her mind, *what am I in for, there are two crazies in the van!* With a rush of air, Georgie opened the sliding door from the outside, holding on to the seat armrest, he pushed his legs and body out the door, a great pop and the van again veered. "Methane gas!" erupted Georgie.

Mr. Vance had hit the brakes but another thunderous burst of methane and the van was on two wheels. Georgie smiled at Mrs. Vance and pulled himself in and sat in his seat and with a gassy bubbly tone said, "I had my seatbelt on all the time!"

"Heather and Jason," screamed Mom, "did you two trick Georgie into drinking that combination of stuff?"

Two faces in the van turned a rapid red. "The van has a hole in the window and a hole in the back of Georgie's pants! The van almost skidded off the road and I know what you're going to say, 'It was just a joke'!" Mrs. Vance had brought a plastic bag with a wet towel in it for emergencies. Georgie's head and face covered with blood was an emergency.

Everyone was shocked and staring at Georgie except Mr. Vance, who was trying to find a place to stop at Button willow, the eighteen wheelers were so numerous and moving every time he stopped. There was a diesel blasting him with air horns. Mrs. Vance yelling, "Stop this thing so I can clean Georgie up!"

Finally on his third attempt, Mr. Vance jumped out of the van, jamming it into park with a crunch. Mrs. Vance in an exasperated voice, "Finally!"

Mr. Vance now staring through the hole in the window murmured, "We'll have to take him to the hospital." The wet wash towel revealed no cuts, no bruises, no gassiness, no scars—just a bloody towel. Mr. Vance said, "impossible," and turned, pulling on his hair and mumbling to himself, while walking back around the van, got in and slammed the door.

The kids still reverberating from the stop except Denis; he stood up and screamed, "You're a robot, Georgie is a robot! Where's the button to turn him off?" Thor grabbed Denis and covered his mouth. While Thor and Denis were struggling, Jason and Heather said, "Sorry mom, Georgie said he could drink anything and he could hold it. We wanted to see if he could."

Mr. Vance, after getting in the van, thought he better take another look at the sliding door. He wrestled with his seatbelt to extricate himself from the driver's seat to get a good outside look at the sliding door. With duct tape and a plastic bag, Mr. Vance gnashing his teeth on the duct tape, tearing pieces off and sticking tape on his left arm, placed the bag over the hole, ripping tape off his arm along with the hair and said to himself, "Please God, don't let this trip be a disaster."

Mrs. Vance from inside the van asked, "What did you say?"

"Oh nothing," replied Victor. The commotion finally settled, but no one got a satisfactory answer about the bloody towel, no cuts on Georgie's head. Denis just stared at Georgie for the next hour. Thor sat with his arm around Denis. Thor kept turning Denis from looking at Georgie. Silence reigned supreme except for the emoting grunts from the driver's seat, low but nevertheless grunts coming from the brain mulling over what to say to the kids, students of course, but what if this leaked out to the press or some adult figures spilled the beans.

Mr. Vance continued the conversation with himself, *it'll probably be my own two kids that leak it using another corny trick on Georgie.* Just as the thought crossed his mind, he looked in the rear-view mirror and there was Jason with a baseball bat in hand ready to hit Georgie on the head, while no one else saw the hit except Heather because they were sitting in the back. The hit sounded like a baseball hitting an aluminum bat.

Mr. Vance stopped the van, throwing everyone forward, he turned and said, "Heather and Jason, get out of the van."

No one had seen the hit but Mr. Vance. Jason opened the sliding door which tore the tape and the bag lose. Mr. Vance again slammed the driver's door as he angrily walked to the back of the van and motioned to his children to meet him ten yards back. His eyes were wild and his speech slurred for the first two seconds. "The only reason that Georgie hasn't retaliated is you're his friends but if you keep antagonizing him, I don't know what will happen. The vinegar and baking soda wasn't enough, I thought you brought the softball bat to play not to hit Georgie over the head."

"We made a secret pact with Georgie, he wants to see just how much he can take without getting hurt," reiterated Heather.

"You what!" cried Victor Vance. Jason and Heather both nodded in a meek way. Mr. Vance put his hands over his face for a moment then started for the van and yelled, "Georgie, come out here."

Victor Vance stood rigid and determined then he walked Georgie back to Jason and Heather, "Yes it's true I could hear every word in the van."

"Why?" said Mr. Vance with pleading eyes.

"I figured on the trip no one would notice," replied Georgie, throwing his hands up into the air.

"Do you realize if the paparazzi or journalists finds out you will never ever have another peaceful moment in life ever, the rest who know you will be subjected to scrutiny beyond belief. Do you understand that?" pointing at each one of his children. "Get in the van and give me that damn bat." Babbling to himself and fixing the tape and plastic bag on the sliding door window, Mr. Vance held the bat under his arm.

Walking stiff-legged, red-faced and moaning, Victor Vance opened the door and plunked down in the driver's seat and crammed the bat between the seats. Mrs. Vance asked, "Are you angry about something?"

Mr. Vance's face twisted in a manner that Mrs. Vance had never seen before and pulled up the bat and showed Mrs. Vance the dent in the bat. Denis stopped singing I'm so wonderful and said, "What's that?" For the first time in his life, Victor Vance thought of something neurotic, *this kid has been sent on this trip to drive me insane* so he turned and faced Denis with a dark disfigured, two-faced repulsive scowl and with a high-pitched voice replied to Denis, "Sit down and shut up!"

The glee suddenly crashed from Denis' manner; he sat like a crumpled, mauled, terrorized swimmer doing the backstroke trying to get away from Mr. Vance but never moving from his buckled in seat.

This is the fifth trip to the Grand Canyon, the idea of ingesting baking soda and vinegar, who has thoughts like that? My adopted kid, his eyes bulged and maybe that was what made him see an auto glass company, he swerved the van without signaling a left turn off the freeway that almost put the van on two wheels. Mrs. Vance punched him in the right shoulder and demanded, "Where are you going, Vic?"

But Victor Vance said nothing and slammed on the brakes in one fell swoop, turned off the ignition, pulled out the key, unbuckled his seat belt and ran for the office of the glass company, before Mrs. Vance could say another word. There were clicks heard all over the van as the kids scrambled to get out the sliding door and bash harmlessly into its pillar and post. Georgie of course was the first one to pull the handle on the auto glass company door without turning it and broke the door jamb and then proceeded to push Dad into the counter. "Dad, are you alright?"

"No," as Victor Vance rubbed his chest. "Get back in the van; you have a hole in your pants!"

Georgie turned and went out as fast as he came in, knocking the entire crew to the ground and Mrs. Vance. Bodies strewn all over the dirty ground, the door now completely off its hinges and on top of the door Denis and Patty is sitting on it. "This trip is going to be a disaster! It's already a disaster," still grabbing his chest and discombobulating.

The man behind the counter said, "Yes sir, that door will cost you a hundred dollars. Now how can I help you?"

Mr. Vance didn't pay any attention to the counter man, he went and told Patty and Denis to get off the sliding door. Denis jumping up and saying, "Are you crazy; even Van Helsing wouldn't do that!"

"Don't you know any other words, Denis?"

"Doesn't this kid ever give up?" Patty stood up did a couple of dance steps. "Kids, you just never know."

"Yes, I'm all right but this ding-a-ling pretended to conduct music on the door and hit me in the nose," she pointed to blood on her blouse. Mr. Vance pulled out his handkerchief and laid Patty back on the ground. Thor pulled his butt out of a puddle and in an angry mood said in a whisper, "Mr. Vance, should I knock this guy out and put him in the van?"

"NO!" Thor jumped back; the no was heard at least a mile away. Now red in the face and mumbling to himself again, he picked up Mrs. Vance, who tripped over the sliding door when Thor pulled up on it, stumbled and staggered to the counter with his arms wrapped around Mrs. Vance. Mr. Vance said, "I need a glass replacement on the sliding door," as he leaned exhausted on the counter while still holding his wife.

The man behind the counter stared for a moment and said, "Drive the van in."

"You got a restroom? The kids need to clean-up and change pants."

"Yes, but we need an adult in there with them," replied the counter man.

"Okay if my wife stands outside the door?" He nodded to his wife that he just released from his grip and allowed her feet to slip on the floor.

"Ah yea." Mr. Vance turned to his wife and helped her up. On wobbly heels, Mrs. Vance, her shoes twisted, herded the kids toward the restroom while Mr. Vance picked up Patty and brushed her off and sent her scurrying along with the others. Laughter rang out from the restroom as everyone discovered the hole in Georgie's pants and realizing that was the cause of the van careening like it did. Denis ran back to tell Mr. Vance that Georgie had farted and made the van go funny,"

"No, he puked first and then farted, Denis, and split everyone's pants in the back."

Denis had a thoughtful look on his face and said to himself yes, we skidded left and then right. Then he said, "How did he do that? I want to try it."

Mr. Vance silently drove the van into the auto glass building, two workers carried the door in.

Then he said, trying not to be angry, "I don't know; ask him! Now why did I say that?" Mr. Vance got out of the van Denis is back in it.

The glass worker looked at the hole and asked, "How did you say you broke the window?"

"I didn't!" Denis thrust the softball bat through the hole.

"Oh, I see," said the man.

Victor Vance nodded his head in agreement than quipped, "Get out of the van, Denis."

"But I want to see him put the glass in, Mr. Vance."

"See him do it from the outside and put the bat back where you found it."

"Yes Mr. Vance," Denis answered in a little voice. Victor and Jan Vance sat on stools at the counter waiting for the damaged replaced window and the door reinstalled and weather stripping; they figured it would cost them two hundred and fifty dollars. They heard a crash in the shop, Mrs. Vance opened the door to the work area and there was Denis. He had fallen on a windshield. Mrs. Vance closed the door. "Better make the total three hundred."

The owner of the business came through the shop door in a hurry. "Get those damn kids out of here before they turn this place into a junkyard."

The owner grabbed a pad and a pencil but Mr. Vance intervened and said, "Will three hundred be enough?"

"Yes," he replied defiantly. "Get the hell out of here!"

Chapter 38

The hum of the van on the open road put everyone to sleep. Mr. Vance was enjoying riding quiet through the woods and occasionally seeing a deer. The cars at this point of the drive were few while the forest and landscape was quieting on the nerves and Mr. Vance had mood music on the radio, that was now putting Mrs. Vance on the edge and Mr. sandman was sweeping across her brow. Her eyes were fluttering, her head was dropping forward when Mr. Vance heard a sound that he had never heard before.

He looked out his window then the side view mirrors finally in his rear view, saw nothing but the noise continued; he gently slowed the van down so that he didn't wake anyone; after all he wanted to keep the down time going. Finally, he started gently driving at two m.p.h.

No one was coming in either direction but the sound was still in the van, it was becoming louder and the entire group was becoming restless while asleep. Strange. He saw in the rear-view mirror Denis floating upward not touching the ceiling of the van; there was that sound again; this time he saw a thin silver-green light flash and Denis settled back into his seat, his safety belt buckled. Then a leaf landed on Victor's right shoulder; he looked over at Georgie asleep but orchid leaves occasionally fluttering from his mouth and sticking to the ceiling of the van.

Thor rose after a flash of silver-green light, a slight hiss, he floated down, a snap was heard, it was the safety belt. Victor Vance again looked over at Georgie asleep. *What else will Georgie think up in his dreams?* Mr. Vance sat staring half at the road and half in the rear-view mirror, when the interior of the van lit up silver-green. Everyone started moaning and one by one they popped up and settled down, kind of like the wave at the ballpark. Solution, *stop the van really quick and wake everyone up or should I just hit Georgie over the head with the softball bat?*

With a sudden movement, Mr. Vance chose the latter. Humm, another dent in the bat. A voice in the back, "What happened?"

Mr. Vance quickly slipped the bat between the front seats. The leaves fell from the ceiling, Mr. Vance didn't hear the noise any more—Georgie was awake. Denis was rubbing his eyes. "I see silver."

Georgie quickly changed to normal. The van was moving, Mr. Vance used his first alternative and slammed on the brakes and yelled, "We're here!" Mr. Vance let up on the brakes quickly so that everyone's head jerked back and forth.

"I should have destroyed that cracker jack box with the driver's license in it before you found the license," said Mrs. Vance, holding her neck and screaming with emphasis on driver's license.

"Get out of the van," demanded Mr. Vance. "Surprise, it's dinnertime at some Podunk restaurant in the middle of nowhere," he continued. "We do have to eat besides I'm getting claustrophobic in the van with all the strange preposterous things happening. I need food and ordinary polite conversation."

As they all got out of the van, Mr. Vance put his hand over his mouth and stamped his foot and said, "Stop everyone and turn around. Georgie, come over here please."

"What, Dad?"

"Look closely at everyone's backside; what do you see; even mom's?" Dad twisted around. "Even me! I'm disappointed, Georgie, I thought you could hold it together better than this," Victor asked without screaming, keeping his temper under control. "You, after eating, will sew all the holes up." He looked up at his Grand Canyon passengers and said, "I want you one at a time to get back in the van and change your britches, Georgie is going to sew them up. Denis, you first then Thor, Homer, Tim, Jason, Johnny, and the two girls last, Heather and Patty." Victor looked at his wife and said, "We forgot to drop Heather and Jason off at Janis' place," he slapped himself on the head. "Georgie and I will save seats in the restaurant."

Mr. Vance wrapped his right arm around Georgie and carried him into the eatery. "Your hole in the pants will have to wait till last."

"Yes, Dad but I was asleep. I didn't know what I was doing."

"I know but what will these kids say to their parents when they get home?"

"I don't know, it may be fuzzy in their minds at the end of the trip," remarked an anxious well-meaning freak Georgie.

"I hope you're right, my crazy son. Let's be normal in the restaurant."

"Yes Dad." As Victor Vance opened the door Dad and Georgie saw the usual sign 'Please wait to be seated'.

A voice came from the kitchen, "How many in your party, sir?"

Victor hesitated for a moment and said, "Ten."

A beautiful girl came out of the kitchen dark in complexion sparkling dark eyes and said to Georgie, "Olompoli ta ta?"

"What did she say, Dad?"

Mr. Vance bent over and whispered, "She asked if you're Indian; say Zuni."

Georgie smiled at such a lovely face and uttered, "Zuni; and I have a twin brother Johnny who will be in a moment. We're on a trip to see the canyon."

"I live in the canyon in the winter on the reservation; we're called Havasupai, our Super reservation is near the west end of the canyon."

Just as she finished, Johnny stepped through the door and said, "Olompoli ta ta?"

"You two do look alike, come down and see us at the Res and I will show you around. What are your names?"

"Johnny Two Buck and my twin Georgie."

"Which one of you is the oldest?" she asked.

They looked at each other but Mr. Vance spoke up and replied, "Thirteen minutes." Just as Red Feather Light-foot began to speak, the rest of the gang burst through the door of the eatery.

Mrs. Vance asked, "Have you got a booth?"

"No, we've been talking with this young lady," Mr. Vance replied.

"Oh, this way," as Red Feather grabbed a bunch of menus and pointed at a booth by the window looking out at some spectacular scenery.

Georgie sat down in awe. "I'll have to explore that."

Mr. and Mrs. Vance stared at Georgie, shaking their heads. "Stay with the crowd; don't go off alone," pleaded Mr. Vance.

"Don't worry, Mom and Dad, I won't," as Georgie slurped his water. The dinner went well; no food fights or titanic spills; courtesy prevailed because of Red Feather's attention and generosity in the serving of food. Mr. Vance asked Red Feather if the little general store attached to the restaurant had a sewing kit. She was off in a flash and returned with it and said, "Will this do?"

Mr. Vance nodded and replied, "Thank you Red Feather how much?"

"A dollar twenty-five no tax, "answered Red Feather. Mr. Vance left a generous tip for Red Feather as the group moved toward the van and took their seats. On Georgie's seat sat pants to sew, Dad gave Georgie the sewing kit with a measure of authority expressed, "You wanted all the Grand Canyon group to have the rip in the back of their pants."

"Yes Dad." Slipping the end of the thread in his mouth, wetting it and into the eye of the needle; Georgie's right hand was a blur. One pair, two pairs, three pairs, then an "Ouch". Mrs. Vance and the crowd looked and Georgie was sucking on his fingers and with his left-hand throwing pants at their owners.

"What happened?" asked everyone.

"The needle got hot!" He then began on the fourth pair of pants.

Denis reached over and grabbed his hand and said, "Your hand is a blur. Hold still. I can't see your hand or mine; how do you do that?"

Georgie looked at Denis intently and replied, "It's an old Indian trick," as he ripped the thread loose and turned the pants right side out. "See," he put his hand over Denis and vibrated his hand under his.

"Oh, that tickles." That seemed to satisfy Denis as Georgie threw another pair of pants to its owner. Mrs. Vance turned from her seat and motioned to Georgie to slow down. He nodded and turned to Johnny who handed him another pair; this time Johnny's. As Georgie turned the pants inside out, Johnny pressed the button on his multitasking watch, the stopwatch indicator, and timed the sewing event. It took Georgie sixty and one-tenth of a second and that was going slow. Georgie finished the sew job in ten minutes.

Chapter 39
The Hoover Dam Crossing

Mr. and Mrs. Vance pointed out the large electric towers that precede the Hoover Dam and as they came to the road leading to the dam, the cars and trucks ride along the top of the dam and as you cross the center of the dam, the enormity is breathtaking. Mr. Vance parked the van and the gang walked to the tiny park where there are two statues about ten feet off the ground on a very large pedestal, everyone admired them.

They are called "Winged figures of the Republic". The students then began walking to the edge to look down at the Colorado River seven-hundred feet below. Denis' attention was on the two statues; he was mumbling various things and for no specific reason, he said, "I wish I could sit between the two statues."

Suddenly, there was a blur from the dam walkway, people wondering where the gust of wind came from on this calm day, it didn't come from one but two directions. Denis found that his wish had come true. He was very content to sit and wave at the people. Everyone was looking down at the water the dam was holding back. Then everyone straddled the time zone, Pacific and Mountain Time and from state-to-state Nevada to Arizona.

Homer said, "I don't feel any different."

Mrs. Vance answered, "You shouldn't; it's just man's attempt to organize."

Thor said, "I suppose there is no line around the equator?"

"No line to mark it. But there is a way to tell what hemisphere you're in by pouring water down a drain."

"That's crazy," Patty said to Mrs. Vance.

"No, it's not; if you ever get to the Ecuador in your life time, you'll find that it is separated by inches. It's the water test, pour water down a sink drain;

it will swirl counter-clockwise, then move the sink just inches south of the equator, the water will swirl clockwise."

"Now that's hard to believe," said Tim the quiet one. Everyone crossed the street or the top of the dam to the elevator that goes deep into the dam. They all piled in, a dam guide closed the door. The elevator began descending into the depths of the dam. Thor turned to the man operating the elevator and asked, "Do you get angry when people call you a dam guide? Do you think they are swearing at you?"

He laughed and with a devious expression on his face answered, "I say it's the darkest dankest hottest claustrophobic place because the cement is still curing after all these years and it creates heat where we're going, it's a kind of hell." Then laughed hideously.

Thor crumbled in his exuberant attack on the guide. The interior of the dam was hot and it was all the guide said, and more.

After inspecting the interior, everyone got the willies and moved quickly to the elevator. Homer dropped to the elevator floor and said, "It's the force ten of Hoover Dam; the explosion hasn't done anything to the dam, but wait I see a crack, water is coming through!"

Mrs. Vance said, "No time for games, Homer, get up!"

"Yes, I will!" The dam guide seemed slightly darker as the elevator reached ground level and everyone escaped into the fresh air, even the dam guide. The group charged toward the van, of course, Mr. and Mrs. lagged behind with the key, the gaggle was antsy but quieted down in respect of the old people only for seconds. As the key clicked in the van door, conversation bubbled over about the concrete in the dam, Patty described it as an impossible number of sidewalks piled up that would've been for girls to play hop-scotch on.

Thor's comment was how did they get it to stick to the walls of the canyon? Mrs. Vance turned from her front passenger seat, "Where's Denis?"

Everyone looked startled with the thought passing their minds: where did I see him last? Then Mr. and Mrs. Vance said in unison, "Where is Denis, Georgie?"

"I left him between the two wing things. He is happy he gets to wave at people. I kind of forgot about him." Georgie scrunched down in his seat in a pleading manner with a meaning of 'please don't continue this conversation further; let's just go and get him.' Mr. Vance turned the van around, Mrs. Vance turned in her seat and didn't say another word. As soon as the van was in front of the statues, Georgie released himself from the seatbelt, opened the side door of the van and ran without showing anything extra and tried to coax Denis down but Denis would have none of it. He was standing up with his arms in the same position as the statue's wings. "Stop flipping your wings and get down here; we're leaving," Georgie said in a pleasant voice. "Look, no one is waving back!"

"They were waving before."

"Forget all that, we have to go," answered Georgie.

Denis finally submits. "Okay, okay, help me down." With a two-hand grab, Georgie helped Denis to the ground. "Hey do that again; you made me float down?"

"No time, Denis, stop waving at people no one is watching." Just then Georgie made a mistake, held Denis by his shirt in the back and carried Denis with one hand, his feet barely touching the ground. "Wow, you're strong," Denis remarked.

"Never mind," allowing him to walk on his own. Georgie let Denis step into the van first, saying, "Boy, is he strong." He continued until the eyes of Johnny and Georgie kept staring at him until Denis got the message and changed the subject to waving at all the men and women and it gave him such satisfaction.

Mrs. Vance said, "Look Denis, your shoe is untied."

"No, it's not. Why are you trying to stop me from talking? I'm only trying to express my opinion."

"But your opinion is less than grand," said Mr. Vance.

"But to me, my opinion is wonderful!"

"To everyone else it's not!" said everyone in the van in unison.

Denis expels this squeaky milk cuddling voice, "You all are trying to shut me down!"

The van in unison again, "Yes!"

Georgie snapped Denis' seatbelt as Denis' lower lip began to curl outward and his upper lip to curl inward. Mrs. Vance turned in her seat and said, "Let's sing happy birthday to Denis."

Denis was nibbling on his right thumb and trying to bite off his thumbnail; the singing rose from crumbled crackers back to a bubbling machine style. While everyone was singing, they were thinking I want to strangle the prick in the morning, in the afternoon, in the evening, maybe just for fun although everyone's hands were in position they thought, no, let his parents suffer.

The pain of Denis was numbed by the arrival of the van at Bright Angel lodge built in 1908; all the children had never seen a large building made of logs. Denis plowed through everyone in the van to reach the van door and stuck his head out, "Uncle Tom's Cabin! I didn't know it's still standing!" The van occupants went ugh and hurried away from Denis. They heard, "Wait for me!"

Mr. and Mrs. Vance directed the students to the registration desk, Mrs. Vance said, "We have a reservation for nine for the Bright Angel cabins on the rim."

The clerk went through the reservations and replied, "Ah yes here it is, you'll be staying in cabins one through four right out the back door of the lodge and to your right."

"Thank you."

"Oh, you'll have to be back with everyone in two hours for the weigh in and at that time everyone must be here who is going on the mule ride to the bottom of the canyon," said the clerk behind the desk.

"Yes, we made sure all the students and ourselves on the trip are under the limit," replied Mr. Vance. The clerk handed all the students and Mr. and Mrs. Vance a brochure on the fantastic trip to the bottom of the canyon.

Patty looked at Homer and replied, "Boy, this is like Jules Vern's 'Journey to the Center of the Earth'; maybe we'll see some dinosaurs."

"Patty, what are in those brownies you've been eating?" He gave his usual nasty look. The band of students and their escort turned right out of the lodge to the immense water carved wonder of the world, "The Grand Canyon."

Patty looked over the edge and said, "Does this fill up in the rainy season?"

Mr. Vance replied, "You're kidding, of course?"

"Does this crack go to the center of the Earth?"

"Yes, when we reach the bottom, we'll be able to see China a moment later," expressed the guide. After the frivolity, the beauty of the canyon penetrated without disturbing the things that children of that age think. It sort of lifted them up and slipped beauty between games and sex and drenched their minds slowly with earthy wonder.

Denis thrust himself through from the back to the front and said, "Foggy bottom!"

Mr. Vance looked down at Denis and replied, "No, mine's free and clear; how's yours?"

"No not that bottom, Washington DC's bottom; it had fog just like this and called it at first Foggy Bottom and now it's called DC."

"There is an Indian village on the floor of the canyon, but hardly a city; besides, those are clouds not fog hanging over the canyon."

"At home Mom and Dad would call them fog."

"Denis, we're trying to get situated in the cabin."

"No fog!" The disparage and exhausted Victor Vance replied, "It's over!"

"What's over?" asked Mrs. Vance.

"The verbal beating!"

"Well, who would have thunk it." Mrs. Vance rolled her eyes as Mr. Vance walked into the first cabin and threw himself on the bed and covered his ears.

Mrs. Vance was up and about going from cabin to cabin getting everyone up. "I thought you were Denis just to get us from falling asleep and get us up," Heather said.

"I want everyone up, we have to go to the weigh-in," Mrs. Vance explained.

Heather and Patty said, "Oh," in their heads and bent down to put their shoes on. "Is everyone up?" Heather asked.

"Everyone but your dad; go jump on his frame and get him up." By the time Mrs. Vance and Patty made it to the first cabin, Mr. Vance was complaining but up.

"Okay let's get there," said the drunk with sleep V.V. His wife grabbed one arm and his daughter grabbed the other and his son tickled his nose with a feather.

The torture got to him and finally opened his eyes, by that time Jason had the feather hanging with the boogers and only the quill end in Jason's hand was showing. V.V. asked, "Would you get that feather out of my nose; you're tickling my brain." A smirk and a smile broke out on everyone's face as Mr. Vance finished his pun and walked majestically, otherwise known as a pole up you know where, so everyone punched and pulled at him until he walked normally. Dramatically, he fell to his knees, there was a pillow of course where he fell and said, "Am I to suffer these indignities the rest of the trip?"

"That is it," Mrs. Vance signaled to everyone to get a pillow and beat the tar out of Mr. Vance.

V.V. began to laugh as he fell to the floor of the cabin with feathers flying around the room became filled with joy and frivolity.

The next thing he knew, the group of students and his children were laughing and picking off feathers, walking to the weigh-in. Their faces changed jovial to contentment then to concern as the scale hit two hundred-and two-pounds. Patty was overweight and cannot go on the mule trip to the floor of the Grand Canyon. Mr. and Mrs. V appeared to be in some agony as Patty got off the scale.

The man in charge of the trips said, "Don't worry, we have other activities for her and we will have a chaperon that will take her to these activities while the rest of the group is on the ride of adventure." The rest weighed below the limit. So, Patty would see the Grand Canyon through the magic of the camera in 3D.

Dinner in the diner can't be any finer than the one at Bright Angel Lodge with Denis the menace. But we were hungry so we'll go with Denis, the non-stop oral pest. As we sat down for dinner, Denis still commenting on the number of feathers flying in the room and trying to estimate how much extra the room will cost. "I ordered coffee," Denis said to the waitress. "Do you have that coffee the little nocturnal cat that eats coffee beans?"

"What?" said the waitress.

"You know, the coffee that the cat eats the coffee beans then poops them out, then roasted then drunk by people with money!"

That gained the others' attention. Denis needed the satisfaction with the ee-you. But the chorus of shut-up Denis heard from the table and several tables around deflated what he gained. "No wonder your mother and father sent you on this trip, who could stand such a mouth!" Patty blared.

Turning red, Denis was about to pontificate with obscenities, Mrs. Vance grabbed his arm and reminded him of his table manners and his behavior on the trip wasn't up to snuff. "You've ruined my appetite," said Mr. Vance.

He stared with blazing eyes for a moment at Mrs. Vance then said, "Yes murder," covered his eyes with his hands then uncovered smiling. Mrs. Vance thought to herself, *A little Dr. Jekyll and Mr. Hyde; I'm going to watch Denis.* The dinner went fabulous after Denis turned into Dr. Jekyll only a few stares at Patty. After dinner Denis lagged behind and occasionally bolted toward the canyon rim trying to get attention but no one even turned to notice what he was doing. So, when everyone got to the cabins, Denis jumped on the bed of the first cabin, which wasn't his cabin, he began bouncing on the bed and chanting grasshopper. Now, Homer was six feet tall and aptly built who took admonishments from Denis, so he said to Mr. Vance, "Shall I quiet him down?"

"No do not touch him, Homer, but we can all leave the room and he won't have an audience."

"Hey," from the bed, "where are you guys going?"

"Does anyone want to play the pebble game? You know the grasshopper guy grabs the stone out of my hand before I close it."

Denis jumped off the bed and pulled a rock out of his pocket. "I betcha I can," he announced.

Thor took the stone and held his hand out flat, stone in the middle, Denis tried six times and failed. Denis took the stone and wouldn't let Thor have a chance. Thor just laughed. Denis was irritated as they walked to the ice cream counter. Denis kept jabbering about the good things he could do. Everyone stayed in front of him so that the incessant cacophony was softened by the distance and chatter. Soon the continuous oral cavity flapping stopped as the soothing and tasty ice cream slid down their throats, they all seemed happy just lapping ice cream.

Bedtime after watching the setting sun and finishing their ice cream honesty finally fell over the face of Denis as he described the ever-diminishing ball of orange and red fire creating ever-increasing shadows the beauty smother words of description.

Meanwhile, back in the mind that doesn't fit the body, that was in Georgie's brain, a plan for a nocturnal journey *but whom shall I take with me? My Indian counterpart or my stepbrother or sister to take on the ride, maybe Denis, I could drop him over? No that's what my real brother would do. I'll take Johnny*, he thought. With just a peek of the sun over the Grand Canyon, everyone slipped into his or her respective cabins. Johnny took the lower and Georgie took the upper. Mr. Vance took the other lower and Thor the other upper.

Georgie looked at his glow in the dark wristwatch; it was two A.M. He slowly floated down to Johnny's side and rubbed his nose. "Johnny," he whispered.

Johnny turned his head and focused on his clone and murmured, "What do you want?"

"Let's find out where Red Feather Lightfoot lives," with words barely audible. Georgie picked his sire up.

"I guess," Johnny murmured softly. "I can call you that," as he opened the window in front of the cabin and gently, slowly moved through. Johnny looked at Georgie, "Hot snot, we made it," as he landed on the sidewalk in front of the cabin with Johnny in his arms.

"Put your arms around my neck, we're going to the west end of the canyon and locate the Indian village so tomorrow before it gets dark, we can find her home without anyone knowing how we arrived at the village."

"Don't you think it's better to find our way in the light of day?" replied his Indian twin.

"You think we should fly around tonight with a flashlight?"

"Someone would probably shoot us down," suggested Georgie. "I have good vision; we'll find our way." Before Johnny grabbed Georgie's neck, he quietly closed the window but not quietly enough because Mr. Vance got up and looked out the window; seeing nothing but black, turned, checked the boys and the makeshift bodies, and went back to bed. The boys had made their beds up so it looked like they were still asleep.

"It's colder than I thought," said the chattering Johnny. "Let's make it a fast trip!"

"Cold wants to kill you!"

"That's a matter of opinion. President Buchanan died after his inauguration!"

"What are you talking about, Johnny?"

"He didn't wear a coat!"

"Who!"

"Look, we have to go back," said Johnny.

"We're not off the ground yet; how can we go back? Stop being so nervous; I've made dozens of trips at night."

"But not one over strange territory where there are no lights."

"Okay Johnny, I'll have to get Dad's keys to the van and get the flashlight that blinks. Johnny, let go of my neck. I have to go back through the window and get the keys out of Dad's pants pocket. Johnny, let go," Georgie said in a whisper. He didn't. Georgie gently grabbed Johnny wrists and pulled his hands apart. Georgie quietly glided back to the window and silently reopened it. "Dad is snoring so no danger of him waking up."

Victor Vance had laid the contents of his pockets on the nightstand by the bed. Georgie hovered for a moment, spotted the keys, grabbed them by the rental tag and moved back toward the window. The keys jingled, Dad scratched his nose and turned to his side and started to snore again. This time the window squeaked as he closed it. "Grab hold," as they flew over the cabin to the van parked under an apple tree, Johnny pulled an apple off the tree.

Meanwhile, Mr. Vance turned over in bed, looked over to see if everyone was still in bed, yes, they were, closed his eyes and went back to never-never land. Georgie turned the key in the van door lock with a big clunk. "Don't tell me I broke the lock?"

"Nope, that is my apple."

"Well, get me one, you hogger," as Georgie fumbled around under some of Dad's newspapers until he found the flashlight.

He turned and said, "I couldn't reach that big fat apple; it's too high; you'll have to lift me up."

"I'll get it," with the flashlight in his right hand, Johnny hanging on Georgie's back he picked that big bugger as they flew back over the cabin and landed on the edge of the canyon. They stood there for a moment placing the flashlight so it couldn't be seen by anyone on the south rim, only on the north rim. Johnny turned it on flash only. Georgie turned so his brother could take hold of his neck. Crunching their apples before their flight. "Hey I've always wanted to say this: up, up and away; no phone booth slighted." As they picked up speed, there was a bad spot in Georgie's apple, blah. "Oh God, what is that?"

Johnny said, "What is what? Something hit me in the right eye," he lost his hold on his brother, "Georgie!" Georgie looked down, Johnny yelled, "More He...lp."

Georgie dropped his apple and dove down in the darkness. Darkness invaded Georgie's head, the reality that certain death was no option; he must find Johnny before he hit the ground or the river. Fortunately, they were in the middle of the canyon so he won't hit the sides. Georgie's eyes were watering now blurring against the wind pressure. He had never dived so fast; his jacket began to flip. Tears began to slide down his cheeks. I see him faintly; darkness consumed his judgment. He can see the rushing water of the Colorado. Georgie said aloud, "I will catch him! I will!"

Something hit him in the face, he brushed it away, it stank something hot and something that smelled but he can't take his attention away from catching up to Johnny before he died. There he was, his arms up, his mouth open, Georgie grabbed his forearms, his hands slipped to Johnny's hands. Georgie's grip slipped more but before Johnny hit the water, Georgie decreased his speed so that the concession was greatly reduced, the rushing water pulled them under and downstream before Georgie can get the energy to pull Johnny out of the water and into the air. There were thuds and bumps; something was hitting their bodies. Johnny said with a shivering note in his voice, "What the hell is hitting us, Georgie!"

"Bats and an owl chasing them," in a protesting growl, said Georgie. By now both were shivering, the water in the Colorado never gets above 55 degrees even on the hottest days until it hits Mexico. Bats, bats everywhere! Johnny said, "Go back." That was all Johnny could say; his mouth seemed to be frozen as Georgie gained altitude and finally, the pelting of the bats subsided as the two left behind the floor of the canyon. Johnny shouted, "You're not going to drop me again?"

"I didn't drop you, you dropped yourself!"

"Did not!"

"Did too!"

"Did not!"

"Did too!" They were shouting back and forth till they turned on the flashlight, by that time they were too cold to talk any more. Until, they both grabbed for the flashlight and Johnny again fell off Georgie's back even though Georgie grabbed his shirt but it ripped. "You did it again!"

"I did not!" After the last drop, Johnny now lay on the edge of the rim on the Grand Canyon. "What do you think I have; a safety belt on my back?"

"You let me fall!"

"Did not!"

"Did too!"

"Stop arguing, we're near the cabin," Georgie asked politely. "I guess I was scared!"

"You were scared, I was petrified!"

"I was praying."

"I don't have superman vision but I'm better than that Monk and Grasshopper on Kung Fu on T.V. Get the flashlight out of your pants so we can put it back in the morning." Slipping back to bed in their wet clothes was uneventful until morning.

Georgie and Johnny jumped out of bed and ran to the bathroom and both boys got in the shower. Dirt streamed down them and into the drain. Mr. Vance saw the mud on their beds, shoes encrusted, white socks now black. Victor hurried into the bathroom, pulled the shower curtain open, both Georgie and Johnny were in their clothes with hand soap. A slight amount of fear slipped into their consciousness. "What the hell happened to you two?" demanded Dad.

Georgie's eyes rolled around a couple of times; Johnny hid behind Georgie. Georgie coughed and put his head under the showerhead; sand streamed down his face from his hair, he then wiped his face dry and said, "We got in a fight with two big Indians; they called us all kinds of names but the two that humiliated us the most are Buffalo shit and urban squaw pee. They both are over three hundred pounds, they picked me up like a butterfly but I sting them like a bee, we all ended up in a mud puddle. Johnny was trying to help; he really got muddy."

"Boy, that's the biggest Indian B.S. story I ever heard!" Just as he spoke, Mrs. Vance came into the bathroom.

"What happened!"

Georgie looked sheepishly and quickly wrapped the shower curtain around him and said, "We fell in the river."

A puzzled look came over Mr. and Mrs. Vance, they said in unison, "What River? There are no rivers here?"

Johnny edged around Georgie, "The Colorado!"

A couple of snickers came from outside the bathroom the boys thought both stories were highly unlikely and you could hear Thor say, "That's a crock."

An angry look came over the face of Mrs. Vance, "Okay what the hell really happened?"

Still wrapped up in the shower curtain, "We wanted to see the Indian Village that Red Feather Lightfoot came from. An owl chasing bats hit us hard. The hit knocked us almost unconscious from the concussion and we simply fell."

The onrush of noise from the T.V. turned the Vances' heads, so Johnny and Georgie grabbed their clothes. Georgie said, "Mom, you are supposed to be taking care of the girls?"

She wanted to say something but the man on the T.V. was talking about strange leaves that covered the ground in front of the cottages on the south rim of the Grand Canyon. In a whisper, "God I didn't, I wasn't spitting leaves!"

"You weren't, I didn't see any," answered Johnny.

The botany expert said, "They're some kind of parasitic leaf, perhaps an orchid or something of that sort. This is desert country, they cannot exist here on the rim." Anxiety swept through the family and Johnny. The broadcast continued: "When a strange sighting occurred over the Colorado River. An Indian was hit by a dead owl on the canyon floor. Before being struck, he heard a scream and a splash."

Mr. and Mrs. Vance turned with their hands over their mouth both Johnny and Georgie had sheepish looks on their faces, "It's true!"

Victor Vance took his hands away from his mouth and said, "Georgie, come here."

Georgie just had put his "Captain Underpants" on. Homer, Denis, and Thor had their noses in the bathroom when they heard an Indian was involved in an accident on the floor of the canyon; as soon as Mr. Vance saw them listening intensely at the bathroom door, he put his right index finger across his throat. The Vance family turned and Johnny pushed through the boys at the door. The three grabbed Jason, who hadn't said a word, and pulled him out the front door of the cabin and started pumping him for information. He had watched the entire T.V. broadcast. He stood there with a deadpan look on his face and said, "I don't know anything more," with a positive look on a negative thought. The entire group of the Grand Canyon school kids hurried from the cabins. Breakfast was quick; everyone was a bit nervous but did want to see their steeds.

Everyone had their equipment, hats and boots and whatever they wanted to take with them, basically candy. After the wrangler sized everyone up and picked the right mule for each person, he then helped each person onto their mule and adjusted the stirrups while spitting tobacco juice and manipulating his chew of tobacco. He talked as though he was the man that will guide them down the Bright Angel trail.

The ten-gallon hat pushed tightly on his head, his beautiful western shirt, leather vest with tassels, Levi's with chaps over without scuff marks, boots made in the cowboy style with doggies emblazoned on them and spurs with bells that jingled. Patty waved goodbye as we turned our mules to descend to the bottom of the canyon and the Phantom Ranch. This was Mr. and Mrs. Vance's fifth trip down the canyon and probably their last because of new school safety rules and the bra episode.

A lady last in line coming down the canyon at the lunch stop at Indian Wells caught her bra on the saddle horn while getting off her mule; no one noticed; she then hit her head on the hard part of the saddle. This jolt prevented her from making a complaint or yelling. It took fifteen minutes before the wrangler or anyone else found her hidden between the mules. She wanted to go on.

Chapter 40
Two Thousand Feet Down

The wrangler took the lead and slowly moved down the trail, he tapped his mule on the rear, everyone had been given a crop made of metal wire with tape on one end and then a loop large enough to put on the saddle horn. Mr. Vance, last in line, the wrangler first in line. Mr. Vance was riding an enormous mule, decided he, she or it, didn't want to make the trip and refused to take one step down the trail. Mr. Vance yelled, "This mule is stuck in park!"

The wrangler twisted in the saddle and yelled out, "Hit that mule with the crop!"

The mule didn't want to move forward; it reared up and then began to buck. Mr. Vance used his crop on his mule's backside again. Now it really started to buck. The trail was five to six feet wide but the mule's right front foot was over the edge of the Bright Angel trail, at this point it was two thousand feet down, the wind blurred the air with dust; there was a silver-green tint in the air, a fury of leaves, the mule was struck by the whirling wind. The mule was moved by the wind and had an apple in its mouth.

Georgie had an apple in his backpack the mule seemed satisfied and went on as though nothing happened. But the tobacco-spitting wrangler stopped everyone, got off his mule, ran up to Mr. Vince's mule to check the cinch on the saddle, the mule turned and spat part of the apple at the wrangler and hit him on the left side of the face, the wrangler spat his chew of tobacco at the mule but hit Victor Vance in the back of his head just under his hat. The wrangler ran back to the log where a pail of water, a sponge, towel and a pooper scooper sat on a log; the wrangler grabbed all the equipment and ran to the aid of Victor.

By this time, Mr. Vance was off his mule with his hat off, the wrangler washed the back of his head, wiped it dry, the pooper scooper was directly behind the mule in question. The wrangler helped Victor Vance back on the mule. There was a thunderous boom; there was nothing in the pooper scooper, the air turned moist and pungent, a man smoking a cigar saw his cigar flashed and burned to a crisp, the wrangler dove for cover; he felt a blast of another kind may saturate and terminate his entire being.

The hideous cloud of mule methane moved slowly away, choking several other people before it dissipated. The wrangler sauntered back to the bunkhouse as though nothing happened but the other cowboys took off running, two grabbed the wrangler and forced him in an outdoor shower with clothes on. Everyone stopped their mules to turn and watch the two cowboys hold him there for several moments then let him go. He sauntered back to his mount. He said in an English accent, "We shall continue. I made a mistake."

The tobacco chewing cowboy, the night before, had given the mules alpha hay. The next morning, they produced methane gas that bombarded people. Apparently, the chewing tobacco-spitting cowboy forgot. Putting him under a cold shower so that he wouldn't do it again.

Down, down the party went to see the wonders of this great chasm in the Earth. But wait, the wrangler stopped the group and turned the mule heads facing into the Grand Canyon. The mules were feeding on the vegetation below the trail and the only thing between you and two thousand feet of air was the saddle horn, the riders were leaning backward and the mules were leaning forward, getting that bit of vegetation before the wrangler finished his monologue.

With some urging, the mules turned back to the trail with a clickety-clack of their steel shoes, snorting and puffing, grinding on their bridle bits, this created an extra heartbeat in all the riders on the trip. Johnny just behind Georgie said, "We fell in that river?" Georgie just nodded his head and said nothing. Johnny let out a gasp, "What were we thinking," still staring at the tiny yellow ribbon called the Colorado River from two thousand feet above. Stunned, Johnny sat in a rhythmic motion of the mule's gait, pondering, *why am I still alive and not floating down the river while fish are nibbling at my toes*! After several switchbacks, Johnny began to enjoy the ride and the beauty of the high desert.

The man behind the wrangler was wearing a green pith helmet and green overalls that matched his helmet, green belt, green cowboy boots no spurs and coke bottle glasses. Next to him a woman in a ten-gallon hat, a mink jacket with little bells all around the collar; they had a constant soft jingle and feathers at the shoulders. The feathers bleached white, sticking out in all directions. The cuffs and collar were white ermine, the collar covered with a blazing red bandanna covered with probably diamonds, just small ones. The cowboy hat was a variety of feathers from small to big.

The wrangler said at one of the scenic stops that she might scare all the birds away thinking she was a bird of prey. Designer jeans with the sparkle equivalent to the sun at the next scenic stop, the wrangler said, "Her pants probably blinded the birds of prey."

She didn't care for his assessment of her clothes and said she would report him to his boss, the wrangler laughed and said, "This is my final trip." She then said a few four-letter words. The wrangler smiled and turned his thoroughbred mule. It looked like an Arabian except for the long ears. Georgie and Johnny dressed as if they were going to school, Levi's with logos on their jackets, straw cowboy hats, plain white t-shirts and sneakers. Jason and Heather both had Levi pants and jackets. Jason had a shirt with a musical group on it and Heather had a pink shirt with a collar and pearls around her neck, no earrings, both had sneakers on.

The lady with the fur coat was riding a palomino mule. Mr. and Mrs. were on quarter horse mules; the rest of the mule train were on Tennessee Walker Mules.

Georgie wanted to explore the walls of the canyon more thoroughly but there weren't any dark places along the trail that he wouldn't be seen flying away from the mule train. The first chance he got was at lunchtime. Johnny, still nervous from the night flight, said, "I'd rather eat lunch on the ground," harshly stated!

Georgie looked at his friend, brother of sorts, thankful for his skin off his thumb that created his being and purported, "I'm not Superman with great vision. I'm a duplicate, the collision was unforeseen." Georgie understood Johnny's concern; he turned to Jason, "How about it?"

"Georgie, you're losing control, can't you see if you keep trying things like this you'll be seen and everyone and his brother will be on your case for the rest of your life."

Georgie really started to get irritated to the point where he said under his breath what a bunch of chicken shits, at that moment leaves shot from his wrists. Mr. and Mrs. Vance, Johnny, Heather and Jason all scrambled to get the leaves off the table and onto the ground. First, they put their lunch bags in front of the leaves and brushed them under the table and mashed them into the ground, destroying their shape. But two leaves managed to escape, a slight gust pushed them into the lap of the lady with the fur coat. She had been looking the other way and laughing at the wrangler's disgusting clothes, dirty from the shower and wrinkled water caper.

Jason, closest to her, grabbed one but the other leaf fell to her other side and floated to the ground. Jason got up from the picnic bench, slightly hitting the lady. Walking around her to the end of the bench getting her attention, her hand hit her plastic knife and fell on the leaf before Jason could mash it, she said, "A leaf saved my knife from the dirty ground."

Jason bent over and picked up the knife that covered the leaf and gave her the knife. "Oh, give me the leaf, young man, that is a strange leaf, I know that's the leaf that was shown on T.V. by that botanist this morning. I wonder how it got to Indian Gardens?"

The Vance family froze as the lady in the fur opened her purse and placed the leaf in her purse and closed it. Victor said to himself, *At least it's out of sight*. Georgie checked his wrists to see if there was a leaf stuck halfway out; sure enough one was. So, he turned the palm of his hands down on the table and whispered to Johnny, "Put your hand under my left wrist and pull the leaf out and mash it on the ground."

He mashed it all right, Johnny turned and pulled his right leg from under the table so that the lady in the fur coat couldn't see what he was doing. Johnny groaned once while he mashed the leaf. Georgie turned his head slightly and said out of the side of his mouth, "What's wrong?"

"Your pant cuffs are filled with leaves; don't move, they'll fall out." Johnny motioned to Heather and Jason, he stood up, and again motioned to Jason and Heather. Mr. and Mrs. Vance were talking to the lady in the fur coat and don't notice that the three moved away from the table and were quietly plucking the leaves from the bottom of Georgie's Levi's and stuffing them in their pockets and then bump heads getting up, both moaning.

Victor and Jan muttered, "What happened; you've interrupted our conversation."

Heather thought quickly. "I saw a dime in the dirt and Jason and I tried to pick it up at the same time."

At that moment a flash of sliver-green flashed across Georgie, V. V. cried out, "Look at that bird crossing the sun; isn't it beautiful." The lady in the fur coat, the man in the green pith helmet and everyone else looked up, while Mr. Vance looked at Georgie. He put his right index finger across his throat then he made a 'T' for time out. Georgie nodded his head and the silver-green across his face dissipated.

The lady in the fur jacket said, "Why are you sweating, Mr. Vance, the weather is just right for a jacket?"

"Hot flashes, more like silver-green hot flashes!"

"Why, I never heard of such a thing," remarked the lady in the fur. The wrangler, busy downing all the food left, paid no attention to what everyone was saying, his eyes fixed on the juice box of the fur coat lady and when she went to the restroom, he knocked it off in one swell gulp.

He began to fashion a cigarette from a bag of tobacco and a packet of tiny rectangular papers in a tiny envelope. He took them from his right breast pocket in his cowboy shirt. He then took this translucent paper, opened the tobacco bag, with a jagged brown tooth, poured tobacco onto the very thin paper, pulled the bag closed, with his lips wrapped around the pull tag and string, that closed the bag of tobacco. He placed the bag in his left breast pocket, making sure the string and tag hung loose outside of his pocket, licked the paper edge, carefully rolled the makeshift butt, twisted the end and he lit it. Cigarette bent in the center stuck to his lower lip as he drew in the smoke.

Watching Heather, Jason, Johnny and Georgie, he brought in a big breath and exhaled at the same time, but the wrangler's lip tore the paper open, the tobacco fell out. The kids put their one hand over their mouth and turned away, except Georgie; he caught the tobacco and put it back in the paper before the wrangler could say shit. The wrangler somehow didn't see Georgie's action, he had been looking down and said, "Why is that wire hanging from your shoe?" He pushed his cowboy hat back, spit and said, "That's not a wire it's a cable. What did they do, tie you all to the bedpost at night?" He sat back and slapped his knees in glee, pondered for a moment and muttered, "That's a joke, ha-ha!"

Georgie smiled and replied, "Old Indian custom to keep the sparks away."

That put the wrangler into a hysterical mode; he got up and started to dance in a cowboy shuffle. Georgie looked at him thinking he said the wrong word but the wrangler stopped and commanded, "Mount up."

Down the trail into the canyon, the eight members of the wrangler's sat in their saddles, creaking and the clanking of the steel shoes on the rock, the beauty of the Earth's wonders pulsating through the arroyos of their minds while everyone was fascinated by the carving of wind, water, and ice on the planet's surface. A squad of runners from Sweden of all places wanted to run by the mules.

Mr. Vance was last in line and said, "If you want to pass, you must pass on the outside not on the inside of the mules or until the wrangler stops us to view the scenery, you may frighten the mules."

The front-runner nodded and replied, "Understood," in a heavy accent. A hundred yards down the trail and after passing three hikers with camping gear, the wrangler stopped the mules; as usual they hung their heads into the canyon to get the few bits of vegetation, they pounded the air with heavy gas, coughing and sputtering, everyone was consumed in a foul smell. The runners as they passed held their nose, the hikers had to sit down and rest. A smirk twisted upward on the wrangler's face and a bit of a laugh as he pointed out some scenic features of the Grand Canyon. The wrangler seemed to be on the calm and cool side of life, a grizzled old coot with precancerous sores on his face and forearms, perhaps sixty or better, with a sense of humor.

After the incident, things went quiet until the mule train got to the tunnel and the suspension bridge. Phantom Ranch is just across the bridge and the Colorado River. The dismount at the corral led to the typical cowboy talk, saying howdy partner, and the bow-legged two-step. The wrangler still had that stub of a butt hanging from his lip, we all smiled when he said, "Morning will be steak and eggs, then up trail," the butt of the cigarette that Georgie put back together flipped back and forth while he talked. A lady was kind enough to lead us to our cabins. In the boys and men's cabin, Georgie literally flew up to the double-decker bed.

Denis, the second in the cabin, watched Georgie glide up to the top bunk bed and muttered in a loud tone and total admiration, "Damn Georgie, show me how to do that!"

Georgie thought, *You crazy show-off, never do it again.* Quick thinking, Georgie acknowledged that one must take baby steps and practice them first. "What do you mean, baby steps?"

"Like this," he slowly got off the top bunk by sliding off the bed to the floor. By that time everyone had stepped into the cabin including Mr. Vance while no one was looking he ran his hand across his throat. Georgie nodded and tripped over his foot and fell to the floor, everyone giggled. Georgie got up and said, "Sorry Denis, I muffed the baby step; some other time."

Denis knew that Georgie was very agile and athletic so he was very suspicious and looked back at Mr. Vance having his left hand around his throat.

Chapter 41

Denis mused over sand, mud and dirty pajamas and now this Johnny can't do the things that Georgie can do. They looked alike but they weren't alike. Denis sat on his bed and tried to think through the differences between twins or were they twins? Denis slowly moved to Thor's bed adjacent to his bunk bed and asked, "Do you think Georgie and Johnny are twins?" in a whisper.

Thor twisted his head in Denis's direction, nodded and replied, "Yes, you're dopey, Denis, they are identical twins in every way; not only that if you took their fingerprints, they would be the same."

A light blinked on, a bell rang and then a light blazed in Denis' head; he always felt a kinship with the great detectives of history; he had his magnifying glass in his backpack. He had brought some baby powder for his tender feet and needed to put some on his beastly cantankerous bipedal phalanges—it felt so good! Mr. Vance spotted the mess on the floor that Denis left and made him clean it up.

"Darn adults, what do they know anyway." Denis looked at Homer, Tim, Thor and Mr. and Mrs. Vance and thought what do they know about understanding the truth, only great detectives know the truth and I'll find the truth, he thought. After dinner, Denis grabbed the two glasses that Johnny and Georgie drank out of the cleanup pan but the waitress saw him take the glasses and made him put them back. He pleaded with the waitress but to no avail, she said, "They had to bring everything down by mule."

Denis walked out of the dining room thinking, while everyone else were laughing and joking. Mrs. Vance noticed Denis' quietness and asked, "What's wrong?"

"Nothing. Oh Mrs. Vance, I forgot my wallet, it must have fallen out of my pocket."

The waitress didn't see Denis come back, as he crept to the table on his hands and knees. Tim turned and mentioned to Thor, "What's Denis doing?"

"He's sneaky and somehow came to a nutty conclusion that Johnny and Georgie aren't twins, some kind of duplicate, like in the movie, *The Last Star Fighter*, where the kid is taken up for training and a duplicate put in his bed and his little brother discovers the duplicate molding into shape in the movie, or it's like *The Man in the Iron Mask*; that is what Denis thinks or something like that. Don't you read anything?"

"That is the silliest thing I have ever heard," replied Tim.

"Haven't you noticed Denis isn't with our group?" answered Thor. "Didn't you see him sneak back into the dining room?" Thor said.

"No," as Tim turned around and walked backwards trying to spot Denis, Sure enough, there was Denis crouched down running as fast as he can to catch up, with the two glasses in his hands. Tim uttered, "What the devil!" Everyone turned around to see what Tim was babbling about but Denis had already caught up and had his hands behind his back. "What are you doing?" asked Tim.

"Oh, nothing important, look a spark on the ground and some green leaves on the ground right behind Georgie," Denis whispered.

"Strange," both Tim and Thor said together. "Wow!" Again, everyone turned around, the sun left the canyon quickly as it usually does. Phantom Ranch is shrouded in darkness the spark was out so no one could see the strange leaves on the ground, but Tim, Thor, and Denis knew. Denis put the second glass down and it struck a rock with a clang; again, everyone turned around, they saw Tim, Thor and Denis bent over. Denis putting something in a glass. Victor Vance now saw what Denis was carrying, he picked the one up off the dusty path way and queried, "Please give me the other glass?"

"But Mr. Vance, I want them for sovereigns. It said Phantom Ranch on them."

Mr. Vance threw the leaf out of the glass and replied, "You can buy a shirt like everyone else." Tim and Thor immediately stuck the leaves in their pockets, ever so slyly averting a confrontation with Mr. Vance. Victor and Jan gave Denis a stern look and ignored the other boys, not knowing Denis had spread his suspicions. He knew he had the answer in his hands now.

Crushed, he sat on his bed head down as Mr. Vance came back from returning the glasses. He thought if the world only knew the truth, he, Denis would be a famous detective. The detective that found the truth about a boy named Georgie, a Zuni Indian that doesn't live with his twin brother and doesn't have the same last name.

Denis flopped around on the bed until he felt comfortable. He then stuck his right hand in his pocket and hit something hard, his magnifying glass… *I'll go straight to the source.* Mr. and Mrs. Vance went for a walk down the only lit path to the pool. Denis went over to Tim's bed and said, "I want to look at your hands. I want to see who has the longest pinky finger."

"Come on Denis, that's the dumbest thing I've heard."

Denis turned so his face was directly facing Tim, so no one could hear or see what he was saying, "This is part of being a great detective, deception and guile. Don't you see what I'm trying to do, I'm trying to put the importance on the little finger, not on the other fingers or thumbs. And in that way, no one will suspect I'm checking prints."

Then Denis took a swing at Tim with an open hand but missed. "What was that for?" muttered Tim.

"For leaving me sitting two hours between those two statues."

"Oh that, you were driving us all crazy," he replied in a practically noiseless whisper.

Denis grabbed at his right hand pulling his little finger toward him, instantly examining his little phalange and saying very loud, "Short, very short." He went to Thor's bed but Thor banged him on the head with a plastic Coke bottle and called him a dipshit. While Denis attended to his head, Thor grabbed the magnifying glass out of his hand, banged him again on the head and threw his magnifying glass across the room. Denis reached out for it but it was no use. Denis pictured it smashed against the wall. He tried to punch Thor.

But Thor caught his fist and twisted his arm behind his back. Mr. Vance angrily responded, "Thor, enough!" A hand came out of nowhere and handed Denis the magnifier. Denis, showing pain in his right arm, dangling, holding the magnifying glass in his left hand. Denis thinking, *Thanks Johnny, no one but the other twin could have caught it.* Both pretended not to know Denis' predicament with Thor.

Johnny and Georgie were playing checkers on Johnny's bed. The pretense of the maligned arm lasted ten seconds, great detectives fake and parry with their opponents to get true information and correct answers. Denis scurried like a rat smelling cheese or part of a banana over to Johnny and Georgie and asked ever so politely, "May I see your pinkies?"

Both Georgie and Johnny stuck their pinkies in Denis' face. "Too close," pushing their hands away. "One at a time," grabbing Johnny's right hand, pulling it toward him.

Johnny pulled his hand back. "Gotta make a move on the checker board."

Denis looked irritated but kept quiet until Johnny thrust his hand back in Denis' face. "I told you not so close." Denis pulled his hand down and put it under his magnifying glass; he examined it carefully, then asked Georgie but Georgie was concerned that he will give him a shock or will shed some plant material, so he continued to play checkers, not paying attention to the now infuriated Denis.

Georgie concentrated and controlled the flora but a slight shock lit up the magnifier as Denis lurched back and said, "Wow, what was that?"

"Oh, just some static electricity," with his left-hand, Georgie pulled a feather from the other side of the pillow and rubbed it on Denis' hair and touched the tip of Denis' nose; his eyes crossed, he tumbled to the floor in a slow-motion mode and slight babbling; a silver-green spot appeared on the tip of his sonze-olla to be exact. "Too much juice, don't you think, Johnny?"

"I should say, Sherlock!"

A tiny squeaky voice said, "What happened?"

Thor, Tim, Jason and Homer perked up as they heard something thud on the floor, but Victor Vance ran over from where he had been reading *Sea Wolf* on his bed. His face full of fear and consternation, he cried out, "What have you done?"

"I slowed Professor Moriarty," answered Georgie.

Mr. Vance helped Denis up and remarked, "Be more careful, you slipped on a banana peel and hit your head on the floor, are you all right?"

"Yea, yes," Denis looked dazed and disoriented while staring at Georgie. Denis crumbled. Mr. Vance helped Denis up again. "Where is it?" he gasped.

"Where is what?"

"The banana peel!"

"Oh, I threw it out the door; I didn't want anyone else slipping on it," remarked the adopted son of Victor Vance.

"Georgie, I want you to go outside and throw the banana peel in the trash can, after all you put it on the floor!"

Georgie hesitated on how to answer his adopted father; because of Denis being so close and listening to every syllable of every word, he said, "Yes," and pretended to have trouble getting up and walked in a ponderous manner out the door. The screen door being held open by a rock, Georgie made sure that his back faced the cabin door so Denis couldn't see him bend over to pick up the mythical banana peel. After Victor Vance helped the now fragile-looking and constantly babbling Denis to his bed and handed him his magnifying glass and his detective kit.

Denis sat there, glazed over, clutching his Sherlock hat that had spent most of its time on the floor. Victor Vance walked calmly out the door and then turned red in the face but spoke quietly, his first inclination was to scream as loud as he could to impress Georgie of the seriousness of his action. "This is your life we're talking about; if you want the whole world to know you're a freak, just keep acting the way you are and soon the pranks will mount into fascinating entertainment, then, like nicotine in tobacco, you'll thirst for more and more until you die trying to perform some enormous stunt."

"I didn't think my action out, Dad, I'm sorry."

"You'll be sorry if you continue on this course."

"It was a thoughtless prank but it did keep Denis from thinking it out that I'm a duplicate not a twin. Denis would have thought it out."

Victor Vance replied, "Denis is not that smart."

"Oh yes he is. I read his school file; his I.Q. is one hundred and forty-six on the Stanford-benoit test."

"Hum, that's high," thought Vance. "How would Denis know by looking at your pinky and Johnny's pinky?"

"Because even twins do not have the same fingerprints and of course, ours are naturally the same except Johnny's right thumbprint. If he gets to the right thumb then he'll really know. He appeared suspicious when I jumped off the administration building and landed behind him with a thud, my landing should have been light. He turned around and was startled especially with Johnny holding on to me. Denis said at the time, 'Where did you come from?' and I said, 'The roof,' thinking he wouldn't believe me. I said it in jest, our hair is messed up and Johnny is red in the face, we are running from Peter and Paul."

"Your really have to be extremely careful on the rest of the trip, what you say and what you do, damn it," Victor Vance whispered. "You have to keep the leaves down and the voltage at nil, God, why did I bring you on this trip! Right now, I want you to go down the trail toward the Colorado River where there's no one in sight and divest yourself of the leaves and get rid of the static electricity with no noisy disturbance and keep the cable along the shoe, not dragging behind."

"Do you want to come with me, Dad?"

"No, I can't, I've got to stay. I'll be back in three minutes or less." Mr. Vance went back into the cabin but before he did, he knocked the rock away from the screen door so he could hear Georgie come into the cabin. The cabin was lit up as though it was daylight; Denis had turned every light on looking for fingerprints. Then as Mr. Vance sat on the bed, slowly the cabin began vibrating, then a rumble, a faint but an obvious noise raising thunder.

No, it was hooves, the horses and mules were stampeding. Victor Vance fell back on his bed covering his eyes with his hands then with his pillow; someone tapped him on his shoulder, he uncovered and said, "What is it, Johnny?"

"No, it's Georgie, Dad, I had an accident, I took off my cable."

V.V. bonked himself in the head then put his hands over his face again and fell on the bed. "Yes, go on, no don't go on!"

"Dad listen," as Georgie pulled V.V.'s right hand away from his eye, V.V. slowly opened his eye. "While I was digging a hole to put the leaves in, I struck a metal object, when I finished digging it out, it's a hatchet!"

V.V. focused his one eye on the object, "No Georgie, it's a tomahawk, see it has a sharp point on the end, a hatchet doesn't,"

"The lights went out," screamed Thor.

Georgie whispered in the semi-dark, "Dad, I rubbed it to clean it. A big flash of light hit me and burned my hair."

"Keep the volume of static electricity low, got your cable on?"

"Yes."

"You stink," Dad said in a very almost inaudible voice. "Go to the bathroom now." Victor Vance slithered off the bed and snaked his way to his suitcase on his belly, he silently searched for the scissors. It took a minute or two before he could see the light under the bathroom door as he snaked his way to the door someone turned the cabin lights on.

A surprised voice erupted—Jan Vance, "What are you doing on the floor?"

"Oh, I dropped the scissors on the floor," he winked at her.

"You got something in your eye?" Hooves still pounding the ground. Splinters flew as the screen door was ripped off its hinges by a horse that came racing through the cabin, the screen door was attached to a horse going out the front door with no sympathy for the inhabitants and furniture. Denis' bed was turned around, smashing into Homer's. There they lay holding onto each other; the rest of the boys were standing on their beds and the girls somehow were in the cabin too.

Mrs. Vance said, "Two horses ran through our cabin and wrecked two beds, fortunately, the girls were in the bathroom, no one was hurt."

The manager in a robe, nothing on his feet, his glasses twisted, as though something ran him over. One lens shattered, he cried out, "Are you alright?"

"Yes, but the doors are gone in the boys' cabin."

Georgie came out of the bathroom, his hair cut, looking like he had a scalp disease. Victor Vance with his eyes closed, scissors still in hand, flopped onto his bed, inaudibly babbled, "Oh God, I'm tired." His right arm bent at the elbow with scissors snapping lying on the bed, the scissors tumbled from his hand and stuck in the mattress.

The manager said, while hopping around on one foot, pulling out a pine cone leaf with a sharp point and said, "It must have been dry lightning!" He put down his foot and yelled as loud as he could, "Those of you that have no doors on your cabins, come with me." Only three cabins had lost doors, the animals were being rounded up by the wranglers. See the good old boys, cowboys, in their long red underwear and cowboy hats, boots, chase the mules and horses. One old wrangler said, after spitting out his chew, "Damn mountain lion!"

While the incident was serious, no one was hurt. Everyone had to pack up their belongings and tote them to a different cabin at three o'clock in the morning but didn't complain. They were too tired and silence came over the group. Denis was so tired that he dragged his luggage on the dusty path to the next cabin. His Sherlock Homes hat crumpled as it hit the pillow, Denis not to move again for five hours.

Chapter 42
Butts Up

Next morning came with a sudden crash and bang on the old cowboy triangle. It had a Phantom Sam atop the triangle with guns a-blazing and saying, "Stand back, men, women first." Breakfast was dark and sullen even with a joke on the porch, Denis barely ate a thing. Thor ate his and the rest of Denis'; in fact, Denis was lying on Thor asleep.

Homer sat there with his fork stuck in the table and didn't move until someone yelled, "Let's go," then he shoveled food for a frantic minute then stood up, grabbed his milk and chug-a-lugged. Mr. and Mrs. Vance tried to put on a good and positive front of carefree delight, but slowly sank until their heads touched the table and one eye opened between the two of them, food was misplaced—some in an ear, some in the hair. One of the waitresses had to pull Tim from under the table, he was snoring so loud everyone thought it was the mules running again, then someone said, "Dry lightning," no one moved.

Sleep-deprived Grand Canyon mule riders barely made it to their mules, the wranglers had to push more butts up onto the saddles than before. The mules were lethargic going up and full of gas; maybe they ate Georgie's pile of leaves and some gassy hay. I think it was a plot the wranglers had to amuse themselves.

Going up the Kybab trail back to the rim, the hikers cringed and backed off from the mules; in some cases they couldn't because one more step and they'd be on a fast journey and a sudden stop. The wrangler in the front, Mr. Vance in back, silently giggled if you looked closely at the silent movement of frivolity in the saddle. The man in the green pith helmet and green jumpsuit had picked up a stick, a long manzanita stick went through some funny gyrations and on occasion used it as a lance and startled hikers, until the added wrangler saw what green pith helmet was doing with the stick, yelled, after he let loose with his chew, "Stop with the stick." He passed Tim and Thor, grabbed pith helmet's stick and threw the stick into the Colorado River a thousand feet down.

By this time, the dust on the trail was swirling in the wind and everyone was coughing; the wrangler yelled out, "Those neckerchiefs around your neck aren't just for pretty. They are to keep the dust from being inhaled, boys and girls," but green jumpsuit and pith helmet didn't have one. The added wrangler made his way back down the parade of riders and sat laughing on his mule through his neckerchief. He wanted to say *you're sure a dumb cuss, pith helmet*, but he didn't say a word. It would have been cause to be fired.

The lady in the fur coat was no longer black but a dusty black-brown, her hat, nearly blowing off, with one hand on the hat, she yelled, "Let's get the hell out of here," as she fits her neckerchief over her nose and mouth with her other hand.

While we'd only been three days and the experience had been exciting and exhausting. The unfamiliarity had set in. The entire group of school kids had diminished in their enthusiasm and seeing swirling dust looking down seeing enormous depths below them, hearing strange sounds and speech provoked an ever-raising fear. If the stick and the dust incident had continued, homesickness would have struck them but fortunately, it didn't and it wasn't until they arrived at Bright Angel Lodge and picked up the overweight student, she broke down and said, "I want to go home, I miss my mom and dad."

Denis answered, "I miss school!"

Johnny and Georgie pretended to stick their fingers down their throats and made puking sounds, not only for school and the principal but also for Denis. Mrs. Vance gave Georgie and Johnny a look that said let's not overdo it. The kids didn't clamor to get in the van because their buttocks hurt; from the mules constantly going downhill, the front of the buttock got well-worn; on coming uphill constantly, the back of the buttock was persecuted to the highest degree.

Even Georgie who could have floated above the saddle paid for it and said, "Any chance I can stand in the van for several hundred miles?"

The rest of the kids nodded at the suggestion Mr. Vance laughed like a chicken being strangled and said, "No, fasten seatbelts and not in a standing position." But before the van started for home, Red Feather Lightfoot appeared from the crowd with gifts. Handmade Indian dream catchers for everyone, she said, "You couldn't come to me, I come to you. I hope you had great fun at me home. May I come to your castle sometime?" Mr. Vance gave her his home address and school address.

Sleep gnawed at everyone from the drone of the speeding van, they came under its spell save the driver Victor Vance, he was having trouble with the purr of the engine. The day and half trip back was uneventful and lethargic. As they pulled into the school parking lot, they had the scare of their lives as Miss. Syndly peered into the van with her evil horrible smile that brought everyone to attention like robots receiving an order to kill. The Principal Miss Syndly said politely, "Welcome back, children, I hope you had a nice trip."

They answered in unison, "Yes Miss Syndly."

"Did you know that President Theodore Roosevelt took the trip that we were on, he was one of the very first to do so," said Denis eagerly before anyone else, they of course were thinking only of sleep and getting back to their parents.

Georgie whispered to Johnny, "Miss Syndly was on the trip with Denis; she is the buzzard above us that crapped on Denis."

They started to laugh historically. Miss Syndly's face turned even meaner. She stared at the Indian boys, they assumed a posture in the van, a vanilla look until they stepped out of the van. They took the easy way out by shaking Miss Syndly's hand and saying how glad it was to see her and the school. The back doors opened as Victor Vance climbed over the suitcases.

Miss Syndly, after the warm greeting from Johnny and Georgie, wanted to help but by the time she got through taking her shoes off, one at a time, standing on one leg, leaning on the van and rubbing her feet, everything was out and parents picked up their child's luggage and whisked it along with their offspring.

Miss Syndly said, "That was quick." She turned around and tottered back and forth, banging her shoes together and jerking forward in an ungainly way then stepped forward, stopping at the gate to put her shoes back on.

Johnny and Georgie did realize their principal walks with pain. Johnny couldn't hold his cruel thought and said, "Do you suppose she knows Long John Silver?"

Georgie replied, "That's not nice."

Chapter 43

The day started like any other school day—shower, clothes, breakfast, books, and brown paper bag lunch, consisting of a sandwich, peanut butter and jelly on sourdough bread, with an apple, tangerine and a juice box. Mr. Vance picked up Johnny at his parents' house. They sat in the backseat of the car and exchanged thoughts on various homework assignments that lasted three minutes.

Then the usual, they talked about their similarities and the things Georgie could do and Johnny couldn't. Leaves out of the hand and fingertips. "Doesn't that hurt?" Johnny asked.

"Well, it feels uncomfortable if I do it more than once in a day. The wrists, where the leaves come out, hurt."

"I can understand the silver-green skin since you were created in silver plating solution but I don't get the change to normal skin?"

"If I concentrate and stay calm, my skin stays normal."

"How do you manage to levitate and just fly?"

"I think it and it just happens; I know it's impossible for humans to fly. You know that beam of light that almost killed Mr. Ritz?"

"Yes, I remember."

"I get a tingling sensation then I aim my index finger if I want it to come out, I think it."

"How do you repel yourself from the ground?" asked Johnny.

"That silver-green beam spreads throughout every cell and forces me upward and when it hits the ground, it's diluted, it won't hurt anyone. I think we flew too high over the Grand Canyon; the beam was weak at that height and that's why the owl knocked us down."

"Couldn't you have saved us from falling into the Colorado?"

"Could have but I was just as frightened as you were; maybe even more because your life was in my hands. Control is impossible; it came as a narrow beam there must be a big hole somewhere in the canyon. I must be careful!"

Days went on with no importance of Peter and Paul kept trying to show how inferior we were as just Indians and they were superior in all aspects. Yet they couldn't catch us, never beat us on a test. The only thing they had over us were the good-looking dumb girls. Summer break was coming up fast and Johnny wanted to take me to the reservation and meet our relatives. He said, "Let's do it for a joke; the reservation is fun; it has wide open spaces we can hunt, fish and make pretty things. My ancestors and partly your ancestors make beautiful objects from silver and turquoise; that's what my dad does at the college."

"Does what?"

Johnny reiterated, "Makes pretty things; Indian Arts and Crafts. Zuni art is famous throughout the nation. There are practitioners of skills that you haven't heard of and things I haven't seen. Let's explore the Zuni art world and the thousands of acres of land and streams."

"Do you think they'll let me on the reservation?"

"They'd let anyone on the reservation. We can stay with my grandfather and grandmother; they may be shocked to see another one of me; we can play a joke on them and keep us a secret, if it's OK with my mom and dad."

School ran down to an agonizing few days and then there were Peter, Paul and Miss Syndly. With four days left, Miss Syndly was totally out of her mind running around frantically solving imaginary problems. Paul and Peter were trying to get their final licks, punches and jokes on us, we held our own. The watercolor paint, pink to be exact, was over the door with a string attached. Georgie saw the paint can coming down and before it could turn over, Georgie batted it. Beth and Babs, ah yes, the string was pulled by the notorious two, the batting of the can struck the laughing babbling girls.

I kept forgetting to say the sexiest cheerleaders in the school but now being under battle conditions, they looked like Van Gogh's paint pallet, remarkably smeared and wonderfully colorful and screaming their heads off. Slapping the hell out of Peter and Paul. The girls were sent to the office for swearing in class. Now Miss Syndly will be involved in her neurotic way, we will be questioned as though Hitler was still alive.

Next period, Peter, Paul, Johnny and I were all summoned to the office. Babs and Beth were still with paint permeating; they were not so jolly personalities. Georgie sat down beside the girls; they got up and began hitting him as hard as they could. He said, "Give it up!"

Immediately, Miss Syndly went into a tirade directed at the girls. Georgie rushed like a blur to the cafeteria, made seven chocolate milkshakes with tops and straws, blurred back and said, "Miss Syndly, your chocolate milkshake is getting warm."

She turned to her desk and replied, "Oh yes, I forgot," she turned around sucking on her straw. Georgie had passed out a shake to everyone and as soon as Miss Syndly saw everyone sucking, she said, "You can't do that; I'm the only one that sucks here!"

Then everyone roared with spastic laughter bordering on hurling; the girls forgot what Georgie did and began kissing him. Miss Syndly sank to the floor behind her desk with her chocolate milkshake in her left hand and her rank coffee mug in her right with the saying, "Don't tread on me, I change Lives!" Spreadeagled behind her desk, of course, with her shoes off, Miss Syndly said, "I will see you all for cleanup after school or there will be hard times." When she meant hard times, she meant it.

Miss Syndly stomped out of her office after school surprisingly because Stinky's feet were so tender. The six were standing in a row facing the administration building on the prescribed squares. Stinky came out and looked at the six—Peter, Paul, Beth, Babs, Johnny, and blur Georgie—with smiles. "Wipe those smiles off your faces! Weed that flowerbed!"

Somehow Peter, Paul, Babs and Beth didn't notice Georgie's cleanup; maybe they saw too much pleasure in each other and barely noticed the two Indians standing beside them. Of course, the girls spoke up first, "We don't see any weeds, Miss Syndly?"

"What do you mean; there's hundreds of weeds in that flowerbed!" Beth blew a bubble and snapped it. Miss Syndly's face turned red with rage immediately screamed, "Take that gum out of your mouth!"

"It's after school!"

"When you're speaking to me, you don't chew gum! Give it to me!" It was a monstrous wad of gum she had collected it from Paul, Peter and Babs and with her gum added, this she thought sexy and the boys would want to French kiss her to get their share of the gum back. Now her fun had gone right into a tissue from Stinky's pocket.

Surging into the forefront of red raging faces, Babs and Stinky were nose to nose, piping hot. In a stare down, Miss Syndly enunciated slowly and clearly, "Police the entire campus now!" She had six plastic bags in her backpack while pulling the backpack around, she took off her left shoe and scratched her foot on her right ankle bone. "I want the bags back neatly folded at 3:50."

Miss Syndly threw the tissue-wrapped gum on the ground and stepped on the gum. Babs jumped up and down in a white teething tantrum, "How could you!"

"Easy," said Miss Syndly.

With hands curled into fists, Babs thought better of slugging Stinky and hopped away, punching the air. The rest of the crew turned away and began picking up debris. In a low voice, Miss Syndly said, "That's right, assholes and elbows."

That night the administration building burned and the fire was blamed on a time-stamp machine that stood on the counter by the attendance secretary's desk. But the next day, there were smiles on a certain four faces only when Miss Syndly wasn't looking. After the fire, it took all that summer to rebuild. The superintendent who sent Mrs. Buckwith, his lover, to a kindergarten through six grade school, was found copulating in Mrs. Buckwith's office with Mrs. Buckwith. The custodian, Tom Hooper, said, "Are you two looking for something on the floor?"

"No, we found it," as they got up from behind the desk.

The custodian laughed and left muttering to himself, "So summer time is for fun for the darlings." The custodian's cacophony disturbed their joy.

But at Miss Syndly's graduation of the seventh grade to the eighth grade, they all had saved the loose-leaf paper and dumped it in the quad. But Georgie looked at the crazed Miss Syndly as she walked with a limp to her office, Georgie sprang into action and picked all the papers up and threw it in the green dumpster.

The second burning of the administration building two years later at the middle school that Stinky, Miss Syndly, replaced Mrs. Buckwith as principal. Mrs. Buckwith's lover and confidante, nicknamed Slippery Jack, made her second assistant to the superintendent. The school year ended with Miss Syndly being told by the president of the eighth grade at the podium to reveal her secret plans after her speech; it was competent, elegant and well-rehearsed; she told the eighth-grade class to empty their lockers. Not knowing what was happening, Miss Syndly stood and clapped while the eighth-grade students going to the high school knowing that no penalty can be exacted. Empty their lockers—the students and had saved all their assignments for the year and dumped them in the quad. Mrs. Syndly walked around in it for several hours and helped the custodians pick up the paper.

Stinky's year was a bust. The day after the school closed for the summer, Miss Syndly was asked to leave the school district or teach classes; she chose to retire. Miss Syndly's asst. principal who was now principal, invited her back as a guest speaker at a PTA meeting and told several lies about her superb career as a teacher and a principal; the parents who knew her from her tenure at the middle school did not clap at the end of her speech; they walked out of the auditorium.

Chapter 44

Georgie sat at the kitchen table with intense thoughtfulness on his face. He looked like he was going over his past. Mr. Vance thought it natural for someone found in a five-gallon bucket. Georgie sat still but rolled his eyes as Dad Mr. Vance sat down with orange juice he got out of the frig and began pouring it into a glass when Georgie abruptly said, "Where is my mother?"

"Your mother is upstairs making beds."

"No, not your wife; my real mother back where I was killed by my murderous brother? I know where my dad is but mother, I wonder if she is still alive after the horrible burns?"

After Jason and Heather heard what Georgie just uttered, they sat down at the kitchen table to hear this unexplained part of the miracle of how and where this mystical occurrence took place. "Again, I'm dreamed being chased but this time I'm on foot and mother is screaming at my brother to leave me along. He got into his pickup, smoked the tires one of the back tires on the truck is thin it went flat, I came out from behind a big garbage container and danced! That really pissed my brother off. My brother got back in the truck and chased me.

"A big clunking noise kept getting louder until I got to the liquor store then I could tell the rim of his truck had cut through the tire. I'm busting through the crowd of drunks and dope addicts; my brother is hell bent on killing me, still directly behind me and suddenly screaming; one body flew past me then everything went dark! I remember hearing yelling, dizziness struck me, awful moans I opened my eyes I'm not on the ground.

"My brother's truck hit his last victim before speeding away. The noise diminished. I twisted as I saw my body beneath me. But what was holding me up? I turned my head—Dad. 'You're dead!' 'So are you,' he replied. And that's all I remember until I found myself in that bucket."

Victor Vance couldn't comprehend the pain and agony that Georgie had gone through in his other life, he spoke, "Georgie, you're not in that life; you're in this life with us and we won't let anything happen even if we meet up with your brother."

Georgie looked up and smiled, "Dad, you don't know what vicious is in the realm of my brother."

"I've never had to struggle so hard to survive," Dad answered. "I guess we'll never completely understand but so far you haven't had any real difficulties and why did you do so many crazy things on the Grand Canyon trip?"

"Depression after seeing my mother in the hospital. I just wanted to expose my anomalies to the world."

Heather slowly gripped his hand and said, "Jason and I will never tell."

Georgie nodded his head in thanks and replied, "Your help in advising me on the ins and outs of school and especially not allowing me to mistreat someone that deserved it. Treating serious situations with leaves is comedy relief."

Dad broke into the conversation with, "What is your mother's name?"

Georgie quickly looked at Dad and thought, *Does he really want to know or am I a toy in his eyes*?

Mr. Vance said, "I really want to know!"

"You realize all this time since I arrived, no one has asked me about my other life; even Johnny hasn't asked me any questions. My mother's name is Joy Martin."

"Your brother's first name?"

"He was born Douglas Edward but didn't like it so he changed it to Joey."

"Legally or just changed?"

"Just changed after two years in juvenile detention; he changed his first name and told mom; Joy Martin is the only name he wanted to hear from her."

Victor Vance sat thinking then asked, "Do you remember your address?"

"Didn't have an address."

"Everything has a number or name."

"The restaurant had a name, 'Joker in Spades Take Out', 52 Michigan Avenue."

"Funny name."

Georgie giggled in response, "So is the food!"

Everyone laughed except Dad; he grabbed the telephone. The rotary dial on the phone clicked as it went back to zero or ABC; it clicked three times for four one one—information. Victor Vance spoke succinctly, "Detroit, Michigan please."

A voice came back, "What number do you want?"

"I don't know the number but the address is 52 Michigan Avenue, Joker in Spades Restaurant."

"You mean Joker in Spades."

"Yes, yes!"

"The number is 1-321-W.E.4-4694."

"Thank you, operator." Victor's voice rang out. "Do you want to call or do you want me to call?"

All that has happened in a year since my brother killed me, tears came to Georgie's eyes. He pounded his fist on the kitchen table, cracking the wooden table; he stood up, he then uttered his thoughts with facial expressions as he did before he could speak fluently and audibly spat out gibberish that no one had heard from Georgie before, at least not in this lifetime. The stutter stopped, "You call, Dad, I'm afraid I'll be tongue-tied and they'll just hang up."

Then Georgie grabbed the telephone while Dad's hand was still on the receiver. The phone receiver yo-yoed back and forth before Dad spoke, "Do want me to make the call?"

"I'm not sure that I want to make the call at all." Georgie picked up a paper napkin from the table and covered his face. "Don't call, all the pain has come back in a cascade of terror. It's making my head hurt beyond belief," shaking and practically vomiting, he turned and with the napkin still over his face, Georgie slowly walked up the steps to his bedroom.

Staring in disbelief, Victor Vance and family with mouths open, gasped at the behavior displayed by Georgie. The first time he had showed remorse and depression of his former life.

Chapter 45

The trip with Johnny and his parents to their ancestral home took three uneventful days so Georgie had time to think about the call. Do I want to know or don't I? It simmered in the back of his mind for days; the only thing that made him come out of his depression was the many times that the Two-Bucks mistaken him for their son. *After a year of my presence, they somehow couldn't get it through their heads there's two not one.*

Georgie was so much like Johnny the only difference was clothes. But the pain wouldn't go away no matter how he tried. It was like a series of car crashes; his thoughts would go to something else then upside down wheels pointing skyward, still spinning. Then pain from the thought of his mother dying in a hail of bullets or being run over for no good reason except to make it so that Joey wouldn't have to contend with anyone but himself.

The arrival to the reservation for Georgie was a new meaning of unlikeliness; first, they had to cross a dried up river except for a trickle at one side. The bed of the river was damp so the car can make it across without any problem. At this point of the trip, the Two-Bucks stopped asking him about his depression and his glum nature. So far Georgie hadn't seen anything to be happy about but their happiness and Johnny was elated he was going to see both grandmothers and grandfathers.

They drove down a street that was like being in a B-western; some tumbleweed dirt road wind kicking up dust and four figures standing at the end of the road. Silver hair flying in the breeze with Indian style clothing and decked out in jewelry fit for kings and queens. Georgie looked at various structures; they would be houses and they were vacant. Johnny jumped out of the car, his folks got out with salutations to greet the two elderly couples.

Georgie sat in the car; they stared at Georgie as though he was a ghost. Ed Two-Buck muttered to the most bedecked elderly, "Dad, I brought someone I want you to meet—Georgie Vance. Do you see the resemblance?"

Georgie slowly got out of the back door of the car and closed it. Georgie asked, "You leave cars in the middle of the road?"

Johnny's grandfather Walking Horse said, "A ghost is talking to me?"

"I'm sort of a ghost in modern terms. I was born ghost-like but I'm real." The elderly Indians moved back two paces from the car and showed fear. Speak Often, Johnny's grandmother, as her name implied moved forward and touched Georgie. Georgie thought about giving her a shock just as a joke but these people were serious so he just smiled.

"Yep, he is real and not a ghost as far as I can determine. What is your name again?"

"Georgie Vance. You do speak English, I thought I would have to learn a new language.? Will you teach me some of the Zuni tongue, Speak Often?"

Speak Often turned her head toward the others, "He sure looks like Johnny in every aspect."

"Yes, I do in every aspect but one," Georgie said, trying to be truthful.

Ed Two Buck rushed over to Georgie. "Don't spill the beans to Speak Often," he whispered.

Speak Often asked, "What did you say?"

"I said they are both teens now," Ed Two Buck swallowed funny, looking at his mother.

"Now Eddie, you know Johnny's birthday isn't until tomorrow." A nervous laugh erupted from Johnny and his parents.

Black Eagle, Lisa's dad, shook his rattlesnake charm and said, "Come on in before you sweat to death and the dust sticks to you. What's this ghost shit, daughter? Can I call you by your real first name?"

"Oss beso shis-d Dad."

"Thank you, January-o-wolf." They went into the Indian structure; it wasn't a wigwam or a tepee but an unfinished building with air conditioning.

When Georgie came in, he said, "Why haven't you finished the building?" to Mr. Ed Two-Buck's dad Walking Horse.

"This is not where we live, this is our ancestral land, we always meet family here then go to our homes."

"Why?"

"Because Indians that have passed into history live here; every Indian in our tribe who dies is buried here. So, no one lives here just every Indian that belongs to the tribe can be buried here,"

Georgie asked Walking Horse, "Yes," as he pointed out the window at a building that was used for funerals.

"How did you become Johnny or Johnny became you?" asked Black Eagle. "We know that Johnny was a single birth. How did you come about?"

"I am a modern ghost just as Speak Often said. The Great Spirit give me a second chance in life. My father caught my soul after I had been killed by my brother. He the Great Spirit sent my father from the promised land to catch my soul and put it in this body with the experiences of my past life emblazoned on this brain. As an infant, I could propel my body without using my legs. I can project a light it is silver-green in color and I found that it is very dangerous. I almost killed a teacher.

"How and why I have acquired this power I don't know, I barely know how to use it. Johnny and I flew around the Grand Canyon and the light scared the canyon walls. I flew too high; the light is weak at altitude over five hundred feet. An owl collided with us and we fell into the river but hit a sand bar. With Johnny hanging on to me, I managed to bounce the light off the walls of the canyon and made it back to the cabin."

Mr. Two-Buck interrupted and said, "Georgie, can I speak with you outside?" He closed the door then in a muffled voice, "Whatever you do, don't tell my parents and Lisa's parents how you were born; they are very superstitious; this will frighten them to no end."

"I see," Georgie uttered. "Mr. Two Buck, I feel a presence, something tugging at me from within. It's Indian in origin and telling me, it happened here many years ago. Some one was killed, it's one of your ancestors."

"How do you know that?" said a very serious Ed Two Buck.

"This entity is saying to me that the murder weapon is buried in the burial grounds of the funeral building. It is a tomahawk." Georgie was thinking, *How could I be a medium? I know little of their history.*

Ed Two Buck was reeling in thought, "No one is allowed on the sacred grounds. The medicine man cannot walk on the grounds unless there is a funeral."

"You see, I don't have to walk on the burial area," Just as he spoke, something pushed him back and he fell to the ground. Georgie, stunned, dripped some leaves from his wrists and mouth and he was breathing hard as though something grabbed him from within his body. "There is a not so benign spirit here protecting the tomahawk from discovery. I think you better ask your parents and Lisa's parents to step out here and explain."

"I'm not sure that is a good idea this has been a secret in my family for a long time."

"The spirit has gone," muttered Georgie. "Wow, that is something I have never experienced before. Mr. Two Buck, why would a spirit be protecting a murder weapon?"

"Because the ancestor that killed my ancestor is one of Lisa's ancestors, her great-great-grandfather killed my great-great-grandmother in a jealous rage because she married my great-great-grandfather after five years of marriage and two kids, but it has never been proven because the murder weapon hasn't been found." Mr. Ed Two Buck was in deep thought. "Will this disrupt their friendship if this killing comes back in their lives or will they want to know?"

Georgie shrugged. Vacillating Ed grabbed his head and said, "No, no, I can't tell them."

Georgie looked at Mr. Two Buck and said, "I would want to know. I'd feel some satisfaction in knowing my brother killed me and the Great Spirit gave me a new life with loving parents and brother and sister that love me. You and your family had a hard time of what to make of me. While Johnny and I look alike, we aren't alike, you and your wife have eventually accepted me. I think your parents and Lisa's parents will accept this ancient matter for what it is ancient and nothing else."

"But how will we tell them without upsetting them; they are still steeped in the ancient ways," said a puzzled Ed Two Buck.

"This spirit is not helping me think; it is very hard to push from my mind. Besides it does not want the tomahawk to be found. Some other spirit is forcing the first spirit to expose the whereabouts of this murder weapon. There is a tug-o-war in my brain right now between these two entities."

Ed can see Georgie being pushed back and forth; he moved to help but the negative spirit nipped at Ed's fingers on his right hand. Ed jumped back. Georgie jumped into the air trying to dislodge the arguing spirits. Georgie flew around the Indian land, screaming as loud as he can at the entities in his brain: "I know the truth so get out!"

Georgie flew to the car and hid in the car by way of the backseat and the trunk. The entities had never seen such a thing and were confused and disappear. Georgie wriggled his way out of the trunk, he looked up at all of the family staring at him. "What happened here, Ed?" said Walking Horse.

"Something crazy," replied Ed. "I don't know how to explain it, I think Georgie can explain it better than I can!"

"Spirits are chasing me so I hid in the trunk of the car."

"But we saw you in the air screaming your lungs out through the window of the wigwam. No one can fly; that is comic book stuff," said Speak Often.

"Yes-um."

"You aren't Johnny, are you, although you look exactly like him.

"No mam, but I am him," replied Georgie. "And you're right, I can't fly. I have a source of power that holds me up, you'll find burn marks all around here on the ground and maybe on some of the buildings. Basically, the entities frightened me. This is unexplained and I haven't had this kind of thing happen to me before. but this time the entities in my brain scared me more than the power that has been given to me. Hence, I used it without thinking, I hope I didn't damage anything sacred to your tribe," Georgie almost pleaded.

Just as he said that, the smell of smoke was in the air. Johnny asked, "Do you have a fire engine on the reservation?"

January-o-Wolf said, "Yes, it hasn't been used in a while."

Johnny and Georgie ran ahead of the not so young Ed, the elderly Indians behind and Ed's wife tripping along on high heels and yelling, "Wait for me!" Johnny had seen the fire engine before on earlier visits. He had a chance to start it. The building was encrusted in dust. Johnny yelled, "This hasn't been opened in three years!" He pulled on the handles on the big doors and yelled, "They're locked."

Johnny and Georgie stood there motionless for a moment. Georgie then ripped open the doors with one pull, falling backward, holding the handle in the air, flat on his back. An eerie popping and cracking of the hinges on the big doors tore apart with a sudden rush of noise and the left big door fell on Georgie, the right big door still standing. Johnny tried to force the little door in the right big door open; it fell directly on Georgie under the left big door with the wooden broken handle in Johnny's hand from the little door. The little door broke away from the right big door.

A slight giggle emanated from under. Now in a sandwich of sorts, Georgie was between doors. Georgie pushed the doors away and said to Johnny, "Get in the cab, I'll push."

Johnny tried to start the engine several times. There were no gauge readings. Johnny yelled back to Georgie to stop. He jumped out of the cab of the fire engine and opened the hood. "The battery is disconnected."

Georgie came around to the front and said, "Where is the battery located?"

"On the passenger's side under the hood." Opening the door of the cab, Johnny smacked Georgie in the face and knocked him flat on the ground again, this time Georgie popped up with a happy smile on his face. "Forget the fire engine, I'll just blow it out," Georgie explained.

"What do you mean blow it out?" Johnny said with a twisted face. "It's ten feet high and on a vertical surface; how are you going to put it out?"

"Watch!" The silver-green light coming out of Georgie's right index finger turned the sandy soil to glass, Georgie moved to put out the fire, then jumped on the wall standing absolutely perpendicular and blowing as hard as he can and shooting the flames with the silver-green light. By this time, the rest of the clan stood watching Georgie blow out the fire. Smoke billowing out quickly, everyone moved away some coughing but nothing like Georgie's that blew him away from the building.

Georgie was now standing on the ground, smoke still swirling around him, the smoke being blown away by a gentle breeze that sprang up. Speak Often said, looking at Georgie now covered with soot and black as ebony, "Where are your shoes and what's that hole in the seat of your pants?"

Georgie answered, "Victims of a burning firefight, ma'am," as he spit some soot. Georgie was still smoldering.

Johnny pointed, "There are his shoes stuck on the wall."

January-o-Wolf started laughing as she turned to talk to Speak Often, Walking Horse, Black Eagle, Mr. and Mrs. Two Buck, Ed the son of Walking Horse and Speak Often said, "How's that for a pair of shoes dying for a cause."

The smoke was getting thinner. Johnny and Georgie, while laughing at the scene, in unison ask, "Where is the closest shower?"

Both shoes came flying at Georgie and Johnny, Georgie pushed Johnny to the ground and stepped aside as the shoes turned around while Johnny grumbled, "Why did you push me down?"

Georgie fell to the ground as a swishing noise came closer, Georgie fired from his left index finger leaves to hide the silver-green light that shot down his shoes and turned them into flakes. A terrifying screech came from the evil entity, Georgie pulled up Johnny. Something smacked Georgie in the face with something Indian, it fell to the ground.

Walking Horse picked it up, "It's just a dream catcher."

The evil entity kicked Georgie in the butt and lifted him off the ground. Georgie shot the silver-green light shielded with leaves another object emanated from nowhere; the ladies said, "Isn't that lovely leaves with old moccasin leather falling from the sky."

Speak Often let a leaf slip into her hand; she stared at it for several moments, cast the old leather away. "This is not from around here," she shrugged her shoulders and sort of pointed at January-o-Wolf, she moved on to show the boys where the shower was in the firehouse. Speak Often dropped the leaf and it scattered in the wind. She said to the boys, "Just call me Jan."

"That my stepmother's name," mentioned Georgie. The boys looked at her and said, "Yes-um."

"The towels are in the little closet by the showers and if you open the door straight ahead, you will find the showers. Run the water for a while, Johnny, it will be dirty."

Grandma January-o-Wolf turned on the main water valve then turned on the hot water heater, Johnny and Georgie walked through to the showers.

"OK grandma, we have things figured out; where's the soap?"

Grandma threw two bars into the showers. After Georgie lathered up, "Okay is your grandparent playing some kind of joke on us?" Georgie demanded clarification.

"No, how should I know? I don't know them much better than you do," Johnny spat water at Georgie. "Hum I can't believe this. One seems to like us." After five minutes of rusty water, the water turned warm and clear. "The spirit helped?"

After the relief from the grit and grime, the boys thought while you're alone, at least Johnny wondered as they tried on various pieces of firemen clothes. "What does the tomahawk that killed his ancestor look like?"

Johnny responded, "It's something the French invented and gave to the Indians a long time ago to kill the British. They made it from the ax, the chopping part, made the handle shorter. The best killing object on the tomahawk is the opposite end, the iron point of the weapon. It's made with true balance."

Georgie rolled his eyes. "I'm not getting into another absurd ridiculous round with those two spirits that just about drive me crazy and caused me to set the religious meeting place on fire."

But just as Georgie said no, the very rusty nasty looking tomahawk stuck in the wall of the fire house. "What was that noise?" There, near the firemen's clothes closet, was the tomahawk sticking in the wall. Then banging of the locker doors for several minutes, a sudden chill went up and down their spines. "Now look what you've done," cried Georgie. "The good spirit sent us the tomahawk."

Johnny walked through the door to the outside, pulled the tomahawk out of the big door, and held it up and came back through to show Georgie. Johnny pirouetted in the air, dropped the tomahawk and screamed, "Something's got me," then the bad entity took Johnny and dropped the tomahawk, Johnny disappeared in the twilight of the evening, screaming his lungs out. Georgie grabbed the tomahawk lying on the ground and jumped up and followed the screams.

The good spirit pushed Georgie forward, throwing him up in the air and saying in his brain in Zuni, go to the religious meeting place. Out loud Georgie responded, "I do not know what you're talking about."

The good spirit appeared and pointed to the meeting place. "How did you do that?" said Georgie. *You're dead and buried*, he thought. Quickly, he moved to the religious meeting place and saw Johnny's head bent back, his body hanging in the air above a hole in the ground. Georgie immediately jerked Johnny away from the evil spirit, it roared with rage, Georgie bounded as fast as he could to Ed Two Bucks' car.

The evil spirit grabbed Johnny and a tug-o-war ensued. Georgie dropped the tomahawk near the car. Lisa and Ed Two Buck came racing out, from the makeshift building, along with their parents; they looked up to see their son with Georgie on one side and nothing on the other side. Johnny was screaming, Walking Horse slipped and fell, Walking Horse was helped up by Black Eagle. Ed Two Buck was there on the ground, which was what Walking Horse had tripped on. Walking Horse saw the tomahawk where Ed was lying.

At the same time Walking Horse was falling, Ed grabbed the tomahawk, jumped in the air with the tomahawk and struck the invisible force with the ancient horrible weapon that had killed his great-great-grandfather who has his great-great-grandson strike instinctively and with fury. Ed got through to this ghost of the past, Ed was not going to let it happen again, and with the same weapon it tried to kill his son. The evil entity howled with an incredible roar and fled.

Georgie let Johnny down easy, Ed dropped the tomahawk, grabbed his son from Georgie and held him tight, as Lisa ran to her son crying. The grandparents surrounded Georgie, Lisa, Ed and Johnny, grimacing suddenly from out of nowhere the good spirit picked up the tomahawk and stuck it in the side of the car just in back of the headlight on the driver's side. "Don't panic; that's the good spirit that did it!"

"How do you know?" said Black Eagle.

"The evil spirit would have stuck it in my head," Georgie gasped, trying to regain his breath. Georgie made sounds that he'd never heard before.

Black Eagle reported, "I think it wants to give us gifts."

"No gifts," Georgie responded. Bones of cats and dogs came crashing down to the ground. More of the Zuni language flooded Georgie's mind, he repeated them to Black Eagle. "Take care of them, those are my pets," moaned the good spirit entity. Georgie said in English, "I don't know what it means." Georgie held up his arms in frustration.

Speak Often asked, "Say the words."

Georgie nodded and spewed some funny sounds in the Zuni language. "It wants you to take care of its pets."

"They're just bones," answered Georgie. A cloud of dust in the dark sky; a spear stuck in the back bumper on the driver's side of the car vertically. "Please let's get out of here before it throws its horse and cattle bones at us!" pleaded Georgie. He grabbed the dog and cat bones and jumped into the open trunk. It was hard to get the trunk closed because of the spear.

Everyone squeezed in and huddled into the little car. Walking Horse said, "My car is behind the building," just as he spoke, a horse skull landed in front of the car.

"Never mind, go!" Ed sped off like a crazy man avoiding falling bones in a very large cloud of Indian reservation dust. At every stoplight, people in other cars stared at them with a curious look; finally, we made it to Walking Horse and January-o-wolf's home, as everyone got out of the car and Georgie got out of the trunk. Walking Horse said to Georgie, "They call me Walter here. Give me the bones. I have a shoe box to put them in so you can keep them."

"But what do I do with the good entity; it followed us here."

"Where?"

"You can't see it, it's in my skull and I am scared it won't come out," muttered a dejected Georgie.

"You're amazing, Georgie, how did you come by these abilities?"

"Well, your grandson didn't want me to divulge my birth date, you see, I'm younger than Johnny."

"Now Georgie," Ed Two Buck reminded Georgie as he wagged his index finger back and forth.

"What's this all about?" inquired Walter.

Ed Broke into the conversation, "Last name is not Two Buck, it is Vance."

"Is that what this secret is?"

"Yes," exclaimed Ed.

Walter turned to Johnny and Georgie and said, "Come in the house and I will feed you, I'm sure you two are starving after all that exercise."

Johnny and Georgie eagerly followed the grandparents of Ed and Lisa. They sat down at the dining room table. January-o-wolf often used just Jan in the outside world. Walter brought cold pizza and soda. The food and drink were gone in a moment. The rest sat at the table and excitedly discussed the events of the day on the reservation.

"Have you seen anyone jump that high and blow out a fire in one fell swoop? Then commiserate with a spirit that throws bones at us," Ed practically spit all over everyone!

"Hey boys," Walter said, "Bart (Black Eagle) and I will take you out tomorrow get some clothes and shoes that fit you."

Jan brought out peanut butter and jelly sandwiches, they were gone in seconds. As Walter handed the boys more sodas, he noticed that while the boys were so different and yet the same, they got along more than brothers. Johnny and Georgie showed their fat bellies to their grandparents, they laughed and said, "Is the T.V. on in the family room?"

"Yes," replied Grandpa. Later Jan went into the family room, both were sound asleep with the T.V. blaring. Georgie must be the one twitching, thought Jan, how can anything bother that kid? Just as she said that, the shoe box slowly rose in the air, it sent chills up her spine. She said in Zuni, "Pets down." After all, the spirit wouldn't know what a box was from its knowledge. The box with the bones gently slipped back to its original position. Then she felt ever so slightly something pass her as she went back to the kitchen. First sheepishly, it pushed the cardboard platter that had the pizza on it. Crumbs on the cardboard slowly evaporated like magic. Jan began to feel the chill on her spine tingle once again. She motioned to the others but they were too busy gabbing.

Then the entity slowly lifted a dish out of her hand while she was trying to put it in the dish washer. A peanut butter blot evaporated like magic. "People," Jan said loudly. The dish fell to the floor.

Walter said "Honey, that's our new China!"

"I didn't drop it on the floor, it did." She then spoke in Zuni to the entity. All that it ate, or a better word, consumed, fell on Bart.

"What did you say to that thing?"

"I told it that it isn't alive so it can't eat and go back and play with its pets," Jan said laughingly.

Georgie heard Jan's voice from the family room. He didn't smile as he walked into the dining room, he said, "That lives most of the time in my head, after all we have a tomahawk in the fender and a spear in the back bumper; either piece of the old weapons could have hurt someone. So don't talk to him about any gifts or war objects. I want everyone who speaks his lingo to teach Johnny and I some Zuni and the entity some English. This thing lives in me and I can't talk to it!"

Georgie grabbed his head in pain and fell to the floor, rolling around and saying out loud, "Help!" Walter said something in Zuni and Georgie's pain went away instantly. Georgie relaxed on the floor and gave a big sigh of relief. "Who said that?" moaned Georgie.

"I asked the entity to come out in the open. Then it or he or she can speak to all present."

He proceeded to engage Johnny and said in his voice, "I get cold outside, I spent a hundred years underground in bitter cold and terrible heat. Tell the Indian council to bury the dead deeper so that heat and cold don't affect us as much," in Zuni.

Stunned, Walter, Sadie, Jan and Bart stammered, "Not Johnny too."

As Johnny's eyes blurred, opened and closed, his mouth began to move erratically. Then through Johnny, the entity evoked, "I won't hurt anyone. I'm just grateful I escaped from Running Wolf after the council sentenced him to death. He was buried beside me; he has tortured me ever since."

Jan began in English asking its name then started over in Zuni, "What is your name?"

"Trotting Fox."

Walter explained to Trotting Fox, "The Zuni tongue of the people is no longer spoken in the land."

The good entity replied, "I speak good."

Walter answered in Zuni, "Only a few speak our tongue. The tongue of the land is foreign to you, but in the land, the tongue you hear us speak that you don't understand, everyone speaks and if you don't learn it, Ed, Lisa, Johnny and Georgie will ignore you forever. They don't speak your tongue; it will be like you're back in your grave alone."

"No, I can't stand lying beside Running Wolf forever, my soul will be extinguished from soaring like an eagle; that's why I'm here! Running Wolf was condemned by the council, that is why he couldn't follow me and torment me any longer. Running Wolf cannot soar and cannot leave our land."

The others were listening intently to the conversation, while some understood, the boys were almost oblivious. Johnny picked up a word or two but Georgie didn't understand a word. Walter asked, "Why didn't you soar to the sun and moon?"

"By the council's orders, I and Running Wolf had to come back to our graves at night and all others could soar."

"What is this tongue called?" Walter looked over to his wife, just mouthed English or American? A blurry but building image began on Johnny while he was sitting by his mother; she turned and screamed then jumped up and said, "Don't do that or I'll kill you! Do it to the other boy."

The entity said, "He is not a true Indian brave. I can feel it in his head."

Lisa pulled her son to the floor and sat on him screaming, "Get out…get out!"

Ed grabbed his wife by the arm; he blurted, "What are you doing?"

She began slapping her son with her other hand. "Don't you see he is trying to take over his body!"

The entity replied in Zuni, "I need a place to rest at night or the council will commend me to the land and I will be back where I started from."

"The not so good entity is pushing us into a corner. Push back, Walter!"

"The essence of my spirit will be sent to the hunting ground."

"Why don't you want to go to the hunting ground?"

In Zuni, "I didn't get to finish life and I want to see more of the land."

"Why did you leave Georgie?"

"He is not Indian although he looks Indian."

"You mean you can actually see us?"

"Yes. I will stay with Georgie, although I don't want to."

A halo effect began developing around Georgie, a feather brought gasps from the group even when he looked at the big mirror behind the couch where Walter, Jan, Sadie and Bart were sitting. Trotting Fox said in Zuni, "Boy, I sure am bony."

Everyone on the couch got up and said, "Damn it, you're dead!"

The entity dissolved and kept quiet. "The impertinence of that ghost!" Jan went on, "That disgusting thing, let's dump it back at the reservation."

Suddenly the entity in Zuni, "Please I beg you, don't take me back to my grave!"

Walter, still standing, replied in Zuni, "If you learn the speech of the land, English, by morning I will not take you back to Zuni land," as Walter threw a Zuni-English dictionary.

The entity replied, "What is this?"

"You figure it out," answered Walter.

Chapter 46

Bart and Sadie, Speak Often left, Walter and Jan went to bed. The boys grabbed the dictionary and slipped into their sleeping bags on the floor in the family room. Georgie said, "We have our own ghost; if we can teach him English by morning, he's ours."

Johnny almost yelled, "We can keep the creeps at school creeped out, and the teachers in wonder."

Just then Jan came in and asked if they were alright. Both said, "Yes fine."

"OK for the night," then she came back in and asked, "Do you want some hot milk with chocolate in it?"

"Well yes," said Georgie and Johnny nodded. Immediately, Jan left and in a matter of seconds, she came back with two cups. Again, Johnny hid the dictionary in his sleeping bag. They puffed up their pillows and sat up. Jan handed them the cups then she said, "Put the cups on the table when you get through."

"Yes ma'am," as they chug-a-lugged their drink and put the cups on the table.

"You guys are fast," as she walked out of the room.

Johnny didn't take the dictionary out until Jan's footsteps faded away, "Now, where is that ghost?"

Georgie: "I can tell you I think he is afraid of the book and the funny marks in it." Georgie moved close to Johnny. "You are the one that speaks some Zuni."

Georgie thought that the entity was between them. Johnny pointed to the word for a greeting in Zuni and said it. Johnny said, "Hello," and pointed to the word hello on the page then to the word in Zuni opposite. The entity spoke the Zuni word for a greeting first, then, he said, "Hello!" The boys looked at each other and smiled and uttered "Wow." The entity mimicked them and said "Wow!"

Then, "What word should we use next?" Both studied the dictionary. "Food, no, tree," Johnny pointed at the word in Zuni then said the word in English. Hour after hour, the boys relentlessly pursued their ambition to take the entity home with them. At eight o'clock the next morning, the boys were fast asleep.

But the entity said, "Hello Jan."

She said, "Which one of you is awake?"

"Me, Trotting Fox."

Jan dropped the tray with the food on it, screamed, and ran to Walter. "It can talk in English," Jan rambled on and woke up Walter, "Get out of bed."

Walter rolled over and looked at Jan and replied, "It's too early to get up."

"You don't understand. Trotting Fox said hello to me in English and called me by name."

That got Walter's attention, he grabbed his robe, while putting it on the entity had followed Jan into their bedroom. "Hello."

"Who's speaking?" Walter demanded.

"Didn't think me could do it, did Walter! Me dead, Trotting Fox couldn't in the new tongue ha-ha English."

Walter blinked in amazement then stared around the room and came onto his wife once again and whispered, "Is that you, Jan, talking to me?"

"No!"

"Me, me take back couldn't speak tongue."

Walter sat back on the bed and shuddered with the cold; the entity hit Walter with his cold breath.

Chapter 47
The Trip Back Home

Going home for the boys was exciting but Mr. and Mrs. Two Buck, Ed and Lisa weren't so sure the word exciting was exactly right with a tomahawk in the fender, the spear in the back bumper, the entity wouldn't part with his treasures. Ed took the weapons and put them in the trunk. The entity put them where he wanted them, this happened several times, back and forth.

"You don't have hands, how are you putting them back and my bumper looks like shrapnel went through it," Ed said with disgust on his face.

"Me need to get food," said Trotting Fox.

"Johnny, Georgie, tell Trotting Fox he is dead; tell him to his face!" Ed babbled.

"He doesn't have a face," Georgie mentioned.

"Alright just tell him."

Georgie spoke up, "You don't need to hunt for food, Trotting Fox, you have no mouth."

Johnny surprised his mom and dad by what he said, "Look, Mom and Dad, these are great Indian artifacts, why not allow Trotting Fox this one concession?"

Ed Two Buck grabbing his hair and mumbling to himself, reluctantly got back in the car. Ed's face was red and the driver's window was down because of the smell given off by the Indian entity. Ed announced, "If he so much as touches those deadly weapons, I'll, well, I don't know what I'll do something to that thing, entity, ghost, whatever."

Everyone went quiet as Ed Two Buck pressed the metal to the floor of the car, he constantly was looking at the gash in his front fender and mumbling again to himself, the whole fender had to be changed. The noise in the car constantly increased. Johnny and Georgie kept laughing at the entity's mistake calling everything he didn't know junk in Zuni. "How did they get that white brave on the wall, funny clothes, ha-ha?"

"That is called a billboard and they are telling you to buy a product."

"What a product? What buy? This buggy goes fast? No horse? You have wampum, we get horse, no space. Let me out buggy, I want to scalp that white brave. Just too many white braves. Me, Trotting Fox scalp them all."

Johnny tried to look at Trotting Fox, he yelled, "Trotting Fox! Go back, Dad, Trotting Fox wants to scalp the guy on the billboard!"

Georgie rolled down the window and propelled himself out of the car while Ed Two Buck turned the car, or buggy in Trotting Fox's words, back. There on the billboard walkway, the white brave had been scalped and Georgie was shouting at the entity as Ed, Lisa and Johnny pulled up to the billboard in the car. Ed jumped out and screamed, "I told you, I will take you back get in the buggy, oh the car!"

"We are two hundred and fifty miles from the reservation," Johnny commented.

"Georgie and the entity, come to the car. Calm down everyone, I got it straight with Trotting Fox, we have to take him back to the reservation."

"Who makes the decisions here, I do," said Ed. "We're taking him back!"

"Me, no do again brave Two Buck me no."

Georgie spoke up, "I 'promise' that is the word you're looking for, Trotting Fox."

"Me promise, Me promise," said Trotting Fox.

Ed Two Buck got out of the car grabbed the tomahawk and slashed at the entity where he thought he sat in the backseat. Georgie and Johnny cringed to the sides of the car. The boys looked in amazement at Mr. Two Buck; they had never seen him so angry. "What will I tell Mr. Vance? Not only does he have a freak of nature, now he has two freaks to take care of. Why haven't you gone to the happy hunting ground?" pleaded Ed.

"Me go to ground Brave Two Buck, but they send me journey."

"For God's sake! Why?"

"Because me come to tell young braves not to fight white eyes they are like leaves on trees. They will die!"

Ed replied, "Did you!"

"Me save many braves, but killed by Running Wolf for not letting them fight, we on Zuni land for many moons."

Ed sat in the car playing with the radio then said, "Well, let's get going." He closed his door and put the pedal to the metal. Johnny and Georgie looked at the tomahawk stuck in the middle of the backseat, they slumped down, Georgie murmured to Johnny, "That's close."

In a whispering voice, "Me no kill white eyes."

"No," said Johnny. "Trotting Fox, you will live with a white brave, squaw and his children."

"Me no," TF said softly.

"I will be living with you in the same wigwam."

"They live wigwam, me see no wigwams."

Georgie thought for a moment, "A new word for you, Trotting Fox, house that is what you see along the trails. How do you see?"

"Me not know, going too fast," responded Trotting Fox.

The car quieted down for a while until Mrs. Two Buck began thinking of sleeping arrangements, she did not want this crazed entity in the same room even if he was a relation to either her or Ed. She thought that there was no way that thing can sleep in the car with the kids. She suddenly turned to Ed and said, "The boys can sleep in the car and we'll sleep in the motel, I won't have that thing looking at me while I'm asleep, it scares the life out of me."

Ed pulled into a nice motel.

Trotting Fox, "What place?"

"This is a wigwam on the trail where you sleep, one darkness on a long journey like our journey home," Johnny informed Trotting Fox. "Let's take Trotting Fox to the soda machine and show him a few tricks."

"TF, come," said Georgie; he inserted a quarter in the machine and a soda slid down and plunked at the take-out spot.

"What noise."

"That's a bottle of soda."

"What soda."

"Boy, this could go on forever." Johnny snapped the cap off in the bottle opener and took a drink.

"Brown water?" asked TF. "Brown water bad."

"No, no the water is made that way," Georgie told TF.

"Why call me TF?"

"That's short for Trotting Fox. You see it is the first letter in your name and your last name."

"What letter?"

"Never mind, I'll tell you later, from now on I'll call you TF." Johnny and Georgie agreed.

"Me Trotting Fox."

"I am Trotting Fox."

"Me know Trotting Fox, me, T.F. Not, Trotting Fox?"

"Well, let's let it go!" Georgie pulled out from his back pocket "Pop Rocks". Johnny drank about a quarter of the soda, then handed the soda bottle to Georgie. He pushed "Pop Rocks" down the throat of the bottle, shook it and fired right through TF. TF sounded like a firecracker. "You know water spirit, got gone bad brown water."

Georgie and Johnny looked at each other and laughed. Georgie asked T.F. to go into the soda machine and push some bottles down, "You want bad brown water?" asked T.F.

"Yes!" Georgie and Johnny nodded and heard a clank and rumble then six bad brown waters crashed to the take out opening, to the delight of the boys. "Let's show TF the ice machine. TF, I want you to sit right here and look up, can you see the hole?"

"Me can't."

"Yes, you can, you don't have a solid body."

"Me Try."

Georgie pushed the handle for ice. The ice came tumbling down. "Death come to get me," said a trembling TF. "Hard water in the hotness summer, me cold."

Chapter 48

The family car of the Two Bucks pulled into the driveway of Mr. and Mrs. Victor Vance's, hoping that the Vance family will accept their new responsibility, that of an Indian entity who hated white eyes. Everyone in the car had a cold feeling stemming from the ice machine negativity. Ed Two Buck and Georgie got out of the car. Jan Vance opened the house door to greet them and hugged Georgie and Ed. While Lisa nervously opened the passenger side door slowly. "Is Lisa sick?" asked Jan.

"Ah no," said Ed. "She's just nervous."

"What about?"

"Well, I don't know how to say this but we picked up another guest. Can he stay at your house with Georgie?" Ed said in a pleading way while Lisa held her hand over her mouth looking almost in tears. Heather, Jason and Dad were playing ping pong in the family room and didn't hear them drive up, but once they heard the chatter at the front door and heard the familiar voices, they hurriedly came to the front door and hugged the Two Bucks and then Georgie, they felt an eerie cold intense feeling that practically made them jump out of their shoes.

"Don't blame me, it is Trotting Fox that made you feel that way."

"Who is Trotting Fox?" asked Jan Vance.

"He is an entity that survived death on the Zuni Reservation. He is two hundred and fifty years old or so."

"Where is he?" Victor had a concerned look on his face. "This isn't funny, Georgie."

"He hates white people! He thinks the war between the Indians and the white men is still going on," almost in tears Georgie said, "Come out, Trotting Fox, and meet my father."

"Me no think he father."

"Me not here."

Victor Vance looked behind Georgie left and right. Georgie giggled and said, "You can't see him."

Jason said, "Why not?"

"Because he doesn't have a body, he lives in my brain."

"Come on, this is getting scary," said Victor.

Jan moved back, "He can't hurt anyone, can he?"

"He can only speak." Georgie kept his fingers crossed behind his back.

"Ed, what did you do to this kid?"

"The only thing I can figure Georgie's brain transmits some extraordinary brainwaves because there were two entities, but one couldn't leave the reservation. This one wanted to haunt Johnny and he knew Georgie's brain is not Indian. We insisted that he stay with Georgie although he preferred Johnny."

"Ed, can't you take care of anything that's Indian!" complained Vic Vance.

"Now look Vic, your primordial soup created this problem," said a red in the face Ed Two Buck.

"I took my problem and faced it. Now you brought this problem back and you want me to handle it."

"Me stay Johnny and Indians, not white man," replied Trotting Fox.

"I refuse to have a freak in my house, you Vic have a freak."

"What Freak?" a voice came out of nowhere.

"A creep?"

"What creep?" asked T.F.

"They're talking about you and me, TF. In a bad way," Georgie said.

The invisible entity began making weird sounds that made the superstitious Ed and Lisa Two Buck leave without saying another word. Victor, Jan, Jason, Heather and Georgie, not forgetting TF, looked amazed as the Two Bucks drove away.

"White man tries to kill me because me am Indian, will kill," T.F. said.

Victor looked around and asked, "Who said that? Did you take up ventriloquism?" demanded Victor Vance.

"No Dad, the entity is real, not make believe or not just a voice I made up while I was away." Tanny came to the front door and began growling. Georgie said no to the dog and she quietened down, but was uneasy.

"Its real Dad holds my throat," a voice said. "No hurt Indian without Indian brain."

A cold wind swept over the Vance family. "Dad, I am the same kid that left home with the Two Bucks and I'm not going to change. I'm younger physically than Johnny but mentally, I'm much older than Johnny and this Indian spirit is good, if only you let him prove himself. He won't eat anything, he doesn't need a bedroom, he and the dog are with me, he will clean up."

Victor Vance put his arm around Georgie and said, "T.F. I'm OK, come."

As they walked up the steps, Jason and Heather said, "Wow, you got to tell us what happened on your trip; it must have been exciting."

"The strangest thing no one lives on the reservation except two spirits. I'll tell you the rest later, I'm starving."

"Me go with Georgie," T.F. said.

Mrs. Vance slipped into the kitchen and made two sandwiches for Georgie. Everyone kept close to Georgie, they wanted to meet a 250-year-old. Mrs. Vance put a glass of milk on the table. Georgie said, "Trotting Fox, meet the Vances—Jan, Victor, Jason, and Heather," he pointed to each person.

"Zuni no like white."

"TF, I won't stand for your hate; these are my friends."

"Sure, they attack you in your sleep?"

"No Trotting Fox, you saw Jan Vance give me food. Now you got me talking funny," Georgie laughed.

"The grandparents of Ed and Lisa are fine people and are just as superstitious as Ed and Lisa, maybe more. They told Trotting Fox that if he couldn't master some of the English language overnight from a Zuni to English dictionary, they would send him back to the reservation with the bad entity in the morning," Georgie responded.

"Now how do you tell something or someone to go back?" asked Dad.

"Ed and Lisa's parents are descendants of the council members and apparently, they have the power to send him back. Johnny, who speaks some Zuni, taught Trotting Fox to speak English by morning."

"Me not something or someone. Me Trotting Fox!"

Victor Vance mentioned just a small thing, "Why would you bring something like this home? It's not like bringing a fish home or a bunny home, but a ghost, home?"

Georgie pondered for several seconds, stopped eating his sandwich, "We thought he could help us at school and help find my brother that killed me and my mother and my dogs."

"Kill is a very serious word in this house, Georgie, you talk as though you hate, just like Trotting Fox. Somehow, someway, you got a second chance for life; now you want to spurn your second chance?"

"I don't want to lose my second chance for life, you all have been so wonderful to me, I'll never forget what you have done in sickness and health."

Chapter 49

It was that morning that came every September, school began anew. Heather, Jason and Georgie sat in the backseat of the car while Victor Vance made his way to the Two Bucks' house to pick up Johnny. Johnny and Georgie acted like nothing happened over the summer. They were so happy to see one another neither Jason or Heather could break into their conversation. Johnny said, "How has TF been?"

Georgie rattled on, "The funniest thing that happened at home, we tried to explain what the toilet is, it took two days. TF thought it was a well. Then he had a hard time understanding what is the white thing around the water. He thought you stuck your head in it to get a drink."

Johnny and Georgie laughed all the way to school. Mr. Vance dropped them off. He had to take Jason and Heather to the high school, it took another five minutes and he said goodbye to Heather and Jason and drove back to the middle school. Thinking to himself, *I don't know how I'll be able to pay for college for those two, then of course there's*...just as he pulled into the school's parking lot.

Victor thought, *There's Georgie in a few more years*. He made it to his classroom, then he looked at two boys that were ready to square off, before he tried to unlock the door, he saw that confrontation had started, he said in a loud voice, "Stop already!"

Some of the crowd disappeared after hearing his voice. Victor Vance ran up to see what the source of the commotion was, he held his head when he saw the giant boys Peter and Paul, daring Johnny and Georgie to punch them, "Come on, you god damn Indians, you got away from us last year, we got you now."

A wind so powerful, it blew dust in Peter's eyes then Paul's. Everyone ran to their classroom thinking tornado, even Georgie and Johnny disappeared. "Boys, what are you doing?"

"Nothing Mr. Vance, we got dust in our eyes and the others tried to help."

"See that the both of you stay out of trouble so you make it to the high school next year."

"Mr. Vance, we never cause any trouble."

"See that you don't."

Miss Syndly stepped out of the Administration building and said, "Are these boys causing trouble the first day of school?"

Peter and Paul looked at Mr. Vance as he answered Miss Syndly's question, "There was some words said between the boys and Johnny and his twin brother but dust got in their eyes and nothing was said after that."

"So, everything is settled?"

Peter and Paul said it in unison, "Yes Miss Syndly." Peter and Paul put on their best smile, "Going to class now."

As Miss Syndly walked around the campus making sure all the new students found their way. Mr. Vance said, "Was that you that stirred up the dust, TF?"

"Yes, me do it, mighty brave Vance."

"Now go find Georgie. I am going to my classroom."

"Where find?"

"I don't know, I saw him go to D wing; there are only four classrooms just look through the door windows." Victor opened his door and Johnny was standing beside him. "What happened?"

"Oh, Peter and Paul were going to punch our lights out."

"Just as I thought."

"Did TF create the wind?"

"Yes."

"Georgie told me that he instructed Trotting Fox to blow at anyone causing trouble for him or me inside or out the classroom. Georgie requested TF, 'Hold anything thrown and throw it back.' TF said when he was young at lessons, they practiced on the reservation, things thrown, catch objects and throw back. Throwing them back is no easy task for TF."

"Where is TF now?"

Johnny signaled with a whistle and TF said, "Me here, brave Vance."

"Don't throw objects back. Do not, Trotting Fox," said Mr. Vance.

"Why so many tepees?"

"Many students," answered Mr. Vance.

"Hard and old dried-up squaw make powwow and talk much bad to brave Vance me no like."

"Don't worry about the dried-up Miss Syndly. Don't say that or sometime you'll slip," replied Johnny.

"Miss Syndly is a nice person," Mr. Vance answered TF. Johnny and Mr. Vance went into the classroom and took the chairs off the tables. Victor Vance's class enrollment was heavy because so many students liked the curriculum he offered and particularly the variety that he offered at the same time. The bell rang and in seconds, students began entering into the classroom.

This was Mr. Vance's tenth year in the classroom and he had been through eight principals and six assistant principals and five counselors. Some were good and some not so good. Criticism of their administrators brought them grief to no end, because some of the not so good administrators got their positions by extracurricular activities. At closed door meetings, some administrators took suggestions and recommendations well and were used when practical.

Victor Vance thought of becoming administrator but he thought he will miss the students and their fantastic ideas and the pleasure of working with them, seeing their creations blossom into something beautiful and being sad if they didn't work out. Things ran through his mind; students filled his classroom with joy as they sparkled and wanted to have new experiences. *My day is full*, thought Victor Vance. *Imagine, a mixture of juice brought me another child, Georgie.*

The students were delighted with the subject matter and the presentation. At the end of the day, Mr. Vance waited for Georgie and TF. Georgie told a tale in an instant, "I answered three questions in math. Two questions in history about the Grand Canyon. Johnny answered on the depth and geology of the canyon. Science wasn't so good; neither one of us knew anything on the periodic table; what's that table about helium and hydrogen and so on?"

"Oh, you mean the periodic table and all the elements we know and one is a secret in this room. We've got to keep our compound a secret."

"I'm not sure what it is," replied Georgie.

"What you were born in, Georgie," answered Dad.

"I am filling with leaves. I need to get rid of them." Georgie walked up to the big wastebasket and shot leaves, he turned silver green and flashed a silver green beam out through the opened patio door up into the heavens.

"Hope I didn't hit any Greek gods."

"Where did you pick up Greek gods?" asked Mr. Vance.

"In the reading class actually, in Mr. Wolfe's class, the guy with the small red rubber ball with a rubber string, he hit Babs and Beth twice and he has a good sense of humor. You know, I could get to like this guy."

"What about you, TF?"

"Me know what red thing is?"

Everyone pointed a finger at TF, of course, at Georgie's head. While Georgie and Johnny attempted to explain, Dad Vance opened a locker and pulled the old paddle and red ball attached with rubber string. He began to bat the ball with the paddle. TF said, "No not me do!"

"You can't do it, Trotting Fox, you have no hands."

"Me do." Victor Vance handed the paddle and ball into the air. The paddle fell on the floor but the rubber string and ball moved toward the door and out. "I go use."

"Wait TF..." but the red ball disappeared down the hall toward Georgie's and Johnny's math class; soon, the math teacher came screaming out of his classroom. Then the history teacher, the same, several seconds later the teacher that started the rubber ball in the head came rushing out swinging his rubber ball around his head attempting to ward off TF's ball. Things with strings got tangled up. Mr. Wolfe finally got the best of TF and came running down the hallway and stopped suddenly.

Something was pulling on the tangled red rubber balls. "What's that in your hand?" asked Victor Vance.

"Oh, that's two red rubber balls, I started out with one; all of a sudden, I was fighting with something in the air and I had two. Something is trying to pull the balls from my hand."

Mr. Vance didn't let on he knew anything of this extraordinary experience. He grabbed the balls away from Mr. Wolfe, wrapped the strings around the balls. Mr. Wolfe pointed his chubby finger at Victor Vance just as Vance gave the balls back to Mr. Wolfe. "By the way, Mr. Wolfe, what is your first name? My name is Vic."

"Aah...ah mine is Fred."

Georgie and Johnny said, "Hi."

Mr. Wolfe ran to his car. "Me wanted reds balls with magic pull and go."

Mr. Ritz came running by saying, "I got to get to the sidewalk."

"Bus loading?" Victor assumed.

"No, cigarette," Mr. Ritz said with a smile.

Chapter 50

Mrs. Weeks, an English teacher, started doing collages with her students, all feminine, and in 1978, that meant taking procession and stand up for women's rights in every way. One week later, Mrs. Weeks' class came out, carrying signs on sticks, stating this week was women's rights week. While they were marching around the campus singing a rights song, Babs and Beth at the head of the parade with the teacher singing as loud she could. Trotting Fox came out of another classroom, he had fallen in love with two squaws, that's right—Beth and Babs.

The vice-principal constantly finding Peter and Paul wobbling and generally looking drunk but they claimed they had been hit with something flashing red, then disappearing. "My head feels like the paddle with a ball attached," as Paul slowly sank to the grass. Peter stood beside Paul holding his head.

The ever-happy entity, sporting new confidence, whacked Mrs. Weeks in the head and hid behind a tree even though you can't see him. While Mrs. Weeks turned around to see who the culprit was, thinking some boy hiding between the girls.

Miss Syndly heard the singing, she stomped out like she usually does knowing Mrs. Weeks barely taught any English in her classroom, walked out of the administration building and stepped in front of Mrs. Weeks and said, "I see you are a member of the 'Women Rights Organization'. I am too." Miss Syndly suddenly grabbed the back of her head and what does she have in her hand—a little red ball with a rubber string. She looked around, heard no running footsteps, no one hiding under the bench. "Funny, something must have come over the building," thought Miss Syndly.

The girls stood in awe, one said, "She does have eyes in the back of her head!"

Miss Syndly made sure everyone made it to class. TF resting in the tree lamenting losing the fun thing, picked leaves, then floated down to C5 Mr. Vance's classroom, thinking he might be able to get another red ball from Brave Vance. Suddenly, he thought first time in two hundred and fifty years other than attacking. It was a sneaky idea. "Me go in great building and take back ball."

Mrs. Weeks had all girls in the class, after a long speech on women superiority, pick up their placards for another outing around campus. Mrs. Weeks picked up a can and some rags and came out of the classroom last. Now her speech upset some of the girls and the others agreed so as the class ended, the girls marched as they always did when they reached the middle of the campus quad, it was the eighth-grade lunch; the girls ripped off their bras and placed them in a nice neat pile.

Mrs. Weeks poured kerosene on the bras and lit them on fire. The girls started running around yelling, "I'm free." The eighth-grade boys saw their chance, groped all without bras and cheered loudly as they passed the girls to the cafeteria. A girl came running to Mr. Vance's class and said, "I'll never do that again, the eighth-grade boys are crazy."

Mrs. Weeks was asked to leave her position as English teacher while the girl's parents stormed the administration building.

Chapter 51

Victor Vance, after all the screaming on campus and accusations flying back and forth in a violent manner that he had never seen before on campus with parents showing up and asking questions that should never be asked at a middle school. The parents had the custodians pinned against the wall. Miss Syndly had so many parents in her office that TF had trouble finding the little red ball and the rubber string. TF heard words that weren't in his dictionary, they seemed to be little four letters that the Vance family never used or the Two Bucks.

The words were used by women screaming or a man's high-volume low voice. Even the noise bothered TF as he searched the office, he noticed prune face or stinky, Miss Syndly heard words like, "Fire that woman before she turns this place into something other than a school," and then more small words that the very old Indian entity did not understand.

No one seemed to notice that drawers were being opened, papers on the desk moved. The commotion in the assistant principal's office was just as loud as the principal's office. Then TF saw it, the rubber string and red rubber ball wrapped around Miss Syndly's right foot and she was trying to shake it off. TF was down on the floor scrambling between feet; of course, everyone was stepping through him. He managed to grab the little red ball, TF said to himself, *How am I going to unravel that rubber string? Maybe I'll tickle her foot or I'll just make a horrible sound and she'll jump up and I'll unwrap the string.*

He sat under the desk and thought, *What horrible sound do I know?* It hit him like a rock, where did the ball come from? It came the Wolfe man. Then from the bowels of the entity. It startled the ten parents as they stared intently at Miss Syndly, they thought they saw some changes in her face, the parents scrambled for the door.

TF unwound the rubber string and slipped it through the half-opened window. The torrent of noise of the wolf call had Miss Syndly on top of her desk, reaching for the ceiling after she stopped screaming. Dead silence in the office, the secretaries left, Miss Syndly left, even the vice principal, all the parents gone. If you looked closely, you could see a red spot coming down the hallway toward C5. Sparking erupted from C5 as the entity approached, lightning struck through the south window of C5 once again.

Smoking letters were carved into the floor of the room. Wide-eyed, Georgie said out loud in a determined voice, "Joey." He stood over the letters, his body shaking, his eyes blinking, Georgie said out loud, "Amazing, first Dad, how do you do it?"

Victor Vance walked over to Georgie and said, "Your hair is standing on end."

Georgie looked up and laughed, "So is yours, Dad."

Johnny and the entity opened the C5 door laughing, the little red ball hanging in the air. Johnny said, "What's that smoking on the floor?"

"It's a name from my past; something I have never spoken of," Georgie said with almost tears in his eyes.

"Me hate light and noise from sky," moaned the entity.

So many bad memories flooded back into Georgie's mind. "I laughed at our hair standing on end but it isn't funny; that's my brother's name," said a now anxious Georgie.

Victor Vance looking at the now smoking letter in the cement said, "Someone sent us a message concerning the killer?"

"Yes," Georgie was almost vomiting. "That must stand for my brother, why would my dad send me a message?" Georgie grabbed a stool and slumped holding his head. "I thought this would never come."

"Georgie, everything can be solved," said Victor Vance.

Georgie looked at his father and murmured, "He must be close."

Chapter 52

Johnny had heard of Billy Mills, the Indian winning many foot races, then a gold medal in the mile of the Olympics and since both had good foot speed; of course, Georgie was without a peer. Both bought the same running shoes. Georgie never outran Johnny, they reported to the coach every day. Georgie couldn't get the name Joey out of his mind. It was like someone took a branding iron and burned the name into his frontal lobe, no matter which way he turned his eyes, it blazed through.

At times, Johnny had to grab Georgie to direct him in the right direction. Georgie began lagging behind the other runners, while Johnny led the pack. This went on for several practices, the coach was ready to ask Georgie Vance to leave, he had ten good runners that included Johnny, who was the top runner. He asked the coach not to let Georgie go; he had the kissing disease and he was just starting to feel better.

"We have ten uniforms, if he continues, he'll have to run in his sweats."

Georgie being the eleventh member on a ten-man squad was not the best position to be in, said the coach.

"Thank you coach, I appreciate it and you won't be sorry," replied the grateful Johnny. He led Georgie away with the coach shaking his head. The days dragged on for Georgie, thinking of the name on the floor, he didn't like to go in C5 even though Dad, Mr. Vance, filled in the name on the cement floor in C5. Miss Syndly inspected rooms daily, once she spotted the name, "Joey," etched in Victor Vance's room, every day gave Dad trouble, every morning. Miss Syndly was at the door, Dad opened the classroom and she said the very same words each morning, "How could you allow something like this to happen?"

Mr. Vance told her the truth, "It is a lightning strike."

"How could two lightning strikes happen in the same place two years apart?" Miss Syndly thought she had him on this one. She thought, *Why is he so popular with the kids, it's just disgusting.*

Victor Vance pleaded his case, "Look at the window, two holes not one, but two. They are too small for a ball and too big for bullet holes, they are from lightning. The first one struck the cabinet, the other struck the floor."

Miss Syndly gave Victor Vance the suspicious eye and left the room. Johnny said, "Good thing she didn't look in the cabinet. That fish eye gives me the willies," exclaimed Johnny, expressing his opinion.

The day before the first cross-country event, the coach called Georgie and Johnny in his office, "Beth and Babs tell me that Peter and Paul are faster than you two."

Beth and Babs were standing by the coach's desk smirking at Georgie and Johnny. "Are you going to take the word of two campus queens who spread indignities throughout the school on a daily basis?"

Beth standing close to the coach's desk asked coach. "What does the word indignities mean, honey?" She threw an eraser at Georgie while the coach wasn't looking. The coach looked back at Beth with a sweet smile on his face, Georgie caught the eraser between his teeth and put the eraser behind his ear.

"Coach, could you look this way, I know Beth is cuter than me, but the problem is Melvin and I are running, not Beth."

The coach cleared his throat and said, "Sorry boys, I'll have to drop Georgie and Melvin."

"I challenge both of them right now," Georgie just about gave the coach a shower.

"Hmm, let's wait till after school." Georgie and Johnny walked out of the coach's office staring at their two obnoxious school mates. Peter and Paul chewed their gum as though they were going to spit it at them. Paul mouthed up, "We'll crush you two after school."

Georgie almost ripped the door off C5 as he turned the doorknob. It was Victor Vance's prep period and he was setting up the shark and fingernail show for the new seventh-graders. "Those two girls get everything they want; they can twist male teachers' minds with their bodies and their facial beauty. Do they have their own hairstylist?"

"Boys, while you're both handsome in your own right, those girls are sisters in something you didn't know because they have different last names like you two. Peter and Paul are not brothers, they think because they are taller than everyone else, they should command all the attention not only from the women teachers but the males also."

"That's what happened; the cross-country coach got hypnotized by Beth and Babs. They told the coach that Peter and Paul are better runners then Georgie and Melvin," Johnny expressed his opinion about Beth and Babs. "They are stinkers!"

"The coach who is in charge of the squad, told Johnny the leader to drop Georgie and Melvin. Georgie challenged Peter and Paul to a cross-country duel after school and thought Melvin would do the same," said the red in the face Johnny.

Georgie looked up at the ceiling where the little red ball rested on the light, "Trotting Fox, if you leave the ball on the light too long it might stick."

"Me move."

Dad Vance said, "It should be no contest, Georgie."

"I think I'll ask TF to come with me."

"Me go," TF chattered.

Georgie and Johnny left to go to math, the entity not far behind. At the door stood Peter and Paul and of course, the campus queens, Peter with a laughing smile on his face and a joyful expression in his voice remarked, "Johnny is going to cut you from the cross-country team." Then a snicker crossed Beth's and Bab's faces. Georgie just stared at all four of them, knowing what will happen in the race.

Mr. Clancy was sitting at his desk and jumped up realizing that his duty was to stand by his door to watch the comings and goings of the students. He looked to his left and sees Peter and Paul blocking the way to his room. Students to the right were OK. Peter looked at his watch and tugged on Paul's sleeve; the bell rang. Peter and Paul ran for the classroom, figuring that Georgie and Johnny would get detention there by forfeiting spots on the cross-country team.

Mr. Clancy saw it differently and gave Peter, Paul, Babs and Beth detentions slips and called the detentions into the office. Mr. Clancy, tired of the comments in class and the feeling of irritation by all the students toward the four, brought cheers from everyone in the class. Mr. Clancy really got hostile when he said, "If either one of you says another word to anyone, you'll get detention for a week!"

Paul sent a note on his charting paper by way of the campus queens stating that this game was not over, knowing that if you punched the time clock earlier then the Indian boys could get one up on them. Paul got up near the end of the class and asked, "Since everyone has their work done, could Johnny tell us about his summer vacation?"

Mr. Clancy looked around the classroom, everyone was on the edge of their seat and ready to go when the bell rang. He reluctantly said, "Yes."

Johnny looked around the room seeing everyone was about to fly from their seats and said, "We took a trip to a Zuni reservation and the most interesting things about the res—" The bell rang and everyone scurried out except Jamie, he ran in and out, he forgot his brown bag lunch under his desk.

"I didn't quite hear what you said about the Zuni reservation?"

"Mr. Clancy, we have to go serve the detention."

"Boys, bring your detention slips up to my desk." He tore them up. "Don't tell anyone I'll write a note to Miss Yerkes the vice-principal that I suspended your detentions, they are on the absent slip."

"Remember now, you put the most hated foursome in the school on detention."

"When they see that we aren't there, they'll plot some other devious scheme to do us in, Mr. Clancy. We have a chance to beat them at their own game in just a few minutes. So may we go now?"

As they walked out of math class, Georgie said, "We'll take the shortcut." Georgie grabbed Johnny around the waist since there was no one on the campus, he lifted Johnny and landed in the atrium of the administration building and they quietly sat down and waited for the Vice-principal to check them off. Minutes later, other students walked in the detention room—a couple of burly kids from the football team, Tad and Mike, the two queens, two kids from the chess club, that started a fight over who won the chess game between the two.

Paul and Peter who sat beside the football players said a couple of words then Mike came over to Georgie and took a swing at him, missed and quickly sat down, Paul with his hand over his mouth. "I thought running backs are quicker than that?"

Mike got up again but the vice-principal opened the door and said, "Ladies and gentlemen, you have one hour," and closed the door.

Immediately, Mike got up, swung at Georgie and missed to the left again, then he missed to the right. Georgie said, "Do you want to try again, Mike?"

"You can bet on that, Georgie."

"You got any money on you?"

"Yea ten bucks," replied Mike in a cocksure voice.

"Put your money where your mouth is!"

"Where's yours?" demanded Mike.

Georgie pulled out his wallet. Mike swung at Georgie again, this time he stuck his fist through the window of the detention room door. Blood spurting from Mike's hand; the vice-principal came in again. "Who started it?"

Beth and Babs pointed at Georgie. "I hardly think so, look how small the Indian boys are. I bet either Peter or Paul instigated this attack."

"I'm the only one hurt," pleaded Mike. He turned his eyes on Paul and Peter, they began fidgeting, Tad moved closer and Mike left the room for the nurse's office guided by the vice-principal. At the hour's end, Peter and Paul were frightened and won't leave the detention room. Mike now with a cast on his hand was seated by Tad and Paul. "How did she know?" Paul said with an excuse me voice.

The detention door opened and the vice-principal said, "Georgie and Johnny can go."

"Sorry about your hand," Georgie politely said. Mike gave Georgie a dirty look but said nothing. Both Johnny and Georgie ran down to C5 with TF following with the little red ball.

TF said, "Me know understand the best thing?"

Chapter 53
The Race

The coach got up to leave when he heard running feet. Georgie and Johnny opened the coach's office door and offered their excuse. The coach put his feet on his desk and looked at the boys. "Do you really think you can beat Peter and Paul?"

Georgie looked back at the coach. "We wouldn't be here if we didn't think we could beat them," Georgie spoke his last word, running feet were heard again outside the coach's office, the out of breath Peter and Paul.

"OK, let's get this over, down to the starting line." The coach took his feet off the table, grabbed his stopwatch and said as the boys stood at the starting line, "This is a six-mile course, it is marked, I expect the winners to be back in thirty-three minutes. Ready, set, go."

Georgie and Johnny let Peter and Paul exit the track and hit the road first but passed them running down Elm Street. They tried to defend their position by throwing some lefts and rights at the Indians but they jumped past like gazelles.

Beth called her mother and told her to bring the convertible. "Bring four quarts of oil from the garage and hurry to the school to pick us up. We'll be standing in the principal's parking spot." Beth and Babs screamed, "Hurry!"

Georgie and Johnny were safely ahead, they saw no problems except the constant bickering from Trotting Fox, "Me beat you when I live. Me no see trails just hard flat rock. Me no see white flat rock when me alive. Me remember black rock, me no remember flat."

Georgie could see the little red ball following them. "Cut the chatter, we are busy."

"No busy what busy?"

Johnny and Georgie said nothing to TF. TF just bounced the little red ball on their heads. They came to a steep hill as they turned on to Maple St., Johnny jumped at the top of the hill preparing to run as fast as he could when they heard cheering across the street. Johnny looked and saw oil on the sidewalk, Georgie grabbed Johnny under his left armpit but staying on his right side and just as his feet were to touch the sidewalk, Georgie said, "Make sure you look like you're running; I will too."

Georgie shot the silver-green light out and caught the oil on fire as the laughs across street in the convertible turned into four-letter words as they ran merrily along. Peter and Paul were stopped at the top of the hill watching the fire. Neighbors ran out, turned on their hoses and washed down the sidewalk. Georgie and Johnny turned onto Old Main St. on the way back to the school, Johnny mustered enough energy. "Hold it down, I'm out of breath, besides we'll set a school record; we don't want to do that, someone might get suspicious."

"You're right, let's let them catch up and just barely outrun them at the end," Georgie replied."

"Slow down and walk a while, Georgie. I'm just normal that's why I'm breathing hard!"

"Yes, yes."

Walking was not TF's favorite. He liked to move through the atmosphere faster because the atmospheric conditions seemed to tantalize something in the electrons, neutrons and protons in his conglomerate makeup. If he moved fast, he felt solid and this made TF happy.

TF can't understand why no one liked his dog in the shoe box just because the dog had been dead for two hundred and fifty years. He tried to resurrect his dog named Arrow. An arrow came down landed on a duck, the dog was under the duck and the arrow pierced the dog too. The duck was trying to fly. The dog was howling and jumping around. Trotting Fox named the duck Arrow too just before he ate it; that is, he tried to eat it. The dog ate the duck. *My dog Arrow is bad at hunts. My dog can no longer do its daffy tricks such as pee on your leg or defecate on your dinner, that wasn't so funny.* Then Trotting Fox realized he shot the dog with two arrows. O the life of the brave. "Me not so much."

"What a memory I have," thought TF.

Johnny looked at the little red ball and said, "Why did you give us the story of the dog?"

"Me have no other to give."

"You mean I have something else to give," said Georgie.

Johnny shook Georgie's shoulder, "They're coming, move faster." Peter and Paul really turned it on.

"Think Billy Mills, Johnny," said Georgie. They ran like they never ran before; they heard their large-footed, not so friendly friends pumping hard to catch up to them. Rounding into the track, they can see the coach, watch in hand, and getting off the bleachers right in front of finish line. Georgie and Johnny running side by side. Georgie helped Johnny along the way, Johnny was sprinting as hard as Georgie and beat Georgie to the finish line. Trotting Fox came in third. Little does Peter and Paul know they came in fourth and fifth.

"Coach, they cheated, something kept hitting them on the head that pushed them to run faster!"

But by this time Trotting Fox hid in a tree out of sight. "Come on boys, that's hardly a believable story."

"Coach, you don't think we'd lie to you?" The Coach gave a Peter and Paul a slow burn look.

The next few days were uneventful in the life of the two school boys, one normal, one different, but identical in looks. Peter and Paul walked around campus slapping each other on the top of the head and saying, "Run faster." This amused the two blond-haired giants. That was what TF called them after the race. "Passed young brave test salty sweat in eyes."

"Where did you pick up that phrase, TF?"

"Me, no word, fake. Me no talk."

"Just keep coming to the English class so we can both figure English out." Trotting Fox tweeted in his ear—damn language. "You know the word language?"

"Me know word from old Indian braves and squaws from tribal land."

Georgie thought for a moment and said, "I think you have learned more in the English class then I have since grade one," said Georgie.

While Paul and Peter lamented their loss. They had a physical complaint, they told everyone they slipped on fiery tar and burned their feet, their butts, of course, they couldn't show their supposed injuries. Babs and Beth took a different tact, they kept teasing Georgie and Johnny by calling them names, not insulting names, because they know that they would get into serious trouble and possibly spend time at the continuation school. So, Beth and Babs thought brush cut, prickly top, grease down. Both Johnny and Georgie liked plaid shirts. Georgie called Babs nice babe and Beth tootsie; these names were spoken in servility. The boys wanted no enemies and didn't want to be antagonistic to anyone.

Chapter 54
Run

The day came for the first cross-country meet at the park. Since Johnny and Georgie were side by side with Peter and Paul, the coach allowed them to compete anyway, the girls were running with the boys at this meet. Three schools, Lincoln High School, Washington High School, and the Long Mountain Middle School. The middle school qualified over a high school, this was very rare. The high school kids laughed at the group from the middle school; they yelled, "No chance," in a group.

They patted them on the head, Georgie said to Peter and Paul, "How does it feel to be low on the totem pole?"

Peter spoke up through the chatter and rowdy high school bearded boys and the girls with their flashy bobbles and beads, "I'm a mouse now, I'll be in that group in a few years."

"Intimidation now?"

"I might not be able to beat you but I know I can beat some of them. The coach wouldn't allow us to be here if he didn't think we had good respectable numbers."

Paul looked at Georgie with horror on his face and said, "The coach did this to get even?"

Georgie looked over and said, "maybe!"

The gun went off, some of the high school kids looked at the intermediate kid runners and laughed, "Later, turtles and rabbits are off."

"Hares stupid!" Beth spewed. One of the very muscular females came back and was about to punch Beth when one of the coaches caught the fist in mid-air and yelled, "Naughty-naughty," and blurted, "You're out, get off the field." He said that after she tried to kick him in the shin. The race led them into a forest that surrounded the park, a wide pathway between the trees expressly for cross-country.

The ladies were falling behind the men with several exceptions, the younger students were falling behind everyone but one exception, Georgie, who was right behind the leaders and gaining, there didn't seem to be any shoving or pushing in the front group of runners, they seemed sincere in their effort until that puny Indian showed up in the middle of the front runners, then all hell broke loose.

"Get out of the way, punk. Fall back, Jack, scam Sam, you're in the way shorty."

Then as Georgie sped up, he noticed a truck in the trees and some kids standing around it, a hand reached out of the truck doling out small packets and money going the other way. He kept running, he looked back, he ran into a tree and laughter spread through the slower high school kids; some had concern on their faces as they yelled back, "He knocked himself out!"

The medics came down the path to pick up Georgie lying on the ground, between two trees, he kept saying, "I saw the ring."

Trotting Fox bopped Georgie on the head with the little red ball while lying on the ground. He sat up with a burst, "I know that ring, TF, follow me." Johnny saw Georgie run through the trees to the street at a speed even TF couldn't match. The truck driver noticed through his rear-view mirror, cars slamming on their brakes nearly causing accidents. The tires squealing something was catching up to the truck in the forest. The driver's speed reached seventy miles an hour, passed a few cars, the truck driver saw no problems behind him.

Georgie knew that even he can't run down a truck at that speed. He made a mad dash back to the race. TF saw Georgie and hit him with the ball, Georgie looked back and said, "Thanks for reminding me who I am. I'm just a weirdly cloned Indian boy."

Johnny screamed as Georgie started coming back through the trees, "Change back!"

He said to himself change what? Then he looked down at his right hand and said silver-green boy. He closed his eyes and concentrated; the next thing he was on the ground. Two medical people were again picking him up. "Look at those two bumps on his head."

Georgie was hosted on to the gurney, the face of his Indian brother appeared and said, "How did you get into this mess? It looks like you're growing two horns like elks back on the reservation."

"Yea, the trees jumped in front of me."

"You can laugh, young man, concussion is the worst when you're forty-five; that's when they gain ground on your brain," the medical man gave his speech as he tried to put Georgie into the ambulance. Georgie flew off the nice portable bed, grabbed Johnny around the waist and said to Johnny, "Pretend to run."

Georgie ran so fast, he was at the finish line before they can get the gurney back in the emergency wagon. Johnny and Georgie were standing around with the other runners after the race when they heard from the forest a loud voice yelling, "I'm not last! I'm not last!" A mildly portly girl appeared from the trees walking to the finish line. She walked fast.

Chapter 55
Hurt

Mrs. Vance took a plastic bag filled with ice and put it on Georgie's large bumps, she tied a strip of towel that Jason tore off a bath towel. "Really mom, before we get in the car, the bumps will be gone."

"Just the same, it's better to be safe and smart." The towel strip and ice fell off.

Victor Vance asked, "What happened in the forest primeval?"

"I saw my brother, at least I think I saw him. I didn't see his face but I saw a hand with a ring just like the ring my brother wore. This person in the pickup truck was handing out small packets. Boys and girls were passing money to the hand with the ring. That ring scared me in so many places my face looked like mincemeat, my chest a shambles. My place in life after we got away from my mother is in a dumpster.

"My mother put Joey in juvenile hall at least four times. He has been incorrigible and I'm afraid he still is. I don't think he has ever considered a regular job. He might hold down a job on the side, he has been trained as a carpenter and an electrician. I saw no signs on the side of the truck. After school, I'll be searching here and the towns around us."

Mr. Vance thought for a moment and said, "I'll drive you if want?"

"No Dad, I don't think this kind of thing you should be involved in, they may fire you and what will this make me, Dad?"

Heather after catching her breath after the race, "Dad, I am sure Georgie in his previous life has much more experience in this sort of affair, besides being killed by his own brother, he wouldn't hesitate to kill anyone that gets in his way."

"Dad, let Georgie look around before any decisions are made, he is very capable of staying out of danger than you are and this bus of a car is the slowest thing on the road."

Trotting Fox was sitting in the car. "Me go with Georgie me like hunt." TF proceeded to bop everyone on their heads with the little red ball.

School became a little less important to Georgie Vance. He had Dad stop at the closest gas station. Victor Vance gave Georgie two dollars to buy a map of the area so he could search in a precise manner. He also asked the gas station manager if he had a brochure of the brand of gas he and others sold. He shook his head yes and gave Georgie a brochure. This encouraged Georgie to ask every gas station owner about brochures. "Dad, I'll run to school. I need to increase my speed; I was slow chasing the pickup."

"OK but don't be late; you know how Miss Syndly is on being tardy, she'll be down to C5 chewing my ear off."

Georgie put the map and brochures in his backpack and began jogging. TF was right behind him, yes, the little red ball was being bounced on Georgie's head. The crowded busy streets had lots of pedestrians and traffic. Not thinking, Georgie jumped over a car and of course, TF, still with the ball, hit a lady jogging. She came up and asked Georgie, "How do you hit me in the head with the ball and jump over a car at the same time?"

"It's a secret, lady." Georgie wanted to turn on the speed but the lady stayed with him for the longest time; finally, the lady stopped breathing hard. Georgie turned the corner then down an alley out of sight, he blasted down the alley stirring up paper and trash. The lady following Georgie couldn't see down the alley and thought how did a wind stir up so much of a mess, where there was no wind? Georgie just barely touching the ground, Trotting Fox held on to Georgie's head, "Me like wind in face, no like things going through me."

"You have no body and no face; how can you hold on to my head?"

"Me know how." Georgie came out of the alley, he saw a pickup truck a man with his hand and arm out the window with a ring on his finger, not thinking he ran up to the truck and checked the ring out and said, "Sorry, wrong ring." The startled man pushed the accelerator to the floor, Georgie jumped over the bed of the truck, causing the driver to slam on his brakes leaving skid marks thirty feet long.

The driver looked around and said, "Where did that kid go?"

Georgie looked at his watch, *I'll be late for school and have to face Miss Syndly*. Georgie bounded down the street aiming to land at the school ground before the PE class came outside. He landed in front of the door and slipped in without anyone seeing him. Miss Syndly was speaking to Colin Syndly, her nephew, he stood up straight, he was at attention, Georgie thought he was going to salute her after they get through talking. She stepped out of the PE office and slyly slipped behind Georgie and said, "You're late!"

TF hit her on the back of the head. "Who did that?" She looked back at her nephew, he was the only one behind her. "You're after school." The students were outside and had surrounded Georgie. He stood in the middle of the class. Miss Syndly came out saying, "I want that tardy student; where is he?"

The students covered his front, back, sides, she tramped around the group like Adolf was still alive. Soon everyone could see her feet starting to give her difficulty walking. She then awkwardly and slowly walked back into the PE building and a semi-silent cheer went up. The students danced with Georgie. Miss Syndly came out, "Alright, jumping jacks, do fifty."

Georgie still had his backpack on, so he put it on the ground and complied. After P.E. class Georgie met Babs and Beth, he walked to Dad's classroom, they asked him why he did so well yet Peter and Paul easily beat him by ten minutes in the cross-country meet? "I ate something that didn't agree with me, I sat down on a tree stump for ten to twelve minutes when I started feeling better, I walked for a while."

Beth and Babs thought that there was something funny going on, Georgie continued walking toward Dad's classroom. He took out the map before he got to the classroom, the girls were slowly following him, they see the map and Babs emoted, "I'll bet that's something we should know."

"Yeah, we'll steal it in math when he goes up to explain some problem, that teacher's pet," responded Beth. "Why can't I go up and explain a problem?"

"'Cause you're too dumb."

"Am not!"

"Am too!"

"Ain't not!"

"Come on, let's get to class before we hate each other again."

Johnny met Georgie at the C5 door and said, "You worried me."

"I didn't run into trouble. I searched Occidental; no sign of the truck." reported Georgie. "I circled the town."

Dad came to the front of the room. Georgie looked up from the map and said, "Where do you think I should search next?"

"Since you were on the freeways to Sonoma, when you were chasing that truck, you should take a look around the small town, he was going that way."

"Oh, if you see Miss Syndly, tell her a story or something that doesn't get you into trouble with the wonderful woman." Georgie thought about running. Passing up cars might cause a strange incident. "I guess I'll ask Jason if I can use his skateboard. I'll put on my tape recorder, the sound of a small engine may work. Dad, where are the sound effects records?"

"There under the counter below the record player, thanks."

Georgie thumbed through and found the right record with the correct sound. He played it and got to the middle of the sound effect; it had a scratch on the record. "At lunch I'll run home and start up the lawn mower, Dad." The bell rang for third period, Johnny and he went to Mr. Ritz's class for science; everyone stood at the door waiting for Mr. Ritz to finish his cigarette on the public sidewalk. This was the only place anyone can smoke.

Imagine, just four years ago they had smoking areas for the seniors at the high school. If students brought a note from their parents, everyone in the world faked the note. As Mr. Ritz came up the hill to his classroom, he put on his shades and said, "No jive, chapter five."

Everyone thought that was cool. Mr. Ritz always let Beth and Babs in his classroom first and let them out at the end of the period bell first. Beth and Babs always gave him a wink which he cherished. On this day, he did try to teach subject matter. He actually bought fifteen pig hearts and was having an activity class. TF said to Georgie and Johnny, "Want to eat heart, me hungry. Hold red ball."

Mr. Ritz talked about what to look for in the hearts. Hearts kept disappearing; there were giggles coming from the students. Finally, teacher's pet stood up, "Mr. Ritz, your hearts are vanishing."

"Don't be silly, I haven't given them out, they are piled in a tray on my desk. I've given them to the teacher's assistant to pass the hearts out."

"Wrong," said Beth as a tray fell off the desk.

Georgie and Johnny were quietly thrashing around in their seats. "What are you pointing and waving at, Beth?" a now disturbed and uncomfortable Mr. Ritz.

"I am pointing at the tray, it was up in the air," said Babs.

Georgie was fascinated by TF action motion. "Yeah, I saw it in the air too." Then a red ball flashed to Georgie and TF spoke, "Me need two hands eat heart."

"I kept telling you your parts don't exist."

"Who are you talking to?" demanded Mr. Ritz. Suddenly, pieces of heart started to fall from the ceiling onto Mr. Ritz's head. The teacher's assistant screamed and passed out in front of Mr. Ritz. The other girls in the class screamed and ran out the door, Miss Syndly tried to come in and was promptly dispatched to the ground on her posterior. She got up, she was back down, back up, back down; this time most of the girls were out of the class, she looked around and saw no one and got back up; boys after hearing a hideous laugh dashed out the door. Some other girls who were not paying attention come running out of the classroom and knocked Miss Syndly back to the ground again. She grabbed a boy by the leg and said, "What is going on in there?"

"Something real creepy and has a horrible voice." Miss Syndly sat up and was pummeled by flying hearts. Georgie and Johnny rushed out of the classroom and helped Miss Syndly to her feet, while she brushed pig hearts off her clothes. She had an extremely agitated look on her face and was about to steam into the classroom with nostrils flared and ears twitching when Georgie said, "Hold it, Miss Syndly, you have a heart stuck in your hair."

"Don't you dare touch that heart! I'll get it later!"

Johnny giggled, "Must be a wig."

"Let's get out of here before she explodes," Georgie said quietly.

"Too late, she's pointing a finger to come in Mr. Ritz's classroom."

"What is it now, Miss Syndly?"

"Don't you take that attitude with me, young man! Now who started all this?"

Georgie and Johnny said in unison, "I don't know, Miss Syndly!"

"Did I hear an echo?"

"No Miss Syndly, we sometimes talk in unison."

"You boys are mocking me," her upper lip began to curl.

"What about Mr. Ritz, he's responsible for the hearts."

A big booming voice cries out, "Me did it!"

Instantly, Miss Syndly fell to her knees, "Please God, I have done nothing wrong."

Mr. Ritz ran out of his classroom. The boys helped Miss Syndly up again.

Chapter 56
Search

Georgie, with a skateboard and a tiny tape recorder, a fiber glass pole with a flag attached on the back of the skateboard. TF was part of the flag with a tiny red ball in the middle of the flag, Georgie's tape recorder blaring as if a hot engine was speeding along through Santa Rosa. The flagpole never meant to bend that far. Trotting Fox had ballooned into an extremely large sack and was lifting up the back wheels of the skateboard.

Georgie turned and said, "Down boy, everyone will think I'm crazy."

Seconds later a siren boomed; it was an ugly noise into Georgie's consciousness, a voice said, "Pull over!"

"Yes officer," as he looked back, Georgie jumped off the skateboard and held onto the fiber glass pole. The police officer skidded his car, it twisted and turned to a stop some twenty-five feet in front of Georgie and the skateboard. The officer backed up, tires smoking. Georgie was jumping up and down and yelling, "My right foot is burning up."

The police officer was thinking to himself, *this is one crazy kid*. "Yes, I am just a little Loony Tunes." *How did he know what I am thinking*, thought the officer.

"You do look like Daffy Duck jumping around like that. What's wrong with you anyway?"

"My foot is hot," replied Georgie.

"Do you know it's illegal to run a skateboard down a highway?"

"No sir."

"Do you have a license?"

"No sir."

Well, you are polite, mentioned the officer to himself.

"Thank you sir."

How does he know what I said to myself? "Your mind is an open book, sir. Sir I'm looking for my older brother, he sells dope to kids and I want him arrested."

"Well, let's talk about you and your motorized skateboard."

"No sir it does not have a motor, I have a tape recorder with motor sounds."

"How can you make it go so fast?"

"I have non-slip shoes on, sir." Georgie put his shoe up, there was nothing left of the sole. "That's why I jumped around; you made me stop at high speed and it ruined my shoe sir."

"OK," said the officer, leaning against the police car.

"But officer, my speed wasn't nearly that fast."

"Look at the skateboard wheels."

Georgie looked down at the skateboard, only steel was left on the wheels. "I see what you mean, officer."

"Get in the car, we are going to the police station." The officer was pleasant and asked, "Why the skateboard?"

"I thought it better then flying and running fast sir."

"You are a nice kid but you're crazy," remarked the officer.

"Thank you sir, for your patience, officer."

He stepped on the brakes, he walked around to let Georgie out of the car and led him into the police station, he remarked to the sergeant at the desk, "I caught this kid on the highway, amazingly going fifty miles an hour on a skateboard and it didn't have an engine and look at this, the wheels are to the steel and his right shoe, the sole is gone." He took off Georgie's right shoe to show the sergeant.

The sergeant yawned, "Spit it out."

"Sir spit what out, I have no gum in my mouth sir."

"Your name, address and telephone number," demanded the sergeant.

"I thought you meant gum sir, like at school sir." Georgie spat out his address.

The sergeant picked up a pencil and began writing, he said, "Anything else I should know, speak up."

"Tell him your address."

"I did."

The sergeant dialed the number, to the astonishment of the officer, "The kid only spoke about gum not his address or I should have my hearing checked."

258

The phone rang three times before Heather Vance picked it up, she said, "Hello."

The sergeant responded, "I have a Georgie Vance here at the police station in Santa Rosa, I'd appreciate it if you come and pick him up."

"Dad, they found Georgie, he's at the police station in Santa Rosa, they want you to come and pick him up."

Victor Vance, Heather and Jason all piled into the car as they backed out, they heard a voice say, "Wait for me." Mrs. Vance was putting the dishes away when the phone rang and didn't know what was going on. Jason opened the passenger side door, got out and let his mother take the seat and got in the back with his sister. Twenty-five minutes later after a big discussion about why Georgie was in jail, Heather said, "They're just holding him until we pick him up."

All of a sudden Mrs. Vance threw up her hands, bashed the ceiling of the car. "What if they ask for adoption papers? Turn around and get the Two Bucks to pick up Georgie. So, we don't have any trouble."

"You think it," Jason whispered, trying to clear his throat from the frog.

Victor swung an illegal turn rocking everyone out of their seats. "Dad," Heather cried, "what are you doing?"

"Going to the Two Bucks house." Minutes later, two cars were on their way.

They stopped in front of the police station. Ed Two Buck got out of the car, a police officer told him to park in the parking lot. The Vances followed, by this time, they had to get out and stretch. Jason pleaded to go in with Mr. Two Buck. Victor said "No".

Jason said, "Johnny is going in with his dad."

Victor Vance just stared at his son, shaking his head. "O Dad!" Ten minutes later Johnny and Georgie came running down the steps with the skateboard, followed by TF and Mr. Two Buck. Everyone gathered around Georgie. The question asked by Heather, "How did you get picked up by the police?"

"I had the skateboard flat out, the wheels began to smoke the police saw me driving slightly erratic, the police officer looked over his donuts on the dashboard and pulled me over. He told me it's illegal to use a skateboard on a highway, heck, I should have run and no one would have noticed. Boy, that was dumb!"

Mr. Two Buck asked, "What were you doing out there in the first place?"

"I saw the ring on a hand sticking out of a pickup truck and thought it could be the brother who killed me."

Johnny queried, "Don't you remember someone was selling drugs from a truck at the school cross-country event, Mr. Two Buck?"

Chapter 57

It was midnight when the Vances pulled into the driveway at their home. Victor Vance sighed and said, "I'm gassed, how about the rest of you?" Just sighs and murmurs as the doors of the car were opened and shut. Mrs. Vance flopped in bed as soon as she made it through to the bedroom door. Mr. Vance said, "No more skateboarding on the highway, Georgie." Then he flopped beside his wife and laid there half asleep.

Heather and Jason sat down at the kitchen table with Georgie. Heather got the cookies and Jason got the milk and glasses. Georgie was pooped and said, "G-wiz I didn't make it to Sonoma, I only made to a police station. I can't drive, I am not old enough. I can run, I'll probably need a pair of shoes every week. I can bounce and sort of fly but I'll be noticed. Then if I sort of fly, there will be phone calls to the police and I'll be picked up as an U.F.O. and that will give Mom and Dad some pain and misery."

"What if it's not your brother, it's someone that has a ring just like the one he wears?" asked Jason.

Georgie remarked, "That could be but what about the Joey burned into the floor of Dad's classroom that got him in trouble with Miss Syndly? I am in trouble with stinky feet Syndly too. Johnny is not, I am, but she doesn't know which one."

They sat at the table munching cookies and gulping milk down, silently trying to think of ways of getting to Sonoma without attracting attention. Heather jumped from the table and said, "Take the bus, that's simple."

"Let's see; I get out of school at three-thirty. I'll call the bus station in Santa Rosa and see what time the bus leaves and the price of the ticket."

Heather got the telephone book and rambled through the book to find the page, gave the number to Georgie. Georgie said, "I was brought up in the slums of Detroit, I don't know how to talk on the telephone, Heather please!" Georgie handed the phone back to Heather after dialing the number.

"Hello is this the Santa Rosa bus station?"

"Yes," the voice said.

"How many buses do you have going to the city of Sonoma?"

The voice at the other end replied, "One at seven AM, one at noon, one at five PM."

"How much is it?"

"One way or round trip?"

"One way," Heather answered.

"It is three dollars and fifty cents," answered the voice.

Georgie looked around and said, "Does anyone have money?"

Jason dug in his pocket. "I have fifty cents."

"I only have a dime, bus rides are expensive," Heather expressed her opinion. "That's out!"

Things were churning in Jason's brain and he blurted out, "The only solution is to hitch hike."

"That's a real thought, don't tell Dad."

Trotting fox said, "Me know what hiccup is." TF caught the rebound off Georgie's head.

"No, it's hitch hike. It means you stick your thumb out along the road and someone will pick you up."

"No thumb, what thumb?" TF laughed.

"You'll see when we try it."

Mom peeked her head in, "What's that noise?"

"Oh, that's Trotting Fox's laugh," Georgie answered.

Heather clucked like a chicken and said, "Strange, very strange. That's the first time he laughed, isn't it?"

"Yes mom," they replied in triplicate.

"Bedtime for all of you, it's one o'clock; it is hours after your bedtime," Mrs. Vance commanded. Heather gave a pleading look. "No Heather, now." Mother pointed to their rooms. "We aren't made to stay up twenty-four hours, even Georgie can't conquer that one."

Chapter 58

Miss stinky Syndly was standing at C5 when Victor Vance arrived at his classroom. The conversation was short, "Where are they?"

"Who?"

"This is not a children's book, Mr. Vance." She stooped down to put baby powder in her shoe.

Victor asked, "Does that help?"

"Oh yes, it helps my feet to slip around, it feels so much more comfortable, Mr. Vance." Then she walked away not realizing that she forgot why she came to C5 for, Mr. Vance twisted the topic. The boys were home free until something reminded her that she was after Georgie.

At school, Georgie and Johnny avoided her throughout the day by peeking around corners and TF hitting her on the head with the little red rubber ball, making her look the other way and escaping, walking on their tiptoes, then running, they made it around a corner and of course, hiding in the boy's bathroom, they had friends looking out the door to if she was close to the lavatory.

Late in the afternoon, in Mr. Ritz' science class, Georgie and Johnny were working in the back of the room, when who walked in but Miss Syndly. Johnny looked up, saw Miss Syndly, and uttered quietly, "Here comes trouble."

The boys were working on a large poster on how more or less electricity effected the mind. Georgie peeked around the poster and tried to suck out a thought from Miss Syndly. So she forgot why she came in the room. She immediately turned around and walked out and didn't say a word, that was not like stinky. Mr. Ritz came back and looked at the poster. "That will never work."

Georgie laughed, "Of course it won't, Johnny and I made it up for fun, Mr. Ritz."

When Miss Syndly walked out of the room and started down the hall, glassy eyed, she walked straight to Victor Vance' s room C5 and said, "Where are Georgie and Johnny at this moment?"

"Well, they should be," he pulls out his desk drawer and looks at their class schedule and said, "science with Mr. Ritz, does that help?"

"That can't be, I was just down there."

"The schedule is in your handwriting."

She squared around and said, "Something strange about those boys." She turned around and marched out as though she had a riding crop in her hand and four stars on her shoulders. She marched back to Mr. Ritz' classroom and said, "All right Ritzie, where are they?"

"Who?"

"Those twin boys with different last names."

"They are in the back of the room."

"They weren't in the back of the room last time I looked."

"Well, take a look now," said Mr. Ritz.

"All I see is a poster." Suddenly, she turned around and walked out. Mr. Ritz scratched his head in confusion. The cleanup bell rang. "Put the projects away," requested Mr. Ritz. When the passing bell rang, Mr. Ritz was already down to his car. A voice from behind a burning bush, where Mr. Ritz threw his lit match. The class before, while running up the hill to his classroom earlier, he had fallen and dropped the lit match setting the bush on fire.

"I see you beat the passing bell, Ritzie," the voice said.

Mr. Ritz, otherwise known as Cracker man, the duffer and puffer. He stuck his cigarette in his left hand, to put it out, then stuck it in his mouth. With a choking voice, he answered, "I had to come to my car to get a Tums; my stomach is killing me." He stepped around to the driver's side and opened the door, he turned his head and spat out the cigarette on the street inconspicuously, moved over to the passenger side seat, opened his glove box, rolled down the window so Miss Syndly wouldn't walk to the driver's side, where the butt lay on the street. "See, I am taking a Tums." Cracker man pulled himself through the window and grabbed her right leg.

She burst out, "I didn't know you cared. What will your wife say, if she finds out about this?"

"No, your right pant leg is on fire!"

"I don't care, just keep patting me down," Miss Syndly said. "Mr. Ritz, what are you doing, keep it up."

"No water, I'm putting the fire out," yelled Mr. Ritz.

"How long is it?" asked Miss Syndly.

Chapter 59

Georgie and Johnny realizing both Mr. Ritz and Miss Syndly were all right and were laughing at how the fire was put out. Johnny took Georgie's backpack down to C5 and gave it to Mr. Vance and told him that Georgie took off to hitchhike to Sonoma. Victor Vance walked around the room picking up things and cleaning and worrying about the way, he now thinks that Georgie found his brother from Detroit. "How the hell did he find his way here?"

Johnny sat down at Mr. Vance's desk, picked up a pencil and pointed it at Mr. Vance and said, "Maybe it's not him."

"If it is him," Mr. Vance speculated, "we are in for some brutal times. Come, let's go home."

Georgie didn't have much luck hitch hiking until an old beat-up car with stickers all over it, one notable one, "Jesus is coming again, boy, is he pissed!" Georgie was thinking a very pious individual; the greeting was, "How the fuck are you, boy?"

Georgie's eyes flicked upward, Georgie said, "Going to Sonoma?"

The man in the car looked up and asked in so many words, "What the fucking hell is that red ball hanging over your head?"

Georgie hadn't heard a greeting like that since his other life, so he said, not mentioning the red ball, "I'm fuckin' fine." As he got in the car, closing the smashed-up door, it clanged shut.

He reiterated, "What's that red ball over your head do?"

"Do you want to see?"

"Yes."

Georgie looked at the driver. "TF, do it."

The ball bounded off the driver's head twice. "How did you do that?"

"Oh, just a magic trick."

Then the driver asked, "What's TF?"

Georgie responded, "It's the name of the trick."

The driver grew silent and didn't speak for several moments, in that time he pulled out a small piece of glass from the glove box. Then from his left breast pocket eased out a small bag like the cowboys used in westerns; it was made of leather but it didn't have tobacco in it. It had white dust. He opened it like a cowboy. "Put some on the glass," he asked Georgie.

"What is that?"

"Want a snort?"

"Thank you, but no." The driver went ahead and sniffed up the entire white dust on the glass, all the while calling the white stuff "White Dragon Breath" and after putting the leather bag back in his breast pocket and the glass back in his glove box, the driver said, "That is sweet."

"Why do you use and who did you buy it from?"

The driver said, "From a guy in a white truck."

TF hit him on the head twice then gave a horrid laugh. The car skidded to a stop almost horizontal to the curb and the driver yelled, "Get out!"

Georgie responded, "TF, laugh again," Georgie mouthed the laugh, TF hurled the little red ball at the driver several times in a flash. The driver tried to peal off in his little car, he couldn't. Georgie stuck his thumb out not realizing he was just one mile from the city of Sonoma. He could see the city limits sign just down the road. He decided to run the rest of the way.

Chapter 60

The little car was going as fast as it can toward Sonoma. The driver who never gave his name to Georgie was fiddling with the leather sack; the "White Dragon Breath" came out and while driving at an enormous rate of speed, threw it at his windshield and he exploded into several four-letter words until he saw the white pickup truck parked at one of the local eateries. He pulled in beside the white pickup, leaving skid marks, his little car ended up leaning on the white truck, the driver got out of the little car on the passenger side, pushed the little car back on all four wheels and ran into Paul's Potluck Diner but walked slowly through the diner around tables, found who he was looking for and sat down.

The man on the other side of the table said, "What the hell are you doing here?"

"There's a kid, an Indian kid, asking about you in a sly way."

"A dumb Indian kid, so what?"

"The strange thing is the kid is magical, he had a little red ball banging me on the head and nothing attached to the rubber string."

"You been using too much of my stuff," replied the man sitting on the other side of the table, in the fancy leather jacket.

"No, no, this kid is after your ass, he is carrying something under the back of his shirt."

"What is it?"

"I don't know, it looked like a 38."

"That reminds me of what Corleone said: Keep your friends close, but your enemies closer. Yeah Joey." Joey picked up the rest of his dinner, rushed up to the counter, asked for a box, paid his check and left. The little car driver followed him out while consistently talking. The man flipped the little car guy a little plastic bag.

The little car driver thought, *I got a free one.* The white pickup sped away into the darkness. The little car guy followed.

Georgie just made it to the Sonoma square. He ran in and around the square then ran down several streets looking. He then stopped at a corner by a gas station. He asked the gas station attendant, "Does a white pickup come in or a little car with bumper stickers all over it?"

"Buddy, do you know how many cars fill up here?"

Georgie gave him a disgusted look and said, "Thank you." He walked over to the water hose and sprayed his shoes. He noticed that his socks were steaming, the tops of his shoes were thin, the bottoms almost gone.

The attendant yelled over, "Hey, don't mess up the area, the boss when he comes back will read me the riot act and kick my ass. If the gas station is not clean on time for the morning customers, I'll get fired!" Georgie helped by putting Clorox on oil spots.

Steam rose from Georgie's shoes as he sped away from the gas station and the annoying attendant. He toured most of the streets of Sonoma, then walked into a bakery closing up for the night, he pulled fifty cents out of his pocket and bought six glazed donuts, it brought back the memory of all the police officers eating donuts at the police station, he laughed. He ate two donuts and got a drink at the water fountain in the middle of the square. The red ball was dunking while Georgie sipped. "Come on TF. let's go home, keep up."

"Me don't know how water goes up, then down in hard basket, then gone?" TF looked under, bounced the red ball below the water fountain.

"Come on, Trotting Fox, you'll never figure it out."

Georgie didn't want to cause any accidents so he kept his speed down to twenty miles an hour. He kept to the sidewalks as much as possible. The red ball no one noticed, the white bag with the two donuts hit several people, once he went through a gang beating up on a kid. Georgie stopped, he told Trotting Fox to give the horrible laugh. Georgie stepped on the kids back at the same time. Everyone scattered as the laugh echoed off a wall, behind the gang.

"The donuts are safe." Georgie picked up the kid, wiped him off with his shirt, gave him two donuts, stuck one in his right hand and one in his left hand and said, "Better?"

The kid replied, "Yea."

Georgie picked up speed; TF hung with him. Georgie slowed down, his feet were extraordinarily hot, so he ran through sprinklers and had steam coming off his shoes again. He said to TF, "Aguascalientes?"

"Me no feet me not hot. Me no water go down not up?"

"I'll tell you later." Georgie and TF began crossing a field with cows in it. He began jumping over the cows and lightly stepping on some of their backs, one cow put her head up quickly and caught Georgie in the groin area, he complained to TF, "Gosh, that hurt! Now I have to go pee." Just at that moment, he was about to cross an electric fence, when he was relieving pain and urine, the electricity went up the urine, Georgie screamed and fell to the ground, into a cow patty. This time it wasn't Miss Syndly who was stinky.

Suddenly, his face was being sandpapered, Georgie opened his eyes, cow tongue, you could use it on wood. He pushed the cow away, into more stinky stuff. "Why don't I open my eyes? I'm afraid of the sandpaper on the face again. Caked in cow dung and urine." Georgie burst out, "I'm an animated cow patty, where is the damn hose, and why the hell are cows on both sides of the fence?"

Chapter 61

Mrs. Vance opened the front door when she heard footsteps and turned the porch light on. "You know how mothers are, did you find the white truck, Georgie?"

"No but I had a ride with a doper, he gave a vague hint." Georgie sat down at the kitchen table. Mrs. Vance handed him a cold soda, she could see he was sweating profusely and dripping on the floor.

"You stink, how far did you run?" asked Jason, holding his nose, he sat down across from Georgie for twenty seconds and left the room. "I ran thirty-six miles at least." Georgie yelled to Jason, "Oh by the way I spent your fifty cents on donuts. I brought one for you and one for Heather."

"I can't stand the smell any longer." Jan Vance grabbed Georgie by the ear with one hand and the other on her nose and escorted him to the bathroom. She threw in a bar of soap, a towel, pajamas and closed the bathroom door. She demanded, "Georgie, get your clothes off, throw them out the window. We'll wash them tomorrow."

Chapter 62
Hid

The man pulled the white pickup truck into a group of trees, along a dusty unpaved road. Uncovered his meal; there wasn't too much left, he quickly downed it and threw the white box out the window. He opened his glove box and took out his custom pistol, it wasn't what you think. It was a 38-caliber air automatic with four Co2 cartridges mounted on the sides of the barrel of the gun. This gave it twice as much velocity that can't be heard at any distance.

This killing instrument was made in Russia. There was no permit needed for an air pistol in U.S.A. Therefore, it can't be traced easily. The barrel had rifle-lings so its accuracy was acute. The clip held forty rounds. With his gun in his hand, he peppered the box, tearing it in half. He said, "Don't let anyone get in my way!"

Chapter 63

The next day, Georgie's shoes were a bit thinner and had no bounce in them. Mom, Dad, sis, and bro sat down at the breakfast table with Georgie. First thing Georgie did was give Heather's dime back. "Thank you for lending me your money."

"Mom, are our lunches packed?" asked the ever-hungry Jason.

"You'll find them in the usual place, son." Mrs. Vance's left hand was holding up her head, her eyes closed, her spoon pressing on her face from her cereal bowl. The three of them got up from the breakfast table, Dad took a last gulp from his cereal bowl and said, "Let's go."

"Oh, wait a minute, we need to get our track shoes and gear, another big cross country is today after school. It will be at the same place, where we saw the white truck. All of us will be exhausted in the middle of the run, because of being up last night, so let's look for the white truck at the same place where it was parked last time," Heather said. "Georgie, call Johnny before we leave and explain to him, he is going to win the race, if he can. The rest of us will look for the white truck," remarked the ever-verbose Heather.

"You didn't take a breath on that one, Heath."

"Oh, shut up Jason, stop trying to make light of something serious."

Georgie was the first one out the door, he looked at the molding around the front door for some unknown reason. While they were driving to school, Jason asked, "Why were you looking at the molding around the door?"

It was like one of the old commercials on T.V. where everyone stops to listen; even Mr. Vance pulled over and stopped the car; everyone stared at Georgie. "Why did you stop the car and why is everyone staring at me? Do I have peanut butter and jelly on my face?"

"What?" Mr. Vance blurted out with a serious look on his face. "Some kind of mark. I.D. Where do you live?"

Georgie looked at everyone with a bright shiny face. "I stuck my gum there last night before coming in the house."

"Did you find it?" Everyone's eyes were focused on him.

"On the dog's nose, I only knew that because Tanny had her nose between her front legs trying to rub the gum off her nose, so I ran over to Tanny in the front yard and there is my gum stuck on the upper part of her nose. I took it off."

Everyone had a good laugh. Georgie turned his head; there on his cheek was gum. This time a belly laugh struck everyone, even the car rocked and rolled. Georgie put a serious look on his face, as Dad started up the car. "Father how am I going to get Miss Syndly off my back politely?"

Victor Vance looked back at his Indian son, "Maybe she'll give up on an obvious mere tardiness, you'd think there are more serious offenses to take care of, son."

"Dad, this is my first tardy; what is she upset about?"

"The only thing that escapes us is a note saying why you were late."

"Dad, I can't say I was chasing a white pickup truck to find out if it's my brother selling drugs to kids?"

"Of course not. Let me think of something that isn't a lie."

"Okay, I thought of a note that isn't a lie, wait until we get to school." Victor Vance pulled up to the high school and let Jason and Heather out and drove back to the intermediate school.

Mr. Vance sat down at his desk in room C5 trying to think of something to write. "Didn't you wash your shoes when you got home last night?"

"Yes."

"This morning your mother tumble dried them in the dryer?"

"Yes, Dad but the tardy was yesterday."

"Oh yes because we slept in, we were up late."

"Yes, I forgot to set my alarm," said Mr. Vance, "That's it!"

"Write that, Dad."

Georgie took the note to the office and gave it to the attendance clerk. "Miss Syndly wants to see you," mentioned the clerk. He thought to himself, *Be calm, she is an old lady giving service to education and keeping ciaos out of the school. What do I have to do with anything except to learn?* He went to her office and listened; he couldn't hear a sound at first then he picked up on "Why are twin boys identical in appearance but different in so many ways?"

Georgie heard from inside the office. He started to walk away from her office door. She spotted his silhouette and with anger threw the door open and said in an irritating voice, "Come in here at once."

Georgie walked in with a smile on his face saying, "Hello Miss Syndly, I got your message from the attendance clerk, Mrs. Rice."

"Yes, I want to tell you about your tardy. I thought you were in P.E. but somehow you eluded me."

"No ma'am, I was absent the whole day. You see we were up late the night before and the alarm wasn't set."

"Now whose house were you at?"

"My father's."

"Now who is your father?

Georgie slowly put his left hand behind his back and crossed his fingers. "Mr. Vance is my adopted dad."

"I thought you and Johnny Two Buck are brothers."

"He is my brother." His crossed fingers tightened, he knew what the next question was going to be.

"Why don't you live with your brother?"

"Ma'am, I thought my parents and Johnny's parents explained all of the details at the beginning of last year. If you look in the counselor's notes, you will find it written down, ma'am. I have to get to class, ma'am."

"You stay here until this is settled." Georgie uncrossed his fingers; he now knew hoping wouldn't work. He concentrated on Miss Syndly's face. She said, "Why are you staring at me like that?"

He suggested, "Because Miss Syndly, it's none of your concern. I hate to be impolite, but you are overstepping your authority in this matter." Georgie got up.

"Okay you can go." *What was I thinking anyway*, as stinky rose from her desk and walked several steps around her desk to the front with shoes in hand and she put them on and scratched her butt.

Down at C5, Georgie said to his dad, "Boy, that woman is persistent, it's like she knows something we don't know."

The working noise in the classroom covered up what Georgie told his dad. "Son, if she finds out, you will never have a normal life."

"Dad, gave me a note so I can get to class." Victor Vance wrote Georgie a very short note describing a helpful situation. With note in hand, Georgie ran to class because everyone was already in. Who was looking out of her office window, oh yes, the one and only! Georgie gave the note to Mr. Clancy. He gave Georgie the usual look, he gave Mr. Clancy the stiff upper lip and sat down at his desk. The Indian clone got out his workbook for math, then Georgie smiled thinking of the way he had turned off Miss Syndly.

D5 door swung open, Miss Syndly had eyes leveled at Georgie, turned and said hello to Johnny. She focused on Georgie, she abruptly stated, "Georgie, will you come out into the hallway please!"

Many of the kids in the class cringed when they heard the voice of stinky Syndly. Georgie walked out the door of D5, it slowly closed. "Miss Syndly, Mr. Clancy is describing a difficult problem and I am missing it."

"You can get it from your brother," she said. "Tell me how can you run that fast? I was day dreaming out my window and I saw this blur."

"Yes, I can run fast and I can jump high; anything wrong with that?"

"No."

"That's why I'm going to win the cross-country race this afternoon, ma'am, and give the school glory and you!" Miss Syndly stood up straight as though she would win the race. "Please allow me to get back to my school work?" Georgie worried the rest of the day about his birth and the things he was capable of doing. *Should I win the cross-country race*? he thought to himself. *Maybe I should stay with Johnny? So everyone will think I'm a normal kid?* He sat pondering his situation not noticing anything around him not even the last bell of the day.

Mr. Clancy, still sitting at his desk sorting papers, he looked up, "Hey Georgie, aren't you going to the cross-country meet? Hey!" But Georgie didn't flinch. Mr. Clancy got up and moved to Georgie's desk, where Georgie was staring into space. Mr. Clancy touched Georgie and got a shock on his right index finger. He ran up to the sink and stuck his smoldering finger in cold water and screamed, "Ouch! Didn't you just flicker silver-green?"

"Ah no sir, I do that when I hiccup, sir." Georgie picked up his books and quickly moved out the door and walked to C5.

There sat the man that took me and didn't allow my birth to scare him. "Dad, today I almost gave myself away twice without thinking about it. I'm scared, Dad, Miss Syndly caught me exceeding human speed. I talked my way out of that one but I really screwed up in Mr. Clancy's class, I was sitting at my desk day dreaming after the bell. Mr. Clancy came over to my desk and touched me. Somehow, I gave him a shock and, in a flash, I turned silver-green and he saw it, but the worst happened, he really burned his finger bad."

"You better go and help him, Georgie. Here's the emergency medical kit, walk, not run, to D5 and help your math teacher. Oh, and give him some absorbing thoughts to the contrary of what he is thinking."

"Yes Dad." In D5, Mr. Clancy sat on a stool beside the sink running cold water on his finger. He opened the med kit and found the burn salve; he was in intense pain.

"I brought burn salve, hold still and turn off the water for a second." Georgie said, "Pain is real and I know it hurts, Mr. Clancy."

"Cut the shit and put the salve on my finger. How the hell did you give me that much voltage and amps?" demanded Mr. Clancy.

"It's a long story." After the salve application and the bandage, Georgie put his index finger on the back of Mr. Clancy's head, it was like acupressure with a mild shock.

The first thing Mr. Clancy said, "What happened to my finger?"

"You burned it sir with a propane torch."

"I did? I don't remember." Mr. Clancy tried to think how it had happened.

"I have to go now, I'm in the cross-country race." Georgie picked up the med kit and walked out, not ran.

Chapter 64

The older kids from the high school snapped and razzed the middle school kids again but Georgie and Johnny, the girls, Peter and Paul yelled and screamed back, "You ain't so hot; you lost the last race, you bums!" screeched Babs.

Beth pretended to twist a dagger in the high school boy's chest! "That's our Beth," quipped Paul and Peter, laughing.

Babs and Beth both chanted, "Go shadows. Middle. Go, go, I couldn't count the times we won."

The starter shot the pistol and they were off as the high school kids tried to cut off the younger group. Georgie cut through and began distancing himself from everyone except one high school boy called Flash MacQueen. Georgie wasn't about to let anyone beat him. He let Flash catch up just to have someone to talk to on the way through the forest. Georgie didn't say "Little Red Riding Hood" or the "Big Bad Wolf", so he thought for a while and came up with, "Hey Flash, do you want to be the tortoise or the hare?"

Flash laughed and replied, "Why, I'm the hare and you're the slow-poke tortoise."

A little taunt won't hurt, thought Georgie. He pulled away about ten feet in front of Flash. He looked back, he said, "Flash, your shadow is thick not thin," Georgie laughed.

"Just for that I'm going to leave you in my dust," promised Flash! Flash sped up but the young Indian boy began bounding in front of Flash. Georgie didn't want to show off too much so he ran beside him and acted exhausted. Flash said, "Stop and fall down, you punk."

Georgie didn't say another word until the end of the race. He began edging past Flash, he said, "Slow poke." A dozen other runners were just behind them as they crossed the finish line. Georgie came over to shake Flash's hand. Flash begrudgingly shook Georgie's hand and asked, "How come you can run so well at your age and your brother can't?"

"I really don't know, Flash." There was some commotion between several officials, Georgie heard static then someone said there were several runners shot, then a voice in the middle of the officials said, "Send three ambulances to the cross-county race at Washington Park. A person or persons in a white pickup truck, license plate, we got three digits AG3. Two wounded slightly and one seriously."

Georgie sprinted down the path where the kids were lying and immediately saw Johnny puking, lying on his back and someone yelled, "He's going to drown in his puke juice!" Georgie turned Johnny over and patted his back, with his feet, then he laid his brother on his back then he saw the holes in his shirt, near his heart.

Georgie picked Johnny up, looked left and right and began running down the path slightly off the ground keeping on a smooth motion. There were no ambulances in sight so he increased his speed, he ran above the officials and over the crowd of onlookers, passing his mom and dad, Jason and Heather, Mom and Dad Two Buck, Georgie yelled, "I'm running to the hospital; it's faster!"

Georgie picked up speed, he calculated that it was three miles to the Memorial Hospital, that was if nothing stopped him, he will arrive in less than three minutes. He passed the ambulances going the other way. Tears began to fill his eyes and sight became difficult, he had to hold Johnny with one arm and hand, while he wiped his right eye then his left. Trouble set in, he couldn't wipe fast enough so he had to stop. His running held up well until he had to stop, he seared off the soles of his shoes.

He stopped, not jarring his brother. "I must run on." Not realizing he had stopped in front of the hospital and wiped his eyes again and ran to the emergency entrance. He left a trail of smoke and smell. His eyes were tearing so badly that he had trouble talking to the nurse, finally, he spoke through with anguish, "He's shot through the heart!"

Two nurses grabbed Johnny and carefully put him on a gurney, red lights flashed and they wheeled Johnny into the operating room, the men in green with masks over the bottom of their faces took off Johnny's shirt. The doctor with glasses asked the nurse, "Oxygen please," as Georgie watched. "What kind of bullets made these injuries?"

"They're not bullets, they're pellets," one doctor said to the other doctor. The one with glasses told the orderly to run the kid down to X-ray, be quick.

Georgie laid on the floor in the waiting room, his hands over his face, his feet bleeding. He heard tires screech outside, he told himself *they're here*. He heard the doors rattle and bang, everyone in the waiting room looked up along with Georgie. Running footsteps filled the hallway to the waiting room of the E.R. A voice crackled, then another, then another, all said the same, "Where is my son?"

Georgie yelled from the floor, "He is in X-ray."

Mrs. Two Buck with a quivering voice asked, "Where is my son, for God sake?"

"I told you he's in X-ray."

The doctor with glasses was running hard down the hallway coming from the X-ray room; he grabbed the defibrillator, almost knocking it over, wrestled it to X-ray. All in the waiting room heard the sounds that they didn't want to hear. Some swearing, some defibrillator noises, some coughing, some sucking air sounds, a rumble, a scrape. Wheels not made to move that fast, a crash, the gurney hitting the operating room doors. The doctor with the glasses walked slowly down the hallway to the group of anxious family members, several crying, the doctor said, "He is alive, he has holes in his heart, I don't know why he is still alive, he has had three transfusions already. We'll need blood; who thinks there's a match?"

"I am, sir," Georgie spoke up.

"Son, you're too young. Anyone else?"

"Yes, I'm his father and this is his mother," said Ed with a strong command. This brought Mr. and Mrs. Two Buck out of the Indian ritual. A very quiet ritual, hum, tears, flowing profusely. The doctor with the glasses asked Ed and Lisa to step into another room.

Georgie asked, "Are you sure you can't use my blood?" to a nurse at the nurse's station.

The nurse looked at Georgie with a trail of blood behind him. "Why didn't you say something?"

"Because I wanted the medical staff to focus on my twin brother." Georgie's shoe tops were above his ankles.

"Young man, let me help you!"

"Yes, you can help me by getting my brother's shoes."

"But you're dripping blood!"

"No, I'm not," answered the Indian kid with the bloody feet. Stunned, the nurse quickly found Johnny's shoes. Georgie sat quietly putting the shoes on. The nurse watched his every move while wiping up blood off the rug. The nurse continued to stare at Georgie. Georgie continued to smile back at the nurse for an hour, until an idea struck him. With his head down, he got up from his seat and slowly moved toward the nurse's station and quietly said, "How does one take a liver biopsy?"

"Why do you ask?" replied the nurse.

"Well, I was reading that they take an instrument, stick it through the skin to the liver and take out a minuscule bit of liver?"

"Yes, that is correct, I just happened to have a catalog with a picture of the instrument."

"Gosh, that's a strange looking thing, it gives me the chills." Georgie said "Thank you," and turned to his dad, he quietly sat down besides, murmuring so no one could hear, "I need the keys to the house and C5. I need to make a replacement part. Where is the ice chest?"

"On the plywood above where the car is parked in the garage."

Trotting Fox was discombobulated, he hit Georgie on the head with the little red ball to get his attention. Georgie put his finger to his lips and quietly said, "No ball, no noise." Georgie motioned to come outside. Georgie stepped quietly toward the door.

Mrs. Two Buck came out of the room holding a band aid on her left arm; she said, "Don't you dare leave, Georgie Vance! You caused all this trouble!"

"Please Mrs. Two Buck, I have to leave!"

Victor Vance said, "I need you to come outside with me, Georgie and Lisa." Mrs. Two Buck didn't go quietly, she threatened Georgie twice and Victor once, before they made it out the door. "Stop screaming, we can't help Johnny by lamenting, while he is still alive."

Between sniffles, wiping her eyes and blowing her nose, Lisa said, "What can we do?"

"Keep our heads on straight and let Georgie do what he has never done before in the history of the world."

After blowing her nose again, "What's that?"

"A replacement part just in case," explained Victor.

"What do you mean a replacement part?" still wiping away tears with her handkerchief, asked Lisa.

The door swung open, out came Ed, holding his band aid. Victor Vance said, "Since the gangs all here, I'll say it again, Georgie is going to make a replacement part. We still have the equipment to duplicate."

"I have to get going, if I'm going to get this finished in time," cried Georgie. At that moment Georgie ran off as fast as he can with Mrs. Two Buck screaming her lungs out, "Stop, stop!"

Ed looked at his wife, "Keep your voice down; this is a hospital."

"We are outside, I don't care; it's my son that I'm worried about."

"No, he didn't say some guy in a white truck shot him," said the distraught Ed. Ed grabbed his wife, kissed her, wiped her tears and said, "Georgie is going to make a usable part for Johnny just in case."

"What do you mean, just in case?"

"You know. Let's go in and sit." While Ed put his arm around his wife, she began wiping her eyes and blowing her nose.

The nurse immediately startled Victor, "Is that your kid that just ran away?"

"Yes."

"Did you know that his feet are bleeding?"

"No, they're not."

"Yes, they are."

"Nurse, I assure you his feet are okay, now please leave us alone." Finally, the chaos subsided and stone silence set in, until the doctor with the glasses came down the hallway and asked, "Who is Johnny Two Buck's mother and father?"

Of course, Lisa Two Buck jumped out of her chair and was nose to nose with the doctor. "Yes doctor?"

"Madam, would you step aside please?" the surgeon asked. "Everyone concerned about Johnny's condition, please step over and make a circle around me," he said. "It will take a number of hours before we can tell if we will be able to save the boy's life. I can tell you he has a strong heart."

Lisa Two Buck really went to pieces.

Chapter 65
Race

Georgie hit the house with Johnny's shoes smoking. He immediately ran to the bathroom and stuck his feet in the toilet. Yes, steam came off his shoes, that is, Johnny's shoes. He then went to the kitchen, looked through the junk drawer and found a skewer. This skewer was eight inches long and sixteenth of an inch in circumference. Georgie then thought he needed a science book, the human anatomy, he went to the family library and found a book on the heart. Five main veins leading to the heart and lungs and five arteries leading away. Georgie loaded up his equipment into his backpack, strapped it on his back, while his shoes still wet from the toilet, his feet do not hurt. He walked to the front door and locked it; he made sure he had all the equipment needed in his backpack.

Georgie ran at top speed toward the school, hoping his shoes stayed wet until he made it to the room C5. While he was running along, he thought back to what Johnny and Dad said how he happened to come about in the vat. The combination of chemicals and his real father who was dead gave me life and a new body, the skin from Johnny's thumb, plus the orchid that fell into the silver-plating solution. He, Johnny, put the plating solution into the cabinet. After Bactine and a band aid was put on his thumb, in the cabinet, the solution produced a cocoon from the skin and the orchid that was inside the cocoon. In that moment, my soul and brain were put in the cocoon.

The conclusion is all I have to do is drop a piece of heart tissue into the silver-plating solution. Georgie jumped over the cyclone fence. Who was dressed in camouflage clothing on a cot asleep, by the door of C5? Snoring like a cow mooing, the ever-determined principal. Georgie landed on his tip toes, hoping against hope that the door doesn't squeak, when he unlocked the door and opened it. That wicked old lady would wake up, he thought, he eased the key into the lock and slowly turned the key, letting himself in the room without a noise.

Georgie was still looking at Miss Syndly through the display case window, he saw her twitch then pop her head up. Georgie jumped back behind the solid door, while she peered through the glass. Georgie for the first time in his new life was in a stress sweat. But the beast that snored like a cow lay back down on the cot. Georgie pondered what to do. *I can't turn on the lights. I can't use the hammer. I'll probably scream when I use the instrument. How am I going to do this?* Then a devious thought came into his mind. *What if I put the ever snoopy, stinky, Miss Syndly, so she can't snoop, but where and how? I could put her on the roof of C5. No, she would probably hear me. What about in her office? I think the boys' locker room is the best place.* Georgie began looking for heavy string, tape, and cloth to muffle her mouth. He knew that the key to C5 was a master key, because Dad had to substitute occasionally on his preparation period. The big towel was in the cabinet, beside the plating solution cabinet. He took the small key on Dad's keyring and opened the cabinet, he took the towel in one hand, the string in his other hand. He began crawling toward the door.

He opened the door, then floating just above the floor making sure the door didn't slam, he glided himself under the cot to the front, easing upward, wrapped the towel around her eyes and tied it tight under the cot. He had ripped off a piece of towel in midflight, while wrapping string around her, holding her to the cot. Realizing now, he failed to get the tape off Dad's desk. He put her down, rushed into the room, grabbed it off the desk, wrapped her securely but with a slight opening so her nose and mouth were free from the tape, but covered with one layer of towel.

Georgie with his hand over her mouth slowly carried her to the boys' locker room and placed her in the middle of the floor. He then tied the cot front on both sides to locks on the lockers. He did the same to the back of the cot so that she couldn't tip herself over.

Now I can get to work, he thought. Georgie looked at the time, nine o'clock, Miss Syndly went to bed early. He decided to turn on the lights. He got the anvil and hammer out of the cabinet in C5. He put the anvil on the heavy wooden table, he took off his backpack and got out the skewer. He figured a four-inch section and pound the skewer flat, bent the end over the anvil, making a minuscule hook. *How small, very small*, he thought to himself.

Georgie realized the skewer was softer metal than he thought, it was starting to get too wide, so he rotated the skewer until the point was hammered, took on a sixty-fourth inch round, well, not completely round. It was not quite like the one in the catalog at the nurse's station, it had a hidden hook inside a tube that had a button and two finger grips, that when the instrument was inserted, you pushed the button forward, it pinched off a piece of tissue. But Georgie's instrument was not the same; the hook was out and will cut tissue until it got to the heart, where it will biopsy the heart and bring back the tissue through the torn entrance.

Trotting Fox did not know what Georgie was going to do to himself. TF was sitting on the ceiling upside down, bouncing the little red ball off the light fixtures, he looked, he saw. Georgie took off his shirt, put the skewer under hot water from the sink in C5, then put some dark orange substance—Bactine—on the skewer, insert the skewer into his chest and screamed his lungs out. Then pulled it out and fell to the floor with an agony-ridden face. "Me die like that, you no do!" said TF.

Seconds passed and Georgie was sitting on a chair calmly looking at a morsel of his heart that was pulsating on the end of the skewer. His wound was closing, Georgie looked at TF, who said, "Me never want you to do that again!" TF came down from the ceiling, looked at the wound—it was gone! Georgie put his shirt back on. The tub of non-toxic plating solution was in front of him. He simply dropped the heart morsel into the tub, stared at the morsel slowly sink to the bottom of the tub. Ten minutes go by, then ten more passed.

The morsel stopped contracting. Georgie had a cold feeling and felt a chill in his gut. *What am I doing wrong?* He put his head in his hands. Georgie jumped up, opened the door, ran down the hallway, put the key in the administration building, opened the door, ran to the secretary's desk, found the phone book and the hospital number. The hospital operator answered, "How may I help you?"

"Yes, I want to speak to Victor Vance who is in the waiting room."

"I'll direct the call to the waiting room and who will I say is calling?"

"His son." The phone made some funny noises, a click and Victor said, "I'll take the call. Hello."

"Dad, I don't know what's wrong, I can't get it to work!"

"Did you plug the transformer into the wall?" said Victor.

"Oh god, that's what I did wrong!" screamed Georgie.

Victor pulled the phone from his ear and said from a distance, "Georgie, calm down and make sure the transformer is on nine volts."

Then Georgie responded, "I'll have to do another biopsy. It's awful pain, Dad."

"I'm sure sorry, son, but if you don't, Johnny is going to die. The doctor said he has only a matter of hours."

Georgie dropped the phone and ran back to C5. He took the skewer, ran to the big sink in C5, turned the faucet on and ran the hot water until scalding hot, he put the skewer under the water, moving it back and forth, turned off the water and watched the steam drift upward, then he held the skewer toward the floor to let water drop off it.

Georgie sat there feeling upset and talking to himself, "I can't let Johnny pass, a person that gave me life. Maybe by accident, but nevertheless a wonderful and a loving friend and companion that I didn't have before." He grabbed the skewer, "Whoops, I can't do it yet." He put Bactine on the skewer. He moved to the cabinet, found the transformer, tightened the wires, then placed them in the non-toxic plating solution. Plugged the cord in the wall plug, now was the time, he picked up the skewer and thrust the makeshift instrument into his chest. Georgie couldn't swallow, he wanted to cough, he knew he couldn't.

He reached his heart, he inserted the skewer, turned the nob and pulled it back out, screamed thinking at least it was not in the same place. A shaft of light burst into the room. No, it didn't come from the plating tub; it came from a flashlight through the display window. Georgie jumped up and put the plating solution back in the cabinet and closed the door on the wires, he raced over to the wall plug, pulled it, zoomed back to the cabinet door, opened it and threw everything in. He was close to the C5 door, before the second knock. Georgie slowly opened the door. "Yes officer."

"Earlier, I saw that crazy principal sleeping outside this door. I asked what is wrong? She said she wasn't sure. That spooked me and I said yes ma'am and left. She's okay, isn't she?"

"Oh yes officer, she was waiting for me, then went home."

The officer turned off his flashlight and said, "What are you doing here?"

"My father left his wallet in this cabinet and he sent me over to pick it up."

"Don't stay too long; the squad car will stop to check the buildings in ten minutes."

"I'll leave as soon as I get his wallet out of the cabinet, officer."

"Okay and goodnight, don't forget to turn off the lights when you're finished."

Georgie waved bye and closed the C5 door. Georgie rushed to the cabinet door hoping that the morsel of heart tissue was developing. He yelled, "Oh god, it didn't!" He looked and the silver sheet of metal was not on the wire. He picked up the tub, put the silver on the wire, plugged the transformer into the wall and wham, a cocoon formed instantly around the heart morsel. Sweat began dropping off his face, this had to be completed within hours. Georgie turned off the lights, picked up the ice chest, ran to the 711, paid the man, he got the ice for Georgie. He ran back to the administration building and called the hospital. "ER waiting room, Victor Vance please."

"Yes, this is Victor Vance."

"Dad, it worked, it's growing. How much time do we have?"

"None, the doctor said he'll die any minute!"

Georgie slammed the phone down opened the door, one second later opened C5 door. Georgie said to himself, *I hope everyone is praying for me, someone, this has to be done now*. He walked over to the tub, slowly covering his eyes with his hands and hoping, *Please, please be finished*. Georgie now shaking and sweating profusely, again, opened the ice chest and washed his face with ice, he then pulled the cocoon out of the plating tub and put it in the ice chest. Georgie turned out the lights, locked the door with the ice chest in hand, he began to pick up speed, a sudden funny feeling came over him. His body said stop, so he slowed to a walk under a street light, oh just a mist, perfect, my shoes or Johnny's shoes won't smoke on the way to the hospital.

Georgie was now racing down the street with TF close behind, "Me take box with hard water and pumping thing. You no sleep and put holes in self."

Georgie turned around now running backward and said, "I can make it to the hospital with the box, TF."

"No, me take box, you home sleep. You sleep one hour."

TF and Georgie turned in different directions. Georgie, exhausted, dragged himself through the front door, floated to the bathroom, dipped his shoes in the toilet one at a time, steam flooded the bathroom, his feet were blistered and his heart hurt. He thought to himself, *What a combination; Johnny and I both have silver hearts, maybe a little green*. His eyes closed while sitting on the toilet. He wobbled and fell on the marble floor.

Chapter 66

A noise that only Trotting Fox can make, created fear in everyone except the Two Bucks and the Vances, a floating ice chest appeared in the doorway. Ed and Victor jumped at the ice chest at the same time, they grabbed the chest, Ed screamed at the doctors. Only a nurse untroubled said in a whisper, "Keep quiet or I will have you both thrown out."

"This is the heart we have been waiting for, call the operating doctor, tell him we have a heart he can use or just parts," said an exasperated Ed Two Buck with Victor rolling his eyes and mouthing the words that Ed said and nodding his head. The nurse looked at them as if they had escaped from a mental institution and demanded to know, "How did that thing float in here?"

"You mean the ice chest?"

"Yes, what do you think I mean!"

"Oh, you mean the super express company?"

"Yes, never heard of it!"

Ed ignored her comments and opened the ice chest and tore the cocoon off the heart, rolled the cocoon up and threw it in the trash barrel, while Victor kept Ed's action covered by throwing his coat in the air, blocking the view of the trash can. Ed turned around with the heart lying in the ice chest, showed the nurse the silver slightly green beating heart. She screamed and fainted directly over the ice chest, the door slammed closed almost catching an artery of the heart.

Another nurse came running and pulled the unconscious nurse off the ice chest with the help of Ed and Victor. The first doctor came out of the operating room and said, "What is going on? The noise level out here is unbearable, we can't think in the Operating Room."

"Doctor," said Victor, "we have something that will keep the boy alive. I don't want to startle you; this is something impossible; can you take the impossible?"

The doctor gave Victor a nonchalant facial expression. "I don't want to hear another sound out of anyone here," announced the doctor.

"You got it," Victor said. Both nurses grabbed the doctor's arms while Ed opened the chest; the nurses pushed his head into the ice chest.

He blinked several times. "Where the hell did this come from?"

The nurses looked at each other for a moment and the first responded, "It floated in here and these two gentlemen say it is a perfect match for the boy."

The doctor looked at Ed and Victor, "It's silver with a green tinge!"

"It's my boy's, take it, use it," cried Victor.

Ed and Lisa Two buck yelled "Yes, yes!"

The doctor blinked again, paused. "Use it, damn it!" screamed Lisa.

The doctor closed the ice chest and took it to the OR, mumbling, "Out of procedure, out of procedure."

"Don't say anything. Crack the boy's sternum."

Years earlier, the second doctor had been to the first heart transplant in the U.S. and ordered the equipment for the procedure. The first doctor while in thought saw the boy's blood pressure dropping, his heartbeat was weak, *look how fast and powerful the ice chest heart is beating*, he said to himself; *it's not supposed to be beating at all, can I do the transplant without killing the young man?* But before he cracked the sternum, he pulled his mask to his neck, put his back to the door, opened it and walked to the waiting room and yelled, "Nurse, I want permission in writing for this procedure."

Ed had a pen in his hand before the doctor got procedure out of his mouth. Dazed, the second doctor who operated on Johnny walked out of the operating room mumbling, "I don't believe it! The arteries and veins on the heart simply jumped on the stubs!"

Ed looked at the doctor painfully and cried, "What's a stub?"

"The part left when I cut the original heart out, a stub of arteries and veins!"

Ed and Lisa now on their knees, "Will he live?"

"The other doctor is closing his chest; your boy should be going to intensive care in a couple of hours and you can see him. Get off your knees, I'm no God!"

Chapter 67

Georgie put his shoes on while nibbling a cookie and thought what Miss Syndly was doing, struggling with her ropes on her cot or sound asleep, then he laughed, he thought, waiting for prince charming to rescue her? Georgie thought he better get over to the school before something happened to old bad feet. He opened the front door, turned to make sure it was locked, walked down the sidewalk, a bright light blinded him for a moment, a voice said, "You all look alike."

Georgie heard a phit, phit, phit, he jumped high in the air, looked down, a white truck! *My brother is cunning and vicious* as Georgie fell to the grass between the curb and the sidewalk. Georgie heard a constant phit as he slid under the truck and came up on the driver's side, put his hand through the window and ripped off the door of his brother's truck! Joey slammed the accelerator to the floor.

Georgie threw the door, hit the back window of the truck, the door stayed fixed in the back of the cab. The smoking tires and the drift around the corner, that son-of-a-bitch showed the ins and outs of driving a modified truck to perfection. *I scared him as much as he scared me.* Georgie thought for a moment, he said to himself *how could he know where I live?*

Georgie looked at his hand, two of his fingers on his right hand were out of joint, sticking straight up, almost at ninety degrees. The second knuckle on his ring finger and small finger. He walked over to the car next door, placed his hand on the flat metal and simply took the heel of his palm, banged his two fingers, they popped into place.

"I should have chased him, I did get his license plate number, Michigan 12Q644." That bugger Joey must have stolen a new truck that someone spent a lot of time on modifying, I know he wouldn't work that hard on anything. After flexing his hand several times, he began running.

Chapter 68

Joey screamed out loud, "How the hell did I miss him, I never missed anyone before?" He grunted and then he grunted again, "How does an Indian kid rip off a door?" He looked down, scaring the people in the car next to him at a stoplight! The man and the woman in the car stared up and he stared down. Joey looked back at the door stuck in the cab, not realizing he was cut up and bleeding. Glass that shattered was lying throughout the cab and stuck in his neck and head from Georgie's blow to the window with the door of the white truck, he drove himself to the hospital where he sent the other Indian kid earlier and followed the other one home.

The second kid ran like a deer, something strange about that one. He got out of his truck, parked away from the emergency entrance to the hospital. Blood streaming down his back and laying a blood trail to the emergency hospital door. His head, neck and part of his back were drenched in blood. He was pulling glass out of his head and neck, while Joey pushed his way through the line, he did say, "Pardon me, I am bleeding, you're not!"

He sat down at the nurse's triage station and said, "I'm bleeding."

The nurse replied, "Let me see your insurance card."

"I'll pay cash."

"Thirty-five dollars please."

Joey took a roll of bills out of his pocket, flipped her thirty-six dollars and replied, "Keep the change," and winked. "Where do I go?"

"The orderly will take you."

A big young man said, "This way." Directly past the grief-stricken Indian parents of Johnny, he gave them a smile, thinking that son-of-bitch better be dead, I know I got him through the heart. He laughed to himself as he passed by. The doctor sat Joey down on an examining bench and began pulling glass bits out of his head. "How did this the happen?"

"I backed into a 4x4 on a house construction."

He didn't figure the doc would say, "Do you have workers comp?"

"No, it is a scab job."

"You must have been going fast for this to happen?"

"Yes, I was angry at the boss," said an irritated Joey. "Can we get on with this?"

"Of course." The doctor continued, he pulled out glass from his neck, then from his back. The doctor spread antibiotic ointment on his head and the rest of the injured areas, until he came to a spot on his neck. "I want you to lay down on the operating room table; you have a piece of glass in your right jugular, Mr., what did you say you name is?"

"Mr. Joey Smith."

"If I pull this out now, you will bleed to death. I must sew the hole up, but I have to anesthetize you."

"What does anesthetize mean?" demanded Joey. "How much will that cost?"

"Three hundred dollars."

Joey asked, "What the hell is the sticky stuff you're putting on my head, doc?"

"It's to prevent infection." Then the doctor began putting a large bandage on Joey's head.

"Okay but get it done quickly, I have to attend to my business."

"Lift up your shirt so I can check for more glass and finish spreading ointment and bandage it if needed."

"Okay but I am in a hurry."

"Yes, yes, just slow down for a second."

Joey exited laughing. The doctor yelled, "You need stitches in your neck." He paid for the antibiotics at the cashier's window. When Joey got to his white truck, he opened the glove compartment and brought out a needle and thread. Threaded the needle, pinched around the glass, stuck the needle in his neck. Slowly as he sewed, he moved his fingers slightly, while he sewed his jugular on the right side of his neck. He had the driver's side window down as he sewed; some blood squirted out the window, hitting passing cars in the hospital parking lot. After he finished sewing, he looked in the mirror—crude but holding, he yelled, "I hope that kid is dead!" Then drove away.

The doctor came out of the operating room and said, "Ed Two buck and all in the waiting room, that son of Ed is a tough customer. Where did you get that heart, really?"

Ed looked at Victor and answered, "He'll tell you all about it."

The doctor asked, "Please tell me?"

"Well, as you can tell, it is a human heart."

"Don't move another step, stay right here." The doctor ran down the hall yelling, "Orderly!"

"Victor whispered, "Come on let's get out of here for Georgie's sake! Can't you see they will find out about Georgie!"

Two cars left the emergency room parking lot with orderlies trying to stop them. Victor Vance said to his wife, "Look back, did they try to get our license plate number?"

Jason yelled, "Put the top down, I'll cover the plate," with both hands, he covered it. Heather was holding his legs. The Vance family car made it to the ramp of the freeway and turned to the roadway. There was a white truck with a police car with flashing lights. The police officer and the man with glass in his head were in the bed of the truck, trying to pull the driver door out of the cab, *that's strange*, thought Jason and Heather. "Dad, Dad, did you see that!"

"Yes, you see something new every day."

"No Dad, that must be Georgie's brother from Detroit! The truck has Michigan plates."

"How the hell did the guy in the white truck get a door stuck in the cab?" mentioned Dad.

"He was in the hospital at the same time, we could have been killed," stuttered Jason. Everyone shrank down in their seats. Then Heather and Jason popped up and looked back. "You won't believe it, Dad, TF put his lance into the cab of the white truck!"

A hideous laugh rang out in the car! Then the lance flew back to the car and was placed on the back bumper in front of the license plate.

Chapter 69

Georgie jumped the gate at the school and landed with a pain in his right foot. He looked at his shoe under the light at the corner, where Dad's classroom was, he leaned on the patio fence. "Now I have a hole in Johnny's shoe." He took the shoe off, found a hole around the big toe. Georgie squeezed, not too much pain, he heard metal on cement, the shoe fit much better, Joey clipped me with one of his customized bullets as he pulled it out. Old ladies go to bed early. Georgie slowly and carefully walked to the boys' gym lockers door; there she was snoring so loud it was practically rattling the lockers.

Amused, he pulled the tape loose that he attached to the lockers so she wouldn't fall off the bed, Georgie carried her back to C5 and carefully put her where she was originally. Georgie jumped back over the fence and quietly made it into the darkness, still hearing the snoring.

Two cars, the Two Bucks and the Vances, pulled up into the driveway of Ed and Lisa, standing there was Georgie. Georgie greeted everyone with hugs and kisses, he even greeted TF with a hug in the air. "How do you greet a ghost with a hug is beyond me," said Jason.

"Dad, mom, Mr. and Mrs. Two Buck, everyone, my brother knows where we live, Dad."

"Both houses?"

"No, just ours, he shot at me and I ripped off his truck door."

"We wondered how that happened; we saw him along the road with a policeman trying to pull it out. TF put his spear through the cab of the truck." A hideous laugh reigned supreme.

"Did the doctor say when Johnny can come home?" asked an apologetic Georgie.

Ed had been sitting in the car steaming, he slowly opened the car door and got out, he didn't want a hug, he just wanted his son home in one piece. "Now how the hell did you make that heart?" demanded Ed. "Not only did you almost kill my son, you saved him from death." Ed gave a rueful smile. "The doctors couldn't save him. The very person my son created unwittingly saved him by producing a heart."

"You got it wrong, Mr. Two Buck, there is the man that started it all unwittingly," Georgie pointed at Mr. Vance and got out of the way.

Victor Vance felt a little nervous as Ed, looking ashen white, he pointed a finger at Victor and demanded a complete explanation. "Georgie was killed by his brother Joey, basically because he not only stammered in his speech but couldn't speak at all. His brother thought Georgie completely incoherent and stupid. Because Georgie's mother couldn't control Joey after their father died, anyway, Joey abused Georgie constantly, he finally kills his younger sibling. Solving Joey's problem of taking care of his brother.

"Joey is now able to sell drugs with complete freedom. Joey is the oldest, the strongest, cunning and viscous was never taught right or wrong by their mother. Joey gets into drugs supporting their mother and of course, Georgie. Georgie is crucified every time Joey has a chance to punch Georgie and throw him in a dumpster, he does it but one more time Georgie retaliates. The next time Joey sees Georgie, Joey kills his dogs and runs him over in front of a liquor store.

"Georgie tells me that something picked his crushed body up and instead of taking him to heaven because I, Victor Vance, and Johnny unwittingly created an extraordinary human being, Ed. Your son saved Georgie's life and now Georgie has saved Johnny's life. I created a non-toxic silver-plating solution. Johnny knocked off an orchid while painfully cutting skin off his thumb and that is how we got Georgie. I'm sure your son will grow up a stronger healthier boy.

"Dear God, will you let us stay at your house tonight?"

Ed scratched his nose, looked at his wife, and said, "What do you think, dear?"

"Of course, they can stay here tonight. The Vance family can stay as long as they want!" Mrs. Two Buck went briskly to the front door, opened it, and everyone piled in. The first one to say something was Trotting Fox, "Me sleep with Indians."

"Oh no you don't, you sleep with the Vances. I am not sleeping with a ghost staring at me all night."

"Not stare," just as TF spoke, "What stare?" The phone rang, Ed rushed to beat his wife to the phone, Ed's big hand managed to slip under his wife's hand and he said, "Hello?"

"This is the hospital, Johnny Two Buck will be ready to pick up in the morning. The doctors are astounded, Johnny has gone out of the room, bummed money off one of the doctors and bought candy from one of the vending machines."

"Give it back right now," cried an infuriated Ed.

"Hello, Mom and Dad, these people are all crazy, I need food, Dad, send me a pizza and hurry, I'll be waiting at the ER door. Help, two orderlies are attacking me, help."

Behind Johnny's voice, "To bed, Johnny!"

"No, no!" The phone went silent.

Chapter 70

Monday morning the Vances were gagging on the egg grind up oak tree acorns wrapped up in a corn tortilla with salsa. "Pardon me Lisa, but what is this mess in this breakfast burrito?"

"Why, that's Ed's favorite breakfast. I thought you might try one. We keep them frozen in the frig."

"Well thank Ed, by the way where is Ed?" asked Victor.

Trotting Fox said, "Like acorn."

"You would."

"Ed went to pick up Johnny at the hospital."

"What, already!" Victor almost broke his coffee cup by slamming it back to the saucer. "I'll wait until they get here, I'll take him to school with the rest of the family."

"Yes, I know Johnny will want to see Georgie, Heather and Jason."

The Vance family put down their breakfast burritos, Jan Vance asked with a terrible look on her face, "Lisa, you don't mind if I go in the bathroom and gargle?"

A voice from nowhere desperately replied, "Me eat."

"You can't eat the burritos, TF, when will he ever learn? He must feel hungry," mentioned Jan.

Lisa ignored Jan's comments. "I know how awful they are, I'll take them out to the garbage."

"Me say no," cried an angry TF.

"So, Ed doesn't think that you didn't finish them."

"Stop following me, TF," Lisa pointed out.

The car turned into the driveway. Johnny jumped out of the car and raced into the house and said, "I feel great," then hugged everyone, his mother first, of course. Johnny chatted with his parents, ate an acorn burrito and said, "Let's go, Mr. Vance, I'm anxious to get to school to see all my friends and I'm glad

I'm still alive." He turned to Georgie and said, "Thank you," as they walked out the door. A wisp of air and a deep giggle rocked the car.

Miss Syndly was poised to pick off the boys when firecrackers went off in the quad. She grit her teeth, put on her right shoe and tried to run to the quad; her left fell off. Actually, this helped her in her quest to catch the unlawful student who lit the firecracker. The student saw that no one was in the office, he lit up another. Miss Syndly hid behind the wooden front gate and peeked through a crack and raced around the gate; when the boy tried to light another firecracker, she grabbed him by his shirt tail and said, "Wait until your mother and father find out about this, Mr. Sam," she gave him a smile that said, "You are in deep trouble. You are in for some work on the seat of your pants, boy. Your writing will be quite a long essay on George Washington. I hope you like to wash and clean the boys' locker room by the gym. It smells awful, I should know," Miss Syndly announces.

Dad drove the car into the parking lot at the south end of the school. Georgie said to Johnny, "How do you feel?"

"I feel fine, feel my heart beat."

Dad unlocked the C5 door. "Gosh, you left it in a mess, Georgie. Help me clean the room up before first period students make it to class." Johnny walked over to the middle of the room, it said JOEY now inscribed in the cement floor. Victor Vance looked up at the window; it had Joey too. "O no we have a criminal's name cut in the window and on the floor!"

Georgie looked down then to the window. TF said, "Bad medicine."

As soon as Trotting Fox said it, the words were slowly wiped away. "Wow Dad, now Miss Syndly can't pick on you. She'll be amazed that we got rid of the word."

At that moment the indestructible Miss Syndly, stinky, walked into the room. "Look at this floooor…what happened?"

Mr. Vance replied, "We filled it, let it dry then polished it until it disappeared."

Miss Syndly took off her right shoe and said, "What about the window," her mouth opened wide and just sort of hung open for the longest time.

"We replaced it." Georgie, Johnny and Mr. Vance nodded.

"Well, that is satisfactory Vance because getting letters out of cement is practically impossible, how did you do it?"

Victor Vance let some answers whirl around in his brain and it came up with technical ceramic. "Chemical formulas taken from the clay industry and magic," replied Victor Vance with authority.

Miss Syndly took her right shoe off again and said, "To change the subject, the other night I was sleeping outdoors on the campus."

"But why would you sleep on the campus when you could sleep on your porch at home?"

"Well, I just like it here," responded the ever creepy stinky. She then said, "While I was sleeping, I had the strange sensation of slowly flying through the air and landing in the boys' gym locker room and later, I flew back where I started here at C5."

"How do you suppose that happened?" asked Victor, trying not to laugh. "Well, you were dreaming, weren't you?"

"Yes."

"Did it really happen?"

"I don't know!" She changed the subject again, "There is always something fishy going on in this classroom, mystical and strange goings-on here!"

Victor Vance looked at Miss Syndly with an irritating look and quietly mouthed the words, "Haven't I always done my job satisfactory and haven't I taken the hardcore students without saying a word? Now can I set up my demonstration for the incoming class!" announced Victor Vance.

"Yes, you may, Mr. Vance, and don't do anything strange or creepy."

"If I hear creepy and strange words coming from students, I'm walking out of this class," said Mr. Vance.

"I will fire you," Miss Syndly walked out the door.

"Why, you buy!"

Quietly Georgie said, "Dad, don't say it, she is still by the door," as the door closed.

Miss Syndly opened the door and asked, "What did you say?"

Victor looked at Miss Syndly and replied, "We have to fix a bicycle when we get home."

She smiled then left and closed the door again. Georgie said, "Wow Dad, that was close, she has a terrible temper."

"Do you know, son, she asked me to run some of the science, grammar videos and cartoons at the next PTA meeting next week?"

Johnny looked at Victor and mentioned, "Arturo Gomez's cartoons are well drawn and clever but are filled with very, shall I say, negative subject matter."

Chapter 71

Joey had gone to the house, 1124 Waterford Lane, to find no one home; he screamed as loud as he could, "You son-of-bitch, you'll never stop me!" Joey took his high-powered air pistol and pumped a thousand rounds into the house. He then yelled, "You screwed up my truck, I will extract blood from your dead body, and I will put it in a squirt gun and spray my victims with it."

Georgie ran by the house several times and the house had no blemishes but the next time he ran by the house, he found it full of holes, Georgie thought to himself Joey must have gotten his truck fixed. Georgie checked with the neighbors and four said they heard screaming but they couldn't make it out and never went out to look. Georgie was perplexed how they were going to get this maniac. *My brother is too dangerous, I will not subject my family or the Two Buck's family to any chancy situation.*

Georgie ran back to the Two Buck's home where Jan and Victor were having diner and asked the two families for a pow-wow. Georgie looked at his family and said, "Our house is almost destroyed. Joey has shot holes all through the front of the house. We'll have to call the police; this is much too serious, Joey is a mad man."

Mr. Two Buck immediately got up from his chair and picked up the telephone and dialed the police, the number was on the roll-a-flex. "Hello, this is Ed Two Buck at 2240 Cherrylawn Lane; my family and my friend Victor Vance and his family are being hunted by a drug dealer named Joey Martin, he means to kill all of us because we interfered with his drug dealing."

The Sargent said, "I will send an officer over as soon as I have an officer free."

"Thank you, Sargent." While Ed was talking to the Sargent, Victor and Georgie were fidgeting and as soon as Ed hung up, "We need to make sure we have our story straight," said Victor. "We met the white truck at the cross-country meet, hidden in the trees, he found out an Indian kid is looking for him through an informant. He doesn't know why the kid is looking for him, he just knows what his informant thinks it is suspicious. I got his truck license plate number; I will turn Joey in for criminal activities."

The officer in an unmarked gray sedan pulled into the driveway on Cherrylawn Lane. The plain clothed officer rang the doorbell, Mrs. Two Buck asked to see his credentials. He was Inspector Hector Gomez of the division of drug enforcement. "Come in, inspector, we have a big problem."

As the inspector sat down, a white truck stopped in front of the house with the passenger side window down. A super air pistol shined in the sunlight and a sharp phit…rattled off a hundred rounds at a time, wounding the inspector and Mrs. Two Buck. "He must have followed me from the police station," said a bleeding inspector Gomez.

Georgie grabbed Heather and Jason and pulled them to the floor, Ed and Victor did the same. Ed crawled to his family room and got his bow off the wall, reached for his quiver, inserted an arrow into the nock-lock, opened a side window and carefully aimed at the truck and air pistol. The arrow from Ed's bow went through the truck's cab and pinned the air pistol to the windshield.

By this time Georgie reached the driver's side of the truck, smashed his left hand through the window of the truck and grabbed his brother by the hair. His brother was trying to turn so that he can pull his weapon from the windshield and shoot at Georgie. Georgie forced his right hand through the glass and covered Joey's eyes. Joey slammed his right foot on to the accelerator; he knew the truck was pointed away from traffic and going straight down the street. Georgie banged Joey's head several times against the glass, his brother fell into unconsciousness, his foot slowly fell off the accelerator.

Georgie ripped out the window, grabbed the steering wheel, and put the truck in reverse. The truck jerked hard, the tires squealed, the truck moved backward. Georgie let the truck roll to a stop in front of the house and put the truck in park. His brother's eyes fluttered and with his eyes closed, he tried to grab the air pistol but it was no use; the arrow won't budge because TF was holding it. "I see your conscious brother!"

"What are you doing, smart ass fuckin' Indian! I will kill your ass! And don't call me brother, you son-of-bitch; my brother is dead!"

"Oh, I'm your brother, you crushed me under the truck. Dad sent me to round up your criminal butt and send it to jail for life!" At that moment Georgie ripped out the ignition wires then forced Joey's hands behind his back, tying them with the wire. He picked up Joey, banged his head on the back window of the truck. While throwing Joey on his belly. Then took the rest of the wire, tied his legs to his hands. "That's what they call a hogtie, Joey."

"You Indian freak, you son-of-bitch," screamed Joey.

"I'm Georgie and don't talk about mother that way, Joey! Mother is in a rest home in Detroit." The sirens screamed down the street. The police were in force—three cars and a firetruck screeched to a halt in front of Ed Two Buck's house.

Six policemen and five firemen rushed to the white truck. Joey with bulging muscles was being held by a boy of twelve and a half. "Son," said the first police officer, "how did you do this?"

Georgie said, "What do you mean, officer?" Then realizing what he was talking about, Georgie pretended to faint.

Joey laughed and said, "This kid tells lies, I have done nothing wrong, officer, I caught this Indian boy hiding behind my truck shooting this Beebe pistol at the house."

A big voice boomed, "This man is lying, he was shooting at the house. Take the weapon in and check fingerprints, officers," the voice was Victor Vance's. "The boy saved us from being hit by the pellet gun. I think you'll find that this man has a criminal record here and in Detroit."

In the house, Inspector Hector Gomez and Lisa Two Buck lay wounded. The medical team on the fire truck rush into the house. Two policemen were holding Georgie from falling to the street. Georgie opened one eye when he heard a door slam and two people talking; it was a T.V. crew from KBBT. Georgie heard a voice say, "This is the man who has been selling narcotics to the kids in the park. Officer, who is responsible for capturing this man?"

"This kid, but he fainted; however, I don't see how he did it." The news lady looked down at Georgie and the two officers that were holding Georgie, he slipped out of their grasp and was gone. He quickly flew under the white truck then crawled to the curb and tried to get to the house but was spotted by a news man standing on the sidewalk leading to the house.

Mrs. Vance ran out of the house and said, "Are you alright?" She grabbed Georgie away from the news man and guided Georgie into the house and slammed the door shut.

"I think someone out there knows my mother and my brother for sure, maybe an officer or two, sort of," announced a wide-eyed and frightened Georgie. "It went so quick, I didn't know what to do. Mother, Mrs. Two Buck and the inspector…are they alright?"

"Calm down, son, you did good. We all appreciate that you didn't say more then you had to."

Lisa and the inspector were out the door on their way to the hospital. Victor, shaken, his voice raspy, "How come he didn't shoot you?" he asked.

"By the way who shot the arrow?" Georgie wondered.

"I did!" said Ed.

"Wow, what a shot, the arrow stuck not in the windshield but in the metal at the edge of the windshield so the arrow nock was stuck against Joey's chest, that's when I put my right hand through the window and covered his eyes, nose and mouth then beat his head against the glass and broke his nose, that knocked him unconscious, wow, that felt good after all the beatings I took from him!"

The doorbell rang, Mr. Two Buck went to the door, "Who are you?" asked Ed.

"Your neighbor across the street." Ed opened the door, lights began flashing, Ed slammed the door shut.

Ed turned and said, "There must be twenty photographers out there."

Jan Vance peeked out the side window, she got a blast of the same. Jan Vance screamed, "Oh my eyes, the light is so bright!" Jason and Heather along with their mother and father went upstairs to look out the windows and of course, Johnny and Georgie bounded up to watch the growing crowd.

Ed, who was already upstairs with a pillow over his face, said in a muffled voice, "The crowd is getting bigger!"

"The neighbors must have told the reporters and photographers what happened plus the police chatter over the radios," said the irritated Jan Vance.

Georgie turned to Johnny, "You're the one!"

"I'm the one what?"

"You are me and I'm you. Does that make sense?"

"No," laughed Johnny.

The noise outside began to diminish outside; after all, it was midnight. Lisa Two Buck turned out the last light in the house and the back bedroom.

Chapter 72

The morning paper had a picture of Georgie holding his brother Joey, a very muscular man, in some kind of death grip. Georgie looked puny beside Joey. Ed looked up from the kitchen table and said, "Come over here, Georgie, look at this picture."

"How did they get that picture?" Vic holding a flashlight. "I'm not sure. Oh, I know, one of the policemen must have taken it, I remember a flash."

Everyone came over to the kitchen table and looked at the picture. Ed said, "An amazing youngster captures a man twice his size apparently with ease. Reporters are anxious to interview this boy." Ed then looked up in thought.

"I know just what you're thinking, Ed," said Victor Vance.

"Then wait a minute, isn't it illegal to use a picture of a juvenile without the parents' consent at a crime scene and put it in the paper?" Then Ed said to Vic, "No, that is not what I was thinking. I think we should take our families and move to your house, Vic, because no one but Georgie's brother knows where it is and he is in jail. Let's take a vote. Who wants to leave the reporters behind?"

"Raise your hand and say Aye," asked Victor Vance.

Everyone said Aye. A stampede of bodies hit the floor hard to get their clothes and bedding, toothbrush and comb. Mrs. Vance looked out the side window again and found no one on the lawn or in a car watching the house. "No one out there," whispered Mrs. Vance.

"Let's go out the back, both cars are in the garage. We'll open the garage doors, glide quietly down the driveway then down the hill with engines off. What do you think, everyone?" said a quiet Ed Two Buck.

Both families agreed. Victor spoke up, "We do have to go to school today, it's Monday."

"Oh Dad, Mr. Vance, do we have to!"

"Ed has to go to work. What do you want to do all day, sit around the house and do nothing?"

"Yes," yelled all the kids.

Lisa and Jan looked at their kids, Jan said, "Do we have to listen to all your chatter and we need rest from the hair-raising excitement," said Lisa in a whisper. "Out, out, too much noise drives me crazy."

"Alright Mr. Vance, drive us to school," the kids whined dejectedly. The cars did their job and when they got to the bottom of the hill, Ed and Vic took their foot off the brakes then put the cars in gear, let the clutches out and zoomed into the morning sun. As they stepped into the air pellet pistol riddled house, Georgie said, "I wonder how much lead is going for these days?"

Everyone gave a smirk and a smile but Jan and Lisa didn't; they knew who had to pick them up.

"OK leave, Lisa and I have a big job picking up the pellets."

Chapter 73

School was sudden terror—Miss Syndly had the school band out in front of the school playing "When Johnny Comes Marching Home." TF tried to keep up with the music as he hung out the window, "Bump-pa, bump-pa."

"Dad, keep driving, go to the high school and let Heather and Jason off," remarked Georgie.

As they drove back, Johnny said, "What is Miss Syndly doing with the school band?"

Then Georgie saw the KBBT T.V. truck hidden between the gym and the auditorium. "How did they find out? How do we go to school, Dad?"

Victor Vance was shaking his head in disgust, "I don't know. The only thing I can think of is Johnny said something at the hospital what school he goes to and you?"

"But the last names are different!"

"Me told them," said TF.

"How did you tell the T.V. people?" cried a totally frustrated Victor Vance.

"Me dropped report card on white truck seat."

"What!" moaned everyone in the car. The noise volume dropped to zero in the car.

Victor stopped the car in front of the high school and let Heather and Jason out. They said, "Good luck." Everyone had a grim look on their faces.

"Me Johnny's report card wrapped around red ball," TF explained.

Victor Vance drove slowly back to the middle school where he worked. He imagined swarms of people, cops and scientist trying to physically test Georgie constantly and reporters, T.V. people attempting to interview him. Day by day, Victor thought, reports would occur in the newspapers on his growth, education, and love life. "Dad, you're going to miss the parking lot!"

"Oh, I was day dreaming." Vance locked the car. The boys began walking toward the hustle and bustle of the campus when a reporter and his photograph jumped out of the bushes and the reporter screamed, "There's two of them! You speak English?"

"Of course, they speak English, you nitwit!" yelled Victor Vance.

Trotting Fox hit both of them with his little red ball from the back so Victor had time to unlock C5 and let Georgie and Johnny in and locked the door. Standing outside the door, Victor Vance said, "Gentlemen, don't you realize that you have to have permission from the parents to interview juveniles?"

Smarting from the hit on the head and the twist in the neck, the reporter asked, "You wouldn't happened to be one of the parents?"

"Do I look Indian to you?" A rush of words turned into no words with jaws set and stares. Victor Vance moved toward the admin building to call Ed at the university.

Two voices yelled, "Wait," realizing their scoop was gone if they let Victor Vance slip away, the cameraman and the reporter boxed him in preventing Victor Vance from escaping their clutches. The school band came marching to room C5 with Miss Syndly and the two policemen in the lead. Other reporters and photographers tried to push their way through the band but Victor Vance escaped by crashing through the band and raced to the administration building to safety behind a locked door. He moved quickly to the phone and dialed… "The Creative Arts building please."

Victor turned, hearing a key in the front door letting Miss Syndly into the admin building with the two police officers. The first police officer said, "Are you Victor Vance?"

"Yes."

"Do you know the whereabouts of one Johnny Two Buck?"

"Hold it officer, I'm making a phone call to the father of Johnny. Ed, you better get over here; the police want to talk to your son."

As Victor hung up, the second police officer asked, "Where is the boy now?"

"Here on campus in my room C5. I'll make a call down to the room." Victor grabbed the inside phone and dialed his number. It rang once, "Hello, Johnny."

"No, this is Georgie."

"You better go to class," suggested Mr. Vance.

Miss Syndly grabbed the phone and said, "Georgie, you stay right there!"

Victor Vance looked at Miss Syndly and smiled. Awful things were going through Victor Vance's mind, he began to laugh. "Miss Syndly, why are you inferring?" asked the first officer.

Miss Syndly gave a sinister smile at Victor and blurted out, "There are two boys and they are identical twins." She gave Victor a smirk, "Aren't you supposed to be in class?"

"Prep period," answered Vance. Victor smiled again.

The police officer said, "Let's go down to your room and Miss Syndly, you stay here. We don't want you to interrupt the interview," said the first officer.

Syndly's jaw dropped to her desk top. The admin door closed and the campus noise came into play and the reporters yelling "There's two of them." The officers, not paying attention to the prattle, said, "How can you stand that bitch!"

Victor looked at them and smiled, "It's all part of the game." They shrugged their shoulders as Victor unlocked the door of C5. Two officers sized up the boys and to them nothing appeared unusual. The second officer queried, "Who is Johnny?" not knowing they had different last names and Victor Vance had no legal document that Georgie was adopted.

Johnny raised his hand from where he was sitting on a stool. The first officer reached into his shirt pocket and pulled out a report card, he said, "Is this yours?"

Johnny walked over to the police officer, looked at the report card and nodded his head in agreement. "We found this in Joey Martin's truck seat."

Victor Vance nodded his head no. Johnny looked at him with a smile and reported to the officer, "Trotting Fox put it there."

"Where is the dog?"

"Oh, he's not a dog."

Victor Vance now had his hands in front of him in the praying position and nodding his head no. "Georgie, should I have him do it?"

"Officers, look up at the ceiling corner by the display case. Do you see the little red rubber ball?" requested Johnny.

By this time Victor Vance was sweating and he had his hands over his eyes. As the officers turned…bop, bop, bop, bop…both officers drew their pistols. Georgie laughed and said, "He's not dangerous. He held Joey's gun against the windshield."

Victor Vance was bent over saying to himself, *I'll be thrown in the loony bin.*

The first officer said, "Come down from there!"

"What come down from where? There's the rubber ball, maybe he's hiding under the false ceiling," said the second officer.

"No, he's not under the ceiling; how can he hit you from above the ceiling," Georgie announced.

Victor Vance realized what the boys were doing, they were putting the capture of Joey on TF. The two police officers began laughing and the first officer replied, "You're trying to tell me that a ghost did in the white truck. Not Colonel mustard in the library with a knife," they both started to laugh hysterically.

"No sir, we didn't capture him; a 250-year-old Indian from the Zuni tribe did," Georgie calmly told the officers.

The officers laughed even harder if that was possible. TF hit them again this time in the forehead, bop, bop, of course, TF hit them as hard as he could no self-righteous Indian ghost would take that kind of laughter from anyone. "Damn, that hurts!" cried the first officer.

The other officer said, "If you do that again, I'll hurt you!" A hideous laugh kept laughing more than the cops. The second officer fired into the corner of the ceiling, but the laughter didn't stop.

"You know me fire me arm."

"No, no TF, you mean you did fire at me with a firearm," croaked out Georgie! Slowly ever so slowly, parts of Trotting Fox's body came together to make a conglomeration of bits developing on the false ceiling, blurry at first and lowering himself from the ceiling. The officers got their mace spray cans from their belt holders and sprayed this blurry skeleton into full focus with ragged Indian horrible smelling not so good Zuni wear.

"My God, I never smelled that before; TF, where have you been keeping it?" cried a coughing Victor Vance.

The skeleton bared its not so many teeth at the officers. The number two officer coughed and spat, "Now this has gone too far! Which one of you tied the criminal Joey Martin up, and I want the answer now!" Immediately, from out of nowhere the two officers fell to the cement floor of room C5 tied up no gag. Victor Vance said, "What do you think?"

Bewildered, the first officer looked up from the floor and asked, "That was quick and wet rawhide too, probably pee."

Victor Vance, Georgie and Johnny, "TF did it in the white truck." First Trotting Fox laughed and the rest joined in with a smile and a chuckle. Georgie and Johnny looked down at the officers, Johnny said, "Sirs, please don't tell anyone about TF."

Victor cut the rawhide to allow the officers to rise. Victor Vance looked at the officers and issued a statement to the officers, "Now are you convinced?" They nodded their heads and picked up their mace cans. "If you really want to know, I did it."

As the officers stepped outside, Miss Syndly had the band play "Stars and Stripes Forever!" The officers straightened their uniforms and were in step to the music all the way to the police car.

Miss Syndly came through the door with a broom in her hand. The second officer walked back and peeked into C5 and said, "It's fitting, don't you think?"

Miss Syndly gave the cop a dirty look, turned around, and said, "Who's the hero?"

Johnny and Georgie looked at Miss Syndly, then at Dad Vance and pointed together at Victor Vance. The last bell of the day. Three days left before summer vacation. Ed Two Buck arrived too late; Victor Vance had protected both boys by confusing the officers and Miss Syndly.

Chapter 74

The court proceedings occurred on June thirtieth; a muscular man seated beside a well-dressed man in a suit, light blue with dark blue pinstripes and a red tie. Handcuffs on the big muscular man with a crew haircut with an ugly scar on his forehead. Joey was jingling the handcuff chain against his belt buckle. Not paying attention to the proceedings. He kept his head down hoping everyone will see his scar and have pity on him.

The judge said over his mic, "Guilty or not guilty?"

The lawyer in the light blue suit with the dark pinstripes said, "Cut the noise, you imbecilic dick, and answer the judge!"

Joey looked up and gave the lawyer the harshest angry look while still staring at the pinstripes and yelled, "Not guilty!"

The security officer, a nonchalant and unworthy of his profession, didn't subscribe to chains around the ankles. The judge said to the security officer, "Where is this prisoner's leg irons?"

He stood up and reported, "I didn't think he needed them, his offense is minor."

"On the contrary," the magistrate said, "he has criminal charges against him for assaulting two Indian boys and attempting to kill their families. Take him back to his cell and chain him appropriately."

The security guard unsnapped his pistol, turned, and looked at Joey Martin. "We are back to your cell. Get up out of that chair."

Joey thought to himself, *I'll get this chump.* The security guard came over to the table, grabbed the chain between Joey's hands and pointed his pistol at Joey. "Get up now!"

Joey, the muscular brute that he was, showed no vicious signs. After getting up, Joey and the guard moved behind the muscular man and they quietly walked to the door leading to the prison cells, the security guard pushed the door open from behind the prisoner. Joey kicked backward with his right leg and caught the security guard in the crotch, he quickly turned as the guard fell to the floor and pulled the pistol out of the guard's hand. While in the minor tussle, a round from the pistol hit Joey in the left side near his hip, Joey hit the guard in the head with the pistol, he turned his gaze at the judge and his attorney.

The judge stood up with his hands in the air. Joey walked up to his attorney and said, "Take that suit coat off." He grabbed the overcoat off the chair next to where he was sitting, the attorney in an angry tone said, "You son-of-bitch!"

Joey smiled and discharged one round at the man who was supposed to defend him. The attorney was now lying in a pool of blood, Joey Martian grabbed the overcoat, so it doesn't get contaminated, part of the overcoat was on the floor near the oozing blood.

Joey looked at the judge with his hands up. "Regretfully, it is your turn, maybe not regretfully." With demonical rage, he discharged two slugs from the revolver at the judge, he crumpled to his chair. Now that the defense was out of the way, Joey wrapped the suit coat around his waist so that he doesn't leave a blood trail, scrambled out the courtroom and rushed to the underground parking facility by the elevator and put on the overcoat. He ran down the parked cars checking the cars to find one that was unlocked. He found a Cadillac door ajar.

Quietly, he closed the door, hotwired it in seconds; guards heard by wireless radio that a prisoner had escaped. Joey moved the car out of the parking spot with ingenuity, while the car was in reverse, slammed the accelerator to the metal, killed the two guards firing at the car. The rounds from the guard's guns set the Cadillac on fire. Joey pressed the electric window button to on, killed the remaining guard in front of the car, while bullets were flying. Crashed the door gate, the flames were not apparent to Joey speeding down a street in town.

He turned a corner and settled to a normal speed so that he was not easily detected. He looked in the rear-view mirror and responded to the fire in the back of the car by pulling into a parking lot, jumping out and running into the building in front of the car. Not realizing what building he was in. The handcuffed muscular man was irritated by the blood trail he was leaving. He hid his cuffed hands and gun in the overcoat.

Joey realized that he was in a museum, an old western museum. He looked around the main lobby and saw nothing that will help him get the handcuffs off. Out of the corner of his eye, he noticed a stairway, quietly, he made his way to the second floor. People on the first floor did not notice the man was concealing something or thought nothing of it.

Joey was desperately seeking some way to rid himself of this prison hardware. He was happier than two pounds of cocaine to sell, he found what he was looking for—a blacksmith shop. He stayed light on his feet, scanned back and forth slyly and quietly, jumped over a four feet wall that housed the entire blacksmith shop. The display showed a fake fire in a bed of artificial hot coals. A manikin with a heavy hammer pounding on a piece of metal on an anvil.

Joey walked through the shop. Grabbed the hammer, "The fuckin' hammer is fake, it's made out of paper and paste," he pushed the manikin out of the way, he picked up the anvil, it was real, and threw it at the wall. A thunderous roar broke the silence in the museum, as though lightning and thunder hit the building. The shattered silence struck an ear-piercing sound, the curator's serene and calm nature was suddenly obliterated. He scrambled out of his chair, he was ruefully interrupted while going over his inventory and contemplating his next acquisitions for the western museum.

The curator standing in the hallway not knowing which way to investigate, he listened with apprehension for the next uproar. He didn't have to wait long. Joey Martin walked through the broken wall and found himself in a display of Indian life. He poked around the display, found an actual tomahawk and spear; they were both real.

Joey said out loud, "Maybe I'll get a chance to kill the two fuckin' Indian kids with these ancient weapons." He went back and got the anvil, set it flat on the floor, sat down and laid the chain between his hands on the anvil, picked up the tomahawk carefully, not disturbing the chain on the anvil, he calculated the distance that he had to work with and began pounding on the chain.

The curator finally decided that the noise was on the second floor. Calmly, he walked back to his office and pressed the security button. He briskly walked up the stairs and when he got to the top step, he hid behind a pillar and watched the big muscular man in the prison uniform pounding on something that he can't quite see because of the wall. The curator thought to himself, *How did the brute get past me? I kept my eyes on the monitors*, he stretched his head out from behind the pillar. After he pushed the security button, five minutes later an audio alarm went off, warning all exits will be closed.

Joey heard the big door in the museum closing, he gave a last whack with the tomahawk. The chain broke, instantly Joey got up from the floor and looked around for some way to escape from the museum. He screeched, "Isn't there something in this fucking Indian junk?" He checked the revolver. "Only two bullets," stuck the gun in the back of his pants.

Joey began to look through the Indian display for a way to rid himself of this place, left the spear by the anvil and put the tomahawk beside the gun in the back of his pants, tightened up the suit coat around his wound. Finally, gazing around the Indian room by twisting in a circle in a frustrating and antagonizing shuffle, Joey saw a grass rope hanging on a whittled branch in front of a tepee, grabbed the rope, tied it to a heating radiator, opened the window, threw the rope out the window; it reached almost to the ground in the alleyway.

Joey checked to make sure his pistol and tomahawk were snug and tight in the back of his trousers. He heard trampling and shuffling of feet coming up the stairway. He checked the rope by pulling hard, he grabbed hold of the rope, got on the windowsill, put his feet on the outer wall of the museum and began his descent to the alley floor. The rope broke after two steps down the wall.

The police found Joey unconscious in the alley, but alive. They called for an ambulance, Joey still not moving and was placed on a stretcher and taken to the hospital. The next day the Two Buck and the Vance family had arrived at the courthouse and found that Joey had escaped and was in the hospital. The families were told Joey died. Georgie asked, "What was the cause of his death?"

"The cause of this man's death was found to be a little red ball stuck in his windpipe and a rubber string sticking straight up in the air," answered the coroner.

"Yes, that is possible, sir," said Georgie.

Dear Agent:

This thriller is one of the better school stories since *Harry Potter*.

Georgie is intimidated by a control freak, his brother. Georgie is younger by one year. Their mother works. This dysfunctional family lives in a basement apartment in Detroit. Joey the older brother has just gotten out of Juvenile Hall. Joey is back to his criminal ways, he sees his brother as someone in his way, this is a bad day for Joey. His brother caused the trouble. Joey simply runs over Georgie with his truck. But he is not dead. His soul is lifted from the ground by the man Georgie loved the most—his father. Georgie looks at him and says, "Father, you are dead."

"So are you, son, I am holding your disembodied soul."

Georgie realizes he is in his dad's arms, he again says, "Dad, you're dead!"

"Son, your brother needs salvation and that is you lying on the pavement." Whiteness falls upon Georgie's soul. He found himself locked in a sphere, a ball, a cocoon. He is silver-green. A teacher in Northern California has a bad day. The state of California eliminates toxic substances from the classroom. He is right in the middle of silver-plating objects for the students in his Craft class for gifts.

Six months later, the teacher comes up with a non-toxic solution for silver plating. Some days later his student assistant, an Indian boy, cuts his thumb over the silver solution container, knocks in an orchid being cloned, while skin and blood fall into the silver-plating solution. Another bad day for the student and the teacher. The solution is not discarded. It is put in a cabinet for the President's Holidays.

The fire department calls the teacher to come to his classroom. "Sir your classroom seems to be on fire, but it doesn't burn, can you explain?"

The fireman said he hesitated to touch the building with water. The teacher, Victor Vance, enters the classroom to investigate with his dog Tanny. Tanny slips and slides across the cement floor to the cabinet, she seems to be comforted. Victor Vance sees nothing wrong in his classroom, calls his dog and leaves. The teacher sends the fire department back to their station.

After the President's Holidays, Victor Vance and his student assistant, Johnny Two Buck, meet at the room, C5, Mr. Vance's classroom. Mr. Vance opens the cabinet door, a strange silver-green light engulfs the room. The light is coming from the cabinet where the non-toxic plating solution is stored. Victor Vance and Johnny slowly sneak up, thinking someone is hiding in the cabinet and trying to steal Mr. Vance's formula.

It is Georgie spared from death, whose soul is transplanted and his intelligence into this twin of Johnny. Georgie stays with his adopted parents, Mr. and Mrs. Victor Vance. Georgie is enrolled at the school where Victor Vance teaches. This twin hunts down his criminal brother, Joey.

Chapter 75

The pellet gun that Joey Martin used ruined the houses of two families. Victor Vance moved closer to the high school and the Two Bucks moved next door. The twins Heather and Jason moved to the tenth grade and followed their dad's ability in the arts. Heather sang and danced. Jason painted and sculpted and also danced. Georgie and Johnny played for the Cotati Tigers, a football team of twelve-year-olds. Johnny beat out Paul for the quarterback spot. Georgie replaced Peter as the wide receiver. Peter went to halfback. While Peter and Paul were much bigger, the speed and agility of the Indian boys obtained their positions on the football team.

The police called and asked Victor if Georgie could help out in the juvenile section and asked Mr. Vance if he had his permission?

"Of course he does, that is if he wants to help."

The next day Georgie went to the police with TF and the number one policeman that TF tied up, Officer Callahan, that chased a criminal. The Vances and the Two Bucks moved from their houses do to the powerful through a rock query and captured him on a daring arrest known as not so clean Harry.

After school and football practice in the boys' locker room, while Johnny and Georgie were dressing, three twelve graders came into the locker room. The one with big brawny arms grabbed Johnny and between popping his bubble gum said, "What's this I hear, you pushed my cousin out his job he had for the last two years."

One of the others said, "Work this punk over, Bone Crusher." He had Johnny by his collar and held him off the floor. Georgie sent a shot of the silver green light at the twelve graders; he felt a pain in his back and dropped Johnny. Johnny kicked him in the calf muscle.

"Why you little pipsqueak, I'll knock your block off." Suddenly, his arm dropped and again a pain in his back. The other twelve grader quickly held

Bone Crusher up before he fell to the floor. Sherman cracked his gum and promptly remarked, "What the hell is wrong with you, Crusher?"

"I had another pain in my back."

Georgie rushed over and helped the bent over Crusher and Benton, the third twelve grader, brushed Georgie away and said, "I was trying to help." He was now thinking, *I better escort Johnny out before they try some new tactic on us*. "So, Paul has his cousin out trying to help by intimidation. What do you want to do about it, Johnny?"

"We better ask your dad and mine." The boys walked quickly out of the locker room and to C5.

"You boys going to run for office this year; we need some honest people in the office of president and vice pres.," asked Victor Vance. "The trash they threw last year in the quad was terrible. The administration thought they were wonderful and so did some teachers but Babs and Beth were pests personified."

The first day of the fall semester went well until football practice. The football coach, Max Brand, decided to get help in his talk. Peter's cousin Allen Boles will help known as Bone Crusher, first thing Allen did was throw a football at Johnny. It knocked him to the ground. When Georgie got to him, he was unconscious. The coach fired Allen Boles on the spot. He laughed as he walked off and gave his cousin, Peter a hidden thumbs up. Georgie couldn't retaliate because of the thirty-six players watched the entire so-called accident.

So, in practice, Peter quarterbacked the team and he wouldn't throw the ball to Georgie, as they worked through plays Denis sat in the stands and watched Georgie and was still trying to prove that there was something strange about Georgie. Georgie noticed Denis in the stands and told Max Brand that he was going to walk with Johnny to the middle school and get a ride home. While in the locker room dressing, Bone Crusher came in again chewing and snapping his gum and said, "Can't catch the ball when thrown at you. What did you say your name is, Johnny square head?" He snapped and cracked his gum and said, "Did they paint one of you red so they could tell you apart?"

That was it for Georgie, he sort of nonchalantly set Crusher's hair on fire on the back of his head. Crusher said, "What's that smell, I never smelled that smell before," crack, crack went the gum.

"Take a look in the mirror," said Johnny.

Both Georgie and Johnny put their hands up. Georgie had the silver-green light bounce off the mirror and burn Bone Crusher's hair. They quickly exited while the crusher had his head in the sink. When they were out of eyesight behind the trees at the school, Georgie picked up Johnny and took to the tree tops and cautiously picked their way through the tree tops and made it safely to the middle school without being seen. They noticed Miss Syndly's and Miss Yerkes' cars and Dad's car in the teachers' parking lot. As they went into C5, they caught a glimpse of Denis but he ducked back behind the wooden door at the front of the school.

Johnny gave Georgie a leery look. "Do you think he saw us come over through the trees?"

"No but I saw him in the stands at practice. Denis the would-be detective has an in with our lovely Miss stinky foot principal of the middle school. Dad, Denis is on my tail again."

"Georgie, just don't do anything abnormal such as catching a football and going for a touchdown. Just watch Johnny's movements and fashion your movements after his." Mr. Vance cleaned off his desk and said, "The police Sergeant Bob Newhouser called and said that they want you at the station as soon as possible."

"Dad, is there any way you can occupy Denis and Miss Syndly while I get to the police station?"

"Yes, I'll go to the admin building and talk about the new science book we're getting and get their interest because I have the only copy, I got it from Miss Syndly, she didn't want to read through it. Denis will be thrilled to see it. I hope he doesn't pull a Sherlock on me." Victor Vance walked down to the Admin Building to Miss Syndly's office and there was Denis rattling on about Georgie and Johnny play at the practice.

Denis went "oops" as Mr. Vance walked in the office and then Denis said nothing. Mr. Vance said, "I'm returning the science book Denis might like to thumb through the book, Miss Syndly?"

Denis looked at Victor and opened his mouth, "I wish to go on the trip next spring, Mr. Vance. Are Georgie and Johnny going?"

"I don't know it depends on how many children want to go and how much my wife will drive." Victor figured Georgie had enough time to make it out of C5 and to the police station.

Georgie opened the door of the police station and said hello to the policeman in charge of drugs and a specialty in child drug dealers. They shake hands and Georgie said, "What's up?"

"We have a problem, some guy in a beat-up car is now taken over peddling drugs to kids. Do you know where he hangs out?"

"I think so, it is a small diner in Sonoma, when I was looking for my brother, I followed him there. What do you want to do, Sergeant?"

"I want you to follow him if you find him, Georgie."

"Can you have someone drive me to Sonoma?"

"Of course, Georgie."

Georgie sat quietly at the diner for two hours and then walked to the door and turned on the radio that the Sergeant gave him. "Nothing to report, I need a ride back." A plain black car stopped in front of the diner and Georgie jumped in. The plainclothes policeman asked Georgie," How did that terrible gangster die that you were related to, son?"

"He was my older brother."

"How did you do him in?"

"I didn't, my friend did."

"Was he arraigned and prosecuted?" asked the policeman.

"No, he wasn't." responded Georgie.

"Why not?"

"Well, I will show him to you, TF. Bump, bump."

"What was that?"

"A rubber red ball that hit you in the head."

"How did you do that?"

"I didn't. My friend did, sir."

"Where is he in the backseat, son?"

"No, look at my right shoulder. Do you see that little rubber red ball?"

"Yes."

"That's him."

"What is he, some kind of chameleon."

"No, he is a 250-year-old ghost."

"Alright get out of the car."

TF immediately hit the police officer in the head and laughed his horrible laugh. "Are you a ventriloquist?"

"No."

"Do you have a tape deck in your pocket?"

"No, but I will show you TF if you wish to see him, he is a stack of bones," Georgie said. "You should park the car, sir."

"No, I'll be alright, just show him to me." *This kid is nuttier than a fruit cake.* The Sergeant picked him to help out. *I guess I'm in for a silly stunt.*

"Okay TF, show yourself." Trotting Fox appeared in front of the policeman and gave the officer the deadly smile, the car immediately smashed into a truck passing by on the right, in the slow lane on the freeway. Georgie stepped on the brake pedal and the driver of the truck did the same. Fortunately, there was just one other car that had to stop behind the collision. The police officer had to write himself a ticket for reckless driving. TF let out another horrible, hideous laugh.

The driver of the truck said to the plainclothes cop, "This has gone too far; you can't intimidate me with that phony laugh."

TF struck the pickup driver in the head not once but twice and gave the laugh and this time both men had physical accidents and both got quickly into their vehicles to cover up their mishap. The officer said to Georgie, "Get in the car."

"Sir I'm sorry the fender bender happened but you wanted to see TF."

The plain clothed officer said, "Don't remind me."

When they arrived at the police station, the plain clothed cop said, "I don't want to drive this kid anymore; he is crazy and that trick and the terrible laugh is unnerving; let him loose, let him wander in a swamp, Sergeant, furthermore, he damn near killed me and I had to write myself a ticket for the accident."

Chapter 76

The gaseous Tanny woke Georgie up the next morning with a burst that sent both to the bathroom. Georgie turned on the shower and they both jumped in. The Vizsla liked to set her head under the showerhead and drink the hot water. He soaped up the dog and himself, they wrestled while the water cleaned the soap, Tanny shook. Georgie grabbed his towel, dried himself and the dog. Then turned on the hair dryer and puffed up his hair and Tanny's around the dog's head. Being a short-haired mutt, the dog got a few laughs when they get to the kitchen.

TF got out of the shower. The Indian ghost poked down the showerhead to see who was pushing the water into the tub. Me pee down this thing and if it comes backs up. After two hundred and fifty years, me can't. I go to the food place. When TF made it to the kitchen, of course, he lay a red bouncing ball on each of their heads.

Dad almost swallowed it but it caromed off his teeth, hit me in the eye and in the nose. Both Jason and Heather filled their cereal spoons and shot at the red ball hanging in space. TF emerged, opened his skeletal mouth, the food went in but fell on Dad Vance's head and TF said, "Me hate white eyes but me like white eyes brat's food, food more."

"No, no, I have to wipe my head off from the rice crispies. Tell TF no more food. Next time I'll bash that skull of his and throw food at my kids, damn, you guys are getting messy in your old age."

In the car Georgie straightened his cable so that he doesn't burn anyone and said, "Dad, are you going to make me a new pair of sandals soon if you look at the bottom, you'll see the car tire rubber is below a quarter of an inch."

"Georgie, I showed you how to run the band saw, cut your own."

"Dad, don't you think you're driving a little slow?"

"I'm thinking about the cereal in my hair."

They stopped to pick up Johnny, he said as he was getting into the car, "Mr. Vance I need to—"

"Don't tell me you need another pair of sandals. I'm having trouble finding old nylon tires."

Georgie stuck his foot up bloated, "Me too."

Johnny said, "Oh."

"This morning, I got a call from a teacher that used to work here. We were good friends and if we wanted to come up to his cottage, on the lake, and go water skiing on the lake?" After the screaming and after the big yes was quieted down, Victor Vance said, "Ready with your gear as soon as school is over and get to the house. Georgie and I will bring the food and drink. Jason and Heather, long-sleeved shirts; you know how much you two burn. Mom will call the Two Bucks. Georgie, Johnny and I will get gas for the car." Victor Vance dropped Heather and Jason at the high school and continued to the middle school and parked his car.

The boys got their books out of the backseat and scrambled to science class with Mr. Ritz. As soon as they walked in the classroom, Ronda and Leia that transferred in, seemed to be taking place of Babs and Beth in Mr. Ritz' eye. The movie that Mr. Ritz was going to show was on the heart. The student assistant turned off the lights.

Leia stood up and said, "All four chambers of my heart are with the class and you, Mr. Ritz." When the student assistant turned on the lights after the movie. Everyone looked up and there was no Mr. Ritz. The bell rang to dismiss the class, as the class left the room, they found Mr. Ritz sleeping under his desk and his head leaning on his chair.

Leia said, "Does that mean I don't get an A for the day?"

Johnny and Georgie were last to leave the room, Georgie gave Mr. Ritz a silver-green shot in the derriere. A giggle erupted from the science teacher. The boys walked quickly out of the room while the next class filed in. The math class had Ronda and Leia. They found that if you were a beautiful female child, you can weasel your way into a male teacher's libido and get reasonable grades by smiling, winking and saying something nice to the teacher. When you left class at the bell, of course, it worked the other way around too such as Peter and Paul.

The reason Paul was the quarterback was, Paul gave Max Brand the same treatment, well not winking, but talking about football plays. The boys hoped that school went fast this Friday so they have a chance to do something new at the lake. But little did they know, they would be pushed and shoved into a plot to steal the school's money for yearbooks. The muscle guy that was cold-cocked by the student with the combination lock in his hand had planned the theft the year before but now out of juvenile hall at the middle school will be sent to the continuation school. He pulled off the heist with a seventeen-year-old who was left behind by his parents at the middle school.

The police caught them one hundred miles going north from the middle school in Miss Syndly's car. She always left her keys in the car hoping someone would steal it. The car had collision insurance; it was a 1952 Fraser. The two delinquents had ten thousand dollars and her gold tooth with the diamond was in the glove compartment.

The muscle guy who was driving the car, Flanagan, Marc to be specific tried on the tooth he found in the glove compartment but spat it out on the edge of the passenger seat. "Wow," Val said, "that's a flashy thing."

The other boy Val Tucker was pushing the tooth around in his mouth trying to see if it will fit on one of his teeth. Marc hit a curb on a left-hand turn. Marc turned to Val and said, "That's nothing; watch this," he drove through an open door at the plaza. The first store he drives into a window, Val goes, "Gulp, I swallowed it."

"What the hell are you talking about?" said Marc.

"Yelp, I can feel it going down my throat."

"What can you feel?"

"The tooth going down my throat." The tires were screeching. Marc was laughing and smoking the tires on the main floor of the plaza, "Wow we're out the north door. No scratches, no bruises. Oh man, the cops are in front of us."

The phone was ringing off the hook at the school and at the home of the Vances. They were out in the car going to Lake Berryessa with the Two Bucks happily talking on the walkie talkies, Georgie and Johnny were talking about water skiing. Johnny said, "Do you think you can get up on the sticks, water skis?"

"I'm going to try, are you? I think it is going to be easier for me than you."

"No doubt," said Johnny. Just as they finished talking, Victor Vance hit an unpaved road and the walkie talkie was shaken out of Johnny's hand.

Georgie said to Heather and Jason, "Hey, when is the last time they filled the potholes in this road?"

"Never," answered Jason.

Heather looked at that boat. "Boy, I sure like his boat."

Mr. Vance drove and Jason remarked, "Oh no, we're driving past it, look at this one, it's bigger than the other one, what is that thing beside it?"

Mr. Vance said, "Isn't it a beautiful fishing boat?"

"Yea Dad, where is the ski boat?"

"Did I say he had a ski boat."

"Why did you bring the water skis?"

"Because that way I could get everyone to go to the lake."

The car turned into a morgue. Jason looked around and said, "I only see a dock and a fishing boat."

"Look closer."

"Let me guess a cottage foundation."

"Correct."

"At least the cottage is under two trees. You can help or you can swim."

"There's no wood," a couple of thuds and a bang. "Here comes the truck now."

Cliff Higgins came out of a tent that had AC; it was noisy but it helped and an electric cooler with lots of drinks and food. The amazing thing about Dad's old friend was his first words, "You can use the boat if you want any time." After unloading the wood, we scrambled to the boat. The water was eighty-five and the air temp was one hundred and ten. Johnny had his Nerf gun it had a holder of thirty-five and an extra cartridge.

Jason took over the outboard, he yelled, "It's full of gas." Heather and Jason had long shirts and floppy hats on. Georgie and Johnny had no shirts and no hats. They putted out to the middle of the lake.

Johnny said, "Go out for a pass."

Georgie flew out of the boat and was standing in the water and Johnny shot ten Nerf bullets in a circle around the boat and Georgie caught them all before they hit the water. As Georgie got back into the putt, a flashy boat came roaring by at spectacular speed. A voice said, "Where did you get that dingy; over at the garbage dump?"

Georgie moved to the front of the boat. Johnny piped up, "Can that thing hit five MP?"

The guy in the flashy boat turned his head so that he could see his face. "It is Bone Crusher, Peter and Paul."

Crusher threw nails at the kids, Georgie caught all the nails while Johnny shot Crusher in the face with Nerf bullets. Suddenly, the putt-putt dingy was not so slow. Georgie replaced the engine with his body. He was pushing on the front of the dingy with a force no one can explain and no one of his family will divulge his secret powers. Georgie had the dingy circling the flashy fast boat of Bone Crusher. Crusher was yelling at Georgie and Johnny. The boys were wearing Indian headbands, Heather as usual screaming and Jason had his peashooter out and was spraying Crusher with dried half peas. Crusher was pulling split peas out of his nose, while he was standing up. Paul jammed the accelerator to the floor and Crusher fell to the deck and was yelling four-letter words at Paul as the flashy boat zoomed away.

Cliff Higgins noticed that his boat was going faster than the engine can put out and said, "How are the boys doing that?"

Vic Vance turned and looked at the dingy and yelled at Georgie, "Georgie, cut that out."

Mr. Two Buck gave the finger across the throat. Georgie and Johnny nodded and the dingy slowed. Vic turned back, wiped his brow and put a handkerchief back in his pocket and picked up nails and shoved them in his mouth; of course, he doesn't want Cliff to question him on the boat's performance. But Cliff grabbed the nails from Vic and asked, "How did they make the dingy go that fast?"

Victor looked up at Cliff with the words, "Georgie paddles fast."

Ed Two Buck said, "All the boys are fast."

"I didn't see any hands and arm movement, Vic, Ed."

"They're quick."

"No one is that fast."

"Better ask Georgie and Johnny."

"Yea, I'll wait until they come in, I don't want to ruin their fun."

Vic grabbed the nails back and picked up two, two by fours and spaced them sixteen inches apart.

Jason was in the water and suddenly he was up on the old water skis. Cliff spat out his gum that he had been chewing all along. Heather was back steering and Cliff said, "You can't do that with my dingy."

"Do what?"

"Pull a water skier."

"Cliff, you must be missing something about your dingy." Vic and Cliff continued building the cottage with Cliff mumbling to himself and Vic pretending not to pay attention. As the wonderful day wore on, the cottage builders stopped for a beer.

Mrs. Higgins, Mrs. Vance, and Mrs. Two Buck were sitting in the AC tent looking out the plastic window. Martha Higgins was saying, "The kids are having a great time."

"Yes, and we are sitting in the tent," Jan turned and asked, "Do you want to get in the heat?"

"Jan," said Mrs. Higgins, "I have a long-sleeved shirt you can wear."

"I like the heat," mentioned Two Buck.

Martha remarked, "Let's rescue the boat from the kids and go out for a swim." Martha looked at Jan and said, "You have the loudest voice, yell at them." A holler at the dock brought the boat in.

The men moved to the tent. "Boy, that cool air feels fine and especially with a beer."

"Look Cliff, I will have to leave earlier because Georgie has to go to the police station, he is on duty in three hours."

"You mean one of the twins?"

"Yes, the one that lives with me." A machine gun sound rocked the tent and the three men fell to the floor of the tent. Cliff whispered, "What the hell was that?"

Victor Vance got up and said, "Oh that's the boys; they have some new toys and they're trying them out."

"You two better get out there because it sounds very bad to me," insisted Cliff Higgins. Higgins doesn't come out of the tent. Ed and Vic corralled everyone and left in the cars leaving Mrs. Higgins standing alone in front of the cottage. She said to Mr. Higgins who was on the tent floor, "All three of us until Vic owned up the boys had Nerf machine guns. Get the AC unit out of the tent. I know where to put it."

Cliff Higgins peeked out of the tent, "What are you talking about?"

"Come out and look at this," she said. "Order the shingles."

"That was a nice thing you did, kids, finishing the outside woodwork on the cottage," said Jan Vance.

"When we get to town, drop me off at the police station," asked Georgie.

The police Sergeant at the desk said to Georgie, "The kid, Val Tucker, swallowed Miss Syndly's gold tooth with the diamond, he is in cell #22 sitting on professional designed receptacle to catch such things. Say son, what is that thing on your head?"

"Oh, that is just decoration Indian style."

"Your job, Georgie, is to get the tooth after Val defecates it. He might hide it somewhere or put it down the toilet. I couldn't get any one else to do it."

Georgie said to himself *why me when I could be out working on who runs the drug cartel here in this state. I'm going to talk to pop Vance. I can help outside of the police station and jail. Just not sitting by a pot to see a gold tooth appear.*

As he walked down to cell twenty-two, TF rebounded the little rubber ball off the prisoner's heads without a word. Georgie saw writing on cell wall #20. I killed my brother Georgie and I would do it again. God Joey, I hope they're burning your ass off in hell. Georgie saw some interesting products that the prisoners were making to pass the time. The police Sergeant gave him some long tweezers to handle the job. *I should have asked for a clothes pin for my nose.*

Georgie said to the juvenile prisoner, "Is your name Val Tucker?"

A slow roll of the lips and spit in the sink and finally a yes came out of the prisoner's mouth, "Yes, why did they send a kid to do the job?"

A smile came over Georgie's face, "Well, they thought some company your own age would help."

"You mean to take a crap in a bucket?"

"Well not exactly, Miss Syndly wants her tooth back and you and Marc ruined the car."

"The car was a pile of junk the only thing that had any value is the tooth," said the kid with it in his colon.

Georgie mentioned to the kid, "Could you move the receptacle to the cell door?"

Val Tucker responded, "Why don't you come in?"

"Wouldn't it be embarrassing to you?"

"No not at all."

Georgie unlocked the cell door and walked in the cell and locked the door. Val Tucker made Georgie look like a dwarf. "Gee, you're a pretty good-sized boy," said Georgie. "Why are you still in the ninth grade, you should be a senior?"

"I flunked, my mother remarried six times and I was lost in the crowd."

Georgie remarked back, "I might be able to get you promoted to the high school if you wish."

Val Tucker looked at Georgie and said you look like a person that I can get out of this jail cell with ease.

"Do you want to try?"

"Sure, why not," he said with a twinkle in his eye.

Georgie gave him a big smile and answered, "I'm not what you think I am and you better pull up your pants before you make a decision."

"You're right about that but what about a fist in the face."

TF hit Val with the little red ball. Georgie caught the right-hand punch and twisted his arm. A scream echoed off the wall of the cell and Georgie mentioned, "You better pull your pants back down and get back on the pot." Georgie let go of his fist. "I want to see that gold tooth soon or I'll sic the little red ball on you, Val."

Val straightened his arm out and declared, "You're a tough little shit."

"Thank you for the compliment, Val. I'm sure you didn't mean that in the good way but thanks anyway." Val rolled his eyes and grimaced as he pulled his pants back down. "TF, pull up the stopper in the sink for washing the tooth," said Georgie. A thud announced the excrement's arrival.

Val got up, Georgie picked up the receptacle and put it in the sink as the contents fell. "Nope not in this load." Val laughed but stopped, the twist in the arm was showing up in his face, a bit of pain.

Val said, "My shoulder was affected by the twist. Did you know that you are not allowed to injure inmates?"

"Yes, I know that," Georgie responded.

His prison uniform was blue, his hair was long but the barber in the prison cut it bald. Val kept rubbing his head apparently, a habit when he had long blondish hair. Georgie asked politely, "Would you please sit on the receptacle? Please sit down so we can finish this boring task. When we complete the search and find it, I will ask the police Sergeant if someone can look at your shoulder, is that all right with you, Val?"

"Yes, I think I need a pain pill." Next an odious sound struck the walls of the cell. A tinkling sound came from the receptacle, Val had done it, he laid a golden egg. Better check that, a golden tooth with an obnoxious odor.

Georgie held his nose as he dumped the contents into the sink from the stainless-steel toilet. Georgie tried to be friendly but he had injured Val Tucker and he resented it. When Georgie turned to leave the cell, Val quietly picked up the stainless-steel receptacle and tried to make a deep impression on Georgie's head. The quick-witted TF bounced the little red ball off Val's left eye and he made a sound that made Georgie swirl in a pirouette move and grab the barrel. "Val, do you really want to get someone to look at your shoulder or is it you just want to get out of here?"

"Both."

"That's two ways to break loose," replied the angry teen. Georgie locked the cell door as he left. "I'll send the nurse."

The policeman at the entrance of the cell block asked, "How is the kid?" as he accepted the key from Georgie.

"Angry. Send a male nurse with an escort. The kid is dangerous."

Chapter 77

The adopted son opened the front door of the Vance home with TF hanging on his head, Georgie said, "Dad, I have foreboding feeling about helping the police in these affairs."

Dad asked, "Why do you say that, son?"

"I feel that could be my dad. After all, if I was still in Detroit, no doubt I would be in some sort of lockup."

"But you say your father helped you."

Yes, I remember vividly."

"What you're saying and expressing I have no experience," said Dad.

"Well, Tanny and I will think it over tonight in bed."

That put a smile on Mom's and Dad's faces. "I'll do my homework before I curl up with Tanny." The dog got up from where it was lying by Dad Vance and licked Georgie's hand and Georgie fondly petted Tanny. Georgie closed his bedroom door so the dog couldn't follow him in, there was a couple of scratches, a wiper and a sound of a body plunked down outside the door. He had been some high school courses along with his eight grade classes. He said to himself that's why I feel that way about Val Tucker. Who would have killed me if I was normal?

Then he thought why am I giving Val sympathy. That settles it. I'm only going to look for the guy in the junky car that my brother gave fixes to. If I find him, maybe I can catch the kingpin who is the buyer and seller of the drugs in this area. I better get my homework completed; Dad will be pushed out of shape if I don't. Georgie opened the door and let Tanny in his bedroom after he finished his math.

At school the next morning, as Dad Vance pulled into the parking lot with Johnny and I and of course TF, two police cars pulled up in the front of the middle school where the craziness happened the day before. I say crazy because who would steal a 52 Fraser but two kids stole Miss Syndly's car.

Georgie wondered how come it took two police cars to deliver a gold tooth and money.

Miss Syndly pranced out the front door of the school. She was glad to get the tooth back and almost all of the money. Miss Syndly thanked the policemen and stuck the tooth in her mouth, while she fiddled. She turned and moved to shake hands with the boys in blue. They were the ones who met Trotting Fox and actually saw the 250-year-old's face. The last policeman, he shook hands and said, "Is that him with the little red ball on his head?"

"Yes, do you need a couple of bounces on your head?"

He smiled and said, "No. I hear you're the one that found the tooth?"

"I didn't like that duty; the kid is violent; I was forced to defend myself."

The policeman then said, "Aren't you looking for the drug source?"

"That's my basic duty," as I said my last words, Miss Syndly interrupted and reminded me to get to class before the tardy bell.

I walked slowly because Miss Syndly was watching my every move. Until I was out of sight then I turned a little shinier silver-green energy and made it to math class before the tardy bell stopped ringing. Johnny was already in his seat, when I blurred into mine. "Hmm," said Mr. Clancy, "I already marked you absent, Georgie Vance, your seat was empty a second ago."

"One of my books fell down and I was under my desk sir."

"Did anyone work out the math problem on page 35?" Mr. Clancy looked around the room; no one had their hand up.

Ronda said, "I tried" and when Leia said, "I did too," Mr. Clancy asked, "How many O's is that, Leia?"

"It's not fair to ask that in a math class, Mr. Clancy dear."

"I have the answer, Mr. Clancy," said Georgie Vance. "Two O's and the math question is plus seventy-five."

"Georgie and Johnny, why are you in this easy math class?"

"Mr. Clancy, the counselor said we are on the line, so he said we had a choice we took trig but the class was full, we ended up here."

"Well, I will have to speak to him, you boys need more abstract math," announced Mr. Clancy. The bell rang and someone in the back of the room threw a paper airplane and Georgie sent a quick silver-green flash and the airplane caught on fire as it sailed toward Mr. Clancy, he didn't see it his back was turned, TF forced it into the trash can and everyone left in the classroom said, "Wow."

Mr. Clancy turned around and found Georgie's foot in the trash can with smoke drifting up. "What happened?"

Georgie looked up and remarked, "There was something on fire in your basket sir. Somebody must've thrown something combustible in it, sir." When he pulled his foot out, Georgie noticed a single mark on his left sandal. He quickly walked for the door and Johnny followed with a grin on his face. When they were in the middle of the quad, Johnny said, "Good thing TF put it in the trash. You got to stop doing kinky things, Georgie."

"Yea but it is fun."

The next thing they know the person that threw the airplane was Denis and Miss Syndly was pointing a shoe at them. "Denis said you set an airplane on fire."

"We're not near an airport ma'am."

"No in Mr. Clancy's room. Denis said there was a flash and the paper plane was on fire and somehow it made it into the trash can by Mr. Clancy's desk."

"Miss Syndly, isn't that against the rules and doesn't Denis get an hour after school?"

"What's that on your head?"

"Oh, it is nothing. I hurt myself playing ball with Peter and Paul and I was stuck by a ball, it cut me, ma'am. This is a special bandage."

"Did you see the nurse, Georgie?"

"Yes Miss Syndly." Georgie made a cut mark where the ball lay on his head and TF left. TF went and pinched Miss Syndly's little toe on her left foot to avoid further questions and an inspection under the bandage. The situation ended up that Denis and Georgie had an hour after school. While the two were sitting on the hour after school bench, two kids came in the administration building front door leading to the sidewalk and the other came in from the quad door wearing Ronald Reagan masks, black shirts, black pants, black shoes, and black gloves.

But in their right hands a cream pie and it was aimed at Miss Syndly. As the pies flew through the air toward Miss Syndly, they abruptly took a one-hundred-and-eighty-degree turn, hurting the assailants directly in their Ronald Reagan Masks. The boys who were wearing the masks had no choice but to take off their masks.

One said, "This is no fun; we are caught."

But Denis jumped off the bench in front of the action and screamed, "You didn't do it," pointing at Georgie. Both of the pie throwers escaped out of the quad entrance door. But Denis kept saying you did the turn.

Miss Syndly grabbed Denis by the hair and pulled him back and blasted him, "Why did you get in the way and turn the pies around for me? Oh, thank you Denis, you're such a sweet child. You Georgie, did you see what Denis did?"

"I'm not Georgie, I'm Johnny."

Denis fell to the floor kicking and punching as the Indian boy fled out the quad door holding his head and saying, "I've got to get away from these crazies."

Georgie caught up with the two Reagan faces and threw them in a mud puddle.

Georgie walked home slowly and calmly, "Oh my god, I left Dad and Johnny at the school." He quickly ran back without breaking the sound barrier and opened C5 door. There was Denis pointing a banana at Dad Vance and in the other hand ten more bananas and he said, "I swear I will crush these yellow things and its friends all over the floor of this room, if you don't tell me the truth, Mr. Vance."

"What truth?"

"Who is the mastermind?" Johnny had a big smile on his face and Georgie grabbed one of the bananas, peeled it and ate it.

Victor Vance said, "Holmes couldn't have done a better job in the office in rendering the pies useless, Denis. The way you alter the course of the pies."

Denis stood with a banana in his mouth staring at Mr. Vance. "How can you say that? Miss Syndly said the same thing."

"Your fierce intellect turned those pies around." The banana dropped from his mouth. Denis began shaking his head no and Mr. Vance shook his head yes. "Denis, I want you put on your Sherlock Holmes gear and find out who is throwing the stars and what is their meaning in the Asian language and the country they came from?"

Denis picked up the bunch of bananas on the floor, Denis was deep in thought for several seconds and bent to pick up the last banana but then his mind flaked out, "I know how the stars came about."

"How Denis, how?" asked Mr. Vance.

"Did you see the picture *Kung Fu* with David Carradine, they showed them in use in the picture and how to throw them properly."

"But we need to know who is throwing them on campus, Denis."

Denis scratched his head then his nose and said, "Okay," he turned to Georgie and asked for his bananas back. And sang out the door "Yes I have no bananas," as the door closed.

Denis immediately went to the library and spread out the Encyclopedia Britannica and searched through volumes ABC. But the librarian walked up to Denis, "Time to close up, put the reference books away."

Denis replied, "Miss Syndly said I could stay and look though the volumes."

The librarian went to the phone and called Miss Syndly and she said, "No, close the library." Denis frowned and his lower lip sagged as he got up and put the volumes away.

The next day, Denis didn't go to classes; he got a pass from Miss Syndly. How he got it I don't know. He must have told a big fib. Denis searched and searched until he came upon the words ninja stars. It said briefly look up the word 'Shuriken'.

"Aha, Eureka, I found it." He shoveled through the pages and said, "Why am I looking in this volume, it's the next one." He rambled through the pages until it hit him smack in the face: Shuriken. A piece of metal shaped like a star; the Asian ninjas used to kill their victims with poison on the tips. He wrote down the description in full. Denis visualized himself as a defender of justice. He walked in a dignified way holding his pass so that all of the security guards could see it and gave them a sophisticated ta ta as he walked by. He opened the door to C5 where Mr. Vance had a class in session. He walked up to Mr. Vance and said, "I found the word."

"Denis, don't you see I'm busy."

"Yes, sir but I found the word," he pulled the paper with the description out of his front pocket, unfolded it and kind of stuck it in Mr. Vance's face.

"Later, out, we are on cleanup; move out of the way," demanded Mr. Vance. It deflated Denis as he opened the door and went out. Denis went to the administration building and walked into Miss Syndly's office.

The cacophony of the students passing from class to class was noisy and irritating. Miss Syndly looked up from her desk, her gold tooth shining from a reflection of sunlight through the window, she put down her pen and asked what he wanted. Denis chirped, his voice changing and cleared his throat and announced, "I found it."

"What did you find?"

"The word."

"And what word is that?"

"The word is Shuriken."

"Never heard it before," said Miss Syndly.

Denis said, "You know the metal things that are stuck in the wood around the buildings. That the malicious students that have thrown in the woodwork around the school. The custodians have to climb up the ladder to pry off the wood. They were used to kill people in China. They put poison on the tips, Miss Syndly."

Miss Syndly thought for a moment and voiced her opinion, "Find some and put the you know what on them. I could use some." She was thinking of the boy standing in front her. Another thought, *I hate kids*. "Get to class, Denis."

"Yes Miss Syndly."

Chapter 78

Georgie and Johnny were warming up for the first game of the season. If you remember, Johnny was quarterback and Georgie was a wide receiver. Peter and Paul were on the team and of course dozens of other boys. Now the coach, Max Brand, was not too sure about Johnny as quarterback; he was much shorter than Peter. While Johnny threw the ball accurately but the height difference in the boys had Max question his change. His first thought was to have an Indian to show that he was using the school's entire staff of boy students.

After the boys pushed the slides and showed the Indian boys were capable of pushing hard, he gave Johnny the football after they ran through the first play. Johnny seemed capable but when Johnny practiced the play in earnest; Johnny did a jump throw. Max had never seen such a throw. The ball flowed through the air in a tight spiral and it ended up in the hands of his brother. He shambled for the end zone all alone.

Max noticed how fast the Indian boy ran and asked him if he would like to be a running back. But Georgie said that he would consider it but he liked wide receiver better. Max said, "Aren't you the boy that killed your older brother?"

Both Georgie and Johnny stuck their heads together in a no. TF bopped him from behind. The coach said, "What the hell was that," as the red ball slipped in back of Georgie's head. The coach looked around but there was no one behind him and he spoke, "That's strange," and thought nothing of it.

The coach took Georgie and Johnny out and put Peter and Paul in the game. Peter as quarterback and Paul as wide receiver. The coach had them run the same play. Now the score was seven, seven. The other team had scored on the defense. A thought rattled around in the coach's brain; I will put Georgie in as running back. "Georgie, take Sam's place as fullback. I want to see if you can get around the corner on the other team." The coach signaled Peter, the end around play next.

Sam came out of the game and Georgie went in at fullback. He was thoroughly pissed at the coach and when the ball was handed to him by Peter, the quarterback, he dropped the ball. The other team member pounced on the football. Georgie came out of the game without the coach's permission and said, "Sorry coach, I was just not ready for the fullback spot."

The coach smiled and said, "Next time."

"But coach I prefer WR. I like running but not in the fullback position."

"Wait, that's why I put you at fullback so you could run."

Georgie realized that he couldn't convince the coach. The next time the Cougars had the ball, Georgie was compelled by the coach to take Sam's place again. As he reached the spot where the fullback stood, Georgie heard some snickering, "We are going to get the ball back," he heard from the other team's defensive line.

Georgie decided to take and run this time. When heard the call by Peter, the defensive line miscued. Five-yard penalty. Georgie was ambivalent and thought to himself, why did I get into football. A second later the ball was hiked. No chance for long decisions. Georgie bounced off a player and then another but decided to fall down when the next player being their safety hit him. Not realizing it, he went twenty yards. The cheers rang out loud. As Georgie got up, all the players were patting him on the back. Georgie ran off the field and wanted to say keep me in the WR spot, but the coach spat out, "Get back out on the field."

"But coach, Paul is in my spot."

"No, he is not."

Bone Crusher came down from the stands and punched Georgie on the chin and broke his hand. Crusher screamed, "What is this Indian made of!"

The coach kicked him in the seat of the pants. Then the coach turned to Georgie and thought he would be on the ground unconscious but he was standing beside the coach smiling. The coach turned white and was nearly speechless. But Georgie played it to the hilt; he rolled his eyes so they turned white and began falling to the ground. But the coach caught him. He pretended to be unconscious, he then began to laugh. The coach stood him up and said, "You're faking it."

"Yes, I am, he missed me and hit the pole that holds up the covering above us."

The coach said, "I swear he hit you."

"Bone Crusher is a friend of Peter and Paul and he will do anything to help them win the starting positions on the Cougar Team."

"I know that, Georgie, but you and Johnny have a role to play for the Indians of northern California. To me I admire with what you put up with not only on the team but at school too. It is strange that you are identical twins but you report to different households. Why is that?"

"Coach, can I get in the game at wide receiver?"

"Of course, Georgie and Johnny, take Peter's place. Quick now, we just got the ball back." The coach signaled Johnny for a pass to his brother. There were only forty seconds left on the clock. Georgie was knocked down twice as he ran, he didn't want to show the impression that he was invincible so he fell down at the five-yard line and called time out. The ref cooperated. He then ran to the coach and the coach put Sam as fullback and Paul as tight end. Sam hiked the ball and pushed through the center of line for the winning touchdown and time ran out.

Mrs. Vance made it out of the stands along with Heather and Jason, Mrs. Vance kissed Georgie and Johnny. Mr. and Mrs. Two buck had trouble getting out of the stands. Kids were cheering in front of them and they didn't want them to stop and of course they joined in. Johnny's parents picked him up and Mr. Two Buck carried Johnny around on his shoulders until the cotton candy man walked out of the stands and gave Johnny and Georgie some cotton candy for winning the game.

Begrudgingly, Victor Vance made it home after going through parents' night at the school and hearing about the game from an excited parent who quickly picked up Sam the fullback and the parent of Sam drove from the high school football field to the junior high to express his opinion how well the boys played together, he just couldn't believe it. No one complained about not being in the game to tackle someone, they didn't spy on the other team and they were polite off the field and on the field. No hatred expressed, just good hard football.

Dad Vance was happy the game went well for the cougars but felt bad for the other team. After talking with Georgie and finding out that Georgie didn't use his abilities to overpower the other team, Dad Vance said, "After all, you went through terrible hardships in your other life, how can you be so kind with a boy beating you over the head with a receptacle that held poop in it."

"Dad, I got to say that it didn't hurt but I never brought up to the Sargent because the things I went through in my other life. I never told you the whole story."

"Well son, I know your previous life was grim. I hope life now is a happy life and I hope it stays that way. I know, Georgie, you have had some exciting experiences already and the great thing is you have everything going for you. Do you think your gifts will continue?"

"I haven't heard or have any signs on either way, Dad."

Chapter 79

"Georgie, you have a phone call from the police station in Santa Rosa," said Dad. Dad Vance handed the phone to Georgie.

"Hello, oh Sergeant."

"Hi. I had a call from an official that wants a short person for a position that you might be interested in, Georgie."

"What would that be?"

"He didn't say outright but this guy is an important government guy. If you have any thoughts of making a buck or two, come down and I will call him back."

"Okay Sergeant I'll have my dad drive me to the station if he is not busy."

"Okay see you soon, son," responded the police Sergeant.

"Dad do you have time to drive me to the police station?"

"Georgie, I do have to study the next chapter in the science book."

"I'll run over but I'll need another pair of shoes, the job is a paying job so I'll buy my own."

"How many have you gone through since you been here?"

Georgie thought for a minute and said, "Twenty-five and a pair of Johnny's. I will be home as soon as possible, Dad, so I'm not tired at school. Bye," as Georgie opened the front door. He stepped out, looked to see if anyone was around then taking off at twenty-nine miles per hour, he made to the corner he upped the speed to forty miles per hour. Then he said to himself the speed limit here was only thirty-five. When he got to the police station, the police Sergeant asked, "Why are you hopping around like that?"

"Hot feet."

The crazy kid. The Sergeant said, "The man that wants to see you is conferring with the chief of police about you and he will be out in a few minutes so take a seat."

Georgie said to himself, *I feel like Miss Syndly*, so he hurriedly put his shoes back on. He had run through water so his shoes were giving off steam. Georgie was brushing away a cloud of steam while a man in a black suit with a white tie came out of the chief's office. *What, I'm talking to a mafia member?* But the man in the black suit put his hand out and announced, "I am Robert Daimler of the CIA," then pulled out a badge and it said Robert Daimler of the CIA #1206.

Georgie brightened up and said, "Am I in trouble?"

"No but you're kind of young."

"Yes, physically I will be thirteen but mentally I am twenty-one."

Robert said, "Are you strong?"

Immediately, Georgie lifted the man over his head. The man over Georgie's head said, "How tall are you? You can put me down any time."

Georgie answered, "I am five foot four," as he gently dropped him to the floor.

"I would like you come to Washington D.C. with me." Then Robert Daimler said, "Do you speak any other languages?"

"No, but one dialect."

"That won't help. Come on."

Georgie said, "Where are we going?"

"We are taking the plane to D.C."

"Hold it, I have to tell my parents goodbye and get some clothes."

"You have parents?"

"Yes, they took me in and I have had a wonderful time with them and their children sir."

By this time the police Sergeant, at the desk, his eyes had to be readjusted he couldn't believe what he had heard. He said, "Take me along for the ride."

Robert Daimler gave the police Sergeant a hairbrained look and said, "I need a police car to drive to his house."

"No need, I will carry you to my place so that you can meet my parents. But only if you buy me a new pair of shoes on the way."

"How will I leave from your place to the airport?"

"You can take a cab, if I don't go."

"You say you will carry me?"

"Yes, I will sir."

"My luggage also?" Robert picked up his things and said, "I have a bag at the hotel, that's okay?"

"Sure," said Georgie, "let's make it to the hotel." Georgie picked him up carrying his briefcase. Georgie walked out of the police station with Robert Daimler in his arms and bounced along the ground to the hotel. He set him down to walk in an appropriate manner into the hotel. He went to his room grabbed his bag, while Georgie sat in the lobby. Georgie looked up from the magazine he found on the table. "Ready?"

"Yes." They walked outside, Georgie slipped his arm under him and off they went and in a matter of minutes Georgie opened the front door of the house he lived in and Mrs. Jan Vance came to the door to see who had opened it and said, "Georgie, you're home and who is this?"

"Mother, I need to sit down. I'm a little winded."

"Well of course, son."

"This is my mother, Mrs. Vance."

"How do you do, I'm Robert Daimler."

Mr. Vance had taken a shower and had put on his PJs and reading the late newspaper. Georgie and Robert came in the living room. "What is this occasion?" asked Mr. Vance.

"Dad, I want you to listen to what he has to say," Georgie said.

"Georgie didn't do anything wrong?"

"No, no, that is not why I am here, Mr. Vance," remarked Mr. Daimler. "Georgie has some thoughts of joining our organization."

"And what is that may I ask?"

"It's a government group."

"I think he'd better tell you, Mr. Vance."

"Georgie, what have you gotten into?"

"Nothing as yet; it is just a thought of the Chief of Police Thor Baxter. The government wants a short person with some color in their complexion to pursue a language we don't speak in this country."

"What language is that?"

Georgie looked over at Robert and he gave him a nod yes. "Dad, you know I have been dissatisfied with school and I have a twenty-two-year-old brain and having to work at an eighth-grade level. I thought this program he mentioned would invigorate me."

"And what program is that?"

"The government has been looking for a short person with a darker complexion and has the ability of learning a language quickly. I think that is me if you let me go?"

"First of all, he didn't talk you into it?"

"No, it will give me money so that I can find my mother and keep her safe and in a good environment."

Mr. Vance thought for a moment and said, "Do you think you can find her again in Detroit?"

"Yes."

"This is totally up to you, Georgie."

Mr. Daimler, after hearing this conversation. "Are you willing to take a chance with me?"

"I just don't understand your relationship with your parents and your mother. That's your birth mother you're talking about."

"Yes."

"Obviously, you are adopted and your birth mother is in Motown. How did this adoption come about because there is some distance between the two towns?"

Georgie put his head down and Mr. Daimler saw the little red ball on the right side of Georgie's head. He then asked, "What is that?"

"Oh, just a trinket sir."

"You do know that your family will miss you and your twin brother will feel lonely."

"Where is he, we could use two," said Mr. Daimler.

Georgie thought to himself, how am I going to explain this? "You two don't get along?" asked Mr. Daimler.

"No, we are great friends, he prefers living with his Indian parents and I had a chance to live with the Vance's and I took it.

"The boy seems to be quite strong," mentioned Mr. Daimler.

"Georgie, you didn't."

"I was asked if I had any good qualities? So, I picked him over my head."

Dad Vance said with a watery eye, "You know we will all miss you deeply."

Georgie turned to Mr. Daimler, "Can I do this on weekends?"

"No Georgie, and by the way can I call you George?"

"My birth certificate said Georgie."

"Oh, can I see it?"

Dad Vance's face turned a little red when he said, "We have none." Dad Vance thought *I have to tell a big lie.* "We were driving in Detroit when we found him abandoned at night. We were coming back from a live show at the Michigan Theater. I had my window down and I heard some crying and it sounded like a baby. I got out of the car and I looked in a trash can and there was a wailing like a banshee baby in the trash can. My children said let's keep him and here he is."

Georgie remarked, "That's the story."

"You said you have a twin brother?"

"We aren't brothers; we just look alike."

"You say you're twenty-two; do you really think that?"

"Not really. I say that because I can answer all the teacher's questions. I frustrate all seven teachers."

Mrs. Vance had been sitting quietly but when she heard all the lies her husband delivered to Mr. Daimler, she interrupted Victor and described the scene with a little more detail. He turned to his wife and said, "What I remember is the trash can having been worked over. Georgie just barely fit in it. He had some bruises but otherwise he was okay. He was wrapped in part of a torn sheet. And it said in pencil Georgie and his mother's name Jessica Martin who is blind. It gave no street address. But the thing I remember most we had to stop to get diapers and clothes also it was steaming hot."

Mr. Daimler said, "This kid is a gem. So I could say Georgie is twenty-one."

Dad smiled and remarked, "You could say that."

"Does he have any other attributes"

"Yes, he is courteous and extremely helpful."

"Do you think he has the ability to learn other languages quickly? I think, I asked it before. Look Georgie, I will be in touch with you at the police station."

"I am playing football on the twelve-year-old team with my lookalike on weekends. He can take my place and vice versa. I play on Saturday at five PM before the junior varsity at the high school in Cotati."

"If I have a chance to see you play on this coming Saturday," as he looked in his appointment hand book, "it looks like a maybe."

Georgie escorted him to the front door. Mr. Daimler said, "If you had a beard maybe I could pass you off as a 21-year-old."

In response to his comment, Georgie said, "Indians do not have beards," Mr. Daimler."

Chapter 80
Day Dreaming

Georgie and Johnny walked into Mr. Ritz's class and the first thing he mentioned, as they took their seats, "Johnny." Mr. Ritz's head swiveled back and forth not knowing which was which.

Johnny answered "Yes Mr. Ritz?"

"Your dad makes Indian jewelry?"

"Yes, he does."

"Any chance I could see him, my wife's birthday is coming up soon. Mr. Two Buck, can we meet after school?"

"I'll see if I can arrange it, Mr. Ritz."

Georgie was looking out of the window with a glum look on his face and was in another world. A voice pierced his ears and he turned his head toward Mr. Ritz and said, "I don't know."

Mr. Ritz said, "I didn't ask you a question, Georgie."

Georgie got up out of his seat and as soon as he opened his mouth, the bell rang. Every one chuckled because it rang as though it came out of Georgie's mouth and it did because Georgie made it so. He began walking out of the room, Denis the investigating nut case was standing by the door as Johnny came out of Mr. Ritz's room first, knocked Johnny on the head with a fungal bat he took from the gym class and did the same to Georgie.

Johnny fell to the ground and Georgie picked him up. A bump rose on Johnny's head. Georgie immediately realized what the hit was for and produced the same lump on his head and summarily fell to the ground, thinking Denis almost caught me and said, "Gosh, I have slow reactions," and of course he said it in a murmur.

Denis piped up, "Hell Georgie, you can't fool me, get the hell up and pick up Johnny."

Georgie thought this was getting ugly. He picked up Johnny and at the same time, he noticed a rock just behind Denis so he moved it over mentally so Denis tripped over it and injured his right ankle. Georgie carefully, lightly gave his right hand to Denis and held him up. "Wow, Denis, we all have bumps."

At once Miss Syndly was directly in front of them and said, "Is Denis hurt?"

Georgie looked at Miss Syndly. "Denis, tell her what happened."

"I tripped over a rock."

"No, tell her the complete story, Denis."

"I did an experiment."

"Yes, you did and what was the test?"

Denis came up with a shit eating smirk, then grunted, then whispered so Miss Syndly couldn't hear what he was saying, "I hit them over the head to see who would fall down."

Miss Syndly said, "Get him to the nurse."

Johnny and Georgie were both bleeding from the head, they pointed to their skulls. She answered, "You two know where the band aids are, get them."

They dropped Denis and started walking, Miss Syndly stamped her foot, pain came to her face, take him too. TF bopped her from behind, she turned quickly but the crowd of students interfered with her vision. So, she grabbed the closest student to her and hauled him into the office before the three boys could get to the door.

David Goldberg, the student she grabbed, was sitting on the after-school bench in tears. Johnny and Georgie helped Denis to the nurse's office. They sit him down and the nurse said, "Denis, what happened?"

"Tripped on a rock and strained my ankle. But I think Georgie did it somehow."

Johnny shook his head, "He didn't watch where he was going."

"Yes, Denis thinks he doesn't do anything wrong," the nurse patted Denis on the head. The nurse pointed at the band aids; of course, the boys knew where they were, they grabbed two and went out the door.

They hopped in Dad Vance's car and waited for him. Georgie fidgeted with the wire on his sandal and made sure it touched the door frame of the car. Johnny straightened the books in his backpack so he could get his hat in the bag. Dad Vance opened the car door, stuck the key in the ignition and said, "Let's get home."

They let Johnny off and Georgie said, "Dad I think I'm going to talk to Robert Daimler and see if I can join the group of agents that support the country."

"Georgie, do you think you can cloak your physical and mental gifts from the agent personnel?"

"I will certainly try, Dad."

"Son, it is your life."

"I really hate to leave you and Mom and Heather and Jason. All of you, Johnny my super friend."

Johnny looked like he had tears in his eyes when they let him off because I told him of the proposition that Robert proposed. I know it is skimpy but I would like to try it. If they let me. I'll tell Mom when we get home.

"Well, we are in our driveway; get out and tell her." Dad looked teared up as Georgie got out of the car. When he got through telling his plans for his future, it was six thirty when Georgie picked up the phone and dialed the Washington number that Robert gave him. The phone rang once and it immediately went to: this message will be recorded.

"This is Georgie Vance and I would like to speak to Robert Daimler on the position he may offer me."

"Robert Daimler is not here. He will call you back. What is your number?"

"Vance residence, 707 555 5554." He turned to his mother and father, "It's still up in the air, he is not there." Georgie went to his room and did his homework. He sat there analyzing what he should do with his life. *I could ask to be put in the 10th or 11th grade or college. Play higher level sports? But that would expose me to the public. Robert Daimler knows that I can take severe blows to the body and the head. He doesn't know of my real weapon and I don't want tell him or other personnel unless I have to. If I do tell and show them, it will be in a critical situation.*

The next morning a life changing call came from DC. "I will send money for your flight." Georgie stared at the ceiling and thought, *That was quick, it's like he does it all the time. Gosh, no more Miss Syndly and Denis will be dejected because his adventures are only from books.*

Georgie went to school for the last time, got out of his dad's car, picked up his books from the backseat. Johnny got out the other door and came around and said, "You will write, won't you?"

"Yes, I will write to my parents, you and my real mother, Jessica Martin if she hasn't given up the ghost." Georgie went to his classes, left his books and when he got to science, told this was his last day and Mr. Ritz didn't believe him and when the final bell rang, Mr. Ritz wouldn't take the science book. Georgie said, "I'll mail the book to you."

Mr. Ritz laughed and said, "Get the hell out of here."

Georgie went to room C5. Johnny and his dad sat staring at Georgie as he walked in the room. Dad said, "Johnny, do you want to drive to the airport with us?"

"Yes."

"Jan wants to see him off."

Georgie had already packed his things in an old suitcase that his mother gave him, it was in the garbage can with him, at least that was how the story goes. Johnny told his dad and mom that his other half was leaving for Washington D.C. now and was it all right if I see him off at the airport in Oakland? Johnny's mother said, "Who is going with you?"

"All the Vance family."

She nodded yes. "The ghost that haunted me is leaving our town?"

Johnny with tears in his eyes choked out, "Aha," turned around and left. They picked up everyone and silently drove to the airport. As they approached the airport, Mrs. Vance turned to Georgie and asked if he had told Robert Daimler what time he was arriving in D.C.

A sudden shocking look spread across Georgie's face. He put his left hand to his face and raked it on all parts of his face. Tears fell from every face. But Mr. Vance as he wiped his eyes and looked into the rear view and saw Georgie's face, his lips quivered and he responded, "I'll call from the airport for you when I take you into the airport desk to finalize your ticket and luggage."

As Georgie got out of the car, everyone followed. They hugged and kissed him, it made Georgie feel bad for leaving. He carried his suitcase and Dad Vance had Georgie's ticket. Once Dad and Georgie made it to the ticket counter and got rid of the luggage, everyone piled into the airport terminal. Johnny grabbed Georgie's arm and spewed out through his tears, "I can't live without you." Johnny stood there in disbelief that his other half was getting on a plane and leaving.

"Don't worry, I will be back in no time, Johnny, my life giver."

All around hugs and kisses again. Georgie picked up his plane pass a C card last to get on. He waved to everyone as he entered the line for safety check. Johnny was the last to leave the terminal, Dad Vance had to come back in to get him, as they went out the door, Johnny kept looking back.

Chapter 81

Georgie Vance glided down the steps and bounced on the tarmac. Robert Daimler hurried to his newfound young man with an extra coat because the snow was blowing across the entrance to the DC terminal. Robert asked, "Didn't you bring a heavy coat?"

"No, I'm tired of those heavy things, Mr. Daimler. But I will buy a coat fitting the weather here later when I am paid."

Robert looked at him and smiled, "None of that," as he navigated him into a clothing store in the terminal. "I am sorry but I just didn't have anything heavier than this football windbreaker."

"Yes, yes look through the jackets."

Georgie picked out a red jacket with blue and yellow stripes. Mr. Daimler said, "No not that, you need something a little more conservative." Daimler grabbed a dark blue jacket with a hood, "Try it on."

Georgie did just that. "Okay it fits," Mr. Daimler rushed up to the counter and paid the clerk. He hurried Georgie to his car and drove a half hour to his house. Georgie put the hood up of his new dark blue jacket as they drove up the driveway. "Why did you put the hood up, son?"

Georgie said, "We are getting out in the snow?"

"No, we aren't," remarked Mr. Daimler, he pushed a button above the windshield, he drove in the garage and two children burst through the door leading to the house. Georgie unzipped his jacket, pushed his hood back, the children swamped Mr. Daimler; they looked about four and seven; the youngest boy sat on his father's foot holding onto his leg; the older boy jumped into his arms. They said, "Pop goes the hamburger."

Georgie responded, "That was different."

Mr. Daimler laughed and so did the children. Mr. Daimler asked, "Are we going to make it in the house?"

They said, "No," and "who is that?"

"That is Georgie Vance, a boy from California. Georgie is going to be with us for a few days."

The boys said, "Oh."

Mr. Daimler chugged along with the kids still in the same positions. Mrs. Daimler met them at the door, while the boys made a mad dash to the kitchen table. Mrs. Daimler had set the table beforehand for a guest. She said, "The plate alongside the boys is your plate."

Georgie nodded and said, "Thank you."

They had a great meal. While the boys were wild out in the garage, their manners were perfect at the table. Georgie smiled at them and asked, "What are the boys' names?"

She answered, "Peter and Paul." Looking at Peter and Paul, he asked them which one was Peter and the oldest spoke up and pointed at himself.

Mr. Daimler stopped eating and said, "The boys go to bed at eight o'clock, we can talk later; you can roughhouse with the boys after dinner if you wish."

Mrs. Daimler passed around the cookies and sat down. Georgie asked, "Do you have a dog in the garage?"

"No," said Robert Daimler. Then a piercing sound erupted and the dishes that were in the cabinet fell to the floor in pieces. This continued and Robert said to his kids and wife, "Get under the table; those sounds are bullets." There was a sudden wind felt under the table and a crash and the garage door fell into the garage. Robert Daimler had pulled out a thirty-eight pistol.

Peter and Paul were screaming and Mr. and Mrs. Daimler had the boys beneath their bodies. A sudden breeze hit them again, a crash outside on the street. Mr. Daimler said, "What was that?" The bullets had stopped flying through the house and a cold wind crept through the door leading to the garage and the electric garage door was demolished.

Georgie got up from under the dinner table and picked up the door and placed it where it belonged and screwed the door into place with his thumbnail and closed the door. The boys and mother came up from under the table.

Peter spoke with a twisted voice, "How did you get the door to stay up?"

By that time sirens were blaring and no one heard what Georgie said. Robert Daimler and Georgie Vance went outside with their heavy jackets on. Found a damaged van turned over.

Four policemen and two police cars, one policeman was putting yellow tape around two trees and the van in the middle. They found the machine pistol and the man, badly wounded from the crash. A neighbor came out from his house and noted, "I was looking out my window watching the snow fall when I saw and heard the gunfire and as the van pulled away, a silver-green light hit the van and no doubt hit the driver and the van was flattened."

The policemen began searching for bullet fragments. Robert Daimler sounded off, "Stop looking here, look in my house. This terrorist shot up my house," complained Robert.

"Sir, is this your house and what do you do?" asked the police officer.

Daimler said to the policemen, "You will find bullets all over the place in my house." One of the policemen hesitated and called in the accident and the other three policemen came into the house to inspect the damage.

"What did you say you did?" said one of the policemen.

"I didn't want to say in front of the neighbor, I'm in intelligence business," announced Daimler. Georgie stood quietly listening to the conversation.

The boys were in bed and Mrs. Daimler said to everyone, "We need a safe house, Bob."

"You are right, Jessica."

The name struck Georgie and he remarked, "Can I help with Peter and Paul?" Georgie spoke quietly to TF, "You okay from the rush in and out of the house?"

"Me feel blown out for such a rush, that white big wheel rolled, you hit it with silver-green, you get in trouble?"

"He was a bad guy."

"Another white eye dead."

"TF, we can only talk when we are alone. So don't speak out unless I ask you to, please."

"Me no do so far."

"And thank you for that, TF." Georgie worried about the machine gun tragedy that turned Robert's house into a shambles.

A truck pulled up in the front of the house. Robert went out and told the driver to go in the alley and park there. He and Jessica had picked up clothing for the children and for themselves. They had taken Georgie's belongings out to the truck. Daimlers picked up their children and exited out the back door with Georgie following. No space for Georgie in the cab. So, Georgie jumped into the back of the truck.

After a few blocks, the driver pointed the truck directly at the Potomac River and jumped out of the truck into a snow bank. A car was waiting for the driver, they sped off. While that was happening, another truck made sure that the Daimler family would make it into the freezing water. Georgie, feeling the crushing blow, braced himself in the back of the truck, unable to know what was coming next. Next, water rushed in.

Georgie made a mad dash and cracked the cargo door open with one mighty shoulder collision with the door. He was now submerged in the river, but swam to the undercarriage of the truck. The Indian boy thought, *Am I strong enough to lift the truck out of the Potomac, who's that in the cement blocks? Jimmy Hoffa? No but the body is recent. They are tidy cement underwear blocks.* Georgie's mind finally picked up on the reality of the state of affairs. He heard screaming from above, the cab apparently was partly above the freezing water line. His feet were on the floor of the river. He was pushing hard to keep the truck from dropping deeper into the Potomac.

Georgie thought how much longer can I hold this position. He struggled to the front of the undercarriage of the truck. He was out of breath, he swam to the surface, the very top of the cab of the truck still out of the water. Robert with his youngest child in his arms. His wife and his older boy appeared. The youngest was coughing and spitting out water. *It reminds me of my other life and my brother.*

He pulled Robert and Paul out of the water. Mrs. Daimler and Peter were starting to float down the river. Georgie shuddered to think of the water temperature, *don't think about it, just jump in and help Jessica and Peter out of the water. Here goes cold to colder*, he grabbed the boy and his mother and placed them on the bank of the river. Slid under the truck and put his back under the oil pan and lifted the truck out of the Potomac onto sand along the river. "It looks like the truck got to the bank of the river by some kind of sorcery," said Robert, not knowing how it slid to the sand.

Georgie was small and wasn't detected under the truck. He didn't feel that anyone should know his capability. He doesn't know how they could, even my parents don't know, they strictly kept my gifts under wraps. Georgie swam downriver and crawled up the bank and thought he would freeze to death.

An ambulance screamed down the road to the accident, he warmed himself up by running back to the collision where he found both boys being wheeled into the nurse's wagon. Two paramedics carefully had them wrapped in blankets and the driver opened the back door and paramedics placed the boys in the stretcher while the other held Mrs. Daimler.

Robert Daimler wrapped in three blankets stood surveying the spot where the truck was pushed into the river. A policeman asked, "Mr. Daimler, is this young man with you?"

Daimler responded quickly, "Georgie, how did you get out of the back of the truck?"

Georgie looked up and said, "I fell against the door and it opened."

The paramedics gave Georgie blankets and he spoke up, "So far, it hasn't been a pleasure to work with you, sir."

"Georgie, I know it looks bad. I'll have to explain later in private." The police knew who Robert was; they had dealings with him before; they hurried Robert and Georgie into a police car. Mrs. Daimler went with the children. Robert asked the driver of the police car to turn up the heater. When they got to the police station, waiting for Robert was the head of the intelligence agency.

"I thought we solved this matter."

Robert reminded the chief, "The person that slipped through our fingers is in Iran when Tasha was poisoned by Sudum."

The man in the black suit with the black tie and white shirt with a black hat said, "Who is this child with you?"

"He is our item who will excommunicate Jerry from the situation."

Vinson Rogers, the intelligence man in charge, said, "You're using a child. We better discuss this in my office in the morning."

Robert Daimler gritted his teeth and requested another safe house for his family and the short Indian man who was twenty-two in mind. Vinson Rogers walked over to the police desk, picked up the phone and dialed a member and talked in a language that just agents understood, he immediately hung up the phone and while walking back, wrote down a street address and gave it to Robert. "This will have to do; you have gone through two other safe houses in the past three months."

Vinson looked at Robert with admonishment in thought, "Look buddy, suck it up and this time don't leave the house for three days or more," his eyes glared viciously with no remorse in his eyes.

"Okay, okay, I did a job for the agency and it backfired. Can I help it if the man had a twin brother who is more devious and more cunning than his brother?"

"Look Robert, we will talk about it manana."

The Daimler family picked up their belongings and Georgie picked up Peter and Paul, they headed out the door of the police station. Vinson Rogers on the phone again making sure that Robert Daimler and family with the little Indian had a secure place to live. He ran to the front of the station and grabbed Robert's hand and said, "The back door, a plain car is waiting. An agent of the bureau is at the wheel of the car."

They stuffed their belongings in the truck, Georgie opened the back door and got the boys in and sat down beside them and of course, they were crying and calling for their mother. Jessica Daimler got in and sat on the other side of the backseat. The sniffles quickly ended, the car was silent going to the new home for a while and then Paul asked for food and Mom Jessica produced a candy bar and split it between the boys. The house was a nice house but not as nice as the other bullet-ridden house. When they settled in and Peter and Paul were in bed, Georgie with a serious look on his face said, "I didn't come this way for a house full of lead, did I, Robert?"

"No, you didn't. One of the men I put in prison did the shooting. He was released three months ago and is receiving money from an eastern nation, probably one of the aggressive Arab kingdoms and furthermore, I was instrumental in a couple of missive guns resting in the mountains, fifty yards long being built to destroy our allies in the east."

Still with a gaze of gravity on Georgie's face, he expressed anxiety, "Do you think this terrorist will find this place?"

"Possibly."

"What about your wife and children?"

"They are going to her parents' house and I won't tell you where it is because I don't know you that well."

Georgie appeared more on the calm side after the conversation.

Chapter 82

That night Mrs. Daimler and the boys were picked up by her parents in the alley behind the house at one o'clock that morning, but not before a squabble broke out between her father and Robert. They almost came to blows. Robert forced the older man into the car. The older man said a few more words but the windows were rolled up and Robert paid no attention and walked back to the house. "He's right and I'm wrong, I beginning to think this position of whatever it is called is not fit for me."

"Mr. Daimler, I have an opinion that I'm putting myself in a bad situation sir."

"Yes, you are but it pays well."

"You say your mother is in the same spot."

"She's in a home for the elderly but she is not that old. Apparently, she assists with the over the hill gang. Now that she is on her feet, she stays in the home in a room with other women."

"If she is doing well, why do you want to move her?"

"I was helpless when I was with her. I know she won't recognize me until I talk to her. When we were together, I couldn't speak and when I could speak, she was blind and sick. And I wasn't allowed in the room so I hid until it was late and no one came into the room, only occasionally but she resisted everything I said because she thought I was dead."

"You do have a problem. But you won't solve it if you quit this position, if you make it through the training course."

"After what happened while I've been here, I'm really thinking about going back home where it is safer."

"Georgie, you can stay at the training center; there is constant protection," answered Mr. Daimler. "I'll drive you over now if you wish, Mr. Vance."

"What time do you go to work, Mr. Daimler?"

"I get up at 5:30, clean, eat, and leave."

"Where should I sleep?"

"Georgie, sleep on the couch; you can shower if you want."

"I shower with my dog; she likes the water but especially likes the hair dryer."

Mr. Daimler gave him a smile and said, "You'll have to find it, I'm new to this place too."

Things were buzzing around in Georgie's head, *should I stay or go home or go to the training center?* He found the guest room and a nice bathroom with towels on the racks, soap in the shower. He went back to the bedroom and there on the bed was his gear. He took out some clothes, left them on the counter and soaked in the shower thinking of Tanny the Vances' dog.

Two and a half hours later, Robert Daimler's special alarm went off throughout the house, set up by the IT agency. Georgie couldn't sleep because of the shooting that had gone on in the other house and the physical strain he went through, his muscles ached from saving the truck. For the first time, he had trouble getting out of bed. He stretched for several minutes and then dressed. Georgie made his way to the kitchen. He found that Mr. Daimler had scrambled eggs and had the ketchup beside the eggs bowl and pointed toward the cabinet where plates were located. "Gee, they had everything set up; you can move from house to house."

"Yes, but they take some out of your check if you get shot up twice in a year and I did. Knock that food off, we will be late."

"I'm a little achy from the river," said Georgie.

"I'm too, let's get to the car."

"A new car."

"Yes, and it has special tires for snow. The agency will set you up with everything if you join the agency," remarked Robert.

"Are you going to tell me why the agency wants a short dark man, or boy in my case?"

"No, they will tell you if you make it through training." The car was quiet as they drove along the freeway or do they call it by that name in D.C., thought Georgie. There were traces of snow as they drove to a gate and a guard said, "Hello Mr. Daimler, you haven't been around lately."

"On a trip," as he showed an ID card.

"Okay sir," and nodded. Robert drove through the gate and immediately it closed.

"This building has every imaginable security device so just follow me, Georgie," said Robert. They got to his own personal parking spot. Robert Daimler got out of the car. Georgie closed the door on his side and jumped over the car from a standing position. Robert said, "I didn't know you could do that."

"There is deep snow on my side of the car and I didn't want to walk in it and this is my first time I've seen snow in a long time." They walked into the building; they were both searched. Georgie said, "Sort of tickles."

After the search, they looked through his wallet and found a picture of his dog, Tanny. The inspector asked, "What kind dog is it?"

"Tanny is the type of dog you see in the National Dog Show. She is a lovable Vizsla. My mother and father had the dog before I was theirs, you see I was adopted."

The inspector remarked, "That is a beautiful animal; you are lucky."

"Yes, I am sir."

Robert spoke up, "We have to see the gentleman in charge."

So, Georgie followed Robert to the escalator. "You know I have never been on one, what's it called, Robert?"

"Escalator." Robert turned to the left and pressed a button and a door opened.

"Now where are we going."

"Up." He pushed a button again—ten.

"What is this called?" Georgie asked.

"Elevator," Robert marveled at the things the boy didn't know. "You're never been in a big city have you, Georgie?"

"No." A buzzer rang and the door opened. "That was quick, oh, gee that is a wonderful view." Georgie stood there for several moments and then Robert nudged him to go. They turned a corner and walked into an office and the man asked them to sit down. The man was wearing a fancy suit, a tie he had never seen before. Georgie asked, "What is that thing around your neck, I have never seen it before."

The man's jaw dropped and he laughed and said, "Son this is called a bow tie." Edgar Slater said to Robert, "This is just a boy. What are you thinking?"

Robert Daimler said, "I know what you think but he is twenty-two mentally."

"Georgie, do what you did to me to Edgar and add something."

Georgie immediately blurred and Edgar was still sitting in his beautiful leather black chair but his head was touching the ceiling, Georgie grabbed one of his shoes and threw it to Robert. He said, "What do you think, Edgar?"

"My bald head doesn't like the ceiling."

Georgie asked Robert to throw the shoe back and as Georgie placed Edgar gently behind his desk. Edgar grabbed a cigar out of his cigar box and said as he was lighting it, "The boy is strong but is he smart enough to carry out the mission. You will have to test his ability, Robert." Edgar suggested, "Can you get a birth certificate?"

"His parents said he didn't have one and was adopted in Detroit. They found him in a trash barrel on a very hot day. They stayed in town for a couple of days and inquired around the neighborhood but no one knew who the boy belonged to so they gave up looking and took him home. That's the story I was told."

Edgar said, "It is a pleasure meeting you, Georgie.

Georgie was taken by Robert to the training center a couple of floors below. Robert pushed six and the door closed. "Now what?" asked Georgie.

"You'll have to fill out some papers. Yes and no and multiple-choice questions."

"I shouldn't have any trouble, Robert."

The elevator door opened and a young man greeted them and asked Georgie to come over and sit by a desk. He handed Georgie a test and he said you will be timed. He handed Georgie a sharp pencil with an eraser and said, "You have ten minutes to finish the test." The pencil was a blur and Georgie finished it in four minutes and thirty-two seconds. The young man with curly dark hair, glasses, a dark brown suit with a red tie said, "I was the fastest on this test before this boy took it but I'll beat him on the number right." The young man introduced himself to Georgie, "I'm Ronny and your name for the record is?"

"Georgie Vance."

"No middle name?"

"No." Robert swiped his hand across Georgie's head and said, "Let's go to the gym and see what you can do there."

Georgie pushed his chair back into place and said, "Lead on to the gym and I will surprise everyone maybe," and swiped Robert's hair and then laughed and remarked, "Touché."

As they rode down to the gym on the elevator, Robert said, "The shooting at the house was from an indictment that didn't go well and the man in the van was the criminal in the case and he had sworn to get even. I really didn't think he would do it."

A buzz and the door opened. Two gigantic guys met them at the elevator door. Georgie asked Robert, "How come everyone meets us at the elevator door?"

"They call ahead to make sure the number of persons entering is the same as exiting the elevator."

"That seems strange, Robert."

"I don't have to explain."

The two exceedingly big men picked up Georgie by the elbows, of course, one each side and as soon as they made it to the gym mats, Georgie flipped them both over on their backs. He then bounced around them. "Robert, am I finished? This is the first time I've shown off in front of people, Robert. I know my mother and dad would be disappointed in me for doing what I just did."

"Georgie, have you ever shot a pistol or a rifle?"

"No."

"The pistol range is in the basement. I noticed that you have the little red ball hidden in your hair, why is that?"

"As I said before, it is a trinket given to me by a relative on my real mother's side."

He thought to himself, *Boy, that is a big lie*. Robert looked at Georgie and said, "What are you thinking just now?"

"Oh, I was thinking that this is an unusual interview for a job. Are we going down to the pistol range?"

"Is this part of the interview?"

"Yes."

"Let's go when you are ready, Robert. I am ready, I've never seen a pistol range." So, they went back to the elevator and Georgie thought out loud, "How long have elevators been in existence, Robert?"

"Oh, I would say two hundred years, Georgie."

"That long." As the buzzer let out a yelp and they got off the elevator, "You'll have to wear goggles and sound protectors."

Georgie asked, "Which way?"

Robert pointed to the little building as they entered the door, pistols hung over the wall in the back of the man with the IT hat on. He instantly responded, "Robert, you know better than to allow a kid on the firing range?"

"He's not a kid and I want him to shoot a few rounds."

Georgie said, "The only pistols I've seen are the police officer's equipment."

The man behind the counter said softly, "I see."

"Let's start with the gun that all the IT agents use." Robert handed Georgie goggles and ear protectors that are on the counter.

The man with the pistol in his hand said, "The clip fits in the bottom of the handle. Pull back the barrel cover and that puts the cartridge into the firing chamber. Use stall three."

Robert showed Georgie to the stall. Robert explained the ins and outs of the semi-automatic weapon. Robert told him to squeeze slowly on the trigger. Georgie fired off eight rounds, Robert brought up the target. The shot pattern was reasonable. Both Georgie and Robert and the range Marshall thought not bad for a beginner. Robert looked at his watch and said, "Enough for the day."

Driving back to Robert's home, he announced that Georgie would be placed in a dorm with other men who want to be IT agents in the next day. "Robert, I think you took a wrong turn; you are going to your old house not the new one."

"You're right," and made a U-turn and then turned toward the new house. Then Robert asked Georgie for the number and street, "The number is 235 West Elm."

"You know it better than I do. Look Georgie, I would really want you to stay with me and my family. If you don't want to go to the Dorm with the other recruits, you can stay. I know the kids would like it."

"I would really appreciate it," Georgie responded.

"Okay I'll inform Edgar that you are staying with me for most of the training. For the language training, you'll have to go to school in another state. They'll inform you about where, what and when." They pulled up in the driveway and Mrs. Daimler came out the garage door to allow her husband in. She had the control unit for the door lift. She had a worried look on her face. Robert said, "Honey, what's wrong?"

"The damn dishwasher doesn't work right."

"You had me scared for a moment. I'm glad that's all it is, honey." Robert's kids grabbed his leg and did the same thing they did the first night. The table was set the same way as the other house.

Mrs. Daimler asked, "What do you think of Edgar and the IT firm?"

"Edgar is a little stuffy puffing on that big cigar and the rest is nice." They all sat down for supper but the boys had watched TV and saw boys load up their spoons with food and shoot it at one another. They had done the same but Mrs. Daimler took their spoons away from them so they pouted the rest of the night. Georgie tried to explain to them that it was not done in real life. No one does that sort of thing. But they didn't go for that thought.

Later the boys found the garbage can in the garage and scattered food on their dad's windshield. Mr. Daimler made them clean it. But as usual kids have trouble doing a good job. So, after their exploits into food throwing, they didn't get cookies and milk and no story. They again pouted but took their punishment and went to bed without crying.

Morning came early with two boys that age, I could hear them wrestling in the master bedroom. Breakfast was quick. Georgie was initiated into training you wouldn't believe and there was no wizard of Oz. The day started with a twenty-mile run and of course, you couldn't believe who was first. Judo was next, the instructor said, "That Judo is essential for the missions you men will need if you get into a tight spot. Jigoro Kano said it is a great mental and physical training of the body and mind. Who would like to put me down?"

A quiet rang out on the mats so Georgie said, "Me sir."

The instructor smiled and said, "Is there anyone else?" All quiet on the western front, the instructor looked around; no takers. "Son, what is your name?"

"Georgie sir."

"Georgie, I probably outweigh you by one hundred and eighty pounds."

"Yes, you do sir."

"Now how are you going to do it?"

"Are you going to attack first, or should I?"

"It is your choice, Georgie."

"You attack first sir, I will defend myself." The instructor Sam Spade, immediately grabbed Georgie's arm but found himself on the mat staring up at Georgie and gasping for air; he remarked, "How did you do that, son?"

"Just the twist of the wrist sir. Would you like to try it again sir; maybe you slipped?"

"Yes, maybe I did." Sam Spade got up and walked over to his desk and pulled a paper from a folder and looked at the other men and read: "A one hundred percent score from an IQ test from this child that is standing in front of you, gentlemen, that has immense strength as you just saw. Anyone question it?"

Everyone stepped forward and in unison said, "I would like to have him as my partner in all of the training."

Sam Spade, the instructor said, "How many of you would like to physically partake in judo with this young man?" None raised their hands. "Georgie, stand aside and let the normal men learn the moves in judo. This assignment is according to weight and size: Johnson and Jordan, Peterson and Goldberg, Jenson, Gerrenson, Stevenson and Belton," as the instructor got up from his chair, he remarked, "Vance, you sit on the side of the mat and watch the moves that I'll show the rest of the team."

"Sir I can act reasonably normal. I know I was picked because no one else volunteered. I don't intend to hurt anyone of the group sir."

"Don't call me sir; it sounds too professional, son."

"I thought this would be difficult," said Georgie. "But you are making it easy. Just call me Georgie's sir, I mean instructor Sam."

"I will send memo to Edgar Slaten that you passed all the skills in Judo and I'm sure you will be sent to the language school next, Georgie."

As the day ended, Georgie met Robert at the car. "How did it go?" asked Robert.

"It went well. They are going to send me to a school. Did you say the language school was in Connecticut?"

"Yes."

"I'll be going there tomorrow."

"I guess you dazzled them today."

"How will they send me; by car, bus or plane?"

"Georgie, they will send you by plane, they need someone your size for a mission," remarked Robert.

"I guess I won't see you after tonight."

"I think the course is six weeks, Georgie. The kids will miss you so don't tell them that you're leaving. I will tell them tomorrow evening. This has happened many times before when sponsored. So, pack up your suitcase because I will take you to the airport," mentioned Robert.

"How far do you think New London, Connecticut, is from here?"

"Oh no, they won't accept you running to New London; they probably would have to buy three pair of shoes and Edgar wouldn't stand for it."

Georgie giggled a little and said, "The shoes and eating on the way is cheaper than flying."

"Believe me, Georgie, they have the money to send you by plane. Oh, by the way has anyone informed you were to get your paycheck?"

"No Robert, do I deserve one?"

"I picked up your check and cashed it for you; here are the dollar bills. Do you want to count it now or in the house?" As he handed it, Georgie saw an envelope packed full of bills!

Georgie looked at Robert driving the car with his mouth wide open and tittered with a, "Wow!"

Chapter 83

The boys were still in bed when Georgie left in a taxi that Robert had called the night before. Georgie had put his money…well, most of it in a small Indian pace pipe bag with TF's little red ball and put the drawstrings around his left wrist. TF objected by bopping the bag on Georgie's head the bag still on his arm. Georgie said, "Ouch, why did you do that?"

"Because that is my favorite hit toy," said TF.

"Trotting Fox, your English has improved immensely."

"Thank you for the compliment, Georgie," said TF.

As the taxi pulled into the airport, TF jostled the ball out the bag and into the back of Georgie's thick hair in the back. "I swear TF, you must be in love with that ball." Georgie went to the ticket counter; the lady took his luggage and he went through the security line and a drink of orange. TF said to Georgie, "How do they make that drank like that?"

"TF, you know what an apple is, don't you?"

"Yes."

"Have you noticed that the color of the juice is sort of a yellow."

"Humm yes."

"This orange color is a fruit called an orange because the skin of an orange in color." Georgie was going down to get on the plane and to other passengers it looked like this poor child was talking to himself. The woman behind Georgie was shaking her head in disbelief that a boy that young was talking to himself. Then Georgie said out loud, "What color is the ball you love?"

The lady behind Georgie tapped him on the shoulder and said, "I hope the trip is taking you to see a doctor, son."

TF had taken the ball out of the Indian bag and bopped the lady on the head twice. She screamed, "Who did that?"

"Ma'am, are you in pain or do you talk to yourself?" She stuck her nose up and walked past Georgie. The ride was short and a limo picked up Georgie after he found his luggage on that terrible carousel. The ride to the school was pleasant and the driver was talkative. He acknowledged that he was the youngest person that he knew of that had attended the school. Georgie shook his hand and thanked him for the ride. As he entered the building, he noticed the gargoyles that did not enhance the building's look. The place looked old itself and he asked the person he saw, "How old is this building?"

"Didn't you read the inscription as you came into the building?"

"Do you know?"

"Yes, 1892."

"Where is the office?"

"Down the hall first door on the left."

"Thanks." He followed her directions and walked into the office. Georgie shook hands with the head of the school and sat in the chair across from Mr. Jon Bronson. He said, "Son, what is your name for the record; we knew you were coming. You are assigned to Dorm A, room 310 and here is your schedule. Your class will start in the morning in this building on the second floor, room 202 at 9:30 AM. I have a Miss Oliver waiting outside this door to escort you and good luck."

"Thank you, sir," and he shook hands again.

Miss Oliver greeted him and walked out the door to the dorm, she pointed to the staircase and said, "I'm not walking up those stairs. I'm leaving and you'll have found your room on your own, goodbye."

As soon as she left, Georgie glided up the companionway and stopped at the landing, walked to his room; there was no lock on the door. He knocked and no answer so he walked in the dark and he could tell there was someone in the room; he said, "Am I interrupting something? This room is 310, isn't it?"

A voice said, "Yes and who the hell are you?" as a girl ran out of the room dressed in a sheet and a giant of a man pulled up his shorts and growled, "You little punk, I am going to mash your head in so you're four inches shorter." The first swing missed. The man said, "Stand up straight so I have a better shot at you."

Georgie picked him up and since the door was still open, he threw him out the door and closed it. However, the muscular man opened the unlocked door and said, "I don't know how you did it but it won't happen again." He stormed into the room and again swung; this time a left hook that glanced off the dresser, but Georgie picked him up and again threw him out the door, this time Georgie

368

could hear him bouncing down the stairway. Georgie picked up the clothes and put them outside the door. The room had a telephone and he called down to the office and asked for clean sheets. They asked why "Somebody has been using the room and it has no lock on the door."

"What room did you say it is?"

"Room 303," said Georgie Vance.

"Who give you that room number?"

"You did."

"Oh, I'll send the key for room 304. 303 is a closet for bedding, sorry."

Suddenly, as he entered 304 again, he was a long time before he wasn't in touch with the world around him because he couldn't speak and no friends and now, he put himself in a position of not knowing anyone in his surroundings in this dorm. Do I really want to do this or should I go back to the Vances? He had turned on the lights in the room, dropped his luggage and flopped on the bed and stared at the ceiling. The night was filled with people on the ceiling staring down at Georgie, especially Tanny, his sleeping partner.

The morning came with Georgie hugging the pillow thinking it was Tanny. *I've got to get over this emotional response I have. I'm sure there is some way to rid myself of this feeling*. He heard a bell thinking it was a call to breakfast. He hurried down to the main floor of the dorm. Who does he meet at the breakfast table but the huge man he threw down the steps! The girl that ran out in the sheet was standing beside him. Georgie smiled and said, "What's for the morning meal? I'm new," trying to be polite.

The big man said pointing at the girl, "We didn't appreciate the interruption." But he didn't look angry and then he said, "How did you throw me like that?"

"It's just a knack I have."

"It's certainly a good knack and I think I will be working with you. My name is Harvey Baton. What's yours?"

"I'm Georgie Vance from California. The weather is cold here." Georgie had put his blue jacket from the airport on because he wasn't sure where breakfast would be in this building or the main hall next door. The giant of a man had on short pants and a tee shirt. Georgie laughed and said, "I guess I'm overdressed for breakfast?"

The girl was polite and said, "Just call me Dianne, Georgie."

They finished breakfast and Georgie said, "The food is different here than it is at home."

"How could eggs and bacon be different in California?" asked Harvey.

At the dorm, a bell rang and Harvey and Dianne got up from the table and told Georgie to follow and Georgie said, "Are you going to the Arabic Language class?"

"Yes." As they walked to the other building, Georgie asked how long the class had been going on; in other words how far am I behind? Harvey looked down at Georgie, "You are short just two days."

"I should be able to get a textbook?"

"Yes," said Harvey, "Mr. Conkite will give you one."

To Georgie it was freezing cold but Harvey still in short pants and tee short loped along like a boxer in training, Georgie floated along but looked like he was running. Dianne was in Harvey's arms. But when they got to the steps at the main building, Harvey slipped on the first step and somehow threw Dianne over his head while Harvey sat grinning on the ice; Georgie was opening the door of the main building for Dianne. Harvey's derriere must've hurt but he didn't show it. He got up and walked up the steps without a thought of the ice on his mind. He caught up with Dianne and Georgie as they opened the door for Harvey and they walked in together. Harvey said, "After all that training, you'd think I could manage the ice without falling."

"You were carrying Dianne; you couldn't see the ice, just don't think about it, Harvey." They entered the Arabic lab. Dianne and Harvey sat and Georgie went and told the professor that he needed a book and his name was Georgie Vance. Georgie sat down and quietly listened to the professor explain the Arabic language and then simple expressions that all the Islamic world uses. After an hour and a half, the class broke for a break.